White Lies and Valentines by Margot Dalton

Divorcée Molly Clarke is a Seattle window dresser with an attitude. So when a company Valentine's Day draw pairs her with the boss's son, she spends her savings on a killer dress and lies through her teeth about her family and life-style. Her date buys her story, but Molly is the one who's shocked when *he* seems to be reeling *her* in, hook, line and sinker!

A Very Special Favor by Karen Young

Joe Masterson and Marly Kendrick had been planning a Valentine's Day wedding sixteen years ago, but Marly had left Joe with no explanation and no goodbye. Now she's living right next door with a little girl called Jaycee. He knows he should stay away, but Jaycee isn't about to let that happen. All she wants is one little favor....

Arrangements of the Heart by Marisa Carroll

The arrangement is purely business. Lori Fenton needs someone to care for her young son while she undergoes surgery. Matt Damschroeder needs cash to save his business. Neither one ever imagines their marriage of convenience could become anything more. But February 14 is drawing near—and Matt and Lori are no match for the magic of Valentine's Day.

My Comic Valentine by Muriel Jensen

This Valentine's Day, Sean Megrath is in for a rude shock. The sexist cartoonist is the target of the Sweet Avenger. The mysterious female vigilante has a delicious recipe for mischief and mayhem planned for Sean, and all the men who done women wrong. Even worse, Sean is struck right in the heart by Cupid's arrow. He's head over heels in lust for his luscious neighbor, Abby Stafford. But Abby is the *marrying* kind!

About the Authors

Margot Dalton, one of Superromance's most popular authors, has written twelve novels for the line. Her books have appeared regularly on the Waldenbooks Romance Bestseller list and, judging from the reader mail she receives, her talent is much appreciated. In addition, Margot is the author of five titles for Harlequin's successful Crystal Creek series, and is currently hard at work on two more. Margot lives with her husband, Ross, in the beautiful province of British Columbia, Canada.

Karen Young, author of six Superromance novels, won the coveted Rita Award for her 1992 Superromance, *The Silence of Midnight.* This title was released as Harlequin's 500th Superromance title, and was also named Best Superromance of 1992 by *Romantic Times.* Karen's next project for Superromance, a ground-breaking family saga that begins in the 1930s, is a worthy successor. Watch for it later this year! Karen, the mother of three grown daughters, lives in Louisiana with her husband, Paul.

Marisa Carroll, otherwise known as sisters Carol Wagner and Marian Scharf, have written eight Harlequin Superromance novels and five Harlequin American Romance novels. In addition, they wrote two Waldenbooks bestsellers for the highly praised Tyler series, and their Saigon Legacy trilogy for the Superromance line earned them the *Romantic Times* Lifetime Achievement Award for best contemporary series. The sisters live in Deschler, Ohio, with their respective families.

Muriel Jensen started writing in the sixth grade and never stopped! She is a regular, award-winning contributor to both the Harlequin American Romance and Superromance lines. *Milky Way,* her wonderful installment in the popular Tyler series, was a Waldenbooks bestseller. Muriel lives in Astoria, Oregon, with her husband, two calico cats and a malamute named Deadline. She also has three grown children.

My Valentine

1994

Margot Dalton
Karen Young
Marisa Carroll
Muriel Jensen

Harlequin Books

TORONTO • NEW YORK • LONDON
AMSTERDAM • PARIS • SYDNEY • HAMBURG
STOCKHOLM • ATHENS • TOKYO • MILAN
MADRID • WARSAW • BUDAPEST • AUCKLAND

HARLEQUIN BOOKS

My Valentine 1994

Copyright © 1994 by Harlequin Enterprises B.V.

ISBN: 0-373-83294-X

The publisher acknowledges the copyright holders of the individual works as follows:

White Lies and Valentines
Copyright © 1994 by Margot Dalton

A Very Special Favor
Copyright © 1994 by Karen Stone

Arrangements of the Heart
Copyright © 1994 by Carol I. Wagner and Marian F. Scharf

My Comic Valentine
Copyright © 1994 by Muriel Jensen

CONTENTS

WHITE LIES AND VALENTINES

Margot Dalton

A Note from Margot Dalton

Writers are people who spend a lot of time looking around at the world, thinking deeply and wondering about the things they see. (Perhaps this explains their unfortunate tendency to forget things in the oven, and to wander out into oncoming traffic.) One of the things I've always been curious about is our fascination with the concept of Valentine's Day.

No other occasion seems to have such universal appeal, regardless of age or position. In fact, during my teaching years, I was interested to observe that children at the grade-school level actually seem to get more excited about Valentine's Day than they do about Christmas. By the time the big day finally arrives, the emotion at school has built to a fever pitch, and all because of the exchange of a few bits of colored paper!

I believe that people everywhere, even the smallest children, get caught up in the enchantment of Valentine' Day because it's the epitome of romance, a day when anything can happen. If you're in a relationship, this is the day when you'll express your feelings in extravagant ways, renew your love, grow even closer to your sweetheart. And if you're alone (or in love with someone who isn't aware of you), this is the day when you're really able to believe that your dreams will come true, when the magic will sweep in and change your life forever.

In "White Lies and Valentines," I've written a story about this sweet promise associated with Valentine's Day and its power to transform even the most humdrum and unromantic existence. I hope all of you will enjoy the same kind of enchantment on this very special day.

Chapter One

"I SEE ROMANCE. I see a tall, handsome man. He's laughing in the sunlight and holding your arm. Oh, my, he's so handsome. And he's *rich*." Grace looked up from the dark mass of leaves in the flowered teacup and leaned earnestly across the table, fixing her niece with a meaningful gaze. "Molly, this young man is tall and blond, and he seems to be *very* wealthy."

"If he's wealthy," Molly said cheerfully, "then he doesn't have to be blond or handsome, Auntie. He can look like a frog and it's okay with me."

Grace Clarke pursed her bright red lips, drew her shawl more tightly around her fat shoulders and looked reprovingly at the young woman seated across from her. "That's not what romance is all about," she said. "Love has nothing to do with money."

"Doesn't it?" Molly asked with mild sarcasm, glancing into the dregs of the cup encircled by her aunt's pudgy, jeweled fingers, then smiling a brief apology when she saw how troubled Grace looked.

"I *hate* drinking tea at breakfast time," Helen said glumly, interrupting the conversation between her sister and her aunt.

Molly gazed at Helen across the cluttered table. "Well, you're the one who's supposed to do the shopping," she pointed out calmly. "You didn't go yesterday, so there's no coffee for breakfast. So you can't really complain, can you?"

Helen's pretty face tensed up. "It's not *my* fault!" she said indignantly. "Can I help it if that awful man's lurking out there? Molly, he's watching me all the time, just waiting for his opportunity. You know he is.''

Molly sighed and poured herself another cup of luke-warm tea, watching as Grace heaved her fat body from the chair and swayed across the kitchen to check on the half-dozen eggs that were being poached in a big saucepan on the stove. "Helen," Molly began gently, taking a deep breath to steady herself. "Sweetie, you know that this is all so—"

"I saw him yesterday morning," Helen interrupted, her gentle brown eyes full of worry. "He was standing right outside the window with a newspaper under his arm, just watching the house."

"He was probably a neighbor, waiting for the bus," Grace commented from the stove.

Molly sipped her tea and sighed again, while Helen glared at her aunt.

At thirty-two, Helen was the younger sister by four years. She had always been dark and petite, the delicate one of the two. After acing her way through school and college, she'd started on a successful career as a librarian, becoming branch head in her mid-twenties. Then all of a sudden she'd developed the bizarre fantasy that a sinister, bearded man was stalking her, planning to seize and torment her in dark, unspeakable ways.

These days Helen was seeing him everywhere—in the supermarket, on the street, at the corner store and hardware store. Any man with a beard seemed to fuel the fantasy and the terror. The result of all this was that much of the young woman's life was now spent cowering in the house, peering fearfully out from behind curtains. She hadn't worked at all for several years, and barely left the house anymore.

Apart from her peculiar delusion, Helen seemed to be a normal, intelligent person with a shy smile and a whimsical sense of humor. Molly loved her sister dearly, though she couldn't help being impatient with her at times. It wasn't just the frustration of trying to deal with Helen's eccentric fears. Molly was ashamed to admit it, but she knew that much of her irritation stemmed simply from the fact that Helen was another mouth to feed. Helen's unemployment insurance had run out a long time ago, and Molly had been providing for her since then.

Molly smiled wryly over the rim of her cup, thinking about the rich young man her aunt had seen in the tea leaves. She allowed herself a brief, wistful fantasy in which a wealthy man would see her on the street and fall instantly in love. He would sweep her off in a long black limousine to a life of luxury, where she could have a big studio of her own and paint all day without ever once worrying about whether the roof needed to be replaced.

This pleasant daydream was interrupted by the arrival of Molly's son, who ran into the kitchen in his bare feet, wearing ragged gray sweatpants and an ancient Galactic Warriors T-shirt. "Charlie, for goodness' sake!" Molly said to him. "Hurry up and get ready for school. You're going to miss the bus."

"Grandpa and I need a pail," Charlie said, cheerfully ignoring his mother. He moved across the kitchen to lean against the soft, pillowy body of his Auntie Grace.

Grace smiled down at her beloved little nephew, her face tender beneath its paint and powder. Grace was always fully made up, even at breakfast, and she wore her dyed black hair pulled back into a dramatic chignon. She also wore bright silk dresses and fringed shawls that she wrapped around her plump body, and masses of beads and jangling bracelets. Although she had to be nearing sixty and was at least a hundred pounds overweight, Grace Clarke still had a smoldering eccentric kind of allure that brought a steady stream of visitors—many of them male—into the faded elegance of the front parlor in their big old house.

Unlike the rest of the family, Molly didn't object to the visitors at all, mainly because Grace told fortunes as part of her daily entertainment. She charged an exorbitant fee, which made her the only member of the household besides Molly who could be said to be gainfully employed.

Grace leaned over and gathered Charlie into a soft, warm embrace. "Such a good boy," she crooned, smoothing his cowlick, her rings sparkling in the overhead light. "I saw a man in your mother's tea leaves."

Charlie lounged against the counter and watched as Grace spooned poached eggs onto slices of brown toast. "What kind of man?"

"A rich, handsome man."

"Like a boyfriend?" Charlie asked with sudden interest. "A real rich boyfriend?"

"Yes," Grace said, giving the small boy a mysterious smile.

Charlie's grimy face brightened. He turned to his mother. "Mom, if you get a rich boyfriend, can he buy me a new skateboard? I want one with—"

"Go wash your face," Molly interrupted, looking at her ten-year-old son with loving exasperation. "And get ready for school."

As she stared at her child's departing back, she suddenly remembered what she'd been meaning to ask him. "Charlie!"

"Yeah?" He paused in the doorway, standing storklike on one foot and curling his toes to avoid contact with the cold hardwood floor.

"Why do you and Grandpa need a pail?"

"There's another leak in my ceiling. A big one, right in the middle."

"Oh, *damn!*" Molly wailed.

Both her aunt and her sister looked at her with helpless sympathy as she buried her face in her folded arms.

The roof had become the bane of Molly's existence. She even had nightmares about it, terrible dreams in which the heavy roof slowly collapsed like some kind of disintegrating monster and smothered all of them beneath its vast mossy expanse.

This big shabby house, now almost a century old, had been home to Molly since her birth, except for those brief few years when she'd been married and lived in Portland. Her ex-husband still lived there, eking out a meager existence selling computer software.

Molly knew that life hadn't been all that great for Charles either since their divorce. He'd married his secretary—the one who had caused all the problems in the first place—and they had three children now, including a pair of twins born just the previous year. Molly had tried very hard not to feel a certain gloating satisfaction at the thought of Charles fathering twins in his forties, but she was only human.

Still, Molly thought, it would be nice if Charles were a little more prosperous. Then maybe he could pay child support occasionally. As it was, she hadn't seen a check from him in over three years. Andrea was almost thirteen now and in desperate need of some new clothes. And poor Charlie talked constantly about a skateboard that Molly could never afford....

"Maybe Walter can do something about the leak in the roof," Grace suggested without much optimism.

"Oh, sure," Molly said dryly, looking down at the egg her aunt had placed in front of her. "You know Daddy—what he'd do is invent a way to divert the water to the basement and use it to generate electricity for his grow lights. Then he could raise tomatoes down there."

Molly's daughter strolled into the kitchen wearing faded jeans and a sweatshirt with a rip in the collar. "Hi, Helen. Hi, Grace," she said, kissing her aunt and great-aunt, then seating herself next to her mother. "Mom, Grandma wants more typing paper."

Molly looked blankly at the girl. "Typing paper?" she echoed. "*More?* I just bought her a ream of typing paper about two weeks ago."

"She says she's been very inspired lately," Andrea reported. "Also, she's been working all night, so she wants her breakfast in bed," she added, turning in her chair to address Grace, whose response was an outraged snort.

Grace had shared this house with her brother's wife for almost thirty years, but the two women had never really grown accustomed to each other, and their small battles raged more or less constantly.

"If Selma Clarke wants her *breakfast* in *bed*," Grace began, her plump jowls quivering ominously, "she can just—"

"Andy, surely you aren't planning to wear that sweatshirt to school," Molly interrupted hastily. "Look at you. It isn't even clean, for heaven's sake."

"It's clean enough," Andrea said calmly. "We're just having science lab all morning anyhow. There's a new leak up in Charlie's room," she added, reaching for a slice of toast. "It's awesome, Mom. Just like Niagara Falls."

"Is Grandpa doing something about it?" Molly asked wearily.

Andrea nodded. "We were just up there looking at it. We think maybe we can use some tubing to route the water down through the little hole by the radiator, and drain it into the basement."

Molly glanced eloquently at her aunt and her sister. "What did I tell you?"

Helen giggled, then sobered hastily. She gave Molly an apologetic smile and began to eat her egg.

Molly glanced at her watch in sudden alarm. "My goodness, I'm going to be late. Andy, make sure that Charlie gets dressed and catches the bus on time, would you please? And change your shirt, darling," she added, bending to kiss the girl's freckled cheek. "Okay?"

Andrea shrugged. "Don't worry, Mom. Everything's cool."

Molly took her old brown overcoat from a closet next to the kitchen door and plucked her umbrella from the stand. "Helen," she said, turning her collar up and drawing a big woolen scarf around her neck, "could you please check the ceiling up in Charlie's room? Make sure they've got something under the leak so it doesn't overflow onto the second floor, all right? If it's leaking right in the middle, water will start running down into Mummy's bedroom again."

Helen nodded. "I'll look after it, Molly," she promised. "Have a nice day."

"A nice day," Molly echoed wanly, bracing herself against the blast of icy rain that battered the kitchen door. "Thanks, Helen. See you all later," she added, smiling at the three around the table. Then she closed the door behind her, plunged into the darkened street and ran frantically toward the bus stop.

THE CITY BUS CHURNED to a halt in slushy mounds of snow and ice next to the curb, and Molly stepped out into a bitter gust of wind. She shivered, huddling into her collar and scarf, half running along the sidewalk toward the store.

Winter had been relentlessly cold and snowy. It was an unusual weather pattern for Seattle, where the ocean breezes usually provided a moderating influence, even in January. But January this year had seemed as bleak and hopeless as her own life, Molly thought with uncharacteristic gloom, still brooding over the leaking roof.

Charlie's room was on the third floor of the big old house, a converted attic space filled with lurid posters, old sporting equipment and strange, discarded science experiments. There were already several leaks in the roof, dripping rhythmically into plastic buckets placed strategically on the floor. Molly was familiar with those leaks and had learned to accept them. The thought of a new one was ominous and troubling, a forecast of more disasters to come.

She sighed and quickened her steps as she reached the huge plate-glass windows of Donovan's Department Store. The windows sent back broken reflections of a tall, slender woman with a delicate pale face, vivid blue eyes and a mass of short chestnut hair that sprang into soft little curls in the dampness of the winter air.

Molly caught glimpses of her image, frowning at her tired and troubled face. She grimaced, seeing how shabby her old brown coat seemed next to the elegant garments on the mannequins. She really should buy a new coat. This one was a disgrace, with its sagging hem and shiny worn patches on the cuffs. But Christmas had been so expensive this year, and she only had seven hundred dollars in the fund for the new roof, which was becoming an urgent necessity.

Absorbed in her dark thoughts, Molly pushed through the front door, hurried across the children's section and descended a flight of stairs to the group of basement offices where her workroom was located. M. Clarke, Artistic Director, read the sign on the old wooden door. As always, it brought a wry smile to Molly's face.

When she'd been hired for this job nine years ago, she'd pictured herself wearing a smock and beret, whirling through the store and passing thoughtful judgments on the artistic merits of window displays and advertising campaigns. In reality, she spent her days dressing and undressing the mannequins, sprinkling artificial snow on the floor and sweeping it up again, stacking cans of tennis balls into shaky pyramids and making posters that advertised huge savings on toothpaste.

She *did* get to help with the design of seasonal window displays for the store, as well as six other Donovan enterprises in the Northwest. But their budget was so limited that they had to keep recycling the same tired props and trying hard to think of new ways to make them look fresh and interesting.

As Molly was hanging her coat and scarf on the old wooden coat tree behind the desk, her door opened and a curly golden head popped into view. "Hi, Darcie," Molly said with a smile, shaking the moisture from her hair. "How was your date?"

Darcie's pretty face twisted into a grimace. "Awful. Just awful. He kept blowing his nose and talking about his mother."

"Not a good sign, is it?"

"It sure isn't. Molly, do you have a perm or does your hair just do that naturally?"

"The second," Molly said, squinting into the little mirror behind the coat tree. "When I was a girl, I really hated it. Now I realize I'm probably lucky, because there's nothing at all I can do with my hair, so I don't have to bother. I just cut it short and forget about it."

Darcie sighed and touched her own mane of bright platinum hair, which consumed much of her free time and a good portion of her meager pay check.

"Darcie, is the supply room unlocked?"

"It will be as soon as I get there. Why?"

"I need to buy another ream of white bond paper," Molly said, flipping though her notebook to see what jobs awaited her.

Darcie paused in the doorway, clutching a clipboard and a pile of pink requisition slips. "Look, Molly..." she began awkwardly.

"Hmm?" Molly glanced up from her scribbled notes.

Darcie shifted on her high heels. "Molly, nobody else *buys* that stuff, you know. They always just sort of...take it."

Molly stared at her co-worker. "You're in charge of the supply room, Darcie. I can't believe you're advising me to steal paper from the company."

Darcie flushed. "It's not that. Whenever I catch anybody lifting stuff from the supplies, I track them down and make them pay. But you're so honest it hurts. And you have...what? Six people to look after?"

"Seven, counting me."

"That's what I mean. It just doesn't seem fair, that's all."

Molly nodded glumly. "Especially now."

"Why?" Darcie asked, her face full of sympathy as she perched on the corner of Molly's desk and gazed at her face. "What's happening now?"

Molly shook her head. "Oh...another leak in the roof, nothing too unusual. I guess I just feel kind of down today."

Darcie pursed her bright painted lips. "Can't the others help you a bit? I mean, there's your kids, but the others are all healthy adults, aren't they? Couldn't they get jobs *somewhere?*"

Molly thought about her family, wondering how to explain them to an outsider, even a sympathetic co-worker like Darcie.

"Well," she began slowly, "Daddy has his disability pension from the army, but it's not much. And I just can't imagine him working at any kind of regular job. He spends all his time down in his workshop, inventing things."

"Has he ever had anything patented?"

"Goodness, no!" Molly said, laughing. "The things he invents are too strange to patent. Daddy designs automatic noodle makers, puppet shows that plug into the cigarette lighter and entertain kids in the back seat, perpetual-motion machines...stuff like that."

"What about your mother? She's got a college education, hasn't she?"

"Yes, but Mummy can't work at a job. She's writing a book. In fact, she's been working on it for fifteen years. That's why I need so much paper."

Darcie stared, fascinated. "A book? What's it about?"

"It's called, *A Comprehensive History of the British Isles,*" Molly said. "Mummy spends all her time up in her room typing and writing in notebooks, smoking cigarettes and doing research. She wears her bathrobe all day long. I've only seen her properly dressed about twice in the past year."

"God," Darcie breathed. "And your sister? She still thinks the guy with the beard is after her?"

Molly nodded wearily. "I thought she was getting a little better lately. But apparently she saw him again yesterday, so now it'll be weeks before she works up enough courage to leave the house again."

"And your aunt? The one who tells fortunes?"

Molly smiled. "Auntie Grace. She's all right. She actually makes quite a bit of money from reading cards and tea leaves, and she gives most of it to me for household expenses. But I still barely make ends meet, and now there's this new leak in the roof...."

Darcie looked at her friend with helpless concern. "Well," she said finally, lifting herself from the desk and heading for the door, "today's the fourth of February. It's the big draw, Molly. Let's go see who we got. Maybe that'll cheer you up."

"Draw?" Molly asked absently. "What draw?"

Darcie stared at the other woman. "I can't believe you forgot about it!"

"Forgot about what?" Molly asked, frowning at the notebook.

"The Valentine's Day staff promotion. They've got all the names, and this morning they're drawing the couples. It's been posted on the bulletin board for weeks now. Practically since New Year's."

Molly shook her head. "I don't know a thing about it. I've been too busy to look at the bulletin board."

Darcie seated herself on the desk again. "It was my idea," she confided, "and I talked the social committee into going along with it. We all agreed that it would really improve relations between management and staff."

"How? What is it?"

"The way it works is," Darcie continued, "they put together all the names of the employees from this store and the managers from here and three of the other stores, and they're going to pair them up."

"Pair them up?" Molly asked. "How?"

"By drawing names," Darcie said patiently. "Couples will be paired with other couples, and singles with singles. Of the opposite sex, of course," she added cheerfully. "It's a Valentine's date."

"Darcie, I honestly don't understand a word of what you're saying."

Darcie sighed. "Your name goes into the 'female staff' bin," she explained. "Molly Clarke. They draw it out, see? And then they draw out a single guy from management to pair with you, and he takes you out on a special Valentine's date. And it's all at management's expense," she added in triumph. "Isn't that a great idea?"

Molly stared at the pretty woman, her blue eyes widening in horror. "Darcie, you actually mean that some poor man from management is going to be forced to take me out on a *date,* just because his name is drawn along with mine?"

Darcie looked offended. "What do you mean, forced? There's lots of guys in management who'd love to take you out, Molly Clarke."

"Oh, yeah?" Molly asked. "Name one."

"Phil Randall, one of the senior accountants," Darcie said promptly. "He's related to Sarah from up in menswear. He told Sarah a couple of times that he'd like to take you out."

Molly shook her head in disbelief. "I haven't been out on a date since my divorce, and that was over nine years ago."

"That's what Sarah told her cousin, anyway."

"Phil Randall," Molly repeated thoughtfully. "Is he the one who looks like a rabbit?"

"No, that's Steve Caulfield. Anyhow, there's lots of neat single guys in management, both in this store and at the downtown office. You know what?" Darcie leaned forward, her skillfully painted eyes widening with dramatic effect.

"What?"

"Even *Kevin Donovan* put his name in."

Molly stared. "You're kidding."

"No, he really did. Rachel Kinsey called and convinced him that it would be a really good thing for staff morale if he did. Isn't that incredible?" Darcie breathed, her voice hushed with awe. "Rachel has more nerve than anybody I've ever met."

Molly was finally impressed. Kevin Donovan was a legendary figure to Donovan employees, even though most of them, like Molly, had never seen the man. His offices were located downtown, away from the commercial premises, and he kept a fairly low profile within the business, though his private life was certainly spectacular.

Kevin was in his late thirties, the only child of old Seamus Donovan, now almost eighty, who had founded the successful chain of department stores. Kevin was the director in all but name, and had recently moved out from the East coast to keep a closer eye on things. He was said to be tall and blond, with dazzling good looks and charm. He drove a silver Porsche, had qualified for the Olympic ski team in his younger days and frequently escorted visiting movie stars to glamorous city functions.

Molly shuddered, thinking about some poor little staffer being forced to go out on an awkward, contrived date with this fabled person. Suddenly she giggled. "Maybe he'll draw Annie," she suggested.

Darcie whooped with laughter at the idea of Kevin Donovan escorting the thin, sour-tempered woman who controlled overdue accounts with a fist of iron. "Yeah. And if he uses the wrong fork, she'll smack his knuckles with her butter knife."

The door opened on their giggles and another head popped in, as elaborately curled and fluffed as Darcie's but a startling bright red. "Hi, Rachel," Darcie said, sliding off the desk again. "What's up?"

Rachel Kinsey stood in the doorway, her lush figure tense with excitement. "They made the draw," she announced in a hoarse whisper.

"Yeah?" Darcie said eagerly. "And? Who'd I get, Rachel?"

"Never mind about you," Rachel said, her eyes moving past the pert young blonde to rest on Molly. "Guess who *she* got?"

Molly's heart sank and her cheeks paled. She felt a slow, ominous tide of dread, and had to force herself to look directly at the tall redheaded woman in the doorway. "Who?" she asked, licking her lips nervously. "Rachel, who did I get?"

"Kevin Donovan," Rachel announced in awe. "Molly got *Kevin Donovan.*"

The leaky roof, her old coat, the grim winter cold and massive heating bills, Charlie's crooked front tooth...all her other worries paled in the face of this new catastrophe.

For a moment, Molly stared at Rachel and Darcie with wide, stricken blue eyes. Then she moaned aloud in anguish and buried her face in her hands.

Chapter Two

MOLLY SPENT THE MORNING at her crowded worktable, cutting out pink orchids and accordion-pleated Valentine hearts for the big window display, her mind still sluggish and numb with shock.

After lunch she carried boxes of pink and white streamers up to the main floor and climbed into the window, oblivious to the curious stares of shoppers and businesspeople who plunged by the plate glass with collars turned up against the icy wind. As she worked, her thoughts raced around frantically like small furry animals trapped in a maze, searching for some kind of escape.

She could tell the committee she was sick...no, the date was for Valentine's Day, which was still ten days away. Sickness wasn't a valid excuse. Maybe she could say she had to go out of town to supervise the spring window displays at the other stores....

Molly felt a brief flare of hope, then sagged in despair again. Everybody knew that she didn't start the spring displays until much later in the month. Certainly Kevin Donovan, who was the big boss of the entire operation, would have her schedule at his fingertips if he wanted to look it up.

And if he was offended by her refusal...

Molly pictured herself losing her job and felt sick with fear. It wasn't much of a job, but it kept food on the table and bought clothes for her children. Well, sort of, she corrected herself, recalling the sweatshirt Andrea had been wearing at the breakfast table.

She smiled wanly at two elderly ladies who stopped to watch her hanging a fat cupid from the central hook. Molly bit her lip and positioned the cupid carefully, wondering what on earth she could wear for this ludicrous "date."

The only decent thing she had was the green wool dress she'd bought six years ago when Andrea had played a piano solo at the school Christmas concert. It wasn't bad, though it looked a little old-fashioned and stuffy....

With a fresh jolt of misery, Molly remembered that her father had spilled a glass of port wine on her skirt during their New Year's dinner. The green dress had a big stain down the front that was still visible, even though Helen had scrubbed the fabric diligently with club soda and toothpaste.

"I just can't afford to buy a new dress," Molly whispered aloud, and the two old ladies smiled and waved at her.

She waved back, then climbed out of the window display and began to gather armfuls of the pink cardboard orchids.

Maybe she could get Rachel to trade with her.

Rachel had drawn Harry Condon, the corpulent director of personnel who called Molly "little girl" and gave chocolates to the typing pool every Friday. Going out on a Valentine's date with Harry wouldn't be so awful. She certainly wouldn't have to worry about the stain on her dress. And Rachel would be thrilled about the prospect of spending an evening with Kevin Donovan.

Now if she could only think of some excuse . . .

Molly's mind raced with newfound hope as she considered this possibility. She was so absorbed that they had to page her twice over the store loudspeaker before she heard her name being called.

"Hello?" she said breathlessly, having run all the way through ladies' wear to take the call on the service phone.

"Miss Clarke?"

"Yes?"

"This is Kevin Donovan. I understand we have a date for Valentine's Day."

Molly's heart thundered and her face drained slowly of color.

"Miss Clarke?"

"I . . . yes," she whispered. "I . . . I guess we do."

"Well, I'm certainly pleased," the voice on the other end continued. "I'm not usually so lucky in contests."

Molly grimaced at his suave courtesy. He sounded just as he'd been described . . . confident and masculine, appealing, polished—and absolutely terrifying. She clasped the phone in mute helplessness, feeling like an idiot.

"I've made dinner reservations at the Breakers," Donovan said. "Is that all right with you, Miss Clarke? Do you like seafood?"

I eat a lot of tuna, Molly told the phone silently, then gathered herself together and spoke into the receiver again. "I . . . yes, I like seafood," she said. "That sounds just fine, Mr. Donovan."

Molly wondered if she'd ever actually met anybody who'd even set foot inside the Breakers. The legendary restaurant on the waterfront was rumored to have a cover charge in excess of fifty dollars, though surely that had to be an exaggeration. Still, it was hardly the place to wear an old woolen dress with a wine stain on the skirt. . . .

". . . your address?" the deep male voice was asking.

"I—I beg your pardon?"

"I was just wondering what time you'd like me to pick you up, Miss Clarke, and what your home address is."

Molly's blue eyes widened in horror. She pictured Kevin Donovan's silver Porsche pulling up in front of their old house with its sagging veranda, Charlie's decrepit "clubhouse" in the front yard made of bits of scrap lumber, and the pair of tires hanging on ropes from the big oak tree near the fence.

"I—I was planning on working late that day," Molly said, crossing her fingers automatically as she told this small fib. "It's a Thursday night, and I'll have to prepare the weekend promotions. I wonder if you could—" she swallowed, then forced herself to continue "—if you could pick me up here at the store? In the lower staff lounge?"

"Certainly," Donovan said. "Would seven be all right?"

"That's . . . that's fine," Molly whispered.

"I'm really looking forward to the evening, Miss Clarke," the man said, sounding almost like he meant it.

"So am I," Molly murmured, crossing her fingers again.

MOLLY CURLED UP on the faded tapestry-covered window seat and looked out at the driving rain which was gradually turning to sleet as the sky darkened and night closed in. She smiled at her mother, who sat in her bathrobe frowning over the sheet of paper in her typewriter and grinding out a cigarette in the brimming crystal ashtray.

"Mummy, dinner's almost ready," Molly said. "Are you coming down?"

Selma Clarke shook her cropped gray head absently, then peered over her glasses at her daughter. Her thin face softened with affection. "I'm all right, dear," she said. "I had a bowl of soup and a few slices of cheese earlier, and Walter's bringing me some toast.''

As if in response to his name, Molly's father entered the room, his plump face cherubic and smiling in the dim light. He carefully set a plate of toast and jam on the typing table, kissed his wife with fond tenderness, patted Molly's shoulder and withdrew, padding off down the hall in his bedroom slippers.

''He's working on a miniature water-powered turbine,'' Selma said proudly. ''It's the cutest thing.''

Molly nodded, watching as her mother lifted a slice of toast with one hand and pecked at the typewriter with the other. ''Mummy, you're working so hard these days,'' she ventured at last. ''Why don't you take some time off?''

Selma shrugged. ''It's going so well, dear. I can't stop now.''

''I understand, but . . .'' Molly fell silent, looking helplessly at the stacks of heavy reference books and mountains of paper that littered Selma's bedroom.

How could she tell her what she was thinking—that her mother was wasting her life? Selma's manuscript on British history had soared by now to over fifteen hundred pages, and nobody was ever going to publish it. Not in a million years. As if the world needed another dry, massive history book . . .

''Is something the matter, dear?'' Selma asked, lowering her glasses and gazing at her daughter with sudden intensity.

Molly flushed and shook her head, got off the window seat and picked awkwardly at her jeans. ''Nothing, Mummy. I'm just worried about you, that's all. You work so hard, and smoke so much, and you hardly ever get outside for fresh air. . . .''

Selma chuckled, a deep raspy sound in the stillness of the littered bedroom. "I'm happy, though," she countered. "I love my history, darling. I'm doing exactly what I want. How many people can say that?"

Molly nodded slowly, smiled at her mother again and moved toward the door. "Are you sure you don't want me to bring you anything?"

Selma shook her head, already immersed in her typing. Molly paused by her mother's closet, casting a speculative glance at the dresses hanging inside. They were all good quality but hopelessly outdated. It had been years since Selma had paid any attention to what she wore.

"Mummy..." Molly began.

"Hmm?" Selma said, munching absently on the slice of toast, her eyes fixed on the page in front of her.

"Nothing," Molly said, leaving the room to head downstairs to the kitchen, where her children's voices were raised in furious anger. Apparently the quarrel had been raging for some time, and involved a set of tools discarded by their grandfather. Each child was noisily laying claim to it.

Grace, majestic in purple silk and a black fringed shawl, was stirring a pot at the stove and enjoying the conflict. Occasionally she added fuel to the fire by saying things like, "I wouldn't let him get away with that, Andy," and, "I'm sure Walter said Charlie was supposed to have them."

Molly sighed and waded into the uproar, all thoughts of elegant restaurants and party dresses banished from her mind for the moment.

"SO WHAT'S ABSOLUTELY your best price, Judy? Your rock-bottom deal?"

The saleswoman pursed her lips and examined the tag on the brown silk dress in Molly's hands. "Eighty dollars," she said reluctantly. "With your employee discount. But Alison would have to approve it."

"Eighty dollars!" Molly's heart sank. She looked at the dress, which was sensibly styled and could be worn on many future occasions, like Charlie's high school graduation, Andrea's wedding, the christenings of all the grandchildren....

"How about this one?" Judy asked, disappearing behind a rack of coats and rummaging busily. "It just came in yesterday. With your coloring, it'll look great. What do you think, Molly?"

"Ohh," Molly breathed, staring at the dress that Judy displayed. "I don't know if it's my style."

"Try it on," the woman urged. "Come on, Molly, what have you got to lose?"

"A new roof," Molly said dryly. She swallowed hard, longingly gazing at the wisp of crimson over Judy's arm. It was the color of a flaring sunset, a hummingbird's throat, the heart of a poppy. It was low cut and frothy, with slim braided straps and little fabric flowers worked into the bodice. It was glamorous and flirtatious, extravagant and utterly unsuitable, and Molly had never wanted anything so much in all her life.

She reached out a cautious hand to touch one of the flimsy straps, then shook her head and carried the brown dress toward the fitting room.

"Molly?" Judy pleaded, following her. "Just try the red one on, okay? Nobody's had it on since it came in and I want to see what it looks like. Just for a minute. Please?"

Molly took the dress, gave the younger woman a rueful glance and disappeared into the little cubicle.

The dress fitted her as if it had been designed and sewn for her alone. The crimson bodice hugged her bosom and drew attention to her curves. Her shoulders looked like creamy marble, while the shimmering silk skirt flirted daintily around her shapely legs. The color highlighted her pale skin tones and brought out the glow of her chestnut curls. She looked demure and sexy, classy and alluring, young again and vibrant with joy.

"Oh, wow," Judy exclaimed as Molly emerged from the dressing room.

"Wow, indeed," Molly said. She was gazing at herself in the triple mirror with a kind of dreamy astonishment.

"You *have* to buy it, Molly," the woman said solemnly. "It would be an absolute crime for you not to own that dress."

Molly's smile faded at the mention of criminal activities. She thought how wrong it would be to deplete the fund for the new roof just to buy this impractical, frivolous dress. And it wouldn't stop there. With a dress like this she'd need new shoes, a different coat, some jewelry... no, not jewelry. Grace would probably be able to loan Molly a necklace and maybe a pair of her showy earrings, dripping with pearls and rubies....

Judy watched the changing play of emotions on her customer's face.

"I'd need new shoes," Molly said unhappily. "And probably a coat, too. I couldn't wear my old brown coat with a dress like this, Judy."

"I know. We have a pair of mat gold sling-back heels that would be just perfect for it. And this creamy mohair coat... Look at it, Molly. Isn't it gorgeous?"

Maybe it was the slim gold shoes with their dainty straps, caressing her feet with a sleek, expensive feel. Or the full sweeping cut of the long coat with its absurdly impractical color. Whatever it was, Molly's resolve suddenly cracked and her good intentions disappeared as though blown away by a gust of wind. "I'll take them," she said recklessly. "I'll take everything. Quick, Judy, tell me how much before I change my mind."

She stood by the service desk, breathing hard and stunned at her own behavior, watching as Judy vanished into the recesses of the store to consult with her supervisor. I've never done anything like this before in all my life, Molly thought with amazement. Never in my life.

She clutched her checkbook with shaking hands, looking at the balance which had grown so agonizingly slowly over the past ten months. The figures danced in front of her eyes and she shook her head, trying to clear her thoughts, struggling to understand just why she felt driven to such rash and uncharacteristic behavior.

Did she actually believe, in some hidden place in her soul, that Kevin Donovan might be attracted to her if she dressed like this, or that something could come of their "date"?

Molly shook her head again, frowning.

She knew that she didn't cherish such dreams, not even in the depths of her heart. Men like Kevin Donovan and life-styles like the one he led were not meant for people like Molly Clarke and her family. She honestly didn't envy Donovan his glamorous life, although she certainly would have welcomed the ability to write a check for anything she needed. No, the red dress and gold shoes, the beautiful coat and this whole burst of rare extravagance represented something else to Molly.

This was the only romantic and exciting thing that had happened to her in many years, and her life after it would doubtless continue on in the same way for years to come. This one evening, with its incredible glamour, its brief, tantalizing glimpse of another world, would shine forever like a beacon over the humdrum landscape of Molly Clarke's existence.

And now that she'd been trapped into it, this evening was going to be her moment in the sun, her adventure of a lifetime, and *nothing,* Molly thought fiercely, was going to dim one single moment of it.

She finally had her breathing under control and her hands weren't shaking as badly as before, but her face was still pale with suppressed emotion when Judy returned, looking miserable.

"It's...it's three hundred and twenty dollars for all of them," the saleswoman said hesitantly, glancing at Molly with abject sympathy. "That's absolutely the best we can do, Molly. The coat alone is almost three hundred retail, and the dress is—"

"That's all right," Molly interrupted, drawing another deep breath to steady herself. "I'll take them, Judy. Can I write a check?"

"Sure," Judy said.

Molly opened the worn checkbook, gripped her pen tightly and began to write.

"Is this...is it for your Valentine's date? With Kevin Donovan?" Judy asked reverently.

Molly nodded and watched the woman fold the shimmering crimson fabric into a dress box. "But not just that," she said with forced casualness. "I'll probably find lots of other places to wear them. PTA meetings, film nights at the library, Charlie's Little League banquet...stuff like that."

Judy caught her eye and both women giggled, then sobered.

"It's just two nights away," Judy murmured. "You're the luckiest woman in the world, Molly Clarke."

Molly swallowed hard and gave her co-worker a wry smile. "Yeah," she said. "Sure I am. Thanks, Judy."

She gathered her bulky packages and hurried off through the store, still shaken and dazed by the enormity of what she'd just done.

Chapter Three

MOLLY SMOOTHED the red dress over her knees, touched her hair nervously, then got up and crossed the shabby staff lounge to look at herself in the mirror again.

A pale face gazed back at her, its blue eyes glistening with fear and excitement. Molly narrowed her eyes and peered critically at the small dusting of freckles across the bridge of her nose, rolling one of her wayward curls over a shaking finger.

I wish I could just die, she thought desperately. *I wish I could collapse on the spot, never wake up, and then none of this would ever have to happen. I wish...*

"Miss Clarke?" a voice said quietly from the doorway. Molly's eyes widened in panic and her heart began to pound. She drew a deep breath and turned slowly to look at the man who stood by the old vinyl couch.

Somehow, Kevin Donovan wasn't what she'd expected.

He was certainly as tall and handsome as everybody said, with shining golden hair and a broad-shouldered, athletic figure. But this man, in his trim gray flannel slacks and impeccable navy blazer, still wasn't the blue-eyed playboy that Molly had visualized.

In fact, Kevin Donovan's eyes weren't blue at all, but a deep brown that provided a startling contrast to his fair coloring. She noted his high cheekbones, an arresting gaze and a wide mouth that curved into a boyish grin when he saw Molly standing by the mirror.

"Hello," she murmured shyly. "Mr. Donovan," she added with an awkward smile.

"Call me Kevin. And you're Molly, right?"

"Yes."

He moved across the room, his eyes softening as he gazed at her. "You look beautiful, Molly," he said quietly. "I'm the luckiest man in the city, escorting a woman like you tonight."

Molly was impressed by the apparent warmth and sincerity of his words, even though she knew it was just good manners. Men like Kevin Donovan were trained from birth to be gentlemanly and courteous, to say all the right things and make a woman feel like a princess. Still, she felt herself flush when he stopped in front of her. Until now the Valentine's date had been just a colorful fantasy, a girlish daydream to while away the dull winter hours. But now the man was here in the room, all six feet of him, so close that Molly could see the fine dusting of golden hairs on his well-shaped hands and smell his subdued cologne. She was suddenly overwhelmed by the reality of the situation.

Molly stood in tense silence, watching while he opened a small, foil-wrapped box and took out a corsage of tiny white roses. Their fragrance made her draw a quick breath.

"Is this all right?"

"Oh, it's lovely," Molly said, touching one of the dainty flowers. "They smell so pretty," she added shyly, glancing up at Kevin, who was studying the pearl-tipped pin attached to the corsage. He looked down and met her eyes, his smile fading to an intense gaze that made Molly feel shaky and alarmed.

His eyes were dark and piercing, and he had the most beautiful mouth she'd ever seen on a man—finely sculpted and powerful, but with a humorous curve.

"Here," he murmured, fitting the white roses against the swell of her breast. "Let me just get this thing..."

Molly shivered at the feel of his warm fingers against her skin, then forced a smile and stood with childlike obedience while he attached the corsage. Clearly it was something the man had done many times before, she thought, wondering why the idea cast a sudden shadow across her mind. After all, this was just—

"Well, shall we go?" he said cheerfully, extending his arm. "Is this your coat, Molly?"

Molly nodded nervously, then watched as he lifted the white mohair coat from the old couch and held it open for her. Suddenly all her brave, reckless feelings came flooding back. She was *glad* she'd bought the pretty red dress and gold shoes, delighted that she wasn't wearing her old brown coat. Who cared about the cost? This one moment of breathless excitement was worth every penny.

And no matter what happened afterward, what grim sacrifices she'd have to make in order to pay for all this, the evening ahead was going to be the most wildly romantic experience of her life. Molly intended to savor every second of it.

LIGHTS GLISTENED and sparkled behind masses of greenery and flowering plants, and gleamed softly from the depths of a huge aquarium that filled one entire wall near the dance floor. Angelfish swam past, iridescent and shimmering in the darkness, pursued by elegant goldfish with long trailing fins.

Molly sighed and gazed at the tropical fish in dreamy silence, circling the hardwood dance floor in Kevin Donovan's arms while the band played "Strangers in the Night."

"Having a good time?" he murmured, his breath warm on her cheek.

Molly nodded and smiled over his shoulder at a tall woman in black silk and diamonds who was dancing with a small, plump man wearing a white dinner jacket.

"Did you like the caviar?" Kevin asked.

Molly, who had secretly been disappointed by her first experience with caviar, nodded again and tried to look critically approving, like a woman who knew fine caviar when she tasted it. "Yes, it was quite good, I thought," she told him.

Kevin leaned his head back and smiled down at her. "I thought so, too," he said. "The caviar is always delicious here."

Molly returned his smile automatically, wondering how often he came to the Breakers. She tried to imagine what it must be like to be Kevin Donovan, for whom an occasion like this was just an average Thursday evening, instead of a once-in-a-lifetime adventure. More than ever, Molly was happy that she'd bought the new outfit. She felt at home among the well-dressed people on the dance floor, as though she were actually a fitting companion for a man like Kevin Donovan. And his admiring glances and compliments made it clear that Kevin shared this opinion.

"So, Molly," he continued, swinging her expertly past an ivy-wrapped column and settling back into the slow rhythm of the dance, "tell me more about yourself. Do you have family here in the city?"

Molly thought about Andrea and Charlie squabbling in the kitchen while Grace stirred a pot of spaghetti sauce at the stove, about her father and his basement full of strange inventions, about her mother's cluttered bedroom and Helen's eccentric fears.

"No," she said promptly, consigning all of them to oblivion without a moment's hesitation. "No, I'm afraid I don't. I'm all alone here."

"Never been married?"

"Once," Molly said. "But," she added, truthfully this time, "it seems like such a long time ago. How about you?"

Kevin shook his well-barbered golden head. "I came close a couple of times, but somehow it never quite clicked. My father always says I'm too fussy, but I don't think so. I want a woman who's a friend as well as a wife, and it seems awfully hard to find her."

Molly felt a brief pang of sympathy for him, wondering how hard it would be to find a loving friend when you had to worry all the time whether women were just after your money. Then she remembered the car he drove, with its rich leather interior, the polished wooden dashboard and discreet brass plate engraved with his name.

No, she thought, gazing at the bright, jewel-like fish, nobody had to feel sorry for Kevin Donovan. His car was probably worth more than the house her family lived in. No doubt the hood ornament alone would buy them a whole new roof....

"Any hobbies?" he was asking.

"Mostly just my painting," Molly said. "I love painting more than anything in the world. I majored in fine arts in college." Well, that was true, at least.

"Really? What do you paint?"

"Nature studies," Molly said. "Realistic scenes mostly, of plants and animals."

"Oils or watercolors?"

"Oh, oils, absolutely," Molly said firmly. "They're a much more flexible medium, I think."

She felt a stab of bitter longing, recalling with startling clarity the smell of turpentine and linseed oil, the rich, promising scent of paint, the warm glow of a fresh white canvas and the feel of a good brush in her hands.

Oh, I want it to be true, she thought in anguish. *I want to paint again. I haven't touched a brush in almost ten years, and I miss it every single day....*

"Do you still find time to paint, even with your job?"

"All the time," Molly said impulsively. "I really don't need the job," she added, giving him a conspiratorial smile. "I just like the contact with people, that's all. But my first love is painting. If I didn't have to go to the store, I'd probably spend twelve or fourteen hours a day in my studio, and forget to eat and sleep."

"Where's your studio?"

"Right in my apartment," Molly said casually, amazed by how easy it was to tell these colossal fibs. "I have the penthouse, and there's a big room with skylights facing north. It's perfect for painting."

Somehow, she didn't feel all that guilty about the lies. The whole thing almost seemed true. She could actually see the big studio with its clear north light and stacks of canvases, tidy shelves of paint tubes and racks of brushes.

"That sounds terrific," Kevin said warmly. "Maybe you could show me some of your work when I take you home?"

Molly's breath caught in her throat and her fantasy world came crashing down around her.

He had to take her home!

She hadn't even thought about it. She just hadn't allowed herself to picture the evening coming to an end, and her world turning into a pumpkin patch again. Molly had somehow thought that they'd go on dancing and talking, eating and drinking champagne and smiling at each other, and then she'd sort of fade painlessly back into reality.

But it was all going to end sometime. Kevin was already talking about taking her home. And of course, with his impeccable courtesy, he'd insist on seeing Molly right to her door. He'd certainly never agree to drop her back at the store and let her find her own way home. She'd told him all those ridiculous lies, and now she was trapped....

Molly's mind raced frantically while Kevin tightened his arms around her and the band swung into a moody rendition of "Love Me Tender."

MOLLY PEERED ANXIOUSLY out the side window of Kevin Donovan's car, searching in desperation for something, anything that she recognized. It had been so long since she'd been down here... not since the party celebrating Rachel's most recent engagement.

Please, she prayed silently. Oh, please, just one measly little landmark. Is that so much to ask?

"There!" she shouted suddenly, causing Kevin to jump behind the wheel. "That's the deli. You turn after the deli."

"Right or left?"

"Umm... right," Molly said, quickly resuming her silent prayers, then warming with triumph when Darcie's big apartment building came looming into sight. "That's it," she said, giving him a radiant smile and bouncing happily on the seat, almost giddy with relief. "That's my building."

Kevin parked at the curb and looked over at her in surprise. Molly felt awkward all of a sudden, as she realized how strange her behavior must seem.

"It's just... it's been a long day. Seems like months since I've seen this place," she told him truthfully. "But it's really been a wonderful evening, Kevin. Just like a dream.''

He smiled at her, reaching idly over to fondle the soft collar of her mohair coat. "That's true. It certainly was." Suddenly he frowned and peered out the window at the apartment building. "You know, that's funny," he commented.

Molly's fingers tightened on the beaded silk evening bag she'd borrowed from her Auntie Grace. "What do you mean?"

Kevin looked awkward for a moment, then grinned. "Well, bosses do have certain privileges, you know," he said, giving Molly a cheerful glance. "When I heard about this date, I have to confess that I looked up your résumé, just to get some idea what I was facing. It was most impressive," he added.

"Impressive?" Molly whispered.

"Your college grades, the art prizes you won, the glowing praise from faculty supervisors...even your scores on the company aptitude tests. Brains and beauty. I could hardly wait to meet you."

Molly relaxed, warmed by the sincerity of his praise and by the comfortable knowledge that every word on her résumé, at least, had been the absolute truth.

"But," Kevin went on, "I was sure the address was somewhere over in the Bellevue area, wasn't it? I seem to remember it wasn't right downtown, anyway."

Molly drew a cautious breath. "Oh, that was when I first moved here," she said. "I stayed with relatives while I was looking for a place of my own, and used their address for my mail. I guess nobody ever bothered to update it, that's all."

Kevin nodded. "No problem. It's just a résumé. Still, I'd better..." He took out a small leather notebook and jotted down the address of the apartment building, while Molly watched in helpless silence, shifting uneasily on the seat.

This was all getting too ridiculous.

"I really wish I could talk you into showing me some of those paintings," he said.

Molly shook her head regretfully. "You know, I never dreamed you'd be so interested in them. I'd really like to show you my work, but I've had such a long day, Kevin, and I have a couple of important meetings first thing in the morning."

He nodded, instantly apologetic, and reached for the door handle. "I'm being inconsiderate, aren't I? Sorry, Molly."

Here it was. The moment she'd been dreading.

Molly forced herself to give a little squeal of alarm, then gazed up at him with a helpless, wide-eyed appeal.

"Molly? What is it?"

"Kevin, I just realized I've done the stupidest thing!"

"What's the matter?"

"I changed clothes at work, and transferred my things from my briefcase to this evening bag, and I—"

"You forgot your keys," he said with a teasing grin. "Right?"

She nodded with a rueful look that she hoped wasn't too artificial. "That's right."

"Well," he said, turning his key in the ignition, "no problem. In fact, it's great. Now I get to keep you with me a while longer."

"Why?" Molly asked in alarm. "What are you doing?"

He shifted into gear and glanced over his shoulder at the slow-moving traffic. "We'll just run over to the store and get them."

"But it's . . . it's all locked—"

"I'm familiar with the night security people. I'm the boss, Molly," he told her.

"No!" she said. He turned to her in surprise. She forced her lips into a weak smile. "Please, Kevin," she said in a low voice. "I certainly don't want to cause all that trouble. I'll just buzz a friend who lives in the building, and she'll let me in."

And dammit, Darcie, you'd better be home, Molly thought grimly. Because if you're not, I swear I'll—

"How will you get into your own place, though?" Kevin was asking.

"Oh, she has a key to my place, too. She often pops up there while I'm away if she . . . runs out of butter or something."

"I see. Well, then, Molly, I guess it's good-night, isn't it?" He got out, came around and held the door for Molly, then strolled beside her up the walk. At the lighted entry he paused, smiling down at her.

He wore a gray tweed topcoat over his slacks and blazer, and his shoulders looked broad and strong and capable. Molly felt a rush of pure physical desire combined with something more subtle—a fierce longing not only for this man's body but for everything he represented.

What must it be like to be the mate of a man like Kevin Donovan, not just for one Valentine's date but for a lifetime? She imagined walking beside him in clouds and storms and sunshine, through seasons and decades, loved and cherished and adored by someone so wonderful. . . .

Suddenly Molly was angry with everything. She felt a helpless fury at the miserable sameness of her life, the weary treadmill in which she was caught and the pitiful yearning for romance that had started her on this whole humiliating charade in the first place.

"Look, Kevin," she said grimly, "there's something I want to tell you about this date of ours."

"Don't say it," he whispered, moving closer to her, so close that she could feel his warmth and smell the masculine richness of his scent. "I know every word you're going to say."

"You do?"

"Yes, I do. You're going to tell me that this is only a first date, and it wasn't even your own choice. But, Molly..."

She drew her breath in sharply and gazed up at him as he put his hands on her shoulders and pulled her gently toward him.

"Molly," he whispered, "this has really been a magic night for me. And princesses have sometimes even been known to kiss frogs on the first date, you know, when there's magic in the air." He bent to kiss her, his arms tightening while his lips brushed softly against hers.

Molly forgot all about her angry resolve to tell him the truth. She melted in his arms, lost in wonder, drowning in the rich sensuality of his kiss.

Only one thought cut through her pleasure and that was a fervent hope that the bank of intercoms was far enough away that Kevin wouldn't overhear the conversation when she buzzed Darcie to let her in.

Chapter Four

EARLY THE NEXT MORNING Molly stumbled off the bus and trudged along the sidewalk to Donovan's, vaguely surprised that the building was still there. She half expected to find her workplace transformed into something from another era—a medieval fortress festooned with banners and ringed by a moat full of swans, or a futuristic silvery pod filled with trailing greenery and flowers not yet seen on this earth.

But the side door still squeaked when it opened and the stairs to the basement were just as crooked and dirty as ever, and the hall was piled full of boxes that never seemed to get moved anywhere.

In her office, the worktable was heaped with a confusion of discarded Valentine hearts and cupids, along with Easter bunnies and daffodils. Molly hung her old brown coat away on the wooden tree and stole a troubled glance at herself in the mirror.

She, too, looked just the same: wide blue eyes, a rueful half smile, pale skin with a dusting of freckles, all framed by her unruly curls. There was no sign of—

Her door swung open and the room was instantly filled with the odor of musky perfume. "So?" a voice demanded breathlessly. "Tell us *everything*, Molly. We're waiting."

Molly turned to see Darcie and Rachel in the doorway, their eager eyes bright with excitement.

She hesitated, wondering what to say. "Did you have a good time?" Rachel asked in hushed tones. "Was he wonderful? Where did you go?"

"He was very nice," Molly said quietly, remembering Kevin Donovan's courtesy, his humor, the way he seemed to understand her shy, tentative jokes and find her witty and charming. "We went to the Breakers."

"Wow!" Rachel exclaimed, seating herself on Molly's desk and crossing her shapely legs. "What did you order?"

"I had lobster Newburg, and Kevin had baked swordfish."

"Kevin had baked swordfish!" Rachel said, digging Darcie in the arm with a pointed elbow. "So it's *Kevin* now. Did he take you back to his place, Molly?"

Molly flushed. "Of course not," she said sharply, pretending to take a sudden interest in a big plastic foam egg containing a blue Easter chick.

"Well, did he at least kiss you good-night?"

Molly's cheeks turned pink. She remembered their kiss, those magical moments in the starry night. Kevin's lips had been cold when they'd first touched hers, but they'd quickly warmed up, a fire had started deep in her heart, shimmering brilliant and multicolored across the darkness like the northern lights....

"Come on, Molly," Rachel urged. "You *must* remember if the man kissed you good-night."

"Geez," Darcie said, jumping into the conversation for the first time, "we haven't heard much about *your* date, have we, Rachel? How about it? Did you and Harry go back to his place and slip into something more comfortable? How does ol' Harry look in a sauna wrap, anyhow? Dynamite, huh?"

Rachel gave her young colleague a sharp look. "If you must know," she said stiffly, "Harry and I had a very nice time. Actually he's quite lonely."

"And quite well off, I hear," Darcie added with a grin. "Think about it, Rachel. Now that you've got your foot in the door, don't blow the chance."

Rachel glared at the other woman, gave Molly a look of exasperation and stalked out of the room, her ample hips swaying rhythmically.

Darcie checked that the door was properly closed, then turned back to Molly with a purposeful stare. "Okay, Molly, cut the crap. What *really* happened last night?"

"Oh, Darcie," Molly said helplessly, sinking into her chair and hiding her face in her hands, "please don't ask me to..."

"It's almost midnight and I'm fast asleep," Darcie said sternly, watching her friend's tumbled mop of curls, "when somebody rings me on my buzzer. 'Darcie!' she whispers, like the cops are after her...."

"Darcie, he was standing just a few feet away! I couldn't—"

"'Darcie,' she whispers, 'please let me into the building. I'll explain tomorrow.' So of course I ask what's going on, are you coming up or what, and she says, 'No, I just need to get into the building. I'll explain everything tomorrow. Please, please, *please*...'" Darcie whined, imitating the pleading tone she'd heard in Molly's hushed voice.

Molly stared uncomfortably at her friend.

"So," Darcie said, lifting a pile of Valentine streamers and beginning to roll them neatly, "what gives, Molly? Don't you think I have a right to know? I actually let a stranger into my building, for God's sake. I could maybe lose my lease for that."

"Darcie... I don't know how to tell you this."

"Try starting at the beginning," Darcie said without mercy. "I've got lots of time. Hell, it's Friday. I won't have to work more than five or six hours overtime if you get going right away."

"It was wonderful," Molly began helplessly, almost in tears. "I felt so great in my new dress and shoes, and after I got over being nervous, I actually started to enjoy myself."

"Is he nice?"

"That's the problem. He's really, really nice. I mean, not conceited or arrogant or anything, just nice. It turns out that we've read a lot of the same books, and like the same music, and even laugh at the same things. I couldn't believe how comfortable I felt with him."

"So why is this a problem? Why do you look like 'lost puppies,' as my little nephew would say?"

"Darcie . . . I did such a stupid thing," Molly wailed, burying her face in her hands again.

Darcie leaned over and put a hand on her friend's shoulder. "Look, hon, we all do stupid things every now and then. 'Specially where men are concerned. So, what was it?"

"I lied," Molly said simply, looking up at Darcie with wide eyes. "Darcie, he was so rich and sophisticated, with his beautiful clothes and car and everything, and I couldn't bear to have him know about . . . about the mess my life and household are in. So I sort of . . . made up a whole different life."

"Whew." Darcie gazed down at the other woman with genuine admiration. "I never thought you had it in you, that kind of dishonesty. This is the employee who pays the company when she takes home a *paper clip,* for God's sake."

Shame flooded Molly, hot and sickening, so that she felt almost nauseated. "I know," she muttered. "It's awful. It's just awful."

"And where do I come into this story? Why were you trying to get into my building at midnight?"

Molly's flush deepened. "I didn't even tell him I had a family. I said that I was all alone in the city, living in an apartment. I told him I had the penthouse," Molly added, smiling weakly, "and that I had a studio up there with northern skylights and spent all my free time painting."

"Actually, a rich Arab has the penthouse," Darcie said cheerfully, "and he spends all his free time up there partying. I heard that his rent is something like three thousand a month."

"Three thousand a *month!*" Molly echoed in horror.

"Yeah. I'm sure your Kevin Donovan must have some idea what a penthouse costs. Wasn't he even a little bit curious about why you'd want to spend your time hanging cupids in windows if you had that kind of money?"

"He did mention it, and I told him that I needed the contact with people to...to provide inspiration for my painting. I said that if I didn't have my job as a form of discipline, I'd just stay in my studio all the time and forget to eat or sleep."

Darcie nodded agreeably. "Sounds plausible to me. So then, when he had to take you home..."

"I was in a total panic," Molly confessed. "I had him pick me up here at the store so he wouldn't see my house, but for some reason I'd never once thought about having to go home."

"You probably hoped the evening would never end," Darcie said gently.

Molly's eyes softened as she smiled at her young friend. "Yes, I guess that's what I hoped. Anyhow, I finally told him I'd forgotten my keys to the building, so if he'd see me to the front door I'd buzz another tenant to let me in. That's when I buzzed you."

"I'm surprised he didn't insist on seeing you safely to your door—a gentlemanly guy like that."

"He wanted to, but I told him I'd have to stop at your place to pick up the spare key to my apartment, and you'd be really embarrassed to be seen by a stranger in your nightclothes. I told him you were shy and modest."

Darcie gave a wolfish grin, obviously tickled by this description of herself.

"And then, after you let me into the building, I just rode up and down in the elevator a few times until I was sure he'd gone away. Then I called a cab and went home. The cab fare," Molly concluded bitterly, "was nineteen dollars. I won't be able to buy lunch for a week."

"But it was worth it, right?"

Molly considered the question, absently rolling a curl around her finger. "At first I thought so, Darcie. It was really a wonderful, romantic experience. But now when I think of all the lies I told him, I just feel so miserable about it all, and terribly embarrassed. I'm almost sick, actually."

"Don't sweat it so much, hon," Darcie said cheerfully, sliding off the desk and heading for the door. "You had a great time and bought some pretty new clothes, which God knows you deserve, and nobody got hurt. So what's to feel bad about?"

"But I told him all those *lies*..."

"Forget it," Darcie said soothingly, smiling from the doorway. "Just forget it. Hell, Molly, you'll never see the man again, right?"

"Right," Molly agreed with a rueful smile. "I certainly hope I don't, anyway."

But alone again in her cluttered office, Molly realized with despair that those final words had been another lie. In fact, they'd been the biggest lie of all.

MOLLY WAS ON HER hands and knees in front of the huge supply cupboard at the side of her office, sneezing and coughing at the dust that billowed from the stacked cardboard cartons. She squinted at the faded writing on the boxes, hoping to find more plastic daffodils.

"Maybe this one...no, it says 'dental health,'" she muttered crossly.

The phone rang, and she extricated herself from the mass, brushing at cobwebs and dust on her jeans and turtleneck. "Hello?"

"Molly? Is that you?" Molly's breath caught and her heart began to pound. She gripped the phone with one hand and rubbed slowly at a smear of dirt on her sleeve. "Molly? It's Kevin. I just wanted to say good morning."

"Good morning," Molly whispered.

"Haven't started all those important meetings yet, have you?"

Molly brushed at another patch of dust on the front of her sweater. "Not just yet. You know, it looks like...like the sun might be starting to shine later today."

I'm an idiot, she thought in anguish. *I'm such an idiot....*

"I think the sun began to shine for me sometime last night," Kevin said, with such warmth in his voice that Molly's knees turned to jelly and she had to sit down in her chair.

"I—I see," she murmured, unable to think of a single intelligent thing to say.

"Did you get into your place all right? Your friend had a key?"

"Yes, everything was fine."

"That's a good idea, leaving the key with a friend in case you forget your own. Still, I really would have liked to see your paintings."

"Maybe some other time," Molly whispered, looking frantically at the walls, the ceiling, her shabby brown coat, the loaded worktable and the piles of discarded Valentine decorations.

"Fine. How about tomorrow?"

Molly's thoughts reeled and plunged crazily. She felt the blood drain from her cheeks. "Tomorrow?"

"Sure. It's Saturday, and even painters with busy careers have to take an occasional Saturday afternoon off, don't they? Let's spend some time together, Molly. You just told me yourself that the sun was going to be shining."

"But I..." Molly tried to focus her thoughts. "I have to do the grocery shopping tomorrow afternoon. We're...I'm out of everything," she corrected herself hastily.

That was certainly the truth. Helen was still afraid to leave the house, and Grace couldn't walk through all the rain and slush. At the moment, the family was reduced to eating peanut butter sandwiches and tinned soups.

"Okay. Let's meet down at the Pike Place market, and you can do your grocery shopping in exotic surroundings. How's that?"

Molly hesitated, her dread mounting with every second.

"Come on, Molly," he urged. "It'll be fun. I'm a great shopper. We'll haggle over the fish, squeeze all the melons and hunt out the very best brussels sprouts. You'll love it."

Molly could see Kevin Donovan's face as vividly as if he were standing in front of her, close enough to touch. She saw his sparkling dark eyes and sexy mouth, his graceful stance and relaxed, easy manner.

More than anything in the world, Molly longed to touch him again, to laugh with him and walk close beside him, to share an afternoon of happy conversation and another of his tender kisses.

But it was such an impossible situation. If only she hadn't told him so many foolish lies! Now she either had to continue the whole farce, which would be impossible for her, or tell him the truth and endure his inevitable contempt. *Oh, God,* she thought wearily. *What a mess I'm in....*

"Molly?"

"Kevin, I really have to go. I've got a million things to do this morning."

"But how about tomorrow? Shall we meet at the pier? How about by the aquarium, say about one o'clock?"

"All right," Molly whispered, her misery rising and billowing around her like a dark, ominous cloud. "All right, Kevin. I'll be there."

Chapter Five

THE FOLLOWING MORNING, Molly was sitting with her son at the breakfast table. Charlie was still in ragged pajamas, his hair rumpled and uncombed. He ate noisily, gobbling a bowl of cereal under the mournful gaze of a fat brown hamster huddled in a cage near the boy's elbow.

Molly sipped her coffee and looked into the animal's bright little dark eyes, feeling a twinge of sympathy. It couldn't be a lot of fun, being Charlie's pet and constant companion.

Andrea fed and cared for her hamster with loving care and scientific efficiency, but Molly suspected that Charlie's hamster led an unpleasantly erratic and eventful life. Still, there wasn't much she could do about it.

"Look at this, Mom," Charlie said through a mouthful of milk and cereal, holding out a catalog for her inspection.

Molly leaned over to peer at the skateboard her son was pointing at with his grubby forefinger. "Yes? What about it?"

"It's awesome, Mom. It's got Thunder Trucks and a super concave board with solid grip tape and the best wheels you can buy. Even if you buy just the deck, it costs more than a hundred bucks."

"How much does the whole thing cost?"

Charlie frowned, peering at the bright photograph. "Three hundred and twenty," he said finally. Molly smiled grimly, struck by the irony of the situation. Charlie's dream could have come true for exactly the same amount that she'd squandered on her own.

"Charlie..." she began.

"Good morning, all," Selma said in a husky voice, crossing the kitchen in her bathrobe, a cigarette dangling from the corner of her mouth. "Has the mail come yet?"

"It's Saturday, Mummy," Molly told her. "There's no mail today."

Selma's face creased with disappointment. She ruffled Charlie's hair absently, stood for a moment peering into the fridge, then closed the door and looked gloomily at the cluttered counter. "There's not a single thing to eat in this house."

"Nonsense," Grace said briskly, looking up from the corner where she was mixing hamburger and onion for cabbage rolls. "Molly went grocery shopping last night and bought a ton of things. What do you want?"

Selma shook her head and wandered out, leaving Molly gazing after her in concern.

"Now she'll work all day without eating anything. I should have bought some cream cheese or something for her."

Actually, Molly had saved a few of the more exotic items to pick up this afternoon while she was with Kevin, just to lend credence to her story about grocery shopping. But, as Grace had just mentioned, she'd already stocked up on general supplies the previous evening. It certainly wouldn't do to have Kevin Donovan at her side while she bought family-size cans of pork and beans, huge jars of peanut butter and sacks of puffed wheat. "I'd *die* for this board," Charlie said with a sigh, forcing a spoonful of cereal through the bars of the hamster cage. The little animal backed against the rear wall and gazed at the food suspiciously.

"Charlie..." Molly began again.

"Yeah?"

"Charlie, did you ever do anything really bad, and then feel sorry about it? I mean, did you ever..." Molly floundered a moment, her cheeks pink. "Did you ever tell a really big fib, for instance, and then not know what to do about it afterward?"

Charlie looked startled, then evasive. "What do you mean?" he asked cautiously.

Molly looked at him in surprise. "I mean, like if you told somebody something about yourself that wasn't true, and they believed you, and then you got into all kinds of trouble over it?"

The boy's face darkened. "I'm gonna *kill* Andy," he vowed furiously. "She said she wouldn't tell!"

Molly gazed at him, bewildered. "Andy? What's she got to do with anything?"

Charlie's expression slowly changed from outrage to a guileless smile. "Oh, nothing. Gotta go, Mom," he added hastily. "Me and Jason are playing Killer Martians today." He grabbed the hamster cage and disappeared, leaving Molly to wonder what role the long-suffering rodent would be required to play in his interplanetary war games.

She turned to find her aunt's eyes resting on her with a look of quiet appraisal. "Is there anything you'd like to talk about, Molly?" Grace asked gently. "Anything bothering you, for instance?"

Molly squirmed a little under Grace's steady gaze. After all these years, she still didn't know what she really believed about Grace's powers of extrasensory perception. But she often had the uncomfortable feeling that Grace understood things that were hidden to others.

Molly longed to bury herself in her aunt's comforting embrace and sob out the whole miserable story. But she was too embarrassed by her own behavior, and troubled

by thoughts of Kevin Donovan with his handsome face
and his sparkling eyes.... "Nothing," Molly said finally. "Nothing at all, Auntie. I'm going out this afternoon," she added with forced casualness. "I'll pick up a
few more groceries, all right?"

"Are you taking the car?"

"I don't think Daddy has it running yet. It's been too
cold for him to work on the carburetor. I'll just buy a few
things and bring them home on the bus."

Molly drained the last of her coffee and hurried out,
uncomfortably conscious of Grace's thoughtful gaze following her as she left the kitchen.

THE CAPRICIOUS OCEAN weather had changed again, with
gentle breezes replacing the icy blasts and sunshine glint-
ing on calm blue waters. In the welcome mildness, Seattle's Pike Place market bustled with color and activity. All
the indoor stalls were open, and many outdoor ones had
sprouted like spring flowers under the warmth of the sun.

On the upper levels, vendors sold everything from ba-
tik to beaded moccasins, while street musicians played and
sang and people strolled among the colorful stalls. En-
chanted, Molly paused to listen to an intense young
Korean playing a Chopin polonaise on his softly shining
violin. Kevin Donovan stood beside her, one arm draped
casually around her shoulders and the other clutching a
half-eaten bag of caramel popcorn.

Molly stole a sidelong glance at him, thrilled by the feel
of his long, hard body against hers. Even in his casual at-
tire of jeans, windbreaker and cashmere pullover, he was
still a commanding presence. His golden head towered
above most of the crowd, and there was an air of calm
authority about him, a sureness in his step, that seemed to
set him apart from other men.

Molly smiled at the young musician, dropped a handful of coins into his open violin case and started to walk away, letting Kevin catch up to her and slide his arm around her waist. He stopped suddenly, drawing her aside to a little stall where turquoise jewelry was being displayed.

"Look at these, Molly," he said, holding out a pair of earrings carved into the shape of crescent moons. "They're exactly the color of your eyes. Let me buy them for you."

Molly glanced at the price tag and her cheeks paled. "Oh, no," she protested awkwardly. "Really, Kevin, I couldn't possibly..."

"Look at them," he repeated. He pulled her close to him and turned her to face a little mirror. He held one of the glistening earrings up to her cheek, his fingers warm against her skin. "They're perfect for you. I'll take them," he said to the salesman while he still held Molly's gaze in the mirror.

She trembled at the look in his eyes and drew her breath in sharply as he turned her around to face him.

"Molly," he whispered, bending his head toward hers. "Oh, Molly..." Then his lips were on hers, and they weren't cold at all on this golden winter afternoon. They were as warm as summer, sweet as honey, rich as the violin music playing softly in the background.

Molly forgot everything, conscious only of the waves of feeling that swept over her body. She returned his kiss, hungry for more, marveling at the sweetness of his mouth, the strength of his arms, the warmth of his big body.

For a long time they stood wrapped together, oblivious to the bustling world around them. Finally Molly pulled away with an embarrassed murmur while Kevin dug in his wallet to hand some bills to the artisan smiling in his stall of turquoise.

"I CAN'T BELIEVE you walked all the way over to the market this morning," Kevin said, stretching his arm along the back of the leather seat and smiling at Molly.

"It was such a nice day," Molly said, avoiding his eyes, "and it's only eight or ten blocks. I enjoyed the walk."

"But what if I hadn't showed up?" He indicated her heavy bags of groceries in the back seat. "You'd have been pretty worn out, lugging that stuff all the way home."

"I was reasonably sure you'd show up," Molly admitted. "You seem like a fairly reliable type."

"I do?" He grinned at her, his eyes dancing, and reached out to touch one of the dangling turquoise earrings. "I'm glad you think so, Molly Clarke."

Again she turned away, peering anxiously out the window of Kevin's parked car. Darcie's apartment building loomed in front of her, and her tension increased as she gazed at the locked front doors with their glass panels gleaming dully in the twilight. It was amazing, she thought dryly, how quickly a person could get used to a life of deception. This time she'd made sure in advance that she had a key to the building.

"So," he asked after an awkward silence, "is this my lucky day? Do I finally get to see those paintings of yours?"

Even though she'd been bracing herself all afternoon for this question, Molly felt her stomach churn with tension. "Oh, not today, I'm afraid," she said lightly.

"Really? Why not?"

"My aunt is staying with me. She hasn't been feeling well lately, and she flew in yesterday from . . . from Utah, to have some tests done at the hospital. I think she's probably sleeping now, and I'd hate to disturb her."

Kevin frowned with concern. "Molly, I'm so sorry to hear that," he said gently, touching her shoulder. "I shouldn't have taken you away all afternoon."

"That's all right. I think she was probably sleeping most of the day. The tests are... they're very tiring."

"Is it something serious?"

Molly shifted wearily on the seat, hating herself for being unable to stop the stream of lies. "I hope not," she said briefly. "Kevin..."

"Will she be staying long?"

"No, she's going home as soon as the tests are done. Probably early in the week."

"I see." He hesitated, then turned to look at her. "Molly, I really want to see you again."

"I don't know if—"

"Molly," Kevin told her earnestly, "I've never met anyone like you. You're such a *good* person. I feel happy just being with you."

Molly stiffened in shame. *Such a good person...*

"Yesterday morning," he went on, "after I'd talked to you and knew I was going to be seeing you again today... Molly, I felt like a kid going on a picnic." He leaned toward her again, his dark eyes full of tenderness. "I can't remember feeling that way about anybody, not ever."

Molly gazed at him with frightened eyes. Now was the time to tell him, she realized. Right now, before things went any farther, she should tell him the truth.

Kevin, I've been lying to you all this time. I don't live alone in a penthouse with a studio. I live in a moldy old house with two kids, two unemployed parents, a wacky aunt and sister and a couple of smelly hamsters. I have no money and no prospect of ever having any, and I haven't touched a paintbrush for ten years. I'm a horrible, pitiful fake, and I know you're going to hate me for what I did, but I...

"Molly," he whispered, his voice husky, "help me out here. Am I rushing things too much? Am I making a colossal fool of myself? Because if you don't feel the same way..."

She did feel the same way, Molly realized in despair. That was the whole problem. She felt exactly the same way. In fact, Molly knew what Kevin meant when he'd described himself as a kid going on a picnic. She herself had never felt such anticipation at the thought of being with someone, or such pure happiness in another's presence.

Who could understand the fickleness of destiny?

In spite of his power and good looks, his glamorous reputation and intimidating wealth, Kevin Donovan was, quite simply, the other half of herself. He was the missing part that had been taken from her at birth, the man whom she'd been craving all her life. Now he was here, and in her foolishness she'd built a wall between them so high and so strong that it could never be bridged.

"Do you need a little more time, Molly? Tell me there's hope for me. Tell me you just need time."

"I...yes," she murmured. "I think that's what I need. If you could let me—"

"Don't say another word," he told her calmly. "I understand. Look, Molly," he added, tapping his fingers on the steering wheel, "I have to go to California tomorrow and attend to some business down there. I'll be back sometime Wednesday afternoon. Can we have dinner together Wednesday evening?"

"I...I suppose so," she said faintly, twisting her gloves in her lap.

"Good. Then I'll pick you up here about seven, all right?"

"Fine," Molly whispered. She was such a hopeless coward....

"Well," he said cheerfully, reaching a long arm into the back seat to gather up the groceries, "we'd better get you home before your aunt wakes up and needs you."

"Oh, yes," Molly said hastily, grasping the smooth brass door handle. "Yes, I'd like to be there when she wakes up."

Kevin stood beside her and watched as she fitted the key in the front door of the apartment building. He crossed the carpeted lobby at her side, then paused with her by the elevators.

Molly gave him a bright smile and held out her hands for the bags. "Thanks so much for the lovely afternoon, Kevin. And the earrings," she added. "I can manage the groceries from here, I think."

"Oh, no. Not this time." Kevin drew her into the empty elevator and reached for the number indicating the top floor. "I'm seeing you to your apartment, at least."

Molly had prepared for this scenario, and she drew a deep breath. "Sorry, Kevin. I have to stop off at my friend's place first. She's got a bad cold, and I picked up a few things for her this afternoon as well as my own groceries."

"Okay. What's her floor number?"

"Seven." Molly brandished Darcie's spare key.

Kevin pressed the number, set the groceries on the floor and gathered Molly into his arms, kissing her with leisurely thoroughness as the car rode upward. "It's probably a good thing you can't take me to your place," he whispered huskily in her ear. "I know you want to take it slow, Molly, but the way I'm feeling, God knows what might happen if I could have you all to myself.''

Molly nestled against his chest, thrilling in spite of herself to the feel of his arms, his lean body, his warmth and strength and maleness.

The elevator stopped and he walked beside her to Darcie's apartment. ''This is it?''

Molly nodded, hesitating. ''She's really got a terrible cold, Kevin. Runny nose, clogged sinuses, the works. She'd be just furious if I brought anybody in.''

Kevin nodded. ''Enough said. I'll go before she catches us. See you Wednesday, Molly.'' He bent to give her another lingering kiss. ''And *next* time,'' he whispered, cupping her chin in his hands and gazing into her eyes, ''you're taking me up to see your etchings, sweetheart.''

Molly shivered at the intent look on his face and the teasing glint in his eyes. She nodded gravely, then watched in helpless silence as he smiled again and strode down the hall to the elevator.

Chapter Six

THE BIG HOUSE ECHOED with a confusion of strange noises, reflecting the varied and colorful interests of its occupants. It was past ten o'clock on a Saturday night, and both children were in their rooms but obviously still awake.

A concert of bumps and thuds on the ceiling overhead betrayed Charlie's restlessness. Molly put down her sewing needle and listened carefully for a moment. She heard a muffled crash, bare feet running on the floor and then another heavy thump, followed by a rapid series of smaller thuds. Basketball, she decided. Charlie was practising lay-ups.

Molly knew that she should go up and tell him to get to bed, but felt too drained and miserable to be drawn into any kind of conflict. Instead she returned to her mending, making a row of careful stitches in the torn collar of Andrea's sweatshirt.

Andrea herself was in the room next to Molly's, playing her flute with more determination than skill. Although the flute lessons were free, Molly sometimes wished the music course had never been offered by Andrea's school. The sounds her daughter was making could hardly be called music, but it was part of the girl's nature to persevere. She would eventually conquer this instrument no matter how much everybody else suffered in the process.

The familiar clatter of Selma's typewriter keys drifted down the hall, a staccato counterpoint to the singsong tone of Grace's voice in the parlor below, where she was reading tarot cards to a hushed group of admirers.

In the room on her other side, Molly heard Helen reciting children's stories to an attentive circle of old dolls and ragged teddy bears. Helen still cherished a fond hope that her tormentor would eventually leave her alone so she could return to work at the library where the children's story hour was one of her favorite tasks. She practiced constantly for the moment when she could resume her duties.

Hollow clatters and faraway echoes in the radiator pipes were the only sign of Molly's father, who had spent the past few days doing something complicated to the heating system.

Molly sighed, dropped her sewing onto her lap again and gazed unhappily at the faded wallpaper above the bed. Finally she put the sweatshirt aside, got up and crossed the room to her old desk, then leaned down to adjust the wad of folded paper under one leg that kept it from wobbling. She sat down and took out a sheet of plain white paper. For a while she just stared at it, chewing anxiously on the end of her pen. Then she dated the note and began to write.

Dear Kevin,

It causes me pain to write this letter to you, but I have no choice. I have been deceiving you all this time, and now I must be honest. You see, I'm not free to become involved in any kind of relationship. I have long-standing and serious obligations that I can't ignore any longer.

The fact is, Kevin, there's someone in my life already for whom I care very deeply, someone I haven't told you about. You came along at a time when I was feeling trapped and restless because of various circumstances, and for a little while I allowed myself to pretend that I was free. It was a cruel way to treat you, and I sincerely regret my behavior.

Molly paused, examining these words with gloomy satisfaction. Thus far, she'd worded the letter so skillfully that everything was the absolute truth, although he would certainly take it to mean something entirely different.

"The essence of a lie is the intent to deceive," Selma sometimes quoted, and Molly knew all too well what her mother meant. Still, if she could escape this dreadful situation without telling any more actual untruths, she might be able to forgive herself. She frowned briefly, then returned to her letter.

I know I should have told you this sooner, but I was too involved in the pleasure of getting to know you and spending time with you. If I were free I would love to see our relationship develop. But I'm not, and there's no use pretending any longer.

Molly's face twisted, and a single tear rolled down her cheek. She brushed at it impatiently and forced herself to concentrate on the task at hand.

It was very wrong of me to deceive you and I apologize with all my heart. Please, please don't call me or try to contact me, because it would only be more painful. I am returning the earrings. Again, please accept my sincere apologies.

Molly looked at the words on the page, longing to add

one more sentence. "I love you, Kevin," she whispered aloud. "I really do."

She could never tell him that, of course. Still, she felt she had to say something. She owed it to both of them, especially since this was the last thing she'd ever tell him.

> Despite what I'm asking, I want you to know how hard it is for me to write this. Kevin, you really are a wonderful man. You are attractive in all kinds of ways, not just physically. In fact, I've never met anyone like you.

Molly knew she had to stop at that or she'd be in danger of breaking down completely. She signed her name hastily, folded the note and put it in an envelope which she addressed to Kevin's downtown office. Then she picked up the turquoise earrings and kissed them wistfully, giving them a sad, final glance before slipping them in along with the note and sealing the envelope.

ON MONDAY MORNING, Molly paused for a long time at the mailbox outside the store, clutching her letter in a panic of indecision. If only there were some other way...

But she knew there was nothing else to be done. She had only two choices. Either mail the letter and end the silly charade with a minimum of discomfort to both of them, or go out with Kevin again and tell him the whole miserable truth, which would also require her to explain why she'd lied in the first place. Then she'd have to endure his veiled contempt, his polite attempts to extricate himself from a painful and embarrassing situation.

Molly squared her shoulders and dropped the envelope into the mailbox, choking back a sob as her letter disappeared into its black depths. Then she turned and trudged into the store.

The letter would be on Kevin's desk when he got back on Wednesday. She remembered him mentioning that it was a compulsion with him to go through all his mail as soon as he returned from a business trip, so he was sure to read her letter on Wednesday afternoon. After that, Molly trusted his good manners would keep him from calling and pressing her for more details or another meeting. Kevin Donovan was a gentleman above all else. He would honor Molly's wishes and her commitment to a previous relationship, and leave her alone.

Alone...

Molly battled another dark tide of misery. She'd never before felt this way, battered by emotion and consumed with strange hungers. She simply couldn't put him out of her mind—his brown eyes and strong, curving mouth, the feel of his arms around her, his husky laughter, even the way his cologne mingled with the scent of his warm skin....

Molly draped her coat on the hook and turned listlessly to the mounds of work on her desk, thinking about the week ahead. Maybe she should just get away, leave a week early and head down into Oregon to help with the spring window displays at the other stores. A change of scene would do her good. But first her father would have to fix their car, a rusty contraption so old and rickety that it was in constant need of Walter Clarke's loving attention.

Molly made up her mind. She'd make all the arrangements and leave later in the week. With some luck, she could probably get away by Thursday morning. That way, if Kevin decided to contact her after receiving her letter, she'd already be gone.

She picked up a discarded pile of Valentine hearts and gazed at them sadly for a moment before packing them away in their box.

THE DAYS DRAGGED BY, and Wednesday morning finally arrived. Molly went upstairs to arrange a display in the toiletry section, piling bottles of perfume and packages of soap in wicker baskets and decorating them with fabric bows.

"Molly!" the floor supervisor hissed at her elbow, interrupting her gloomy thoughts.

Molly folded a length of paisley ribbon and took a pin from her mouth. "Hmmm? Did you say something to me, Audrey?"

"Guess what?" Audrey whispered. "Guess who's in the store?"

Molly shook her head and returned to her task, wondering if some stuffed Easter bunnies would look nice sitting in the baskets with the perfume. Or would that be too cute?

"It's *Kevin Donovan!*" Audrey hissed, leaning forward with barely contained excitement. "Harry's bringing him around to meet some of the staff. God, he's good-looking."

"Kevin Donovan?" Molly echoed blankly. "But...but he's..."

"I saw him a couple of months ago at a Christmas charity ball, but he's even more gorgeous close up," Audrey murmured, oblivious to Molly's white face and shaking hands. In her excitement, she'd apparently forgotten about Molly's recent Valentine's date. "Look, here they come," she exclaimed, standing at attention behind the atomizers and trying to look casual. "Pretend you don't notice them, Molly."

But Molly wasn't capable of pretending anything. She was staring, openmouthed and stunned with shock, at Harry Condon and the tall blond man who strolled next to him among the boxed soaps and perfumes.

Kevin Donovan wore light brown slacks and an expensive creamy sports jacket that blended perfectly with his golden hair. He was tanned and debonair, blue-eyed, smiling and attractive.

Molly had never seen the man before in her life.

Chapter Seven

MOLLY DIDN'T KNOW how much time had passed, or even how she'd managed to escape to her office after being introduced to Kevin Donovan. She sat huddled in the basement room, her face in her hands, struggling to make some sense out of the confusion in her mind. "Oh, God," she moaned, recalling Harry's jovial introduction.

"This is Audrey Schick, the floor supervisor, Mr. Donovan, and of course you don't need an introduction to little Molly Clarke, do you? I believe you two had a date recently."

The man's blue eyes had widened with surprise and interest, but he had controlled himself well. Molly was sure the others hadn't even been aware of his mildly arched eyebrows, his quick, appraising glance at her before he smiled courteously, murmured some pleasantries to the two women and moved on to the housewares section.

"Your *date!*" Audrey had breathed in rapture. "Molly, I forgot all about it! What was it like? Isn't he *gorgeous?*"

But Molly was already hurrying away, running back to her basement cubbyhole like a wounded animal. She writhed in misery at her desk, remembering that curious look on Donovan's face. Had he already read the letter? She'd mailed it Monday morning, and this was early on Wednesday.... No, Molly decided grimly, that little pleasure was probably still ahead of him.

She pictured the man sitting at his desk, with his snowy shirt cuffs and perfectly knotted tie. He would open the envelope and remove its contents. His elegant features would twist in distaste as he read those hysterical scribbles from some poor woman who apparently felt great fondness for him but was rejecting his attentions by pleading a prior commitment.

Hmm...the window dresser, was it? The tall, dowdy one with the messy curls? he would think. And then he would look at the *earrings*...

Molly moaned aloud once more, then grimaced with pain. Possible courses of action, all wildly improbable, tumbled through her mind.

She could call Donovan's secretary, explain that a letter was arriving in the day's mail that had been posted by mistake, and ask if it could be held back until she could come over and pick it up....

Molly discarded this possibility as soon as she looked at her watch—it was almost noon, and the day's mail would surely have been opened and distributed by now.

Maybe she could make an appointment to see Donovan on some pretext, then seize an opportunity to look through his mail when he was out of the room.

Molly recognized this plan as being even worse than her first idea, partly because it wasn't likely to work, but mostly because there was no way she could bear to confront Kevin Donovan's smile again. Never again.

There was no doubt that the man she'd met this morning was Kevin Donovan. The *real* one, Molly corrected herself grimly. He was obviously on familiar terms with Harry Condon, the director of personnel, and other senior people at the store.

So who was the handsome, dark-eyed scoundrel who'd kissed her with such convincing passion? Where was he now? Laughing at her somewhere, amusing a group of his friends with the story of how thoroughly he'd tricked a shabby, gullible window dresser?

And *why?*

She realized that this question tormented her most of all. More than the contemplation of her own foolishness, even more than the embarrassment of having Kevin Donovan see that ridiculous letter, Molly was seared by the knowledge of the other man's treachery and the fact that she hadn't the slightest idea what he stood to gain by deceiving her so cruelly.

MOLLY UNLOCKED THE DOOR to her home and entered the front hall, listening to the midafternoon sounds of the old house—the clacking of typewriter keys, muffled footsteps overhead, the murmur of a television set somewhere, distant banging on the radiators.

Molly went through the kitchen and down the creaky back stairs to her father's lair, which was filled with assorted tools and various unrecognizable mechanical devices.

Walter and Andrea were both there, working intently. Molly's father was perched on a stepladder, doing something to the controls of a metal storage tank strapped to the ceiling, while Andrea was trying to direct a hose into a drain on the floor.

"Andy?" Molly said, looking at her daughter in confusion. "It's just past two o'clock. Why aren't you at school?"

"Teacher's meeting." Andrea looked up, wiping a cobweb from her hair. "Grandpa and I are draining the radiators. He thinks there's an air lock somewhere."

"Oh," Molly said.

"How about you? Why aren't you at work, Mom?" Andrea asked, straightening and brushing dirt from her knees as her grandfather climbed down the ladder.

"I . . . I felt a little tired and sick, so I decided to come home early," Molly said.

Walter Clarke looked at his daughter in concern. "Is it something serious, dear?"

Molly shook her head. "No, I'm fine, Daddy. I've just been working too hard lately, and I . . ." Her voice trailed off.

"Well," he said cheerfully, "I think we've found the problem here. The whole system should be operating properly by tonight."

"That's good. Daddy, I was wondering . . ."

"Yes, dear? Andy, hand me that vise grip, would you? I'll just tighten this valve, and we're all set."

"Now Grandpa and I can go back to working on the perpetual motion machine," Andrea told her mother. "Last time, we had it running for eleven hours before it stopped."

"It was just slightly out of balance on the outer wheel," Walter said. "If we adjust the weights, we should have it. The first sensible design in the history of the world."

Molly looked from one to the other. "Everybody in this house is crazy," she said, trying to smile. "Daddy, did you get the car fixed?"

"Partially. It's not perfect, but it should take you safely on your trip. Then we're going to have to look at a major servicing, though. Possibly a new transmission."

Molly nodded wearily, not even daring to ask what a new transmission might cost.

"Well," she said at last, "I think maybe I'll just pack my things and leave this afternoon, then. That way I'll be down there and ready to go to work first thing in the morning."

Walter's mild blue eyes took on a sudden look of concern behind his bifocal lenses. "Are you sure, Molly? You still won't get there before dark, and if you haven't been feeling well . . .''

"I'm all right," Molly said hastily. "Really, Daddy. I think I just need a change of scene, that's all. But I do want to get started right away. The weather's good, and the roads are still clear at this time."

Her father nodded, his face still troubled as he attached the vise grip. But by the time Molly had received his final instructions about the car and climbed the stairs to begin packing, he and his granddaughter were once again absorbed in the problem of adjusting the flyweights on their perpetual-motion machine.

They didn't even notice her departure.

MOLLY SAT IN THE CORNER of the room, making obscure doodles on her clipboard while controversy raged all around her. It was Friday, two days after her disastrous encounter with the real Kevin Donovan, and she still hadn't fully adjusted to the shock of that moment.

She was in a conference room at the larger of the two Portland stores, surrounded by a group of floor supervisors, advertising people and junior executives, none of whom could agree on a theme for a spring campaign.

Molly doodled a Valentine heart and stared at it gloomily, thinking about the humiliating letter she'd mailed to her boss and how he must have reacted when he read it.

After many hours of lonely introspection in her cheap hotel room, Molly had begun to understand a number of things. She realized that Kevin Donovan, heir to the Donovan chain, had certainly been in on the joke. After all, the handsome impostor who'd escorted Molly to the Breakers had been using Donovan's business card and credit card. And he'd even driven Donovan's silver

Porsche on both occasions. The cruel deceit had obviously been some kind of joint effort.

But why? Was there a smoke-filled room in a disgusting men's-only club somewhere, filled with trophies from practical jokes played on unsuspecting women? And was her letter the latest item on display along with stolen bras and panties for cigar-smoking tycoons to ogle and paw?

Molly shuddered, then jerked to attention as she heard her name. "Yes?" she said nervously. "I beg your pardon, I guess I... missed the question."

"Black and white," one of the copywriters said patiently, sighing and rolling her eyes. "We're talking about a spring theme in black and white."

"Well," Molly began cautiously, "that's certainly different...." She hesitated, thinking hard, all the Kevin Donovans in the world briefly forgotten. "Actually, I like the black-and-white theme," she went on with growing enthusiasm. "Checkerboards, stripes, spirals, maybe a few splashes of color."

"Splashes of color?"

"Spring flowers," Molly said eagerly. "Hyacinths, tulips, daffodils... maybe scarves folded to look like flowers against the black-and-white background. Very clean and fresh."

There was murmur of startled approval. The planning committee broke into little groups to discuss Molly's idea while she returned to her notepad. She drew an arrow through the Valentine heart, piercing it cruelly, then added drops of blood falling into the void below. Big, rounded, perfect drops of blood, like shiny tears...

Had the other man, the brown-eyed heartbreaker... had he turned up and waited for her Wednesday night in front of Darcie's apartment building?

Probably not, Molly decided. After all, he was part of the hoax. He knew everything that was going on. In fact, she realized with fresh indignation, he'd even been allowed access to her employment résumé.

"Molly Clarke?" A young secretary popped her head in the door.

"That's me," Molly said. "Over here."

"Phone call," the secretary said. "It's from the main office in Washington," she added, trying to sound casual as if she made this announcement every day. "Actually, it's Kevin Donovan."

Molly was aware of the abrupt silence in the room, the scrutiny that every eye gave her movements as she left with the secretary.

"Just take it there," the young woman announced, waving her hand at a desk phone. "I'm off on my coffee break."

Molly stared at the phone like a small bird eyeing a snake. She had no idea which of the two Kevin Donovans was on the other end, or what either of them could possibly want to say to her. "Hello?" she whispered shakily, feeling like a child summoned to the principal's office for some unknown crime.

"Miss Clarke? Molly Clarke?"

It was the real one, the elegant blue-eyed playboy. Molly realized with a wave of relief that she dreaded him far less than the other one.

"Yes, Mr. Donovan?"

"There seems to have been some confusion here in my office, Miss Clarke. Did you send me a letter earlier in the week?"

Molly swallowed rapidly. "I...yes, I believe I may have," she whispered, attempting to create the impression that she routinely mailed out dozens of letters and his just might have been one of them.

"Was it anything important?"

Molly felt a surge of disbelieving hope. "Oh, no," she said. "Not at all. I think it was...only a sort of report about the recent Valentine promotion, that's all."

"Well, I'm relieved to hear that. You see, my secretary logged the letter in but somehow it vanished before I could read it, and we can't locate it anywhere. My secretary believes she must have inadvertently sent it out with the trash on Wednesday afternoon."

Molly felt another dizzying flood of relief. "Oh, that's...that's wonderful!" she said, picturing her embarrassing letter dropping unread to the bottom of some massive landfill.

"I beg your pardon?"

"I mean," Molly said carefully, "it's very nice of you to let me know about this, Mr. Donovan."

"It was a little difficult to locate you. Your supervisor apparently had no idea you'd left for your duties at the other stores."

"But I left a note for him," Molly said.

Hadn't she? Or was she falling apart completely?

"Well," Donovan continued smoothly, "there's no harm done. My secretary contacted your family who told us where you are, then cleared it with your supervisor. How long do you expect to be in Oregon, Miss Clarke?"

"Probably...probably till late next week. I want to finish all the planning here before I come back, because after that we'll be quite busy with the main store at home."

"Good. We look forward to having you back. And, Miss Clarke..."

"Yes?"

"If there was anything important in that letter, please feel free to write me another one."

"Thank you." Molly drew a deep breath and gripped the phone in her hand. "Mr. Donovan?"

"Yes?"

Who was he? Molly shouted silently. Who was that man with the beautiful mouth and the laughing brown eyes, the man who held me and kissed me and turned my world upside down? You know his name, don't you? Tell me who it is. Tell me why he did that to me. Please, please tell me who he is.

"Miss Clarke?"

"Nothing. I'm sorry. Goodbye, Mr, Donovan," Molly said. She hung up the phone and walked slowly back into the conference room under the avid gaze of her co-workers.

Chapter Eight

MOLLY DROVE UP to her house late on Friday afternoon, sighing with relief at the thought of a warm bath, sleeping in her own bed after nine days on the road, and a quiet weekend at home before facing her regular job once again.

Not that weekends at home were that quiet, she thought, peering at the big house as she came to a halt behind a van parked at the curb. The place looked strange, even shabbier than she remembered—as if she'd been gone for years instead of days. But she'd called home twice and Charlie had assured her that everything was cool, so she assumed no major disasters had taken place in her absence.

Molly got out of the old car, opened the trunk to haul out her suitcase, then looked up in astonishment as a head topped with a bright red knitted hat popped into view over the peak of the roof. It was soon followed by another in a checkered cap. The two heads conferred earnestly while Molly stared up at them with her mouth hanging open.

"Hello?" she called hesitantly. "Hello?"

Two faces swiveled to gaze down at her.

"Who are you? Why are you on my roof?"

"We're tearin' the shingles off," the checkered cap shouted down at her.

"Split all to hell, them shingles," the red hat added cheerfully. "Worn right out."

"But you can't . . . why are you . . ." Molly floundered, looking around in confusion.

Gradually other things began to register in her mind. The truck across the street bore the label of a roofing company, and large bales of new brown shingles were stacked neatly at the side of the house, next to the chimney.

"Oh, for goodness' sake," she muttered grimly, grasping her suitcase and marching up the front walk. "What *now?*"

Molly let herself into the house, hurried through the foyer and then stopped in shocked amazement. Selma Clarke sat on the couch in the parlor, pouring tea into a flowered cup. She wore a well-cut tweed suit, her good pearls and some subtle makeup, and her hair looked freshly styled.

A blond woman in a green dress sat opposite her, reading from a clipboard in her lap, while a pair of young men with long hair and blue jeans were aiming a television camera at Selma as she poured gracefully from the china teapot.

She caught sight of Molly standing in the doorway, waved shyly then returned to the task at hand. Grace marched in, wearing her best silk caftan, smiled at the camera in queenly fashion and seated herself next to her sister-in-law on the couch.

The camera followed Grace's movements, too, then panned back to Selma.

"Mrs. Clarke, where do you get your ideas?" the blond woman asked.

A hideous scraping noise echoed through the house, followed by a series of bumps and crashes from high overhead. "Mummy, there are *men* on the *roof*," Molly whispered urgently. "Who are they?"

"Cut!" one of the young cameramen called.

Everyone turned to look at Molly. "They're roofers, dear," Selma said calmly. "Charlie's ceiling is leaking and

Walter said the shingles are all worn out, so I told them to come and fix the roof.''

Molly shifted her gaze to the blond woman in the chair, the young men with the television camera, then back to her aunt's impassive face. ''I see. And who's paying for it?'' she asked, struggling to keep her voice level.

''I am,'' Selma said. ''I hope I didn't do anything wrong, dear,'' she added anxiously when she saw the stunned expression on Molly's face. ''It's just that Charlie's room is so damp, the poor little dear, and I really think it's unhealthy for him.''

''I don't believe this.'' Painfully conscious of the strangers in the room, Molly set her suitcase down and approached her mother. ''It costs thousands of dollars for a new roof, Mummy,'' she whispered. ''How could you possibly—''

''Your mother sold a book, Molly.'' Grace reached out to grasp Selma's hand and hold it warmly.

Molly gaped at them, almost as startled by this show of affection between the two women as by Grace's words. ''Her book? She sold her *book?*''

''Not *the* book,'' Grace corrected. ''*A* book.''

''I don't . . . I don't understand.''

''Look,'' the blond woman said quickly, ''I think we have enough material here. Let's call it a wrap and come back later if we need more. Thank you both,'' she added, giving Selma and Grace a dazzling smile. She beckoned sharply to the two young men in jeans, who quickly packed up their equipment and trundled obediently after her to the van parked at the curb.

Molly stood at the window and watched them go, then looked at her mother.

''It was just . . . you see, dear, I started to . . .'' Selma floundered briefly, drew a deep breath and sipped her tea.

"I love doing historical research, and I wanted to think of a way to make it come alive for others, too. So I started inventing characters and putting them in actual historical situations, jotting notes about their feelings and observations, you see?"

Molly shook her head in confusion. "Not really, Mummy."

"Well, last year I sent some of my notes to an editor and she suggested that I organize them into a...a novel," Selma concluded awkwardly.

"A novel?"

"Historical romance," Grace said with relish. "Wonderful stuff. You should see what this woman's been writing, Molly! And we never even suspected, although I must say I've been seeing prosperity in her cards for quite a long time."

"But I don't..." Molly stared at her mother, her eyes widening. "Somebody *bought* one of these novels? They paid you actual money?"

"Ten thousand dollars," Selma said casually.

"Ten thousand dollars!" Molly exclaimed.

"That's just an advance against royalties, of course. And then the advance on the other two should be—"

"The other two?" Molly interrupted, battling an escalating sense of unreality. "There's more than one?"

"Well, I still need to do the final drafts on the second and third books, but the publisher's willing to go to contract with a synopsis and sample chapters."

"And then you'll get...you'll get another ten thousand dollars? For *each* of them?"

Grace beamed. "Isn't it wonderful?"

Feeling dizzy all of a sudden, Molly went to sit down in one of the shabby velour armchairs.

"Actually," Selma said thoughtfully, "Phil thinks the advance should probably go up with each book. He's checking into it today with a friend of his."

Molly looked blankly at her mother. "Phil? Who's Phil?"

The pounding on the roof cut through the silence that followed. Just then, Charlie entered the room from the kitchen, sighing dramatically and dragging a huge newspaper bag at his heels.

"Flyers today," he announced. "I'm *dead*." He paused beside the couch and looked with sudden interest at a plate of cookies next to the teapot.

Molly smiled at him. "Hi, sweetie. Come and give me a big hug."

"Why?" Charlie asked, stuffing a chocolate cream in his mouth and slipping several more into his jacket pocket.

"Well, because I haven't seen you for a long time," Molly said. "I've been away almost ten days."

"Oh, yeah," Charlie said. "You left just before Phil came, right?"

"Who's Phil?" Molly asked again.

"I believe Phil came the same day Molly left, didn't he?" Grace asked Selma. "Or was it the day after?"

"It was the day after," Selma said. "The same day I heard from the publisher. In fact, I remember showing the letter to Phil."

"*Who's Phil?*" Molly shouted.

The others turned to look at her in mild surprise. Charlie came over to lean against her chair, smiling down at her. "Phil got me a paper route," he said. "I make forty dollars every two weeks, so Phil says I'll be able to buy my skateboard by the time school gets out."

"But I still don't know—"

"Molly!" Helen came running into the room, cheeks pink with happiness, dark eyes shining. "I thought I heard your voice!"

"Hi, Helen," Molly said, surprised by the vivid glow on her sister's face. "You look so pretty. What's happening?"

"I just came from the interview," Helen said breathlessly. "And I have to wait till next week, but the librarian told me in confidence that he's sure I've got the job! Of course, I'll have to start at second clerk level," she added, turning to look at her aunt and mother, who both nodded indulgently. "But with my qualifications, I should be able to work my way up really quickly. And," she added, folding her hands in ecstasy, "I get to do children's story hour right away! Isn't it *wonderful?*"

Molly shook her head, feeling dizzier and more disoriented with each passing second. "Look, how long have I been gone, anyway? Does anyone know who I am?" she asked plaintively.

"What's the matter, Molly?" Helen asked in concern. "Aren't you feeling well?"

"I'm fine. Just a little dazed, I guess. Helen," she asked cautiously, "how can you . . . I mean, what made you feel confident enough to apply for a job? Aren't you still afraid of . . . of . . ."

"That man? He's gone!" Helen said happily. "Look, Molly."

She opened her handbag, rummaged in a side pocket and took out a folded newspaper clipping. Molly read it in growing astonishment. The photograph showed a grim, bearded man who had been convicted of sexual assault and sentenced to nineteen years without parole.

"Phil found it in the paper," Helen said. "He showed me last weekend. The man's gone, Molly! He's locked up and he can't hurt me. I'm free at last."

Molly stared at the clipping, awed by the obvious simplicity of this solution. Why hadn't one of the family members thought of it? If any man with a beard could trigger Helen's fears, then locking any bearded man safely away was likely to allay those fears.

She looked up slowly, gazing at her sister's glowing face. "Who's Phil?" she asked.

"Here he comes now," Charlie announced with pleasure, looking out the front window. "Hey, everybody, Phil just drove up."

Chapter Nine

WHEN MOLLY SAW THE MAN in the doorway, she forgot everything else. Her mother's book, Helen's job, the new roof and her family's sudden astonishing prosperity, all vanished from her mind as she gazed at him in stunned silence.

"Hi, Molly," he said, shrugging out of his jacket and smiling at her across the room. "It's good to see you again." The waning afternoon light shone on his golden head, and his dark eyes were warm with emotion as he gazed at her.

Molly's family crowded around the tall man, all vying for his attention. Charlie brandished a collection book and a handful of money in his face, Helen clutched his arm and told him about her employment interview, and Grace hugged him with cheerful energy, recounting the story of the television crew while Selma questioned him eagerly about his inquiries regarding publishing contracts.

"Hey," the man said, laughing. "One at a time, okay? I've hardly even said hello to Molly yet."

She sat frozen in her chair, trying to think of something to say. But he filled her whole world. There was no room for words or thought. The last time she'd seen him, he'd been striding down the corridor in Darcie's apartment building. Now he was gazing at her over the heads of the three women and the little boy, looking at her hungrily while she gripped the arms of her chair, her head spinning with confusion.

"I love you, Molly," he said, his voice husky.

"Who...who are you?" she whispered. Molly wasn't even aware of her family staring at her in surprise. She could see nothing in all the world but the tall golden man who crossed the room and held out his hand to her.

"Come with me," he murmured. "I want to talk to you."

She stumbled to her feet and followed him down the hall to the kitchen.

He closed the door and gathered her into his arms, sighing blissfully. "Oh, Molly, this feels so good," he whispered against her cheek. "It seems like a year since I last held you."

Molly struggled in his arms, almost overwhelmed by the familiar scent of him, the warm, remembered feeling of his arms around her. "Let me go!" she said sharply, pulling away from him. He released her at once and she stood by the table, hugging her arms in nervous silence, and afraid to look at him. "I don't even know your name," she muttered.

"I'm Phil Randall," he said gently. "Sarah's cousin. She works in menswear," he added when Molly looked up at him.

"But how did you—"

"I'm an accountant at Donovan's," he went on. "In the downtown office."

Molly began to have a glimmer of understanding. "And when they had the contest..." She floundered, her cheeks hot with embarrassment.

"When Kevin drew your name, I went rushing into his office and asked if I could take his place."

"Why?" she whispered.

"Because I knew it was the only way I was ever likely to get a date with you," Phil said calmly.

"But why did you have to lie? Why didn't you just ask me out, like any normal person?"

"I did," he told her. "Twice since last summer, as a matter of fact. I called and introduced myself, and asked if you'd like to go for lunch or dinner. You just brushed me off, said you were too busy."

Molly stared at him for a few moments. "I don't even remember," she said finally. "That's what I always say when people ask me out."

Phil touched her cheek with a gentle hand. "I know. Sarah told me. So when this contest came up and Kevin drew your name, I decided it was my big chance."

"And he...he knew all the time?"

"Of course. He even loaned me his car and his credit card so I could really impress you."

"I felt like such a fool when I realized you weren't Kevin Donovan," Molly said in a choked voice. "Like both of you were making fun of me behind my back."

Phil looked at her in surprise. "Nobody was making fun of you, Molly. As a matter of fact," he added with a reminiscent grin, "after Kevin met you, he was actually a little annoyed with me. He said if he'd had any idea how attractive you were, he wouldn't have let me take his place."

Molly's cheeks flamed again. "He called me in Oregon and said he never saw the letter I wrote. Was that a lie, too?"

"Kevin's a gentleman," Phil said quietly. "When that letter came to his office he knew it was for me, so he gave it to me unopened. Then he called and told you it had disappeared, because we both understood how embarrassed you'd be if you thought he'd read it by mistake."

Molly stared up at him, reeling from this new shock. "*You* have the letter?"

Phil patted his shirt pocket and smiled at her. "Molly, when I saw what you said in that letter, I was the happiest man in the world."

"But I said . . . I told you there was somebody else."

Phil waved his hand in dismissal. "I knew that wasn't true. What mattered to me were the other things you said. Oh, Molly, darling . . ."

He pulled her into his arms again. Molly closed her eyes in despair, fighting an urgent longing to yield to his embrace.

"Please," she whispered. "Please, don't do this." She pulled away and moved across the room to stare blindly out the window, her eyes burning with tears. Phil walked up to where she was standing, but didn't touch her. "It was so awful," she said, trying not to cry. "You let me tell you all those ridiculous lies about myself, and now I just feel . . . humiliated."

"Oh, Molly," he whispered huskily, moving closer and gripping her shoulders. "Molly, don't feel that way. I knew why you were making up a life for yourself, sweetheart, and it made me love you even more."

She whirled to look up at him, the tears trembling on her cheeks. "What are you saying? How could you love somebody who lies?"

"You weren't really lying. You were just dreaming, that's all. Look, Molly," he told her earnestly, "I loved you the first time I saw you, at the company picnic last summer, and I've made it my business to find out all about you. I know how hard your life has been, and how much you've sacrificed for this family. When you told me all those things I understood what you'd given up, and it made me ache for you all the more. And," he added, drawing her into his arms again, "I was flattered, too."

"Flattered?" she murmured unhappily against his chest. But this time she didn't pull away.

"I knew you must like me a little, or you wouldn't have bothered trying to impress me. I think that's why I kept teasing you about your apartment and the paintings and everything, seeing how long you'd keep it up."

Molly stiffened in his arms again. "And when were you planning to tell me the truth, Phil? How long were *you* going to keep lying?"

"I didn't know," Phil admitted. "I was walking a tightrope, too, Molly, because I didn't want to lose you by embarrassing you, and I was waiting for just the right time. When I got that letter, I knew there was hope for me. I called right away and they told me you'd already left for Oregon. I didn't want to contact you down there and deal with all this over the phone, but I was almost dying, waiting for you to come home again."

"So you decided to fill in the time by getting to know my family," Molly said dryly.

Phil grinned. "I told them you and I were really serious about each other, but you were shy about telling anybody so I had to come around and introduce myself while you were away."

"And they believed you?"

"Absolutely. They just gathered me in and made me part of the family. Grace said she'd already seen me several times in your tea leaves."

Molly's lips twitched a little as she looked at him. "Well, you seem to have worked some wonders here," she observed, "just in the short time I've been gone. I wouldn't be surprised if Andrea came walking in right now, wearing a party dress and high heels."

As if on cue, the basement door opened and Molly's daughter appeared, clad in grease-stained blue jeans, a baseball cap and a baggy plaid shirt of her grandfather's that hung almost to her knees.

Phil and Molly exchanged an eloquent glance. Phil shouted with laughter and Molly joined in, awkwardly at first but with rising merriment.

"Hi, Mom," Andrea said. "Hi, Phil. What's so funny?"

"Nothing," Phil told her hastily, swallowing a chuckle. "I was just telling your mother a joke."

Andrea crossed the room to get a glass of milk from the fridge. "Hey, Mom," she said, "pretty cool about Grandma's book, right?"

"Really cool," Molly agreed, brushing away her tears and giving the girl a misty smile.

"Andy, what's the current record?" Phil asked with interest.

"Sixteen hours and eleven minutes," Andrea told him, after draining the glass and wiping her mouth.

Phil arched an eyebrow and whistled.

"The perpetual-motion machine," Andrea explained when she saw her mother's blank expression. "We had it working perfectly, but then Charlie's stupid hamster brushed against the wheel and it stopped. Grandpa and I are resetting the flyweights right now." She set her empty glass on the counter and vanished into the basement again.

Phil watched her go, smiling fondly. "I love this place," he told Molly.

"Where do *you* live?" she asked him. "I don't know anything about you."

"Oh, come on. You know lots about me," he said with a glance that made her knees feel suddenly weak and shaky.

"I mean—"

"I know what you mean." Phil sat on one of the old wooden chairs and drew Molly onto his lap, cuddling her tenderly. "Actually, I live just about a mile from here, in a house a lot like this one."

Molly drew away and gazed at him in surprise. "Really?"

"Really. In fact, we've had pretty similar lives, Molly. We went to the same high school and everything, but I was a couple of years older so we never met."

Molly shook her head and relaxed into his arms again. "Do you have a family?"

"Not much. There's Sarah's family, my cousins, but I was an only child. My mother died when I was a teenager, and then Dad died of cancer last year. I came back to Seattle to look after him when he was sick, and just stayed on in the house after he died."

"And it's a big old house like this?"

Phil grinned. "It's in better shape, but it's quite similar. There's even a work crew on my roof right now," he added cheerfully, cocking his head and listening to the distant thumps and crashes.

Molly smiled. "You're getting new shingles, too?"

Phil shook his head. "I had the roof replaced last year."

"Then why is there a crew on your roof?"

"I'm having a couple of skylights installed," he murmured, kissing her. "Facing north. I think my attic's going to make a very nice studio."

Molly stared at him, wide-eyed with shock. "Phil..." she whispered.

He kissed her again, with growing passion.

"This is all... it's just moving so fast," she protested.

"*Fast?*" he echoed in disbelief, his lips on hers. "Does this feel fast to you?"

Molly nodded, giving in at last and responding to his kisses with hungry pleasure.

"Well," he whispered, "it feels to me like I've been waiting a lifetime for you, woman. I've been dreaming about you every night and wanting you every day...."

Molly shivered in his arms. A wave of feeling swept through her body, warm and sweet and tremulous. She recognized it as happiness, a wondrous, soaring joy that surpassed anything she'd ever known.

"Molly," he murmured.

"Hmm?"

"I want you to get dressed up. Go put on your pretty red dress, all right? You and I are going out on the town."

"We are?"

"I've made dinner reservations at the Breakers," Phil said.

Molly leaned back to smile at him. "What's the occasion?"

"It's Valentine's Day," he told her huskily.

"It is not. It's already March."

Phil gathered her into his arms and buried his face in her tumbled curls. "That may be. But, sweetheart, tonight you're going to be my Valentine."

And Molly knew that this time, he was telling her the truth.

A VERY SPECIAL FAVOR

Karen Young

A Note from Karen Young

Valentine's Day has always been one of my favorite holidays. This was especially true when I was a little girl. All during the week of February 14, valentines would be dropped into a decorated box in the schoolroom, and on the big day, the teacher would pass them out. All were eagerly opened and read, enjoyed and exclaimed over while we consumed Kool-Aid and cookies brought by thoughtful room mothers. It was a party, and parties were not occasions where shy and inhibited girls like myself usually shone. However, marking a valentine and slipping it anonymously into the box appealed to me. Of course, the best part was watching "my valentine" receive it. Maybe there would be a shy look exchanged, or a tentative smile. Or—somewhat dismaying—an eye-rolling look to heaven. Whatever transpired, it was a time of excitement and joy, the first lessons in learning to reach out to other human beings in friendship and love.

Naturally, when I began thinking of a story to write for Harlequin's Valentine collection this year, I knew my story would have to have a little girl in it. And so Jaycee was born. She is not shy and inhibited—far from it. But she is just as caught up in the magic of this special holiday as I once was. Appropriately, she becomes a matchmaker. And the two people marked by her Cupid's bow are happily reunited in love again . . . on Valentine's Day.

Chapter One

JOE MASTERSON pulled up in front of his house and sat for a minute, waiting for the sudden shower to slack off before making a dash for his front porch. February in New Orleans, sixty-eight degrees and raining. He thought momentarily of his sons in New York and wondered if they were up to their little rear ends in snow. Probably. That's what the weatherman dished up for New Yorkers this time of year.

He had his front door unlocked when he noticed his mailbox. And it had something in it besides junk, for a change. Two somethings, one long and legal-looking and the other pink and prim-looking. He frowned and pushed the door open. Bad news usually came in the mail. Another of life's little lessons he'd learned lately. A glance at the return address on the legal-looking one confirmed it. Laura's lawyer.

Tearing the envelope open, he scanned the words and swore. Low. Explicitly. Bitterly. She was taking the boys to England in the summer. She hoped he wouldn't be difficult about it. Grim-faced, he read on. She knew he was counting on having them, but the experience would be so rich for them, so educational, so...

Crumpling the letter, he leaned his head against the wall and closed his eyes. When his fury eased, he swallowed—hard—and tossed the paper. Later, much later, he would call Laura. This time, they were definitely in disagreement over what was best for his sons, and he wasn't going to roll over and play dead. What could be better for two young boys, aged four and six, than a summer spent

with their father? In his book, that was a hell of a lot more
enriching and educational.

As he scrubbed a hand over his face, the pink envelope
fluttered to the floor. He looked at it without interest before noticing it was unstamped. Bending over, he picked
it up. The return address was two doors down. The old
Kendrick house. At least, that was who'd lived there for
as long as he could remember. He himself had only moved
back into the neighborhood a week ago. He'd put off
paying his respects to Mrs. Kendrick. Somehow, at this
point in his life, he wasn't quite up to a conversation with
Marly Kendrick's mother.

No danger of that. This obviously was not from an
adult. Marly would be...what now? Thirty-four. Only six
months younger than he was. Absently switching on a
lamp, he studied his name and address, written in child-
ishly rounded script, and tore the envelope open. Inside,
whimsical characters decorated the single sheet. He read
the first couple of sentences and immediately forgot the
charm of the stationery.

Dear Joe,
My name is Jaycee Kendrick and I am eleven years
old. You probably haven't noticed me, since you've
only been in the neighborhood a week, but I recognized you right away. Not from the New Orleans
Saints, but from my aunt Marly's high-school yearbook. I have a tiny little problem and I wondered if
you would do me a very special favor, since you used
to know my aunt and all. You see, my Girl Scout
troop is having this dad-and-daughter dinner. With
dancing! So, I need a dad, but only for one night.
And since I don't have a real one anymore and Aunt
Marly isn't married, I thought you might do me this

little favor. Otherwise, I'm going to have to go with Richard Bradley, but he's Aunt Marly's friend, not mine. Thank you very much.

> Your neighbor and friend,
> Jaycee

P.S. My name is really initials and is short for Jennifer Carol.

Joe's hand dropped to his side, and he stared for a second or two at the ceiling. Marly Kendrick was living two doors down from him. In the house where she had grown up. Both of them back in the old neighborhood. And this kid—he glanced at the pink note again—Jaycee Kendrick, was her niece.

Heading for the kitchen, he slipped the note back into its envelope and dropped it on the countertop where his mail usually collected until he had the time or inclination to deal with it. He would have to deal with Jaycee Kendrick's invitation sooner rather than later, he guessed.

He'd have to refuse, naturally. There was no way he could face a thing like that, a bunch of giggly little girls and their fathers, all full of pride and blind love.

He knew about pride and blind love, of course. Every time he thought of Nick and Matthew, he felt it. But he was the father of boys. He didn't know a thing about girls. What the hell would he talk about with a little girl?

Muttering, he yanked the fridge open and took out a beer. Swallowing a mouthful, he stared through the kitchen window past the neighbor's unfenced backyard to the shady, landscaped lushness of the property owned by the Kendricks. Looking at it, he wasn't sure what he felt.

Son of a gun. Marly Kendrick.

"Jaycee?" Marlena Kendrick pushed the door of the attic wide and blinked a moment to get her bearings. The place was dim and musty, but she heard a rustle and then a familiar sniff followed by a canine sneeze just before Beau, Jaycee's golden Labrador, appeared. He looked at her with his tongue lolling and his tail wagging. "I know you didn't come up here on your own, fella," she said, rubbing his big head. "Where is she?"

"I'm just looking at this old stuff, Aunt Marly." There was an excited note in Jaycee's tone.

Following Beau, Marlena stepped gingerly over a fallen coat tree and picked her way through cobwebs and the dusty miscellany that had found its way to the attic over the years until she reached the dormer window. It was the second time in a week that she had discovered Jaycee in the cluttered hideaway. "What on earth, Jaycee? I've been looking everywhere for you."

Jaycee gave her a rueful look. "Gosh, I'm sorry, Aunt Marly, but some of this is too neat! Look at these yucky old hats." She pulled a wide-brimmed relic of the forties from a box and put it on her head. "How do I look?"

With her arms crossed, Marlena studied her at length. "Like Bette Davis with a French braid," she said dryly.

"Who?"

"She was a film star in the thirties."

Jaycee's face lit up. "I look like a movie star?"

"Well..." Smiling, Marlena gave her nose a tweak. "Let's just say if it was Halloween, you'd be ready."

Wrinkling her nose, Jaycee tossed the hat and began rummaging through another trunk. "There's great stuff in these old things, Aunt Marly. When I was up here a few days ago, I found some jewelry and perfectly good evening gowns, like for proms and all. Aunt Marly, did you ever wear this?"

She grabbed a print granny dress with deep lace-trimmed flounces that Marlena had worn to her first dance. She had been in the eighth grade and her escort was Randy Wiggins. With a smile, Marlena recalled the misery and delight of that evening.

And then her eyes fell on the book that was uncovered when Jaycee moved the dress. It was her high-school yearbook.

"I found that, too," Jaycee said, her voice cautious as she watched Marlena's expression. "Can we look at it?"

"It's only a yearbook, Jaycee," she said, wishing she had put the thing under lock and key. "High school seems a lifetime ago."

"But isn't high school a special time? Especially your senior year?"

Marlena looked at Jaycee. "How did you know it was my senior year?"

Avoiding Marlena's eyes, Jaycee looked down at the book in her hands. "I already looked ... when I was up here before."

Ruffling the little girl's bangs, Marlena laughed softly and sat down in the window seat. "You don't have to look so guilty, honey. There's nothing private about an old yearbook."

Jaycee looked up. "Really?"

"Really."

"Oh, boy!" With a relieved sigh, Jaycee wiggled into a spot beside Marlena and opened the book. "I was hoping you'd say that, Aunt Marly." She began flipping pages. "Here you are," Jaycee breathed, gazing at Marlena's senior picture. "Oh, you're so pretty, Aunt Marly."

"Do you think so?" With her head to one side, Marlena studied the photo. "Every girl in my class had the same hairdo: long and straight and parted in the middle.'' She chuckled. ''The natural look, you know.''

But her smile faded as she looked at the picture of herself taken on a day in May sixteen years ago. Thick tawny hair, amber eyes, even features, mouth a little vulnerable even then. Pretty? She'd never felt pretty. Maybe because she had been so painfully shy, naive beyond belief. By the end of her senior year, of course, she was none of those things, except possibly shy. Thanks to— She pulled her thoughts up abruptly. A trip down that particular memory lane invariably reminded her of the most crushingly unhappy time of her life.

''I'm getting to the best picture,'' Jaycee said, turning pages rapidly. ''Here!''

Marlena's heart gave a lurch. She should have realized that Jaycee would find this one.

''It's a Valentine Day dance, right, Aunt Marly?''

''Yes.''

''And that's Joe Masterson standing beside you, isn't it! You look so happy.''

As Joe Masterson's sweetheart, how could I have been anything but the happiest girl at Ben Franklin High School's Valentine Day dance? Joe, star athlete, quarterback of the football team, handsome, confident, sure to succeed. And he did, spectacularly. Without me.

It hurt even now to look at the picture. Inside the heart-shaped frame trimmed in roses and lace, she stood beside Joe. The photographer's command to smile had been unnecessary. They had only to look at each other to smile.

Marlena touched the page, tracing the letters beneath the picture: ''Sweethearts Forever.'' She, petite and fair, and Joe, big and dark, caught forever in that moment in time. The day the picture had been taken, Marlena had believed in forever.

She felt Jaycee's eyes on her face. "Can I ask you something, Aunt Marly?"

Marlena braced herself. After three years as Jaycee's adoptive parent, she knew pitfalls abounded when Jaycee started asking questions. "What is it, Jaycee?"

"A week ago, when Joe Masterson moved in just two doors down from us, why didn't you tell me that you used to know him?"

Marlena stood up, taking the book. "Because there was no reason to. Besides, it hasn't even been a week. The man just got here." She tossed the book back into the box. "Now—" she gave Jaycee a bright smile "—how about chicken and dumplings? That's why I was looking for you, funny face. It's dinnertime."

"You're not fooling me, Aunt Marly."

"Fooling you?" Urging the girl and dog along in front of her, Marlena shooed them out of the attic.

"You want me to stop with the questions. That's why you're acting all flustered."

"I'm not flustered, I'm hungry." Marlena yanked playfully at the French braid. "So hustle it, kid."

Jaycee squealed and ducked a playful swat, then with Beau at her heels, skipped down the stairs and preceded her aunt into the kitchen. "Did you go steady with him, Aunt Marly?"

Closing her eyes, Marlena breathed in deeply. "Yes, I went steady with him." Her face set, she handed Jaycee two plates. "Here. Make yourself useful."

"Why didn't you marry him?" Unaware of Marlena's stricken look, Jaycee plunked down the plates and turned to get silverware from the drawer. "I bet you could still be friends."

"Jaycee—"

Beau woofed and padded out of the kitchen, heading for the front door. "If you married him, you'd probably be rich and famous, too, just like him."

Marlena turned from the refrigerator with a carton of milk in her hand. "Wha-a-at?"

"I just said—" The doorbell rang and Beau woofed again, louder, his territorial statement. "I'll get it!" Jaycee said eagerly.

Marlena watched her disappear down the hall. Her niece knew better than to open the door to a stranger, so Marlena busied herself getting their dinner on the table and trying to put Jaycee's remark about marrying Joe Masterson out of her mind. She nearly had one weekend in February sixteen years ago. All the plans had been set, the blood tests taken. Joe had the ring and the license and the money for two nights in a motel. But then Pete Giarrusso had stepped in, and her whole world had shattered like too-fragile glass in careless hands.

Just as she poured Jaycee's milk, she heard the deep rumble of a man's voice. Wiping her hands, she sighed. Surely Richard hadn't chosen their dinner hour to drop off those files. She'd told him—

"Aunt Marly, look who's here!"

Marlena looked up into blue, blue eyes. The towel fell from her hands. For days, she had imagined this. Worried about it. A reunion with Joe Masterson was bound to happen sooner or later, but not now. Not this evening.

When, Marlena? When you can finally think about him without your heart tripping over itself? When you can see him on television without aching?

"Hello, Marly."

She nodded, barely. "Joe." Her voice was a hoarse, scarcely recognizable parody of her usual tone. "This is a surprise."

As Joe and Jaycee entered the kitchen, Beau trotted alongside him, his tail affectionately thumping against Joe's long jeans-clad legs. Usually when a man entered the house, Beau had to be forcibly restrained. When Richard visited, he had to be banished to the bathroom for the duration.

Joe glanced at the set table. "Have I come at a bad time?"

"No, it's only dinner," Jaycee said, obviously delighted. "We have it every night."

Joe laughed, meeting Marly's eyes. And then his smile gentled to match the husky tone of his voice. "It's been a long time, Marly. How have you been?"

"Fine, just fine." Her own eyes were taking in everything about him. She'd forgotten how tall he was. And big. How powerfully male. Joe had always possessed that special something that made feminine hearts beat faster. Just as hers was pounding now. It was a good thing he couldn't read minds. She cleared her throat. "And you? How are things with you?"

He shrugged. "So-so, I guess." One corner of his mouth quirked upward. "Still trying to get used to life after football."

"Yes, I read that you'd retired."

"I went kickin' and screamin', as they say."

She almost smiled. "Well, not exactly kicking, as I recall. That trick knee finally folded on you for good."

"Yeah."

"I'm sorry."

He shrugged. "All good things must end."

She thought of his marriage. Was that one of the good things that had had to end?

She took a deep breath. "Is this a social call?" She glanced at Jaycee. "Or has Jaycee been pestering you?"

"Jaycee?" He looked down at the little girl and found her watching them closely. "No, we haven't met until now." He reached for something in his shirt pocket. "Actually—"

"I don't pester, Aunt Marly," Jaycee said, offended. "I know that famous people don't like nosy neighbors, so I would never do that."

"Ah, but would you write a letter?" Smiling, Joe waggled a pink envelope at her.

"Well . . ." Jaycee darted a wary look at Marlena.

"What's going on here?" Marlena demanded, looking at them both suspiciously.

Joe handed over the envelope. "Maybe this will explain everything."

Marlena took it, holding his eyes a second or two. Then, looking down, she focused on the words.

Joe watched Marly, noticing the length of her lashes and the thick bountiful vibrance of her tawny hair. He had always liked her hair. He remembered the way it felt when he'd filled his hands with it, buried his face in it, inhaled the fragrance of it. He caught himself up sharply and turned his gaze to the window. He wasn't here to fan the flames of an old infatuation. Marly had given him his first taste of heaven and his first taste of hell. He wasn't about to be lulled into something crazy just because he had a little history with this woman. Besides, it was history he'd worked a long time to forget.

"Jaycee, how could you!"

Jaycee's eyes were glued to her sneakers. "It wasn't so bad, Aunt Marly."

"It was presumptuous and . . . and . . ."

"Desperate?" Joe supplied.

Marlena wheeled on him. "Do you mind! This is between Jaycee and me."

"It's Joe's business, too!" Jaycee said.

Marlena closed her eyes. "It is not Joe's business."

"It is so! I invited him, so I think—"

"Jaycee-e-e . . ."

"Wait a minute, wait a minute." Signaling with his hands like a referee, Joe called a halt to the argument. "Let's all just calm down here, why don't we? Marly? This whole discussion is over a moot point. I came over to respectfully decline Jaycee's invitation. It's—"

"Oh, no-o-o!" Jaycee wailed.

He turned to her. "I'm sorry, sugar. It's not that I wouldn't like to take you to that dinner. It's just that—"

"It's not a dinner! Didn't you read my letter? It's a dance! I need a daddy to dance with me." She whirled on Marlena, who was forming a reply. "And not that dumb old Richard, either, Aunt Marly. I hate him!"

"Jaycee!"

"Well, I do!"

"If you don't control yourself this minute, young lady, you're going to be grounded."

"That's not fair!"

Marlena propped her hands on her hips. "Is it fair to put a perfect stranger on the spot like this?"

Joe shifted uncomfortably.

"He's not mad," Jaycee said, looking confidently at Joe. "Are you, Joe?"

"Enough!" Marlena's patience dissolved. "Joe, don't answer that. Jaycee, take Beau outside for a few minutes."

"Aw-w-w, Aunt Marly—"

"His leash is hanging on the hook at the door."

"I know where his leash is," Jaycee grumbled, yanking it down and clicking it onto the overjoyed Lab's collar. "C'mon, Beau. We're being banished 'cause they want to talk *private* stuff. When things get interesting, I *always* have to leave." Looking wounded, she opened the door and, with dragging footsteps, finally left.

"I feel like such a grump sometimes," Marlena said in the thick silence following Jaycee's departure. Only after she said the words did she regret revealing her insecurity to Joe, of all people.

"Oh, I don't know," he said reassuringly. "I'm thinking a bright kid like Jaycee would probably eat your lunch if you gave her half a chance."

"She's a handful all right," Marlena said wryly.

He cleared his throat. "It's not really my business, but where are her parents? She's Jimmy's daughter, right?"

"Jimmy and Stephanie both died in a car crash New Year's Eve three years ago. A drunk driver."

"God. I'm sorry."

"It still seems . . . unbelievable. One minute they were a beautiful, happy family and the next, Jaycee was an orphan."

"Tough for you, too," he said, seeing the too-bright sheen in her eyes. She nodded mutely. He crinkled his eyes suddenly, as though looking backward in time. "You know, when I think of Jimmy, I always see him with that guitar of his. I never came over here when he wasn't plunking on it or holed up in his room listening to rock music so loud that his hearing was probably permanently damaged." He shook his head. "I'll bet he became a pharmacist or an accountant or something, huh?"

"Not really. He and Stephanie went to California, both of them convinced he could make a living with his music."

"And did he?"

"No." She smiled softly, thinking of her brother. "But he kept thinking he would, kept believing in himself. He dreamed really big, and Steffie dreamed right along with him. I often wonder..."

"What a waste," Joe said quietly.

Marlena went to the door and checked on Jaycee, needing a moment to compose herself. She was relieved when Joe asked about her mother. "She's remarried now and lives in Seattle, of all places. My dad died the year I graduated from Boston College."

"I knew that," Joe murmured. "Pete mentioned it."

Oh, yes. Pete Giarrusso, Joe's uncle. And manager.

"How is the barracuda?" she asked, unable to resist the barb.

"Okay. I don't hear from him much." Joe moved to the kitchen door and, with his back to her, pulled the curtains aside to look out. "He's not with me anymore. We parted company a few years back."

She stared at him in surprise. "I never thought he would let you off the hook."

Joe said curtly, "It wasn't his decision to make."

She laughed, a short sharp sound. "I'll bet he didn't see it that way."

He turned and looked at her. "What is this? Do you have some kind of grudge against Pete? Did he ever hurt you in any way?"

Hurt her? *Hurt* her? She stared at Joe for a moment, thinking of the last time she had spoken to Pete Giarrusso. He had handed her an envelope containing two checks and a one-way bus ticket to Boston. In return, she had signed away her happiness.

Had Pete Giarrusso hurt her? Yes, to the quick. Did she hold a grudge? Not really. She had only herself to blame.

"I'm sorry," she said, blinking a little to banish old ghosts. "Enough about Pete Giarrusso. I guess I get a little grouchy about this time of day."

"And I've interrupted your dinner." Joe looked as though he'd like to make a run for it, but he tapped the pink envelope against his palm. "But we need to talk about this."

"Not really." Marly glanced through the glass on the kitchen door, but couldn't see Jaycee. "I'll take care of it. Jaycee just didn't realize how inappropriate it was, asking you something like this. She's been going through some of my old things in the attic and she found the yearbook." With a shrug, she shook her head. "I guess that and the fact you'd just moved back to the neighborhood gave her the idea."

"Well . . ."

"She's like a friendly puppy, never thinking that she makes people uncomfortable. I've given her the safety lecture about talking to strangers, of course, but—"

The door flew open, startling them. Jaycee was outraged. "He isn't a stranger, Aunt Marly! He was your high-school sweetheart. How could he be a stranger?"

"Jaycee, I've warned you about eavesdropping."

Jaycee plowed on. "So he's not a stranger. Besides, it's two whole weeks before the dance. We can get to know each other just fine in two weeks. Then we wouldn't be strangers." Her eyes, big and appealing, went to Joe. "Would we, Joe?"

He stared into her upturned face, then gave Marlena a shrug. "What the hell, Marly," he muttered, rolling his eyes.

"Joe!"

"Hurray!" Jaycee cried, and threw her arms around his waist while jumping up and down. Joe lost his balance and sat down heavily in the chair behind him, but he was grinning.

"Oops, sorry." Jaycee calmed instantly and assumed the company manners that had been lacking since Joe had knocked on the door. "Would you like something to drink? Iced tea? No, beer. Aunt Marly, do we have any beer? We probably don't because Aunt Marly is mostly a white-wine person. That's what all her friends drink, too, except Richard." As she said his name, her nose wrinkled. "*He* drinks sparkling water." With her head to one side, she studied Joe. "You aren't the sparkling-water type, I don't think."

"No," Joe managed, swallowing a smile. The kid was a pistol. "Beer's fine."

"We don't have any beer," Marlena said firmly, her look and tone quelling her precocious niece. "And you have homework upstairs in your room, Jaycee."

"I haven't even had dinner!" Jaycee howled.

"And you may not for at least a week." Marlena pointed to the stairs. "Go!"

"Oh, all right." She gave Joe an anxious look. "I'm in trouble, but you won't let her change your mind, will you?"

Using two fingers, Joe made an X on his chest. "Cross my heart."

"Thank you, thank you, thank you! 'Bye." As she scrambled up the stairs, Jaycee flashed him a smile as bright as sunshine. "See you later!"

Marlena faced Joe, her hands on her hips. "It was totally unnecessary to encourage her like that. Jaycee takes a promise seriously. I'll be the one who has to pick up the pieces."

"I meant what I told her," Joe said, "and I usually keep my promises."

"Since when?"

Her expression took him aback. "What the hell does that mean?" he demanded.

"What do you think it means? You can't deny that you broke more commitments than you made the last year you played football. Personal and professional. Your public image is pretty tarnished, Joe."

"Do you always believe everything you read?"

"Not necessarily. But I can also speak from personal experience, and I'm just warning you that I won't allow you to sweep into Jaycee's life and charm her socks off while you're feeling expansive, then when it's suddenly inconvenient, bow out with a breezy apology."

He laughed shortly. "Hell, Marly, why don't you just say what you think."

"I don't believe in mincing words where Jaycee's concerned."

"Then believe this. I said I'd take her to the Valentine thing and I will. Furthermore, her idea for us to spend a little time together before the big night sounds reasonable to me. How about I pick her up tomorrow—it's Saturday—and we'll spend a couple of hours at Audubon Park."

She studied him at length, giving Joe the uncomfortable feeling she was seeing beyond the facade that usually hid his real feelings. What did she see? *He* didn't even know his real feelings. But it stung more than he expected to know she didn't respect him. It was surprising to find Marly still had the power to hurt him.

"Why are you doing this, Joe?"

He was wondering the same thing himself. He flashed his much-publicized smile. "Hell, to save her from the likes of 'dumb old Richard,' I guess." Marlena's beautiful eyes lit with golden fire, and he knew he'd have to pay for that taunt. Settling back in his chair, he realized suddenly that he was looking forward to tangling with Marly Kendrick.

AT THE TOP of the stairs, Jaycee flung her arms around Beau's neck. "Did you hear that, Beau?" she whispered ecstatically. "I'm going to the dance with Joe Masterson, the *famous* one-and-only pro quarterback, Joe Masterson. *And,* he's taking me to Audubon Park tomorrow. I can't believe it. Just an hour ago, I was going to have to go to the dance with *Richard.*" She grunted, trying to avoid the dog's slurping tongue. "Oh, Lordy, this is super! Wait'll I tell Melissa. She's going with her uncle. I'm glad I don't have one of those."

She craned her neck suddenly, trying to hear more of the conversation in the kitchen, but could only make out the sounds of their voices, none of the words. "Oh, shoot! I hope they don't start arguing again. If Joe doesn't watch it, Aunt Marly might change her mind." She chewed on her lip and chanted with her eyes closed, "Think positive, Jaycee. Think positive."

When the voices below remained calm, she relaxed against the big dog. "Boy, I was really scared there for a minute. I was afraid Aunt Marly would hang tough and just hustle Joe right on out the door and out of our lives." She screwed up her small face, recalling the words they'd exchanged. "I was right about them, Beau. They're star-crossed lovers—you just wait and see if they aren't. I'll bet there's some deep dark secret why they didn't get married when they graduated from high school. Just think. They could be celebrating their anniversary with a bunch of kids and we would all be living here together. Wouldn't that be a hoot!"

After a second, she straightened with a new thought. "I'm going to beg him to take you with us, Beau. You get to do your favorite thing. Just remind me not to forget your Frisbee.''

She caught the dog by the scruff of his neck and looked sternly into his face. "And this time, don't be running over to anybody's picnic stuff and gobbling up their hot dogs. The last time we went, you got in trouble doing that."

With a whimper, Beau made another slurp at her face, but she dodged it. Since she couldn't hear anything more, anyway, she decided she might as well go into her room and start her homework. She wanted to have something finished when Aunt Marly brought her something to eat. Which was a sure thing. She never stayed mad very long.

Smiling faintly, Jaycee sighed, deeply satisfied with her day's work.

Chapter Two

THE MOMENT Joe hauled himself out of bed the next day, his uncertainty about his suitability as an escort for Jaycee resurfaced right along with his body's usual protests. Rising in the morning was always an ordeal. His trick knee was stiff and sore until he worked it out. Almost as bad were the countless other muscles and joints that had suffered years of punishment over the course of his career, and they hurt like hell. Dragging himself into the bathroom, he smiled grimly. Over-the-hill pro athletes had aches and pains other people could only imagine.

All of which skewed his outlook somewhat every morning. It was hard to be optimistic when you were only thirty-five years old and your bones creaked like an octogenarian's. Today was no exception. His first thought was that he'd committed himself to something stupid. Jaycee was a bright precocious child—a girl-child, furthermore. He didn't know any more about girls this morning than he'd known yesterday when he'd knocked on Marly's door to politely decline Jaycee's invitation.

Marly.

Raking a hand through his hair, he braced his arms on the bathroom sink and stared at his battle-scarred features. He had admitted the truth to himself last night when he'd lain wide awake a couple of hours past the time when he was usually dead to the world. Marly was the reason he had promised to escort Jaycee. Even with their grim history, he was still drawn to her.

But, hey, it was too early in the morning to deal with that. Reaching for the taps in the shower, he turned the water on and stepped into the warm spray, relishing the soothing effect. After a while, he identified the other feeling that had been with him since he'd awakened.

Anticipation. He had made up his mind last night. He was going to persuade Marly to go with him to the park. He wanted to see her again, spend some time with her. After all these years, Marly still had the power to bewitch him.

"THIS WAS NOT PART of the plan, Joe."

"You're having fun, aren't you?" Joe sprawled on the bench beside Marly and grabbed the towel Jaycee had brought for Beau. "Is doggie sweat all over this," he asked, holding it up, "or is it safe to use?"

"It's safe, for now. But when Beau gets out of the lagoon, watch out. He's usually dripping water and some very questionable vegetation."

Marly watched as he scrubbed the towel all over his neck and face, drying his eyes and hair. After caving in to Jaycee's wheedling to play Frisbee with Beau, he'd spent thirty frazzled minutes trying to keep up with dog and girl.

"Has she ever considered pro sports?" he asked, watching Jaycee's antics with the dog.

Marly laughed. "Only soccer."

At a command from Jaycee, Beau plunged into the lagoon to retrieve something that resembled a tennis shoe, then lunged out of the water trailing a bedraggled lily pad from his neck and clearly expecting Jaycee to chase him.

Chuckling, Joe tossed the towel aside and relaxed against the back of the bench. Almost against her will, Marlena studied him. He was still breathing hard, and his skin was flushed. She could smell the musky masculine scent of hot male. To her surprise, her own body quickened suddenly, and she turned away, but it didn't banish the picture that had seared itself into her mind.

In high school, Joe had been attractive, but his looks then had been nothing compared to the appeal of the mature man. Even with rumpled black hair and disreputable faded sweatshirt and jeans, he was still mouthwateringly sexy. There were small scars here and there—souvenirs of his years on the gridiron, she supposed—but they only added to his rakish charm. It was no wonder that in his heyday, legions of women had fallen for Joe Masterson. Did he miss that? she wondered.

"I can't believe I let you talk me into this," she grumbled, turning her eyes on Jaycee. "I've got a thousand chores to do on Saturday mornings."

He rolled his head to look at her, his smooth sensual mouth quirked. "Women's work is never done."

"Yes. Laundry, cleaning, errands, you name it."

"Entertaining Richard."

She whipped around. "No, not entertaining Richard. That's hardly a chore."

"No joke?" He was looking straight ahead, his fingers locked together on his flat stomach. "I got a different idea from Jaycee's description."

"Jaycee is a child. I can't imagine why she says the things she does sometimes. I—"

"The plain truth, you mean? Kids are funny that way."

"No!" Hearing herself, Marlena breathed in deeply. "She doesn't dislike Richard, not really. What is there to dislike? He's a nice man, well-mannered, intelligent, hardworking—"

"Boring."

"No!" She studied her feet a moment or two, unable to prevent a smile. "Well . . . actually . . ." She cleared her throat and shrugged. "Maybe just a little bit . . . ah . . ."

"Boring?"

Still smiling, she shook her head. "You haven't changed a bit, have you?"

"In sixteen years? God, I hope so."

"You're still incorrigible. You still say exactly what you think, even when it's outrageous."

"It's outrageous to say Richard Whatzizname is boring?"

"Bradley, Richard Bradley. And since you've never met him, yes, it's outrageous to assume he's boring."

With his eyes following Jaycee and Beau, Joe appeared to think that over. "So, tell me something about Richard Bradley that'll make me change my mind."

"I have no intention of discussing my...Richard with you."

"Hmm." He shifted suddenly, draping both arms across the back of the bench. "Is your divorce a closed subject, too?"

She glanced at him quickly. "How did you know I was divorced?"

"Jaycee might have mentioned it."

Marlena sighed, knowing it was probably true. Without any prompting, Jaycee would eagerly fill in the details of her aunt's life if Joe encouraged her. Why would he be interested, though? He'd walked out of her life sixteen years before and never looked back.

"What happened, Marly?"

Marlena fixed her gaze on the fountain that graced the center of Audubon Park. The hiss and flow of the spray was mesmerizing, or was she just trying to avoid Joe's intense scrutiny? She never talked about her divorce, never hinted to anyone how painful the failure of her marriage had been to her. Because she'd already had one failed relationship in her past, she'd tried desperately to save it.

"None of my business, hmm?"

"Right." She flicked at loose paint on the bench with her fingernail, then looked straight at him. "My brother and his wife named me as Jaycee's guardian in the event something happened to them. As it turned out, my ex-husband didn't want the responsibility of a child."

Joe frowned. "Did they name you without your knowledge?"

"Of course not. They asked and we said okay."

"We?"

"Yes, Charles and me. We agreed, but when it came right down to it, he claimed he never really thought it would happen."

"Charles."

"Yes, Charles Kingsley."

"Dr. Charles Kingsley, the famous plastic surgeon? The guy who's always tacking and tucking the body parts of the rich and famous? That Dr. Charles Kingsley?"

"Yes, that one. I thought that when he got to know Jaycee he would change his mind. He didn't."

"Was it Jaycee in particular," Joe asked, studying her profile intently, "or kids in general?"

"Kids in general," she said, shrugging. "There are people who feel that way, you know." But Joe wasn't one of them. That was one thing about him she felt sure of. When they were dating, they had talked endlessly about the home they would share, the babies they would have. They'd even chosen names. In the months after their breakup, there had been a great gaping hole in her life as she'd searched for ways to compensate. She'd felt so empty, so lonely. Years had passed before she could even consider another relationship.

"And just look at us now," she mused aloud with a quick brittle smile. "You had the traditional marriage with two kids, not me."

"I'd hardly call my marriage traditional," he said dryly.

"Oh? Since we're talking frankly here, what about your divorce? How long has it been?"

"Almost three years."

She thought a moment. All the news about his knee and forced retirement had hit the press three years ago. Had he lost his career and his marriage at the same time? That would have been difficult, even for Joe Masterson. Unless he'd walked away from his wife and kids as easily as he'd walked away from Marlena sixteen years ago. "Your children are boys, aren't they?"

"Yeah." He shifted suddenly, bringing his arms down. With his elbows resting on his knees, he stared at the ground. "Nick's almost seven and Matthew's four."

"Four? But that means..."

"Yeah, he was just a baby when she split."

She felt a rush of sadness, quickly stifled. She didn't want to feel sympathetic. She didn't want to feel anything. "Is she remarried?"

"Laura?" He laughed shortly. "Within a week of the final decree."

"And your sons are with her?"

"Yeah, in New York City." He reached down and scooped up a penny lying in the grass and sent it zinging toward the fountain, where it plunked in among the water lilies. "Don't tell me you didn't see it in the papers. Big scandal, Laura Masterson and Alex Landowski, the pro-turned-sportscaster from Detroit. He was waiting in the wings when they wheeled me out of recovery after that last surgery. As soon as my loving wife found out I wasn't going to be negotiating another big-bucks contract, she was out of there."

"Taking your children?" In spite of herself, Marlena felt shocked.

He laughed again, not very humorously. "*And* the Mercedes. As well as half of everything else that could remotely be described as our worldly possessions."

"Well . . . she was your wife."

He nodded. "For nine years."

"What went wrong?"

"My knee."

"Your knee?"

"Yeah. My knee gave out and I was no longer in the spotlight. That meant *she* was no longer in the spotlight. She'd married me for the glory, and when she saw it ending, she looked around and found Landowski—whose career will keep him in the spotlight indefinitely, I guess. And Laura, too, indirectly. Which is what she wants."

"I'm sorry," she said quietly.

He shrugged. "It happens. Hey—" he straightened, then reached out and rubbed the back of his fingers against her cheek "—it's okay. I didn't mean to get on that subject. Guaranteed to ruin a good mood. I ought to know. At least my marriage wasn't a total loss. I have the boys."

"How often do you see them?"

"Not nearly enough. I have the usual visitation rights, a weekend once a month, alternate holidays and six weeks in summer. But with them living in New York and me here in New Orleans, from a realistic standpoint, it's not very practical."

"Have you considered moving to New York?"

He shrugged. "What's the point? They started out in L.A. Then it was Chicago. They're in New York now, but in a letter from Laura yesterday, I learned they're going to London, England, for the summer. London! She wants the boys to spend three whole months there. Enrichment, she calls it." He looked away for a moment, watching a young father across the park teaching his preschool-age son how to ride a bicycle. "I wasn't around to teach Matt how to ride a bike," he said softly. "When he learned, it was the first thing he said to me the next time I saw him."

"A lot of divorced parents have the same kind of problems, Joe."

"I know. But somehow that doesn't make me feel better." His expression was one of bewilderment. "How the hell can I be a decent father if I never get to see them?"

Joe Masterson, anguishing over his responsibilities as a father. It was the last thing Marlena had expected to deal with when she'd let him drag her out to the park with him and Jaycee this morning. She felt an almost irresistible urge to reach for his hand and hold it tight. She felt like pulling his head down and having a good cry with him for the moments, important and otherwise, in his sons' lives that he would never share.

"You miss them," she said softly.

"Yeah, a lot."

"And you love them."

He stared at his hands linked between his knees. "More than anything, Marly."

"Then they know it," she said, seeking to comfort him. "Kids can't be fooled about these things. You'll just have to keep trying, be there for them when they need you. That's all you can do."

They fell silent. His love and concern for his sons, thought Marlena, seemed deep and unshakable, at odds with the man she'd known sixteen years ago. The man who had professed to love her and yet had forgotten her so easily. Then again, he hadn't loved her with the same intensity that he obviously loved his sons.

Another thing that didn't make sense was his tarnished public image the last year he played football. She wondered now if he had been physically unable to handle his schedule. Knowing Joe, he probably preferred his public image as a hell-raiser to one of an aging over-the-hill jock.

When he turned to look at her, he somehow managed a grin. "See? I'll bet you didn't think there was anything positive about having an ex who wasn't interested in sharing custody of Jaycee with you."

She laughed wryly. "I guess I didn't. I'll count my blessings tonight."

"Speaking of which, here she comes right now." Looking beyond Marlena, Joe shot his arm straight up just in time to catch the Frisbee Jaycee zipped over their heads. Pushing off the bench, he handed the Frisbee to Marlena and grabbed the towel. "Come on, you two. Time to clean up and head on out of here."

Jaycee's feathers fell. "Aw, Joe, do we have to?"

Bent low, briskly rubbing Beau's soaked fur, Joe gave her a look of mock surprise. "You aren't hungry after this workout?"

"Oh, neat! Are we having lunch together?"

Marlena stood up slowly. "I don't think—"

"I thought a couple of Ruebens and maybe some root beer at the deli past the park on Carrollton."

"Hurray! It's my favorite." She turned big eyes on Marlena. "Please, Aunt Marly, can we?"

Joe looked at Marlena. Later, she blamed it on the conversation they'd had sitting on the bench. They had wandered into very dangerous territory, exchanging details of their past like that. How she'd let it happen, she didn't quite understand. Definitely there would be no more intimate talks.

JOE REFUSED an invitation to a party that night and, instead, went alone to a restaurant on St. Charles that made fantastic poor boys. He wanted to ask Marly, but knew better. Lunch at the deli was pushing it. She had agreed only because of Jaycee. Anything more would have backfired and probably jeopardized his long-range plan. He intended to get to know Marly again.

It was not unusual for him to spend an evening alone, even on a Saturday. He had a lot of acquaintances, but few true friends. In fact, the best friend he'd ever had was Marly. He had wondered about that sometimes in the years when she was no longer part of his life. She had left a hole, an empty place, that no one else had ever been able to fill. That had to be the reason he'd poured out his heart to her today in the park.

After an overstuffed shrimp poor boy and a beer, he walked the mile and a half back to his house, cutting through Audubon Park to Walnut Street, savoring as he always did the unique beauty of the Garden District.

Even in February, the famous neighborhood was a riot of color and fragrance. The leafless Japanese magnolia was in full lavender bloom, pink azaleas alongside white bridal wreath brightened spots in nearly everyone's garden; and pervading overall was the citrusy scent of sweet olive. New Orleans-born and -bred, he was as familiar with the flowering trees and shrubs as he was with the street names.

He reached the elaborate wrought-iron fence that enclosed his own property. He loved this place. Sixteen years ago when he had lived there, it had belonged to his uncle Pete. Joe had been shocked when Pete had sold it without saying anything to him the month after he'd signed the scholarship offer from LSU. Then, just three months ago, he'd discovered it was on the market again, and he'd jumped at the opportunity to buy it. It had been expensive, as was everything on Walnut Street, but it had been renovated by the former owners and was really something. Compared to the way it had looked when Joe had lived there with Pete, it was a showplace. Every time he opened his door, he congratulated himself again on his good luck.

Just as incredible was finding that Marly still lived two doors down.

Her house was more modest, but that had been true even when they were kids. Her folks had just barely managed to make ends meet. Her father, he recalled now, had been a sickly man. Joe could still see him, his face strained from being in constant pain, his skin pasty, his body so thin that his bones seemed too big for his size. He wondered now when Mr. Kendrick had passed away—sometime after he and Marly broke up, he knew. Things hadn't been easy for Marly at home, but she'd never complained. Suddenly he felt a rush of outrage that Kingsley had deserted her over something totally beyond her control. Had he expected her to turn her back on her own orphaned niece? What a jerk.

As Joe unlocked his door, he hoped she had at least managed to get a decent financial settlement out of Kingsley.

Tossing his jacket onto the sofa, he realized that Marly had been in his thoughts almost constantly since he'd left her and Jaycee after lunch. It felt right, having her in his thoughts, just as it had felt right being with her today. He had told Marly about his resentment toward Laura as naturally as he'd always confided in her. It was just like it was when Pete used to ride him at home, pushing him at sports, nagging him about his grades, setting stupid curfews, interfering royally in his life. Marly had been understanding and soft and feminine and loving then. After an hour with her, he never felt as battered and pulled and pressured. Through Marly's eyes, everything took on a different perspective. She hadn't been able to solve his problems, and he hadn't expected that. Hadn't needed that. He had just needed *her*.

That was why he had nearly lost it when he discovered what she had done.

Why? He must have asked himself that question ten thousand times, and he was still no closer to an answer.

When he came out of the bathroom, his phone was ringing.

"Joe, Pete here. How are you, man?"

Head bent, Joe pinched the bridge of his nose. "Doing okay, Pete. And you?"

"About the same, about the same." When Joe said nothing, he went on, "Say, Joe, there're a couple of folks here in Houston talking about putting together a weekend in the Big Easy. I thought you might want to talk to them."

"I think I'll pass, Pete. But thanks, anyway."

Another short silence. "Are you sure, Joe? There's money to be made with these people. They're interested in diversifying, and they've got the money to do it with. Fact is, the casino planned for New Orleans interests them a lot."

"It doesn't interest me, Pete." Joe shifted restlessly, looking around his big empty bedroom. "Look, I've got to run. I—"

"You're still ticked off at me, aren't you?"

"The truth, Pete? Yeah, I am."

"You tossed away a lot of money with that idea, Joe. A bunch of rowdy kids who don't appreciate—"

"It's my money, Pete."

"Yeah, well, a lot of my sweat went into making you what you were, kid."

"I didn't notice you sweating out on the playing field," Joe growled, "or busting your kneecaps. Or practicing ten hours a day, rain or shine."

"You're a wealthy man today because of me," Pete shot back. "If I hadn't stepped in, you'd probably be locked ball and chain to that Kendrick gal with a bunch of snot-nosed kids, struggling to make payments on a house and some old Chevy, instead of a paid-up Corvette in your garage. So don't come at me with—"

"Wait a minute." Although soft, Joe's tone stopped Pete. "What was that about Marly Kendrick?"

"Forget Marly Kendrick. That was a dozen years ago, Joe. She—"

"Sixteen."

"Huh?"

"It was sixteen years ago when I knew Marly Kendrick."

"Aw, Jeez. Are you still thinking about that broad?"

"Tell you what, Pete—" Joe clenched the phone in a grip that turned his knuckles white "—if you refer to Marly as a broad again or insult her even indirectly to me *ever again*, you'd better leave Houston for parts unknown, because I'm driving over there and *beating* an apology out of you. Do you read me, man?"

"Hey, yeah, yeah. I hear you, Joe. I didn't mean to pull your chain like that. I always knew that little girl could get you riled. But, hell, Joe, she's out of your life now."

"I just spent the day with Marly." Joe wasn't sure why he told his uncle, maybe to see what reaction he got. Remembering Marly's hostility when he'd mentioned Pete, he wondered if there was more to Marly's abrupt departure from his life than he knew about.

"You're seeing her again?" Pete's voice rose in disbelief.

"Yeah, Pete, I am."

"Jeez, well . . . hell, I don't know what to say, man."

He sounded wary suddenly. Joe visualized him mopping sweat from his face.

"How long's this been going on?"

"None of your damned business!" Joe snapped.

"Oh, uh, sure. Well, guess I'll let you go now. I—"

"What did you mean when you said if you hadn't stepped in, Marly would be part of my life now, Pete? How did you step in?"

"Like you said, boy, we're talking sixteen years here. I don't exactly recall—"

"Think. Think hard, Pete."

Pete released a long hissing breath. "We might have had some discussions about the time you were deciding on your offers. You had the whole friggin' world at your feet, man, you know. Eight major schools panting for you, the press watching, the pros waiting in the wings. You didn't need to be bound by promises made to a dowdy little high-school girl, Joe."

"You *bastard!*" Joe was breathing hard. Fury was a red haze, obscuring his vision, roaring in his ears like an overloaded freight train. "What did you say to her? You'd better answer me. Damn you! What did you make her do, Pete?"

"I didn't make her do a damn thing. A big check speaks louder than words of love," Pete said sarcastically.

But Joe didn't hear this last. He'd already slammed down the receiver. He paced the room, his thoughts racing. He was familiar with his uncle's high-handed interference in his personal life, but *this!* Raking both hands through his hair, he stopped. The magnitude of the transgression floored him. Pete, his uncle, a man he'd once trusted with everything—his life, his future, his happiness—had somehow engineered the tragedy that had cut Marly out of his life.

Chapter Three

ALTHOUGH MARLENA was already undressed, she wasn't in bed when she heard the knock on her front door. She had known that sleep would be a long time coming that night, and she had sorted through a stack of paperbacks before choosing a mystery. It was not a night for a juicy romance. She was unsettled by the feelings that had been stirred up after spending most of the day with Joe Masterson. She was also unwilling to examine her feelings right now. Maybe later...

The knock came again, more insistent now. She left the sofa and headed for the front door. Through the leaded glass, she saw a tall man, powerful shoulders hunched, fingers thrust in his jeans pockets, head down as though staring at his feet. Joe.

With her heart thumping in her chest, she hesitated only a second or two before opening the door.

They stared at each other without a word. In the filtered light from the street, he looked formidable and... angry. Marlena's hand went to her throat, but she stepped aside to let him in.

"I know it's late," he said. His eyes were dark and unreadable.

"Yes," she said, "it is."

"Is Jaycee sleeping?"

"Of course. It's nearly midnight, Joe."

He glanced at the book in her hand. "You were reading?"

"What is this, Joe?" She knew she sounded impatient, but it wasn't impatience she felt. She felt crowded, as though opening the door to Joe might start something she wasn't sure she was ready to handle. "It was Jaycee who was to spend time with you, not me."

"I just... Look, could we talk a minute, Marly? Then, I promise, I'm out of here."

She searched his face, but it told her nothing. With a small shrug, she pointed with the book to her living room. "It'll be best to talk in there. Jaycee's a light sleeper. With her imagination, I'd rather she didn't know you're here." She laid her book facedown on the coffee table, then perched herself on the edge of the sofa.

"I wanted to talk about the reason we broke up, Marly."

She was caught completely off guard. "What?"

"Sixteen years ago, why we went our separate ways. The way I see it, Marly, we had everything going for us."

"Sixteen years... I can't believe this. Did you come over here in the middle of the night to talk about ancient history? Couldn't you have waited till daylight?"

"Something happened tonight that made me start thinking about ancient history. I need some answers, Marly."

"No."

"No? What do you mean, no? We haven't—"

"You heard me. So if that's what you wanted to talk about, that's all I have to say." She stood up to brush past him, but he caught her arm. "*Don't*, Joe. Let me go!"

He stepped back, putting out a conciliatory hand. "I'm sorry, but...please, I'm not trying to dredge up old hurts or anything like that, or to place blame. I think I've already accepted that whatever you did, you must have felt it was for the best. I remembered how you reacted when Pete's name came up yesterday. I talked to him tonight on the phone, and something he said sent me off like a rocket. Incredible as it sounds, I'm beginning to suspect Pete had something to do with breaking us up, but I want to hear it straight from you.''

"What did he say?"

"Nothing much, because I didn't want to give him a chance to lie. I know from experience that he'll say anything to cover his tail. That's why I broke with him several years ago.''

Marlena rose and went to the dark window. With her arms wrapped around herself, she looked out. Here it was, the conversation with Joe she had imagined hundreds of times. But that had been years ago when she had still dreamed that he would not let her go. That he would search until he found her, and when he did, they would talk. Then everything would be the way it had been. They would reaffirm their love and then they would be together for the rest of their lives.

Keeping her back to him made it easier to talk. "I just don't see the point in rehashing all this," she said in an unsteady voice. "It's too painful."

"Why did you do it if it was so painful, Marly? That's the question I asked myself sixteen years ago. I must have lain awake a thousand nights trying to figure out the answer to that one.''

"I needed . . .'' She swallowed thickly, but forced herself to turn and face him. "We just needed the money so much. And the way he put it, the distraction of a wife would be something you *didn't* need just when the opportunity of a lifetime was being dropped into your lap.''

He was staring at her. "Wait, wait." His hand cut through the air as though to slice through a murky haze. "He? Who are you talking about? Pete? And what money?"

"Of course I'm talking about Pete. Who else? Why are you acting like this, Joe? You know what money I'm talking about, damn you! How do you think I feel? I was faced with a horrible choice, but it's over and done with now. I've put it behind me."

"You've put it behind you."

"Yes! Yes, I've managed to—"

"You killed our unborn child and you've managed to put it behind you." His voice was deadly soft.

"Killed..." Her hand went to her heart. "What are you talking about?"

With his eyes on the ceiling, Joe took a few deep breaths, calming himself. Then he looked at her. "I didn't manage as well as you, Marly. Even now, with two sons of my own, I still wonder about the baby you aborted." His tone was quiet, almost mesmerizing Marlena. "I wonder if it was possibly a little girl. If I'd been given a chance to know her, to love her, would she be with me now? Sixteen and beautiful, probably about the tenth grade, high school." He rammed his hands into his pockets before challenging her with a look in his blue eyes that was utterly condemning. "You know what I'm saying, Marly?"

"No," she whispered.

"Why so shocked? Isn't a man allowed to have feelings about his aborted child?"

"I didn't abort your child!" she cried. "How could I? I've never been pregnant with your child, Joe."

He was silent a full ten seconds. "Say that again."

"I don't know why you ever thought that. I never had an abortion. I would never make that choice." Her mouth trembled. "I...I... My God, it seems like I've longed for a baby forever. And...and...to hear you accuse me..."

"Jeez..." He sank onto the sofa, looking blankly around the room. "I thought... Pete said you... He showed me the hospital bill." Joe shook his head. "I was furious all over again because I had to pay for it while you scurried off to the other side of the country and enrolled at Boston College just as though you'd had your appendix removed."

"How could you think such a thing about me? Didn't you know me well enough to know I would never even consider aborting a child?"

"Pete told me—"

"Pete. *Pete!*" She dashed a tear from her eye in disgust. "And did you believe it just because he said it? Why didn't you come to me? Ask me? Who was Pete Giarrusso that his word made you believe such a...a...an abomination?" She stared at him, stunned.

"He showed me the bill," Joe said, still trying to take it in. "Your hospital bill. He took money from my account to pay it."

"That bill was for my father's medical treatment, Joe."

He was stunned. "What?"

"You really didn't know, did you?" Suddenly her outrage was spent. She sat down on the sofa, leaving a little space between them. With her hands pressed tightly together between her knees, she drew a shaky breath. "It's a long story—I'm certainly not proud of it. When I look back, I'm still not sure I did the right thing. I lost so much."

Her gaze drifted to the dark window again. "Pete had been hinting for a long time that marriage wasn't a good idea for a young athlete with a promising future. I knew, of course, how much you wanted to play professional ball. You had all those scholarship offers and there was the marriage restriction to be considered."

"Marriage restriction?"

"You know, that the best schools discouraged marriage. Your choices would have been severely limited if we'd gone ahead."

His mouth fell open. "That's crap! Who..." His expression cleared. "Pete again."

"Right. And I believed him. I believed all of it."

"You had your own scholarship! We could have managed!"

She went on as though she hadn't heard him. "Still, I think I would have resisted everything in spite of it all if he hadn't promised to pay my father's medical bills. His cancer was in the last stages, do you remember that? There was a sizable shortfall with the insurance. My mother was a basket case trying to cope. She worked a full-time job, and she had Jimmy and me to worry about. I did have that small scholarship, but it wasn't going to come close to paying full tuition and room and board at any school.

"Pete had a ready answer," she said bitterly. "Dad's medical bills paid in full, plus tuition and expenses at the college of my choice, provided it was at least a thousand miles away from LSU."

She looked sadly at Joe. "You'd made your decision by then. LSU, right here in Louisiana." She shrugged. "Of course, there were conditions. I was never to contact you again, never see you, never write you or call you."

With a whoosh of his breath, Joe eased back on the sofa. He was speechless.

"Even so, I thought *you* would call *me,*" she said quietly. "Why didn't you call, Joe?"

He shook his head helplessly. "Anger, I guess. I was hurt, too, if you want the truth, Marly. I had this ring, the blood tests were done, there was no reason for you to—"

"I didn't!"

"Yeah, I know. Now."

"Besides, we used protection," she reminded him "Always. We were very careful. You more so than I, i seemed sometimes."

"Not because I didn't want kids eventually, but be cause there was so much I wanted to do, *needed* to do—to take care of you, give us a secure future..."

He came up off the sofa and began to pace. "God, can't believe this. I can't believe we both let him manip ulate us that way. It's my fault," he said bitterly after a moment. "My ego was too big to fit on a football fielc about that time. I was so caught up in the hype spouted b those scouts, and Pete tapped right into that. He knew me too well. He had me convinced I was the next Joe Na math."

"You were," Marlena said quietly. "Look how suc cessful you became. You fulfilled everyone's expecta tions and more." She smiled softly. "My heart broke al over again every time I watched you on the field."

He looked at her, shaking his head. "How could yo stand the sight of me, thinking I had just walked away My God, we were going to be married after the Valentin Day dance."

"I know." Marlena said, clutching a cushion to he chest. "Why do you think I was so horrified when Jayce conned you into that father-daughter thing on Valentin Day, of all things?"

He stopped and bent to touch her cheek. "I should hav gone to you the minute Pete told me that filthy lie. But was just feeling so...so miserable. I had that stupid not you sent and my ring returned and...and our baby de stroyed, or so I thought. My whole world turned upsid down, and it was too late to do anything about it." He sa down again and caught her hand when she touched him lightly on his thigh. He squeezed it fervently. "All lies."

She had a quick heart-wrenching picture of Joe reading the brief note she'd managed to compose, trying to read between the lines. "My favorite fantasy used to be that you wouldn't believe the note. That you'd tell Pete the scholarship wasn't more important to you than I was. That you'd come to Boston and we'd get married just as we'd planned. The best part was we'd just show up in New Orleans and tell Pete to go take a hike. I'd taken his money, but we could have paid it back."

"Which is exactly what I did," Joe said, studying their clasped hands. "Tell Pete to take a hike, I mean. Only it was about a dozen years too late."

"He saw me as a threat, I suppose," Marly said.

"Not really." With his free hand, Joe traced the line of her cheek, then caressed the warm skin of her neck before withdrawing. "He wanted to manage my career and the money I was sure to make as a pro. A wife was an expensive irritant, from Pete's point of view—then and later. I'm more than familiar with his philosophy on the subject," he said wryly.

"At least you finally saw through him." As she spoke, Marlena shifted slightly and pulled her hand from his. "I'm human enough to feel good that he got what was coming to him."

"He didn't get what was coming to him. For what he did, he should have been horsewhipped."

"It's over now, Joe. Behind us. It seems like a century ago in some ways," she said softly. "And in others..."

"Yeah."

They fell silent, occupying the same sofa in the same room where they'd first kissed. Both were thinking of the emotions that had driven them then. Hot tempestuous young love, frenzied moments of sexual stimulation followed by hours of agonized frustration, until they had finally succumbed.

She remembered it as though it had happened just last week.

Her mother had been at the hospital and Jimmy had been at a rock concert. Outside, it had begun to rain softly. Thunder had rumbled deep and low in the distance as they discovered the ultimate satisfaction to be found in making love.

She had dreamed of it for years afterward.

"You look wonderful," Joe said now, as though he couldn't hold back the words another minute.

"So do you." She touched a small scar on his cheek and smiled softly. "A little harder, a little battered, but still very handsome. How did you manage to hold off all those groupies?"

"I had a wife, remember?"

"Yes."

His eyes, as he watched her, were dark with unspoken needs. She knew it wasn't Laura he was thinking of.

He settled back on the sofa, smiling faintly. "Fill me in. What did you study at Boston College? Where do you work now?"

"Physical therapy. I work at St. Luke's."

"The children's hospital."

"Yes."

"So you work mainly with kids?"

"Yes, I do. And I love it."

He shook his head ruefully. "I really have done you an injustice all these years thinking what I did, haven't I?"

"It wasn't your fault."

"I should have followed up. I should have—"

She leaned forward and touched his knee. "Hush, Joe."

Their eyes met and held while a sudden flurry of wind rattled the windows of the old house. A storm seemed to be building, adding to the charged atmosphere inside. Looking into Joe's eyes, Marlena found that her heart was suddenly thundering in her chest. She wasn't sure she was capable of handling the emotions that were rioting through her.

"Marly, I want to—"

"No." She scrambled to her feet, clutching a small pillow from the sofa. "I don't think we should say anything more tonight, Joe," she said shakily. For a few seconds, Joe didn't move. He looked at her steadily as though trying to gauge whether she really meant what she said. Inside her, a tiny hope fluttered like the petals of a flower unfurling in early-morning sun. But caution won out. She was not going to be seduced by the past.

"Okay," he said, and stood up. He watched her fold her arms around the cushion, holding it like a shield. When he spoke, it was softly. "You look scared, honey, and there's no need. We have unfinished business, you and me, but this time we've got time to get it right. And there's no one to interfere."

He touched her cheek. "I'll see you in the morning."

"No, Beau! Stay!" At Jaycee's fierce whisper, the dog sank back on his haunches with a whimper. She hugged him apologetically and then flopped down on her belly beside him, her chin on her elbows. "If you go charging down the stairs, they'll know we're up here."

She strained to hear, but could only make out the soft tone of her aunt's voice and the deeper rumble of Joe's, no words. As usual. Oh, shoot! she thought. But it would be taking a big chance to sneak down and openly eavesdrop. Aunt Marly had a serious thing about snooping.

"What do you think, Beau? How's it coming? Are they warming up a little to each other? I think they are. I'm almost positive they are."

She wrinkled her nose and then *really* strained to hear something. Anything. "Wonder why Joe's here tonight? It's got to be serious, otherwise he could have just called on the phone. But he waited until I was out of the way and the coast was clear to say something *significant*. That's what it is, Beau. Something *vital* to their blossoming relationship."

Her breath caught in a quick gasp. "I bet I know what it is! They're talking about the reason they broke up way back then. That's good, Beau. Communication is the key to a successful relationship. That's what it says in all those articles in *Cosmo* and *Redbook* Aunt Marly's always reading."

Downstairs, the sound of voices was suddenly clearer. Joe was at the door. "Oops! We gotta move it, Beau." Scrambling up from the floor, she caught the dog before he made a dash down the stairs. Before she hustled off to her own room, she couldn't resist a quick peek at the two adults.

"Just look at that, Beau," she said softly, a smile curving her lips. "They've gotta say good-night, but they don't want to. Know how I can tell? It's the way they're acting. Joe looking at Aunt Marly really *deep,* you know? And Aunt Marly with her arms wrapped around herself like that. I bet they want to kiss, but they're just too shy. Remember, today was only their first date since they were reunited."

Tilting her head, she observed them through the rungs on the stair rail with near clinical detachment. "As they say, tomorrow is another day. It's Sunday, too. When I'm in church, I'll try to think of an excuse to get them together again.''

Turning with reluctance, she motioned for Beau. "Come on, Beau, I guess they need a *little* privacy."

Chapter Four

THE RICH STRAINS of the organ lifted in the Invocation as the congregation quieted and settled back with a few coughs and a general shuffling of hymn books. Conversation ceased gradually until a sense of reverence pervaded the vast sanctuary. The eleven o'clock service at the First Presbyterian Church began.

Marlena idly studied her bulletin while Jaycee and her friend Melissa paged through the hymnal searching for the next song. Other worshipers suddenly shifted along the pews to make room for a late arrival. Marlena looked up speechlessly as Joe Masterson, murmuring apologies and flashing his killer grin, worked his way over knees and feet and finally paused beside her. With a lift of his dark eyebrows, he asked permission to sit beside them. Jaycee, quick to seize opportunity when it knocked, scrambled sideways, practically sitting on Melissa. After only a slight hesitation, Marlena sighed and made room for him.

"What are you doing here?" she demanded in a fierce whisper.

"Attending church," he returned, standing with everyone else for the first hymn.

Flustered and thrilled at the same time, Marlena stared straight ahead. Beside her, she heard his voice raised in song. It was rich and true and deep, just as it had been sixteen years ago, when he sang along with the Rolling Stones or Billy Joel as the music blasted from his car radio.

The hymn ended and they sat down to listen to the sermon. But the minister's words were lost on Marlena.

Nothing registered except Joe. With his shoulder touching hers, she became a receptacle of sensory messages. He looked gorgeous in gray slacks and a pale yellow button-down shirt beneath a navy blazer with gold buttons. He smelled delicious, too. His after-shave was intensified by his masculine heat, which was almost physical, reaching out like a powerful force field, enclosing her, warming her, driving her crazy.

As though sensing her thoughts, he turned to look at her. His grin, when it came, was slow and mesmerizing. When he saw the flush on her skin, it faded and his eyes darkened. That was when he took her hand and laced his fingers with hers.

And that's how they stayed until the benediction.

SOMEHOW OR OTHER, Joe managed to be with Marly at least a small part of every day the next week. He took Jaycee to the movies, but when they went to eat pizza afterward, Joe dropped by to pick up Marlena. She took Jaycee to soccer practice on Tuesday, and Joe appeared. He fell easily into a familiar role, yelling good-natured advice to the referees right along with the other dads on the sidelines. On Wednesday, Jaycee's Girl Scout troop met at a house that was within walking distance. Joe just happened to be there when Marlena went to get her. Commenting that she looked tired, he took them to the deli on Magazine Street, where they picked up seafood gumbo to go. What choice did she have except to invite him in to eat it afterward?

"Do you have any kind of job?" she asked him. It was eight o'clock Thursday night, and she was at the library to pick up Jaycee, who was doing research with Melissa for their science project. He'd shown uncanny skill in learning Jaycee's schedule and had appeared in his Corvette just as Marlena was leaving her house to go to the library. He'd insisted on driving.

"Nothing that might interfere with getting to know Jaycee before the dance," he said.

"You don't work at all?"

"Depends on what you mean by work."

"You used to say you wanted to be a coach someday."

With his shoulders wedged into the space between the wheel and the door, he shrugged. "Well, as they say, that was then, this is now."

She stared at him. "I would think now is the perfect time. A hundred schools—or colleges, for that matter— would jump at the chance to hire a man with your professional credentials. I'm assuming you're financially secure, so you wouldn't necessarily have to take the most lucrative job. Think of the role model you could be to disadvantaged kids."

He looked away from her. "A coaching career is a dream I left behind with the pro ranks."

She shook her head, confused. "You lost me, Joe. I guess I don't get the connection."

He moved suddenly and pushed a CD into the slot. "How about a little Michael Bolton?"

She put her hand over his to stop him. "Wait a minute."

"No? Then how about Harry Connick, Jr.?"

"No! Forget music, for heaven's sake. I'm trying to ask about your real life, Joe. What are you going to do when you grow up? What have you got going that makes it worth the effort of getting up in the morning?"

He gave a short harsh laugh. "Not a lot, short of a miracle, that is."

"What?"

"Nothing. Look, Marly—" he leaned back and rested both hands on the steering wheel "—this is something I'd rather not talk about, okay?"

Work was a sensitive subject? Studying him silently, Marlena realized that to him, it was. She had somehow stumbled onto forbidden ground, but she wasn't sure why. He had talked freely about his ex-wife, his separation from his sons, even about his break with his uncle. But on this subject, he was touchy and defensive. It had to be that he was still hurting from being forced to leave pro ball. She flushed with embarrassment over her clumsiness. She didn't normally invade a friend's privacy.

"I'm sorry," she murmured. "I don't have any business passing judgment on the way you've chosen to live your life. Will you—"

"Hey, Melissa, it's Joe and Aunt Marly!" Jaycee suddenly materialized beside the Corvette at Joe's window. "Are we going somewhere neat? There's this movie—"

"No, Jaycee, we are not going to a movie tonight," Marlena said firmly. Jaycee's disappointment was almost comical. "We aren't going anywhere except home. That is, if you've finished work on your project."

"Aw shoot, Aunt Marly, I don't see why we—"

"Okay, squirt." Joe pushed open the door and stood up smoothly. "You heard your aunt. Time to wrap it up." He glanced at Melissa. "Have you got a ride, honey?"

"Yes, sir, my mom's just driving up."

He gave a wave and a smile to the dark-haired woman in a gray minivan pulling into a spot two cars away, then waited while Melissa walked over and climbed inside. Meanwhile, Jaycee got into the Corvette, sharing Marlena's space, as there was no back seat.

"You two okay?" he asked, glancing over to check their seat belt.

"Fine," Marlena returned, ignoring Jaycee's back-pack poking into her ribs. It was only a ten-minute drive home. "What do you do when your sons visit you? This is hardly a family car."

"I've got a Land Rover. Stays in the garage most of the time."

"Oh." Well, she thought, he might not have a visible means of support, but he obviously didn't have to worry about money. She anchored her arms around Jaycee's waist as the Corvette peeled away from the curb and melted into the traffic on St. Charles.

"Can we ride in the Corvette to the Valentine Day dance, Joe?"

"Sure, squirt, why not?"

"Well, Aunt Marly will probably have on a special dress and I didn't know if it'd get all scrunched up, sitting like this."

"*You'll* have on a special dress, too, love," Marlena said, giving her a quick squeeze.

"Wait a minute here." Joe stopped at a red light and looked at them. "I thought this was a father-daughter thing and no mothers allowed. How is it that Marly's going?"

Jaycee gave him a long-suffering look. "Oh, Joe. Who do you think will serve the punch and cut the cake and all? And take care of, you know, mother stuff? Kristin Steward *always* gets sick and throws up, no matter what."

"Not to mention kitchen duty," Marlena muttered.

"Also mother stuff?" He gave her a teasing look over Jaycee's head. "Women's work is never done." When she rolled her eyes, he just laughed and gunned the Corvette.

In minutes, he pulled over to the curb in front of Marlena's house. Jaycee flicked the seat belt open and tumbled onto the sidewalk. Behind the fence, Beau began barking enthusiastically.

"I'm going to let him out, Aunt Marly!" she said, dashing to the gate. "He's been penned up for *hours!*"

"Careful! Be sure to. . ." Marlena sighed. "Oh, well. It's like trying to hold back a tornado." She gave Joe a wry smile as they got out of the car. "They both have so much pent-up energy it's better to let them run it off outdoors than try to keep them quiet inside the house."

With his hand at the small of her back, Joe walked her up the sidewalk. "I have the same problem when the boys are with me."

"When will you have them again?"

"Soon." He followed her up the porch steps and waited while she found her house key. "A whole week at Easter."

"Nice for you, right?"

"Yeah." He looked up as Beau came tearing around the corner with Jaycee chasing him. "Uh-oh, looks like Beau's slipped his leash. Here, boy!" He started down the steps.

"Catch him, Joe!" Jaycee hollered. "He's headed next door. He saw Mr. Wiggins's cat!"

As the Lab raced ahead of her, Joe made a grab for him, but Beau easily swerved out of reach. Joe turned—and felt the instant slash of white-hot pain as his knee twisted and gave way.

"Joe!"

From a haze of agony, he heard Marly's shocked voice. It was always like this when he was unlucky enough or, in this case, stupid enough to forget he didn't have a knee anymore, only a surgically reworked facsimile.

"Joe, what's wrong? How are you hurt? Jaycee, go call 911!"

"No!" he barked. "No, for God's sake, that's all I need, the whole town to..." He breathed in deeply, leaning back against the edge of the old-fashioned steps. "Just don't call anyone. I'll be able to get up in a minute."

He knew he was probably as gray as death. He always lost color and began to sweat when he hurt the damn thing.

"You can't get up!" Marlena said in a tone Jaycee knew never to argue with, but even as the words were out, Joe reached for the wrought-iron railing on the steps and was levering himself upright, his weight on his good leg.

He managed to struggle to his feet, but his face was strained and his lips white. He looked at her. "Mind if I come inside a minute or two?"

Her expression held concern and openmouthed disbelief that he'd even asked. "Jaycee, go into the house and get some ice from the freezer and put it in a plastic bowl. Then get a couple of towels from the bathroom and put them on the coffee table in the TV room. When you've done that, go fetch Beau."

"Yes, ma'am." After a quick scared look at Joe, she flew to obey.

"I think we'll probably be able to get you up these steps if you just lean on me," Marly said. Without waiting for him to agree, she slipped one arm around his waist and looped his right arm over her shoulder. It was his right knee that was injured. She hesitated before they moved, looking at him.

"Not a pretty sight, huh?" He knew he looked like hell. It was pointless to pretend otherwise.

"I've seen worse."

She was a professional. He recalled with irony what her job was. If he had to collapse in anybody's yard, he should be glad it was Marly's. But he wasn't glad, not by a long shot. He felt betrayed by his own body, short-changed and bitter. He was no longer strong and healthy, no longer the agile, physically superior athlete he once had been.

"I need to go home," he said between clenched teeth.

"How?" she asked simply. "You've nixed 911."

"Just give me a hand to my car and—"

"Don't be ridiculous! Even with an automatic, you couldn't work the brake except with your left foot. How would you get out and climb the porch steps to your front door? There are only three here. You have at least ten. And then what? You've probably got pain pills for these occasions, hmm?"

He grunted, not looking at her.

"But you've been told—cautioned, I imagine—that after an injury, you need first aid before zonking out with pain medication."

"I don't zonk out," he growled, wincing as he shifted to keep his balance. "I hate that stuff. I only use it as a last resort."

"And if we don't get you out of those jeans fast, your knee will swell so much that only scissors will get you out of them." Her face softened with her voice. "Listen, Joe, I'm good at this. Let me help you. You should get off your feet immediately—you know the drill."

He swore softly and vehemently.

With a small sound, she tightened her arm around his waist. Was it a little hug? He wasn't certain, but he realized he needed one, especially if it came from Marly.

"Now, up we go," she said, and gently nudged him up the first step.

THE NEXT MORNING, Joe came awake slowly. His body was steeped in a deep peaceful lassitude, heavy and weightless at the same time. Utterly relaxed. He could hear his own heartbeat, strong but unhurried, and his breathing, slow and even. He couldn't remember ever waking up and feeling so...so good. With his eyes closed, he drew a long deep breath and thought of Marly.

He was in her bed. The scent of her was all around him, on the pillow, in the bedclothes, on his own skin. Slowly and hopefully, he turned his head, but she was not beside him.

She had insisted on going to his house last night and getting gym shorts so that she could strip him to take care of his knee properly. After an hour of ice packs, she had offered her own bed and treated him to an hour of massage. She had called it therapeutic. He called it blissful torture.

He didn't remember much after that. She had persuaded him to take one of the narcotics he loathed, and that was the last he knew. Until now.

He pushed the covers aside and with a groan agonizingly got to his feet.

Slow, slowly does it, buddy. Don't want to crash on the floor and show the ladies in this house what a wreck you really are.

Not that he had any secrets from the lady in charge now. After last night, she knew everything there was to know. She knew his knee was destroyed. She knew how he had to baby it every day for the rest of his life. She knew he was not the man he'd once been and never would be again.

Moving very carefully, he made it to the bathroom.

Marly was waiting for him when he got out.

"Hi," she said, smiling and looking like a tawny-haired angel in a pink T-shirt and no bra.

"Hi yourself." His mouth was suddenly dry, in spite of the long drink of water he'd consumed. The T-shirt was oversize but still showed enough of her sleek long legs to remind him that in all his experience, he'd never seen better.

"Everything okay?" she asked, giving him a quick once-over.

"Yeah, I'm fine."

"As fine as you ever are in the morning."

He shrugged. It wasn't a question.

"Tough getting up, hmm?"

"I manage."

"Then if you can manage to get back into bed, I'll just check that knee."

"It's okay," he said, still propped in the bathroom door frame.

"Joe . . ." She drew his name out like a caress.

"It's a little tender, but—"

"Lie down. This is my job. This is what I do."

"Taking in lame athletes?" His fierce look stopped her in her tracks as she moved to help him. With a bitter twist of his mouth, he reached for the corner of a dresser and began shuffling toward the bed.

He sank gratefully onto the mattress, swallowing a groan. With a glance, he saw she wasn't fooled. She gave him a gentle push, sending him backward against the pillows, then waited until he lifted his good leg onto the bed before helping him with his injured one. Tucking a pillow under it, she began removing the ace bandage.

"Looks all right," she said, studying it professionally. She probed a little here and there, glancing at his face when she expected him to feel it, but his expression remained impassive.

"Hang in there," she advised, beginning to work the knee in a gentle bend, then skillfully kneading the thigh muscles above it. "I know it hurts like hell. I guess another pain pill is out, huh?"

With a negative grunt, he threw his arm over his eyes. Usually, after an incident like this, the pain in his knee was so enveloping, so all-encompassing, that he was incapable of much of anything for a day or two. He should get up and go home, and he would in a minute. But what she was doing felt too good. Her hands moved with magical skill, finding a taut muscle, working it, stroking away the stiffness, neutralizing the throbbing pain.

To distract himself, he watched her from beneath his arm, thinking again how much more beautiful she was now than she'd been at seventeen. He had always been enthralled with the shape of her face—perfect cheekbones, long lashes a shade darker than her tawny hair, and clear golden eyes. He'd never seen eyes like Marly's, not ever. Eyes a man could get lost in. He fought back a fierce desire to touch her. He wondered what she'd do if he dared. Was she aware of him at all?

Apparently not. She worked with single-minded concentration, devoting all her attention to the task at hand. He almost laughed. He was used to women noticing him, actively pursuing him. He was considered reasonably attractive, and just to look at him, he seemed in good shape, which was all that mattered to most of the women he'd been with since his divorce.

Not Marly. She was more intelligent than that. More intuitive. She looked beyond the public image. Even after sixteen years, he knew that wouldn't have changed.

Her intelligence had been one of the things about Marly he'd found sexy as hell. It shone from her eyes, lit her expressive face as they talked. It was the spark that made their conversations lively. When she was eighty, she would still be a woman of beauty, but better than that, she would still be a woman of substance. What the hell had been wrong with Kingsley that he hadn't had the sense to hang on to her?

With his eyes closed, Joe pictured her as she'd been last night, her eyes dark with concern, her mouth soft and compassionate, her hands... He couldn't come up with a word to describe Marly's hands. Wonderful, yes. Healing, no doubt. Mesmerizing, oh, yes. His body was beginning to send him messages. Erotic—that was it.

"God, that feels wonderful," he said, allowing himself a few minutes of sheer bliss. "Let's get engaged again."

She chuckled softly. "So you'll have a live-in masseuse?"

No. A live-in lover. He almost said it, but caught himself in the nick of time. He wanted to make love with her again, he realized. Yes. Definitely. The sooner the better. But it meant too much to tease about.

"Well, the answer's no, anyway," she said after a few minutes.

He didn't know how long it was before she said, "Is this why you haven't considered a regular job since you retired, Joe?"

He opened his eyes. "What?"

"Your injury. Your knee. It's far more damaged than the publicity about you revealed. Any quick twisting movement can bring you down like a tree. Is that why you don't want to coach?"

"Can you think of a better reason?" he said defensively.

"That's not a reason, it's an excuse. You can be a perfectly fine coach with or without perfect knees. Or, if not a coach, anything else, for that matter."

He turned his head to look out the window. "Haven't we had this conversation already, Marly?"

"Your life seems so unfocused, Joe. You don't *do* anything. Not once in the past week have you mentioned anything worthwhile going on in your life. Why is that?"

"I have enough income to live on without punching a time clock every day. Some people even consider me lucky, being able to live like that."

"Do you?"

"Do I what?"

She sighed. "You know what. Do you consider yourself lucky that you don't do anything with time you've been given?"

It was a curse, but he wasn't going to admit that to Marly. "We don't all have your altruistic nature, Marly."

"You did once," she said softly.

"I don't anymore," he growled.

With her hand along his jaw, she turned his head so that he was forced to look at her. "Honest? Cross your heart?"

A heart-stopping moment passed as they stared into each other's eyes. "Why are we arguing about this when we're in a bedroom for the first time in sixteen years?" he murmured, his voice suddenly rough and low. He caught her wrist and placed a warm kiss on her palm. "Do you realize we never made love on a real bed before?"

"Are you trying to change the subject?"

"Me? Why would I want to change the subject? I love having my life-style trashed and my ego trampled. It's just peachy hearing you toss out my shortcomings like used go-cups after a Mardi Gras parade." He dropped her wrist and looked away again. "You sound like Laura."

Marly frowned. "Laura thinks you're squandering your talents?"

He sat up abruptly and rested his elbow on his good knee. "Why am I sitting here listening to this?" he muttered, running a hand through his hair. "Look, Marly, you just don't understand. As an athlete, I'm washed up, finished. Even a high-school team needs a healthy coach. Hell, a high-school team *especially* needs a healthy coach."

"You'd be healthy. Who says you need to be able to do a fifty-yard dash or the high jump? You'd give the job itself your all, I know it. I know you," Marly said with complete sincerity.

"You don't know diddly. How long do you think it would be before I'd take a misstep and fall on my rear in front of the kids? What if it happened in a big game? Jeez, I can just see it now—Big-name Coach Trips Over Own Feet. Unable to Rise. Fans Howl."

"You're wrong! That's negative, self-defeating baloney! You'd be a wonderful coach. Kids would hang on your every word. They—" She stopped as he started getting out of bed. "What are you doing?"

"What does it look like I'm doing? I'm getting the hell out of here." Bracing himself on the side of the dresser, he looked around the room. "Where are my pants?"

Silently, she pointed to the closet. He lurched from the dresser to a chair, then yanked the closet door open. He was pale and unsteady on his feet, but stubbornly determined.

Behind him, Marlena's voice was soft. "Joe, have you ever thought it might be your life-style that makes Laura hesitate to leave the boys with you when she goes to England?''

With his jaw clenched, he gave her a hostile look and snatched at a wire hanger holding his jeans.

''If you squander your time on the golf course or in sports bars or haring around in a Corvette, what kind of role model is that for Nick and Matthew?''

God, why didn't she just take a knife and stab him through the heart? It couldn't hurt any worse. Balanced on one foot, he tried to pull the jeans from the hanger. He was all thumbs, and his knee hurt like hell.

''Are you sure it would be in their best interests if you did have them with you for a whole summer?''

Still silent, he made a quick swipe as the jeans slithered off the hanger, but he wasn't quick enough. They fell to the floor. Leaning against the doorjamb, he clenched his jaw and tried to scoop them up. And lost his balance.

Marlena jumped just in time to prevent him from crashing to the floor. Without a word, she waited until he was steady on his feet and then backed away. She glanced at the jeans. ''How are you going to get them on?'' she asked quietly.

He stared at her, hearing everything she'd said through a haze of anger and frustration and searing pain. ''How the *hell* do I know!'' he yelled. Balling them up, he threw the jeans across the room.

She looked at him, her eyes dark with compassion. ''It really does hurt, doesn't it?''

''I'm all right,'' he said.

''Not your knee, Joe. Your career. Losing your sons. Your wife's desertion. All of it. It's okay to admit you're in pain. But sooner or later, you're going to have to get beyond it.''

He gave her a dark look. "I got enough preaching last Sunday, Marly. And I've heard all this before."

She returned his stare steadily, as though trying to reconcile the man she was looking at with the youth she'd once loved. Joe shifted uncomfortably under her scrutiny but stubbornly refused to back down. She was disappointed in him, but he should be used to that. His fans, his agent, Pete, some of his business associates—practically everybody he knew had taken a shot at him at one time or another during the past three years. But what the hell did they know? How many of them had been in his shoes?

And why did Marly's opinion matter more than anybody else's?

"Fine," she said, bending over and picking up his jeans. "You're anxious to get away, so I won't try to persuade you otherwise. As a pro in *my* field, I'd advise you to stay off that knee as much as you can, but then you already know that."

She handed him the jeans and stood silently as he balanced against the dresser and managed to get them on. He was sweating and his knee throbbed like mad, but he finally managed to dress. When she had gone to get his things the night before, she had thoughtfully remembered to bring his crutches. He despised them, but accepted them now as she held them out without a word.

BY THE TIME Joe made it up the steps, unlocked his front door and let himself into his own living room, his teeth were clenched against the pain. He went directly to the bathroom and washed down a couple of pills, then stretched out gingerly on the extra-long sofa in front of his big-screen TV. He thought fleetingly of the pain-free moments he'd enjoyed as he awoke that morning. He told himself that it was probably just his imagination that his pain had eased magically during the time he had spent with Marly.

And not just the pain in his knee . . .

Chapter Five

"JOE WANTS to take me to the zoo tomorrow, Aunt Marly. Is it okay?"

"Tomorrow's Thursday, a schoolday, Jaycee."

"We're going right after school," Jaycee replied. "We'll be home by six, he promised." She watched Marlena jerking cabinet doors open, one after another.

"Where is that pot?" she muttered, irritated because she was running late. Spaghetti, she decided, and a salad. She had sauce left over from last week in the freezer, so it would be quick and easy.

"Looking for this?" Jaycee asked, holding up the pot she'd pulled from the dishwasher. Marly took it and held it under the faucet, filling it quickly.

She had been delayed by two new patients who had arrived for their first physical-therapy sessions. Both were accident victims, brothers who'd been thrown from a car when they were rear-ended. Neither had been wearing a seat belt. She must remember to remind Joe never to neglect buckling Jaycee up. If he ever spoke to her again.

Jaycee took a radish from the salad ingredients beside the sink. "He said he'd come to the school and pick me up if you'd write a note to say it's okay. It is okay, isn't it, Aunt Marly? Please, please..."

Standing at the stove, Marlena frowned. "Is he up to it, Jaycee? It takes a couple of hours to walk the zoo."

"He knew you'd ask that," Jaycee said sagely. "He said he's fine and to tell you he has a walking stick." She giggled suddenly. "He plans to wear sunglasses and a hat so nobody'll recognize him."

Marlena found a package of spaghetti noodles in the pantry. "How about a false nose and a mustache, too?" she muttered, closing the door with a thump. If he wanted to hide the real Joe Masterson from the world, why not go all the way? And why did she care?

"Are you mad at Joe, Aunt Marly?"

"Of course not. Why would you think that? I haven't even seen him since last Thursday."

"That's why. Because after he fell and hurt his knee and you fixed it, he—"

"I didn't fix it."

"Well, massaged it all night, he—"

"I didn't massage it all night!"

"Okay, okay." Jaycee made a refereelike gesture with her hands, a habit picked up from Joe. "What I meant to say was, you gave him your bed and did your physical-therapy thing, which took all night, because you were in there with him when I went to sleep and when I woke up really early to go to the bathroom, you were still there."

"I slept on the couch that night, Jaycee."

"Oh."

"You didn't really think I spent the night with him, did you?"

Jaycee shrugged. "I guess not. But you like him, don't you?"

"Yes, of course I like him. We're old friends."

"I sort of thought maybe you and Joe might want to be more than just friends."

Oh, Lord, here it was again. Marlena busied herself at the sink, washing the salad ingredients. "Want to get down the plates and start setting the table?" she asked, slicing cleanly through a tomato. "This will be ready in a jiff."

"Drop the subject, huh?"

"If you don't mind."

Jaycee obediently reached for the plates and set them on the table. Looking oddly mature, she said, "I wish you wouldn't treat me like a baby, Aunt Marly. I know about the things grown-ups do."

Marlena's knife stilled. "What things?"

"You know." Jaycee shrugged. "Kissing and stuff." Then, before Marlena could decide how to reply, Jaycee said, "It's okay with me if you and Joe want to do that. Actually, I think it would be better if you were married and he could just live with us and you could sleep together all the time. There wouldn't be any problem with it then, would there? And we could be a family. But if you need a little more time . . ."

Marlena realized her mouth was hanging open. She closed it abruptly. "Jaycee, come over here and sit down."

When they were both facing each other, Marly began gently, "Jaycee, I know how much you would like to be a part of a real family again. I think that would be very nice, too. I'm sorry that I can't just wish on a star and make it happen. Life isn't like that, sweetheart."

"I know that, Aunt Marly," Jaycee said, nodding agreeably. "But I still think Joe would make a perfect husband for you and a wonderful daddy for me."

Exasperated, Marlena said, "We've known him less than two weeks, Jaycee. That's hardly enough time to choose a . . . a pet, let alone a husband and father."

"*I've* only known him two weeks. *You've* known him forever, and that's long enough to choose. Besides, in just two weeks I've decided he's great. He's perfect for us."

Marlena closed her eyes. "Yes, but what does Joe think, Jaycee? You can't just arrange people's lives for them like that."

Jaycee appeared to consider that. "I think he likes me...a lot, Aunt Marly. And I know he likes you."

Oh, sure. So much that he's avoided me for the past week. Marlena rubbed a finger between her eyes. "Honey—"

"He talks about you all the time. He asks me lots of questions about you and your job and Richard. He doesn't like Richard much, I don't think. And he *despises* Uncle Charles. That's one reason I think he has special feelings for you." She added ingenuously, "He's sort of jealous of them."

"Jaycee—" Marly said faintly.

"You should have heard what he said when I told him you didn't get any money from Uncle Charles when you got divorced. He was really mad."

"Jaycee!"

Cocking her head, Jaycee looked directly into Marlena's face. "So, what's wrong with hoping we'll be a family someday?"

Nothing. Everything. "Trust me, Jaycee," Marly said, pushing her chair back and rising. "This is not something you need to be meddling in. You'll just have to take my word on that."

Wanting to end the discussion, Marly quickly busied herself putting the final touches to dinner. She had been thrown off balance by Jaycee's remarks. Was the child really thinking of her and Joe in a sexual sense? Lord, what next? Marly had always been frank and open about sex. Jaycee knew about the egg and the sperm, about the difference in boys and girls, about her own miraculous reproductive system. But Marlena had never gotten really specific about exactly what went on in the bedroom. It must be because of her past with Joe and that ridiculous picture in the yearbook that Jaycee had leapt to the conclusion that she and Joe could just pick up where they'd left off.

They couldn't. She herself had given up that dream.

She grabbed at the spaghetti pot just as it was about to boil over. The fact was, Joe hadn't even spoken to her since that scene in her bedroom. He wasn't a man who took criticism well. Although why he should be asking questions about her and passing opinions on the men in her life, she hadn't a clue. Avoiding her company for days wasn't the way a man pursued a woman.

ON THURSDAY, Joe took Jaycee to the zoo. Marlena picked up a pizza after work and was just getting home as they pulled into the driveway. The Corvette came to a stop and she watched Joe lean over to help Jaycee out of the seat belt. Both were laughing at something he said. He climbed out and waited with his hand extended to Jaycee while she got out of the car. A tug on her French braid made her squeal and giggle harder, then with her arm casually tucked against his side, they walked together across the yard.

In just two weeks, they had indeed forged a friendship, Marly thought. They were no longer strangers. The Valentine Day dance was tomorrow night. After that . . .

Jaycee spotted Marlena and broke away from Joe. "Aunt Marly, you should have come! We saw the albino alligators. They were neat! Solid white and spooky-looking. Like ghost alligators." In high spirits, she hugged her aunt, nearly upsetting the pizza box. "They're famous, you know."

"I know." Marlena smiled, then let her glance drift to Joe as he walked toward her.

"Hello, Marly." Taking off his sunglasses, he tucked them into the pocket of his pullover. He was favoring his knee, but hardly enough to notice. There was no sign of a walking cane.

"Joe. How are you?"

"Fine."

Jaycee dashed to the fence, where Beau was barking a frantic welcome. "The groundskeeper recognized Joe and we got to ride in a golf cart!" she hollered over her shoulder.

Marly smiled at him. "One of the perks of fame?"

"Luckily. After about an hour, I was thinking up excuses to stop at every bench and rest." He motioned toward Jaycee, who was clipping a leash on Beau. "But don't tell the squirt."

"She probably knew," Marly said. "And she knows how touchy you are about it, so she probably just pretended right along with you."

He shook his head helplessly.

"I know the feeling," she said, grinning wryly. Handing him the pizza, she unlocked the front door.

"Runs in the family, huh?" He waited for her to go inside, then followed, using his elbow to close the door behind them. Tossing her purse on the table in the foyer, Marly took the pizza box from him and headed straight for the kitchen. Joe hesitated only a second before following her.

She set the box on the table. "You didn't let Jaycee talk you into buying any junk food at the zoo, did you?"

"No way." He held up both hands, palms out. "I know the rules, ma'am."

"Good. Are you hungry? It's just pizza, as you see. Pepperoni and cheese, but there's plenty if you want to stay." She was moving while she talked, taking down paper plates, finding napkins, setting glasses on the counter. "Jaycee and I never finish a whole one."

He studied what he could see of her face. "I wish I'd known it would be this easy," he murmured.

With her hand on the refrigerator, she looked over at him. "What?"

"Getting back into your good graces. I was afraid I'd ruined everything—losing my temper, slamming out of your house like that, storming off home without thanking you after you'd worked a miracle on my bum knee."

"Hardly." She shrugged. "Besides, I provoked you."

"I behaved like a juvenile." He looked down at his feet, and when he met her eyes again, she saw the effort it took for him to talk about it. "You happened to push a few buttons that are guaranteed to send me into orbit." He grinned crookedly. "The worst part is, you were right."

"No," she said, shaking her head. "After talking to you while we waited for Jaycee at the library, I knew that you were sensitive about losing your career and everything that went with it. You have a right to your feelings. I don't know why I pushed it."

She turned back to the open refrigerator. "Would you like a beer with your pizza?"

"A beer?" He moved closer until he was standing beside her.

"Light or regular, take your choice." She wouldn't meet his eyes.

"You have beer? The white-wine-only lady is stocking beer?"

She stood stubbornly in front of the refrigerator, her back to him. "I have beer, Joe," she said evenly.

He moved until he was behind her, close but not touching. His mouth was right at her ear when he murmured, "You bought beer especially for me."

Her heart was pounding like a drum. "You don't like white wine."

"You've got that right." He nuzzled the skin beneath her ear and ran both palms up her bare arms.

"Joe," she breathed, leaning against him. As he began stringing little kisses along her neck to her shoulder, her whole body flushed with pleasure.

"I..." She lost whatever she'd meant to say as his hand slid around her waist and flattened against her stomach. She whimpered as he cupped her breast with his other hand. Then all thought left her as he buried his face in the nape of her neck.

"Do you know how long I've wanted to touch you like this?" he demanded. She made a soft inarticulate sound as he pulled her close, fitting her perfectly in the cradle of his thighs.

For the longest time, both luxuriated in the moment, neither moving except for the gentle rocking motion initiated by Joe. For Marlena, it was heaven to be enfolded in his warmth, his strength. She felt safe, protected, cherished. She had needed that for so long. To find it in the arms of Joe Masterson filled her with wonder.

"What are we doing, Joe?" she whispered weakly.

With his eyes closed, he inhaled deeply. "Don't you know, Marly? From the moment we met again, this was meant to be. We were lying to ourselves to think it wouldn't happen. Even Jaycee knew."

"Jaycee's a child!"

"But smart enough to see what's in front of her nose. I don't want to walk away from you after the Valentine thing is over, Marly," he said urgently. "I want to stay and see where this takes us."

She rolled her head restlessly. "I'm not going to be one of your groupies, Joe."

"That remark is so cockeyed I can't believe you even said it." He turned her suddenly so he could look into her face. "Marly, no woman has ever known me the way you know me. No other woman has ever heard me cry over my sons. No one, male or female, suspects how the future scares me stiff. Just you. No other person has even suspected who I really am. No one but you. I'd be a fool to throw all that away again." He peered deeply into her eyes. "I'm *not* going to throw that away twice."

She searched his face anxiously. "I'm scared, Joe."

His arms tightened convulsively around her. "I won't hurt you again, sweetheart," he promised, dropping a kiss on her hair. "I swear it."

She shook her head. "Don't," she whispered. "Don't make promises, Joe. There are too many pitfalls. You, of all people, should know that."

"Maybe so, but I'm not afraid of them when I'm with you, Marly."

For a long moment, they were lost in simply looking at each other. With her heart beating fast, Marlena knew he wanted to kiss her. It would feel so right to be in his arms again, to feel the passion that had always flared so naturally between them. She wanted it, she realized. She wanted it desperately, more than she'd wanted anything in a long, long time.

Joe was bending to touch his mouth to hers when the shriek of car brakes outside startled them. Both of them froze and the moment was shattered by the crashing of the front door as Jaycee burst inside screaming for Marlena.

"Aunt Marly! Joe! Come quick, come quick! It's Beau!"

Without waiting for Jaycee to reach the kitchen, Marly pushed away from Joe and headed for the front door at a run. Her heart slammed in her chest as Jaycee raced to her, crying hysterically, flinging herself into Marlena's arms. "What's wrong, Jaycee? Tell me, love."

"He's in the yard, Aunt Marly," she sobbed, her arms tight around Marlena. "Go help him, please. He's still alive, but he can't get up." She was shaking with terror. "I don't want him to die, Aunt Marly."

Above Jaycee's head, Marlena looked at Joe helplessly. "Stay, both of you," he ordered, moving past Marly. "I'll go check and see what's what. Jaycee..." Pausing, he touched her shoulder. "I'll take care of him. He'll be all right."

As he left, Jaycee lifted tear-drenched eyes to Marlena. "That car h-hit him...and...and...h-he didn't even stop!"

"Shh, baby." Marly hugged the small trembling body to hers. "Joe's going to... He'll see to everything."

"I know." With a sniff, Jaycee seemed to pull herself together. She straightened and looked anxiously through the doorway to where Joe was crouched beside Beau, whose tail thumped a weak welcome. A couple of men from the neighborhood approached. In a few moments, the men helped Joe lift the dog gently and place him in the back seat of Marly's car. After a word to one of the men, Joe turned and headed back toward Marly and Jaycee.

Marly squeezed Jaycee's hand. Beau was still alive. Beside her, Jaycee stood silent and still. "He'll be all right, I know he will," the child whispered fiercely. "Joe promised."

"THE VET WANTS to put him down." Marlena's voice was low and unsteady in the small treatment room where they'd been banished to while Beau was examined. Distant yapping came from the inner regions of the animal hospital. The combined smells of disinfectant and room freshener made her stomach roll sickeningly.

"No." The denial came swift and final, from Joe. "It's crazy to even consider it. What the hell does that guy know? Beau's a member of the family. What would Jaycee do without him?"

"Oh, I don't know what to do!" Marlena thrust her fingers through her hair and paced the floor. They had been waiting for more than two hours while the veterinarian assessed the dog's injuries. The fact that he was still alive was miraculous, but even if he survived, his quality of life was questionable. "He'll never run and jump again," she murmured in distress. "Or do the things he lives for."

"He lives for his relationship with Jaycee," Joe said flatly. His own vehemence surprised him, but he knew putting down a dog like Beau was a rotten alternative. "Where is she?"

"In the bathroom. I'm glad she didn't hear Dr. Rutger. I don't want her to have to make such a difficult choice."

"I think you're making a mistake, Marly," he said quietly. "She has a right to participate in that kind of decision."

"What decision?"

Marlena and Joe turned sharply to find Jaycee standing in the doorway watching them anxiously. Her small face was tear-streaked and pale. "He didn't die, did he?" She looked from one to the other, but spoke accusingly to Joe. "You promised, Joe. You promised he would be all right."

Joe went to her, lowering to his haunches to look her in the eye. "He's not dead, sweetheart. He's badly injured, though." He glanced briefly at Marlena. "Badly enough that the vet has suggested we might want to ... to ..." He tried unsuccessfully to clear his throat. "We might want to put him out of his pain."

Her eyes wide and scared, Jaycee pressed her fingers to her mouth and shook her head wildly. "You mean put him to sleep forever?"

Marlena's heart twisted. "Jaycee—"

"No!" Jaycee's denial was as vehement as Joe's had been.

Marlena came over and sat down on a chair beside them. "His leg is broken in two places, Jaycee. His hip is badly dislocated, maybe broken, and it might never be normal again. He's in terrible pain."

Jaycee wiped at her tears with one hand. "Can't they give him something like Joe has for when his knee hurts?"

Joe and Marlena exchanged a look. "Well, yes," Marlena said reluctantly, "I suppose so. But his injuries are so extensive that it will be a long time before he heals. Even then, he won't ever be able to do the things he used to do with you, Jaycee."

"I don't care," Jaycee retorted. "At least I'll still have him as a friend."

"Oh, Jaycee, you just don't realize—"

Jaycee backed away angrily. "I do realize, I *do!* I don't think *you* realize what you're saying, Aunt Marly. If Beau was a person, instead of a dog, you wouldn't be acting like this. What about the people you work with every day? They can't ever be the same again, but you don't just give up on them. What about Joe's knee? He can't play football anymore, but he can still do a million other things. I heard you tell him so last week when you were fighting."

"That's different, Jaycee. My patients, Joe—"

"Why is it different?" Jaycee demanded. "Because Joe's a person and not a dog?"

"Yeah, Marly," Joe put in quietly. "Why is it different? The way I see it, Beau will just have to find other things to do. Isn't that what you've been preaching to me?"

"Beau is a dog, Joe," Marlena said evenly.

"And because his world is suddenly turned upside down, because he's less than perfect, we should just write him off?"

"No, of course not! He's—"

"Crippled? Playing on an uneven field? The effort will be too much?" He was shaking his head, compelled to say words that until a few days ago were just that to him— words. "That dog's got a lot of heart, Marly. Don't sell him short."

"An uneven field? A lot of heart?" With her head to one side, Marlena studied him shrewdly. "I somehow get the feeling we aren't just talking about Beau here."

He grunted, not ready to admit anything. "There are a lot of things a good dog can do besides chasing Frisbees or fetching a stick. He's still loyal and true and capable of loving the people who love him."

"Right," she said, her eyes soft. "He's still able to do all that."

"Are we still talking about Beau?" Jaycee asked, studying them with an odd expression.

"Are we?" Marlena asked, looking at him.

Joe stared back. Hell, no, this wasn't about Beau. At least not totally. It was suddenly as clear to him as a Monday morning practice drill the reason he'd been offended—no, outraged—by the idea of putting Beau down. Both the dog and Joe had a lot of life left in them. Why it had taken him two damn years to see it, Joe wasn't quite certain. He just knew that suddenly he was ready to believe it. To believe in himself again.

Jaycee stirred, sniffed and looked at them both. "So, we're gonna go tell that vet to fix Beau, aren't we?"

With his eyes holding Marlena's, Joe squeezed Jaycee's small shoulder. "You better believe it, squirt. That rascal will be up and chasing Mr. Wiggins's cat in no time."

Jaycee swiped at her nose. "You think so?"

He ruffled her hair and grinned. "Yep. Word of honor." He turned his gaze and smile on Marlena. "How 'bout it, Aunt Marly? Shall I go and inform the good doctor?"

Marlena waved him off, then with a smile, she reached for Jaycee's hand and pulled her down beside her. Locking her arms around her, she gave her a warm hug. "Joe is absolutely right, sweetheart. Even if Beau can't run as fast or jump as high, he is still your best friend."

"I know." Jaycee leaned trustingly into Marlena's embrace. "I knew you'd see that it's all right as soon as you thought about it. It's just like Joe. When he came back to you after all those years, he couldn't do the things he used to do, but you love him, anyway, don't you?"

With her forehead touching Jaycee's, Marlena closed her eyes. "Yes."

"And you don't care if he can't play football and stuff, do you?"

"No, I don't care."

"Me, neither." With a sniff, Jaycee pulled away and sat down on a plastic chair. With her head cocked sideways, she spoke pensively. "With Beau to set him a good example, I bet Joe will quit worrying about stuff now."

Taking a seat beside her, Marlena hid a smile. "I think you're right, sweetheart." Her heart suddenly much lighter, she slipped her arm around Jaycee and they settled back to wait.

MARLENA HAD just finished showering when her phone rang that night. Frowning, she hurried to pick it up before Jaycee woke up. If it was bad news about Beau...

"Hello."

"It's me, Marly."

"Joe." She sat down on the side of the bed. "I was afraid..."

He swore softly. "I'm sorry. I didn't think. Beau's doing great. I called a little while ago."

"Me, too." She pulled the towel from her head and freed the damp weight of her hair. Slowly, she began to rub at it, wondering why he was calling. Not that it mattered. Even at the midnight hour, she cherished the chance to share the moment, just the two of them, while the rest of her world—and his—slept.

"I know it's late," he said huskily. "Did I wake you?"

"No." She put the towel aside and reached behind her to stack a couple of pillows behind her on her bed. "I just got out of the shower." At his quick intake of breath, she closed her eyes, then curled into the pillows and held the phone close to her mouth. "Is something wrong, Joe?"

"I just needed to hear your voice."

Her heart turned over. How many times had he said those words to her? How many hours had they talked on the phone while her mother and Pete had assumed they were sleeping? In those days, they had always been there for each other. Why, at the end, had they stopped talking, stopped listening to each other? "There is something wrong, Joe. What is it?"

"I called Laura tonight."

With an aching throat, she stared for a moment through the dark window. It was a starry night. "Are your sons okay?"

"Yeah, it was nothing like that." She sensed his tension and waited. "I mean, it was about Nick and Matt, but not in the way you think. I told Laura I wouldn't object if she wanted to take them to England this summer."

She paused. "That's not the way you felt last week."

"She caught me off guard last week. I was disappointed at first, and ticked off, I guess. I said some things I probably shouldn't have."

She smiled. "Who doesn't when they're ticked off?"

"Marly..." He hesitated, and she sensed that what he wanted to say wasn't easy. "I've been thinking about everything you said. You were right that Laura feels cautious about turning the kids over to me. She thinks I'm not settled enough. She thinks I haven't adjusted to a life without football, at least not well enough to have the boys with me for long stretches at a time."

She heard him shift restlessly and guessed that he was talking from his bed. She turned slowly onto her back and imagined him there. Did he sleep naked?

"Marly?"

"I'm here."

"She's right, Marly. I hate saying this, but you're both right. I could have been a better role model for my sons, but I was too busy feeling sorry for myself. I should have gotten my stuff together a hell of a lot sooner than I have. I'm embarrassed when I think of the time I've wasted. Ashamed, too. I—"

"Wait. Wait just a minute. Stop beating up on yourself." Marly propped herself higher against the pillows and assumed the tone she used with Jaycee to deliver a stern lecture. "Your life as a sports superstar was almost storybook perfect, Joe. When everything that came with that life-style was suddenly withdrawn, it was natural to suffer some kind of withdrawal. It's okay to sink a little when bad things happen, especially when we've done nothing to deserve it.''

''It's not okay to wallow in it as long as I did.''

''Isn't 'wallow' a bit harsh?'' she asked softly, twirling the phone cord through her fingers.

''Okay, let's say I moped and moaned. A lot.''

She chuckled. ''Whatever. Besides, I know you better than that. I don't believe you've done nothing worthwhile since football.''

He hesitated. ''Nothing like a regular nine-to-five job, but...''

''But you haven't spent three years doing nothing?''

''Well...''

''You haven't led the hedonistic life-style that people think you have?''

''I'm involved in a couple of things I guess you'd call worthwhile.''

She smiled into the phone. ''Such as?''

''This may shock a few of my critics,'' he warned, his voice taking on a teasing note.

''I'm willing to be persuaded.''

''I'll remember that,'' he said quietly, and suddenly his tone was rich with promise. Listening to him, Marlena realized that the bitterness she'd lived with for years in the rare times she'd allowed herself to think about Joe was gone. And the disillusionment that was her legacy from her unhappy marriage to Charles was also fading fast. She felt free suddenly, full of anticipation and quietly unfolding joy. Joe had always been able to bring her joy.

''So, tell me,'' she prompted.

''It's not much.'' He cleared his throat. ''Along with another couple of Saints players, we do a clinic thing for special kids, furnish them with equipment, a gym, a safe place to blow off steam.'' He paused, sounding a little embarrassed. "There're a lot of talented kids who don't have the advantages I had."

"Are you talking about inner-city kids?"

"Inner-city and suburban. They're everywhere. We scout around the area, talk to coaches and priests and school counselors. It's a shame to waste a promising young athlete—a promising young *life*—for any reason."

She was silent for a moment. "Then you are coaching, after a fashion."

"I guess. After a fashion."

"I'm impressed, Joe. Why on earth have you let me rattle on about your not doing anything?"

"Because you were half-right. The clinic doesn't take much time." She heard a soft metallic sound and realized he was probably nursing a beer. "I miss competing," he said suddenly.

"You don't have to tell me that. It's always been food and drink to you."

"Yeah. Well, starting in August, I'll be changing that. I'm signing on as head coach for the Trojans."

Marlena's mouth fell open. "The Trojans in mid-city?"

"Yeah. I called tonight and confirmed it. We've been talking about it for some time now."

The high school was part of the Orleans parish system, and with its huge enrollment came all kinds of head-aches. Marlena recalled a couple of spectacular incidences of violence the past year involving handguns. Joe Masterson could be a powerful force for good at the school, and a wonderful role model.

"You'll be a great coach, Joe," she said softly. "Those kids will be over the moon when this gets out. They'll probably play their hearts out for you, just wait and see." She shook her head helplessly. "I can't believe you're doing this. Wait'll Jaycee hears it. She'll want to go to school there when she's old enough, even though it's out of our district. And the publicity! The newspaper and talk shows will be all over you. They—"

"God, I hope not!" he said. "The school board and the administration promised to keep it under wraps as long as possible. I made it a condition before accepting the job."

"The moment you show up, there'll be a huge reaction, Joe. You'll have to expect that. But all of it will be positive."

"You think so?"

He was pleased. She heard it in his voice. "That's twice in two minutes you've impressed me, Mr. Masterson," she told him, smiling.

They fell silent then, both reluctant to say the words that would end the call—and the intimacy.

"I'm looking forward to tomorrow night," Joe said at last.

His low tone feathered over Marly's skin like a caress. In a voice that was whisper soft, she said, "It was really sweet of you to do this for Jaycee."

"It wasn't only for Jaycee. You know that."

"Yes."

His voice dropped. "Do you remember the last Valentine Day we spent together?"

"Yes," she murmured.

"And the plans we had for that night?"

"Joe..."

"Remember?"

Plans to mark the beginning of their lives together. A teenage marriage. A honeymoon weekend. She would never, ever forget. How could she?

"Marly?"

"I remember."

She heard the sound as he drew in a breath. Gathering his nerve? "We're being offered a second chance, Marly. Not everyone is lucky enough to have that."

"No," she breathed.

"This time, we're not throwing it away, Marly."

"Joe..." She squeezed the receiver, closing her eyes against the rush of emotion released by his words. The promise of a future with Joe Masterson was a dream so sweet it frightened her.

"That's a promise." She imagined him nodding firmly, and her mouth curled in a tiny smile. "I'll see you tomorrow," he told her.

"Good night." Leaning over, she gently hung up the phone.

Chapter Six

MUCH TO JAYCEE'S DELIGHT, Joe Masterson was the star attraction at the Valentine Day dads-and-daughters dance. From her station behind the refreshment table, Marlena watched as he and Jaycee danced and laughed and cut up right along with everyone else. He was playing his role to the hilt and Jaycee was loving it.

To make matters perfect, he had driven with them to the vet's to pick up Beau earlier that evening. Now, contrary to his earlier doubts, he seemed perfectly at ease in a roomful of little girls. Over Jaycee's head, he winked at Marlena. She realized that there were very few situations where Joe wasn't at ease.

Her throat tight, she watched Jaycee's beaming smile. From the moment of their arrival at the dance, Jaycee had basked in Joe's reflected limelight, shamelessly taking credit for roping him into the event in the first place. Marlena sent a heartfelt thank-you heavenward. For once, Jaycee could pretend to be just like the rest of her friends.

Most of the dads had recognized Joe on sight. It was amusing to Marlena to watch them gamely juggle their responsibilities as escorts for their little girls with their natural inclination to cluster around Joe like men in a TV beer commercial. If it was like this three years after his retirement from the Saints, she could only imagine his life when he was still playing football.

She was just as affected by his magnetism as everyone else. The difference was that, unlike these people, she always had been. And tonight, if she was truly reading that look in his eye, Joe was feeling the same thing.

He had been doing it all night long, looking up and catching her eye. Especially when the music turned nostalgic. With a roomful of thirty-something parents, only so much Bon Jovi or New Kids on the Block was tolerated before someone demanded something from the seventies. And then the memories swamped her like water rushing through a floodgate. When their eyes met, it was as though they were alone, two people connecting momentarily, their thoughts suspended while their emotions rioted. At those moments, the music, the ebb and flow of the crowd, the thread of the conversation—all went unnoticed. Until something drew one or the other away.

But as the evening wore on, they kept drifting together, pulled by the desire building between them. It seemed natural for Joe to take her hand, to chuckle with her over something that amused them both, to speculate about someone at the party. Or he would slip an arm around her casually, wanting an introduction to Jaycee's friends' parents. He fit into her and Jaycee's world just as though he'd always been part of it.

Of course he had always occupied a secret corner in Marlena's heart. She could admit it now, and it was...wonderful.

JAYCEE THREADED her way through the crowd, looking for Melissa. Standing on tiptoe, she spotted her near the refreshment table drinking her umpteenth cup of punch, and waved wildly to catch her attention. Gulping it down, Melissa nodded and headed toward Jaycee.

"We were supposed to meet after this song," Jaycee reminded her impatiently. "Did you forget?"

"No, I was thirsty after that last dance. I just love 'Jeremiah was a Bullfrog,' don't you?"

"Yeah, but we've got more important stuff to do." She headed toward the bathroom, pulling Melissa along behind her. "We need to finalize our plans."

"I thought we already did that."

Jaycee rolled her eyes toward the ceiling. "We did, but we've still got to be sure things go right." She pushed the door open, checked the two stalls for other occupants, then turned to Melissa. "Did you clear it with your mom for me to sleep over tonight?" she asked.

"Sure. Just like we planned."

"Good. I've already asked Aunt Marly." Jaycee moved a little closer, looking pleased. "Have you noticed the way they've been acting tonight?"

"Who?"

"'Lissa! Joe and Aunt Marly, that's who."

Melissa shrugged. "Well . . . they look like everybody else's folks to me."

"Right!" Jaycee said triumphantly. "Only everybody else's folks are married to each other." She got a stubborn look on her face. "Which is exactly what we want to happen to Aunt Marly and Joe. They just need some time together to sort of...you know, move things along. That's why I'm spending the night at your house. Then they'll be free to do what comes naturally, or whatever. Me and Aunt Marly discussed this a couple of days ago and we—"

"Discussed what?"

Jaycee huffed impatiently. "Man-and-woman stuff. If you'd just pay attention when I tell you someth—"

"You discussed her and Joe making out?" Melissa squeaked in a shocked whisper.

"No, silly! Well, maybe when you get right down to it, that *is* what we were talking about." She nibbled at her lip for a moment, thinking. "My plan is to just leave them alone together, and from the way they're looking at each other tonight, I'll bet they won't spend the time just talking.''

"Maybe," Melissa replied, then added, "Or he might drop your aunt at your house and just go on home. It's pretty late already."

"Don't even say that!" Jaycee propped her fists on her hips. "How many times have I told you negative thoughts are a dead end, 'Lissa? We've got to think positive."

"It wasn't negative thinking," Melissa muttered. "It was just 'maybe' thinking."

"Okay, okay." With a waggle of her eyebrows, Jaycee rubbed her hands together gleefully. "It's just a matter of time now."

"I guess."

"I *know*," Jaycee said firmly. "Remember, think positive." She pushed the door open and listened a moment. The first few notes of "You Are So Beautiful" floated through the air. "Okay, it's the last song. I don't want Joe to see me, 'cause I want him to dance this one with Aunt Marly."

Melissa craned her neck, trying to see over Jaycee's shoulder. "What's happening?"

"He's gonna ask her!" Jaycee said in an excited whisper, watching Joe look at Marlena. Things were going to work out, Jaycee was sure of it. She couldn't wait to see Beau and tell him everything.

WHEN JOE COCKER'S classic love song began, Marlena's heart skipped a beat. A flood of memories poured through her, precious and bittersweet. An evening sixteen years ago, another Valentine Day, another dance, another time.

You... are... so beautiful... to me...

Across the room in conversation with one of the fathers who coached Jaycee's soccer team, Joe looked up. His eyes met Marlena's and held them. And she was left breathless.

Joe murmured something to the soccer coach and began to make his way toward Marlena. Heat curled deliciously through her as she waited. Sixteen years had not banished her ability to read that look. Rife with lust and anticipation, it linked with her own rising desire and sent her thoughts flying in a dozen directions. She yearned to be alone with him.

And then he was standing before her, looking deep into her eyes as the slow sensuality of the song throbbed around them. People chatted and laughed, snippets of conversation floated unheard. Little girls whispered and giggled. Beside them, a few couples began drifting onto the dance floor. Joe and Marly had eyes and ears only for each other.

"Dance with me, Marly," he said. Without a word, she took his hand and followed him, going naturally into the circle of his arms. Closing her eyes, she dreamily matched her steps to his, and it was as though the sixteen years had never been.

"It's true, you know," he said huskily, holding her close.

"What?" she breathed, nestling her head against his chest. Idly, she sifted her fingers through the hair brushing his collar.

"You are so beautiful . . . to me."

Her heart turned over. "Joe . . ."

"When can we leave, Marly?"

"Are you bored?" She tried to lean back and look at his face, but he held her fast.

"No."

"Is your knee bothering you?"

"It's not my knee bothering me, Marly." With his hand on the small of her back, Joe slowly ground his pelvis against hers. Marlena drew a quivering breath, wrapping both arms around his neck and pressing her face into his shoulder.

"The party's almost over," she whispered, shamelessly savoring the feel of him, hard and urgent, thrusting against her softness.

He planted a slow kiss on the side of her neck. "Thank God somebody turned down the lights."

She laughed shakily, her senses humming. The song was nearly over. Desire and love and need tied her insides into a knot. She wanted to turn her face into Joe's chest and simply follow him anyplace in the world he chose to go.

"Jaycee's spending the night with Melissa," she told him softly. "We can leave whenever you want."

Joe went still for a second, then buried his mouth in her hair, muffling a groan. "Now. Let's leave now."

They left the dance floor, threading through the crowd until they found Jaycee and Melissa and Jean Browne, Melissa's mother.

"Joe and I are leaving now, Jaycee," she said. She gave Jean a distracted smile, intensely aware of Joe's hand possessively around her waist. "Jean, are you sure this is okay with you?"

"Positively." Jean scooped up a stack of paper cups and stuffed them into a plastic bag. "It's their treat for helping me." She eyed the leftovers on the table with exaggerated dismay. "Remind me to volunteer to decorate or serve next year, not clean up. I wasn't bright enough to think of it this year."

"Well, if you're sure..."

"I'm sure. Go, go." She shooed them away, calling, "Nice to meet you, Joe."

"My pleasure, Jean." He flashed his famous grin.

"Do a good job, Jaycee," Marlena cautioned.

"I will. We'll finish this in no time," Jaycee said, poking Melissa in the ribs. "Right, 'Lissa?"

"Oh . . . yeah. Sure."

"Have fun, then." Joe bent and kissed Jaycee's cheek. "Thanks for inviting me, squirt. I had a great time as your dad."

Jaycee beamed. "Really, Joe?"

"Yeah, really, sweetheart." He chucked her under the chin. "So, if you and 'Lissa have things under control, your Aunt Marly and I are out of here."

"We do!" both girls chorused. Then Jaycee added, "See you tomorrow. Late tomorrow."

JOE SEATED Marlena in the Corvette, then closed the door and came around to the driver's side. As he settled behind the wheel, he looked over at her. "Do you get the idea that this evening's ending was orchestrated by two eleven-year-olds?"

Marlena rolled her eyes. "Definitely. But I was hoping you wouldn't notice."

"That Jaycee." He shook his head, chuckling. "We have to get up early to stay ahead of her."

They looked at each other, their smiles meshing. Joe still hadn't started the car. The scent of her perfume lingered in the air, sending a bolt of desire through him. Their smiles faded, leaving both looking deeply into the other's eyes. "We owe her one this time, right?" Joe said gruffly.

Marlena nodded slowly, her gaze fastened on his mouth.

"Marly..." It was a groan, wrenched from his soul. He looked away, then rubbed a hand over his mouth. "Do you want to stop somewhere for a drink?"

"Not really."

With his hands resting on the wheel, he looked straight ahead. "Okay." He cleared his throat and reached to turn the ignition. "Home, then."

He pulled out into the street with a screech of tires, but quickly curbed the recklessness. He didn't want to wrap the Corvette around an oak tree tonight of all nights. Slowing at an intersection, he waited for a red light.

"I didn't really want a drink, either," he said, startling Marly from a dreamy contemplation of his hands, strong and brown, on the wheel. "I thought the evening would never end."

"What?"

"You heard me. I kept looking at my watch, wondering when we could decently leave. I couldn't wait to get you alone. If Jaycee hadn't stepped in, I would have thought of something."

She stared at him. His words swept through her in a trembling wave. He was talking as though he found her beautiful and feminine and desirable. She *felt* beautiful and feminine and desirable. Her doubts and hesitation about being with Joe, trusting him again, suddenly vanished like dust in the wind. She just wanted a chance to love him again.

"I wish we weren't hemmed in with all this traffic," he said hoarsely. "I wish we were on a country road somewhere, or up on the levee, where I could stop and pull you across the console and kiss the daylights out of you."

"Joe..." Her breath shuddered out, trembly and faint.

"Or better yet, make love to you." He risked a look at her and found her staring at him with her mouth parted and her eyes as bright as the twinkling lights draping the live oaks at City Park.

"Me, too," she said huskily.

He groaned. The light changed and behind him a driver honked impatiently. With a curse, Joe gunned the Corvette and they took off.

In ten minutes, they were at Marlena's house. Joe shut the engine off and turned to her. Their eyes locked. His were dark and turbulent, every trace of his casual charm vanished. The air inside the car was suddenly as heavy and seductive as a New Orleans summer. "Here we are."

"Yes."

He picked up her hand and rubbed her knuckles back and forth against his mouth. "I want you so much, Marly," he said hoarsely. "I don't want to go inside for a drink or a friendly chat or anything like that. Hell, once I get inside your house tonight, I'm going straight for your bedroom, lady. I've waited so long to feel this way again that..." He shook his head. "I thought I never would."

"I know," she whispered. "I feel the same way."

"No, I don't think you know..." Closing his eyes, he buried his mouth in her palm. Then his gaze moved back to her face and the desire he saw there caught in his throat. He whispered her name. "I love you, Marly. I think I always have."

Tears sprang to her eyes. She uncurled her fingers and covered his mouth. It was warm, tempting. She wanted to lean toward him and kiss him. "I love you, too."

His breath shuddered out in a relieved whoosh. "God, I was afraid..." He stopped, shaking his head. "Can we go inside now, sweetheart?"

Marly's heart began to hammer painfully in her chest. If she said yes, it meant she was ready to claim that second chance he had talked about last night. No, it meant *they* were claiming that second chance.

"Yes." With a smile, she reached for the door handle.

He got out and was around to her side almost before she was out of the car. As she stepped onto the pavement, he shoved the door closed and caught her around the waist. Together they hurried up the walkway. Joe nearly lifted her off her feet as he hustled her up the steps to the porch. While she fumbled with the key, he crowded close, but she didn't feel intimidated. She felt wanted, needed.

With his mouth at her temple, then her ear, she closed her eyes, the lock forgotten. The rushing heat of his breath caused streaks of pleasure that weakened her legs until she thought they might fold right under her. They would have, she suspected, except that his arms were around her, holding her up.

"Marly, you're killing me," Joe groaned. "For God's sake, hurry. Let me..."

But with a whimper, she finally shoved the key into the lock and pushed the door open. The house was dimly lit by a small lamp on a side table. The moment the door clicked shut behind them, Joe hauled her into his arms. Keys and change hit the floor as her pulse fell with a soft thump. She lifted her face to his eagerly, and without any thought of finesse or style, he covered her mouth with his in a deep hungry kiss.

Sixteen years fell away as though they had never been. There was a fierce intensity to his plundering of her mouth. She wrapped her arms around him, holding him tightly, delighting in the honest male need that claimed him. Answering it with matching fervor.

The fire that raged in him burned just as brightly in Marlena, fed by years of fantasies, countless lonely nights. How long had she lain awake while empty hopeless mem-

ories had seemed like all she would ever have of Joe Masterson again?

He tore his mouth from hers, but still held her fast,
their bodies pressed together. "I've ached for this for so
long," he told her, his lips frantically skimming her cheeks
and nose and eyes. "I can't believe we're finally—"

"We are, we are," she breathed, throwing her head
back as he kissed his way down her throat to the cleavage
bared in the deep V of her dress. She dropped a kiss on his
hair as he reached behind her for the zipper. She hadn't
worn a bra, and when he pulled the dress off her shoulders, her breasts were suddenly free, heavy and throbbing, swollen and aching for him.

"Marly, Marly," he whispered hoarsely, bending his
head and pressing against her softness. "Sweetheart,
you're beautiful, perfect. I've dreamed of this."

She was pressed against the wall, his lower body pressed
tightly into the soft cleft of her thighs. Without thinking,
she buried her hands in his thick silky hair. Joe braced his
elbows against the wall and nuzzled the soft fragrant val-
ley between her breasts. Closing her eyes, she shuddered
with need.

Suddenly she was desperate to touch him. Her hands
went frantically to the buttons of his shirt, tearing them
open while Joe yanked at his tie. With a soft ping, the top
button hit the wall behind Marlena as she tugged the shirt
from his shoulders.

Joe made a noise somewhere between a laugh and a
groan, a sound of pure unadulterated pleasure. Having
Marly tear the clothes from his body was a turn-on like
nothing he'd ever felt before. He gasped as she rubbed her
palms over his chest, flicked his nipples with her tongue,
kissed his shoulders and neck and ears. Cupping her head,

he allowed her free access, glorying in her unrestrained feminine lust.

"I can't believe this," he whispered, weakened with the passion unleashed between them.

"It's true, it's true," Marly moaned. "Oh, Joe, the time we've wasted."

He pulled away abruptly then, catching her hand. "Come on."

She blinked in confusion, but stumbled after him down the hall to her bedroom. At the bed, he released her, but only to finish unzipping her dress and stripping it off her. He took a second to admire the white satin garter belt and sexy stockings before pulling them off and tossing them aside, too. Next, with his pulse thundering in his ears, he stripped away her panties.

There was no time to savor the riches he'd uncovered. Marlena was fumbling at his belt, finally managing to unbuckle it before pushing his pants and shorts down over his hips.

"Hurry," he rasped, lavishing frantic openmouthed kisses over her taut breasts while he worked one of his shoes off using the toe of the other.

When finally they were both naked, Joe took the one step backward, bringing him to the edge of the bed. Pulling her down with him, they fell together with Marly sprawled on top of him. For a second, he drank his fill of the sight of her. Tawny hair framed her face in wild disarray, her amber eyes were glazed with passion, her lips moist and swollen from his kisses. Joe was enthralled.

With a growl, he closed his arms around her, hungry for the taste of her again. He held her tightly, seeking her mouth, then sent his tongue deep, echoing his screaming need for physical completion. Cradled in his open thighs, she yielded to the pressure of his hands, spread wide on her buttocks. His throbbing sex nestled snugly between her legs. With every stroke of his tongue in her mouth, he rocked against her softness. Lost in her spiraling pleasure, Marlena went willingly as he shifted, taking her with him as he rolled over.

"I can't wait much longer, sweetheart," he told her hoarsely.

"Don't wait, don't wait..."

Her plea destroyed what was left of his control. His hand swept down her body and slid between her thighs. They groaned in unison. She was soft and moist and ready for him. Bracing himself above her, he found his place, and with a cry muffled against her throat, he entered her Sighing, Marlena cupped his hard buttocks and arched her hips to draw him deeper still. Eyes locked, they remained like that for a heartbeat. Then with a moan, Joe began to move.

She wanted to savor the moment, to wring every last atom of pleasure out of it, but the intensity of her feelings quickly overwhelmed her. She had waited too long. Reality was too wonderful. She felt the imminence of her climax.

Above her, Joe was chanting her name in her ear, a loving litany that made her soul sing. Then the love that had been secreted away in her heart for more than sixteen years erupted in a brilliant splintering climax. In seconds, Joe followed her over the edge.

THEY LAY for a long time entwined in a tangle of arms and legs, savoring the aftermath. When his heartbeat slowed enough, Joe reluctantly rolled his weight to the side, but he wasn't willing to let her go. As long as he lived, he didn't ever want to let Marly go again.

"This wasn't supposed to happen," he said, his lips next to her temple. He felt the tension that made her go still and quickly hugged her reassuringly. "No, sweetheart, that didn't come out right. I mean, we weren't supposed to wind up in bed before..."

He gently eased her away and bent over the side of the bed, where he'd dropped his pants. Picking them up, he rummaged through his pockets until he found what he was looking for. When he turned back, she was sitting up on her knees watching him.

"...before I gave you this."

"Ohhh... Joe." She held out her left hand and he slipped a beautiful emerald-cut diamond on her third finger.

He brought her hand to his lips and kissed it. "Sixteen years ago, I couldn't afford an engagement ring," he told her. "This time, I want you to have all the trimmings. I want to give you everything, Marly. I don't think I can ever come close to telling you just what you mean to me, but I intend to spend the rest of my life trying."

"Is this a proposal?" Marlena asked, smiling through a sheen of tears.

He flicked a tear from her cheek lovingly. "Yeah, it's a proposal."

Her smile faded. "Are you sure, Joe?"

"I'm sure I love you. I'm sure no one has ever suited me as well as you. I'm sure I want us to live together and play together and raise Jaycee together. I'm sure I want us to have other kids together." He took her in his arms, then leaned back on the pillows, cradling her close to his heart. "Is that sure enough?"

"Oh, yes, it's enough." With a sigh, she turned into his warmth, thinking of all the nights they would share in a future that was suddenly bright. She smiled. Jaycee would be over the moon.

"Did you hear something?" Joe asked, cocking an ear toward the window.

"It was probably Beau— Oh!" With a groan, she rolled away from him suddenly. "We forgot to check on Beau. He's supposed to have one of those tablets the vet gave us." She started up, but Joe stopped her.

"No, stay here. I'll take care of it." He got to his feet and pulled on his pants, not bothering with his shorts.

"They're in the kitchen above the sink," Marlena told him. "In a little white envelope."

"No sweat. Back in a minute." He didn't turn on any lights until he was downstairs just in case Marly's neighbors were looking. A half-naked man in her bedroom would not look good for a single woman raising a young girl.

Thinking of Jaycee, he chuckled as he flipped the light on in the kitchen and shook a tablet out of the envelope. Opening the refrigerator, he rummaged around in the meat drawer until he found what he needed. If he wasn't totally off base, he thought, closing the refrigerator, Jaycee had a very accurate idea what was going on between him and Marly tonight.

He let himself outside quietly and picked his way across a stretch of patio to Beau's doghouse. The big Lab made a soft snuffling noise and Joe crouched quickly beside him before he could struggle to his feet.

"Whoa, boy, take it easy. It's just me," he said, stroking the soft ears while he ran his hands gently over Beau's bruised middle and bandaged leg. The dog's tail thumped weakly. "How ya doin', my man? Missing your best friend, I bet. But she's with Melissa tonight, buddy, and it's for a good cause." He offered the tablet wrapped in a cold cut. "Look, I brought you a treat. Olive loaf, straight from Langanstein's."

With one gulp, the dog downed the cold cut and tablet.

"Good boy." On his haunches beside Beau, he rubbed his hands over the dog's ribs and shoulders. "You're gonna be okay, boy," he murmured, carefully avoiding the injured leg. "We all are, Marly and me, Jaycee and you. This is a big night. It took sixteen years, but she's finally wearing my ring." His hand stilled as he looked into the soft dark eyes of the dog. "Get well fast, Beau. We're having a wedding!"

With a grunt, Joe got to his feet, then with a quick proprietorial look over the shadowy shrubs surrounding the yard, he walked back to the house and went inside.

WHEN THE KITCHEN LIGHT went out, there was sudden furtive movement in the depths of a huge azalea planted against the detached garage. Just then, the lights from a passing car swept over the yard, revealing a small ghostly figure in a baggy white T-shirt darting across the patio to the doghouse.

Jaycee let out a shivery breath as she dropped to her knees beside the Lab. "Wow, did you hear that, Beau? They're engaged! We're gonna be a family!"

Beau licked her hand.

"Just like I planned." Wide-eyed, Jaycee stared at the closed back door. "It worked, Beau, it worked." Scrambling for a bit more room, she wriggled her little rump into what space was left beside the dog. It was a damp evening and she couldn't stay long. She needed to get back to Melissa's house, which was only half a block away. If Melissa's mom woke up and found Jaycee missing... But she'd just had to know!

"A wedding, Beau," she said softly. "Is that awesome or what?"

She began rubbing the dog's ears. "I'll tell you something, Beau. It was just a matter of time and positive thinking. Lots of positive thinking, Beau. That's the secret, I always say."

She caught his face between her palms and rubbed her nose against the Lab's. "We're gonna be so happy, Beau. You just wait and see. When I saw that picture of Joe and Aunt Marly in the yearbook and then he moved just two doors down, I knew it was meant to be."

She looked up at the second-story to the window of her aunt's bedroom. The draperies stirred a little like they did when you close an inside door. Then she heard voices— just barely—one quiet and deep, the other feminine and soft.

Jaycee smiled and hugged the big dog tighter.

ARRANGEMENTS OF
THE HEART

Marisa Carroll

A Note from Marisa Carroll

If I were to make a list of holidays I could definitely do without, Valentine's Day would be at the top of the page. At least, that's the way I and my sister, Marian— the other half of the Marisa Carroll team—used to feel.

In Northwestern Ohio, where we live, Valentine's Day comes at the absolute low point of the year. It is usually cold and blustery, snowy and very hard to get around in. My husband, Joe, and I never plan anything special for that day. If we do, the weather is sure to spoil our fun. And for Marian, her son's birthday, which happens to fall on February 14, has always taken precedence over romance.

That's the way things are for Lori Fenton in "Arrangements of the Heart." Getting through each day, doing her job and raising her son are far more important than affairs of the heart. She hasn't got time for Cupid and flowers and heart-shaped boxes of candy. She hasn't got time for love.

Or so she thinks. Until she marries Matt Damschroeder on Valentine's Day. Then everything changes. It happens this way in real life, too.

Now that my children are grown, my husband and I take winter vacations that usually include Valentine's Day. Last year his present to me—and mine to him— was a visit to the ancient Mayan city of Tikal. Marian's son is a junior at Bowling Green State University and no longer requires birthday parties. In fact, he now has his pilot's license and has promised his mother he'll take her flying on Valentine's Day this year, just the two of them—weather permitting, of course.

Ain't life grand?

And so from Marian and myself, may all your Valentine's Days be filled with love and laughter and clear sunny skies.

Chapter One

"I KNOW you don't want to hear this, Lori," Dr. Gertrude Bengtson said with a trace of her native Austria still evident in her voice despite nearly fifty years of living in America. "But I don't advise putting off the surgery much longer. Your condition is stable at the moment, I admit. But since cardiology is not my specialty, I can't say with certainty how much longer that will be the case."

"Danny says I have a broken heart," Lori said, turning from the window to face her friend. She tried not to let her fear seep into her expression or her words.

"He's a very bright boy." Gertrude smiled. She had coached Lori's son into the world eight years ago. And advised her to keep him when everyone else urged her to give him up for adoption to her boyfriend's parents. Lori had been young and penniless and devastated by her lover's refusal to claim their child. All she knew was that she wanted to keep her baby and Gertrude's staunch, practical support had given her the strength to stand by her decision despite the pressure exerted by Danny's wealthy and influential grandparents. The two women had been friends ever since.

"You are absolutely certain surgery is my only option?" Lori asked, banishing terrors of the past to concentrate on terrors of the present.

Gertrude looked at her with faded blue eyes, full of wisdom and shrewd intelligence. "Yes. I would not recommend the procedure otherwise." The wall behind the elderly physician's cluttered desk was lined with diplomas testifying to her years of training and experience. The complete confidence Lori had in Gertrude's professional abilities didn't make the doctor's plain speaking any easier to hear. She crossed her arms in front of her to hide the trembling in her hands.

"I don't want to leave the city," Lori said. "Can't you recommend a surgeon here?" They'd had this conversation before. Numerous times.

"Of course. If the surgery itself was my only concern. But it is not. I'm treating all of you, Lori, not just your heart. I want you out of New York. Away from the city and from your work," Gertrude stated flatly. "You're skin and bones and you're heading for a complete physical collapse. You're killing yourself inch by inch."

"And you're being melodramatic," Lori said, smiling, but not quite bringing it off. "I'm a single mother with no family of my own and a fatherless child. Stress comes with the territory."

"You're a thirty-two-year-old workaholic with a serious heart condition and a young child to raise. If you want to live to see your grandchildren, you will do as I tell you without any more argument. I'm not sending you to the ends of the earth, you know," Gertrude said, sounding slightly exasperated. She shook her head. The heavy knot of gray hair piled on top slipped a little sideways and she pushed it back with an impatient hand.

"No," Lori agreed. "Only to Ohio."

"My brother-in-law is one of the best cardiovascular surgeons in the country," Gertrude reminded her more gently. "And the Ohio State University Hospital is famous around the world."

"And both your brother-in-law and the hospital are six hundred miles away from New York City and Carter, Finkbeiner and Strauss, Investment Brokers."

"Exactly." Gertrude nodded, pleased with Lori's answer. "You can move into my house in Willow Creek. The house is a bit big for only you and Danny, but it's well kept up and easy to heat. The Damschroeders live just up the hill. They're fine people. They'll take good care of both of you. Serena Damschroeder's mother was my best friend when I first came to this country before the war. She'll be just the person to watch over Danny while you're in the hospital."

"I don't like uprooting him from his friends and his school. This is the only home he's ever known. It could be very traumatic for him."

"Losing you would be far worse." Gertrude stood up. She was a tall woman, broad in the shoulders and hips. She was forty years older than Lori, forty pounds heavier and topped the younger woman's five and a half feet by several inches. "Do you intend to tell Danny's father and his grandparents about the surgery?"

Lori glanced sharply at her old friend. "I have no idea where Danny's father is," she said. "The last I knew, he was touring New Zealand with a rock band no one ever heard of."

Gertrude dismissed Danny's perpetually adolescent father with a snort. "What about Charles and Lydia?"

"One of the reasons I'm considering this move to Ohio is to distance myself and Danny from his grandparents." She felt her shoulders sag under the familiar weight of old fears and animosities and made an effort to straighten her back. "My illness is a perfect reason for them to start insisting again on being made Danny's legal guardians. If they find out how serious my condition is, they may start demanding physical custody of him, as well. I'm not up to dealing with that right now."

"You still haven't forgiven them for what happened after Danny was born, have you?" Gertrude asked.

"No," she replied. "I haven't. I don't think I'll ever forget how they marched into my hospital room with their lawyer and demanded I give them my son. I remember thinking the lawyer's tie cost more money than I had in all the world. They threatened to take him away from me, Gertrude," Lori reminded her friend, although Gertrude knew what had transpired on that day eight years ago as well as Lori. "And when that didn't work they offered me money to give up my son."

"I admit they handled it badly."

"They handled it as they handle everything. With threats and power and money."

"And so for eight years you have pushed yourself to acquire as much power and money as they have in the mistaken notion that it would keep your son safe."

Lori's laugh was short and clipped. "This conversation is getting entirely too Freudian."

"They love Danny as much as you do."

"Gertrude, please." For a moment Lori had felt herself reverting to the scared and penniless new mother she'd been the first day she met Charles and Lydia Michaelson. It was a draining emotion that sapped her strength and her will to fight. She didn't want to feel like that again. Ever. "I don't want to discuss the matter further."

"We'll say no more about it, then," Gertrude replied, although Lori knew she did have a great deal more to say on the subject of Danny's grandparents.

"Thank you."

Gertrude waved her hand. "Someday when you are as old as I am you will understand them a little better, I think."

"Perhaps," Lori said to avoid prolonging the subject.

"It's too bad that by then it will be too late for all of you." Gertrude, dear as she was to Lori, could never resist having the last word. Lori would miss her dreadfully when they moved to Ohio. She would make the move, she knew, for Danny's sake if not her own.

"I suppose we could relocate during Danny's Christmas vacation," she said, bringing the conversation back to the present dilemma, as she turned once more to the view of Manhattan visible from Gertrude's office window. The trees in Central Park were still green, the sun bright and hot in a hazy blue sky, although it was the middle of September. "I can have most of my clients transferred to other associates by then. And the Clifton merger should be wrapped—"

Gertrude spoke quietly but forcefully from her chair behind the big desk. "You will go now, Lori dear. You are fifteen pounds underweight and dangerously run-down. I want you to rest and relax and build up your strength and your body's defenses before the surgery."

"For how long?" Lori groaned aloud.

"A minimum of four months," Gertrude said, coming out from behind her desk to signal an end to the conversation. "You can afford it, and heaven knows Carter, Finkbeiner and Strauss owes you a leave of absence. You've barely taken a day off work in the eight years I've known you."

"I have responsibilities," Lori began.

"Don't give me any more argument or I'll make it six months."

Lori bit her lip but didn't say a word.

"Good. You are stubborn but you also have a great deal of common sense. You know when to fight and when to back off. You will need both of these traits in abundance over the next year.'' Gertrude nodded approval. ''You will do fine.''

''Will I, Gertrude?''

''Of course.''

''I hope you're right. Okay. Go ahead and make the arrangements with your brother-in-law,'' Lori said.

''I knew you would make the right decision. Now, come. No more talk of things that must be faced because they can't be changed. It's lunchtime. I'm exceedingly hungry, and you must eat to keep up your strength. Come with me to lunch.''

Lori shook her head. ''I don't have time.''

''Make the time,'' Gertrude said softly. ''My treat,'' she added with a smile.

''In that case,'' Lori said, smiling, too, because if she didn't smile she just might start to cry. ''How can I refuse.''

LORI AND DANNY ARRIVED in Ohio the second week in October. The low, rolling countryside was a mixture of yellows, oranges and greens, the weather still warm and sunny, although Lori knew from what Gertrude had told her that the Midwestern winters could be fierce. Lori reminded herself to call this the Midwest, not the East. Ohioans didn't care to be referred to as Easterners. For them the Midwest—what she'd always thought of as Iowa and Nebraska and maybe Illinois—started at the state line. The Ohio state line.

''Hello, Ms. Fenton. May I come in?'' a voice asked from beyond the old-fashioned wooden screen door that opened from the kitchen onto the back porch of the Bengtson house. The voice belonged to a short, plump woman, somewhat past middle age with a mop of curly dark brown hair liberally streaked with gray and a twin-kling smile that was hard to resist.

"Please do." Unannounced visits from neighbors were something else Gertrude had told her to expect. She skirted the big metal table—all chrome and gray For-mica—and opened the door to admit her visitor. Lori sti-fled the impulse to let the wooden door slam shut behind her with a satisfying bang the way Danny had been doing ever since they had arrived.

"I would have stopped by sooner, but I wanted to give you and your son a chance to get settled." Her guest was carrying a covered casserole that smelled heavenly. She held it out to Lori. "Welcome to Willow Creek Farm. I'm Serena Damschroeder."

"Thank you," Lori said, surprised and pleased by the offering. "I'm Lori Fenton."

"I know that," Serena said with a laugh. "We've been expecting you. I hope everything's satisfactory."

"Yes." Actually Lori was slightly intimidated by the big old house. She'd lived in apartments all her life, most of them small and cluttered. Her few kitchen implements and appliances barely filled a single section of cupboards. Her bed and dresser were lost in the high-ceilinged bedroom under the eaves. Her metal-framed, high-tech, uphol-stered conversational grouping and big-screen television looked ridiculous in the front parlor with its bay win-dow, lace curtains and flowered wallpaper. Only Danny, with an eight-year-old's eclectic accumulation of toys and possessions, seemed at home in his new surroundings. She put the casserole in the old round-shouldered refrigerator and shut the door. "We're settling in just fine."

"Is there anything I can do to help? Or I could send one of the girls over? I have four daughters, you know."

"You do?"

"Only Dede—she's the youngest—is still at home. But the others are close by. And I have three sons," Serena added proudly.

"Seven children?"

"And four grandchildren."

"My goodness." Lori was an only child. Her parents were dead. She had no other family that she was aware of.

"The Damschroeders all have big families," Serena said, pulling out one of the shiny red-upholstered kitchen chairs at Lori's invitation. "You only have one child?"

"Yes. His name is Danny. Daniel. He's eight."

"I saw him get on the school bus this morning, just as if he was used to it. He's an adorable little boy."

"I think so," Lori said with a smile.

"Gertrude Bengtson told me you're going to be needing someone to help out now and then. And later on to stay with Danny when you're in the hospital."

"I'd be grateful for your recommendation."

"Why, me, of course," Serena said without hesitation. "I'd love to have Danny around. That big old house up the hill is too empty sometimes. Danny and my oldest grandson are just about the same age. They can play together."

"I... Thank you," Lori said, making up her mind just like that. In New York she had spent weeks interviewing candidates for Danny's baby-sitter. Today all she had to do was look into Serena's laughing good-natured face and the decision was made. "I'm sure Danny will get along with you just fine."

"Good." The older woman smiled, well-pleased with the arrangement so far. "Now is there anything else about this place you need to know?"

"I'm not certain how to deal with the furnace." The October afternoon was warm and golden, but by this evening it would become damp and chilly. Before the week was over, the weatherman on TV had said there would be frost. The furnace was a huge, old cast-iron monster of a thing, crouching at the bottom of the cellar steps.

"Don't give it another thought. Bill Houston from the hardware was out here to check it over last week. It'll do you fine this winter. Matt will be over to light it directly."

"Matt?"

"My son Matthew. He looks after the place."

"I believe Gertrude did mention him."

"Matt's a good man. He can fix most anything. And he's single," Serena said.

A shadow darkened the screen door. "Did I hear my name taken in vain?" a man's voice, low and pleasant, asked.

"It was no such thing," Serena said, turning in her seat. "I was just describing you to our new neighbor."

"Please come in," Lori said politely.

"I never realized knowing my way around a toolbox and being single were such assets," Matt said, opening the door.

Serena ignored the gentle gibe. "Matt, this is Lori Fenton," she said, making the introduction.

"How do you do?"

Matthew Damschroeder was tall and broad shouldered and looked right at home in the too-big kitchen. He had a sharp blade of a nose, a strong jaw and a shock of unruly brown hair above dark-lashed gray eyes. He was carrying a blowtorch and a wrench and screwdriver in one hand and a rolled-up newspaper in the other. He set them down on the kitchen table and held out his hand, tanned and work roughened. No man Lori knew had hands like that. "Welcome to Willow Creek Farm, Ms. Fenton."

"Thank you." Lori watched her own small hand disappear inside his, felt the strong pressure of his grasp and pulled away just a little too quickly to be friendly, she realized too late. Matt Damschroeder's dark brows pulled together over his gray eyes in a quick frown. She'd have to remember that here a handshake meant more than just a polite, perfunctory greeting between business associates.

"Matt's just a holler away if you need anything," Serena chatted on. "He lives in the barn across the road."

"In the barn?" Lori had noticed the red barn on the other side of the county road that ran in front of the house, right away. You couldn't avoid seeing it. It dominated the view from the front windows of her house. Danny considered it "awesome." And Lori had to admit she found it impressive, as well. It was freshly painted, well-maintained with the added attraction of the date worked into the gray and black roof slates that proclaimed it was built in the first year of the twentieth century. There was also a beautifully lettered sign out in front that said: Damschroeder Equipment Repair, Matthew Damschroeder, Master Mechanic, Owner.

"Matt fixes things," his mother explained, catching Lori looking in the direction of the barn. "Big things. Combines, corn pickers, diesel trucks, tractors. His father and brothers still run the farm. That's us at the top of the hill." She pointed out the doorway toward a white clapboard farmhouse, even bigger than Gertrude's, with a wide, wraparound porch, tall narrow windows, sided by green shutters, and a dark red slate roof. "Willow Creek Farm. We used to be a stop on the stagecoach route from Columbus to Cincinnati."

"Ms. Fenton will find out all about us soon enough," Matt said, giving his mother a push toward the door. "I'll get the furnace lit and then why don't we give her a chance to get settled in for the night." Lori felt herself flush. It was disturbing that this man, this complete stranger, had so easily discerned the pain and fatigue she tried so hard, and usually successfully, to keep hidden from the world.

"Oh, dear, I am sorry. Here I've kept you yakking in the kitchen for ages." Serena's plump face expressed remorse.

"I'm fine, really," Lori insisted.

"I'll leave just as soon as Matt lights the furnace," Serena said, brightening once more. "Hurry, Matt," she instructed her tall son, as though he were to blame for the delay.

"Yes, ma'am," he said, giving his mother a salute. "It won't take but the blink of an eye." Suiting action to words, he disappeared down the cellar steps. Five minutes later he was back. "All taken care of. The thermostat's on the living room wall, in case you haven't noticed."

"I found it last night," Lori informed him.

"Don't worry if that old relic down there rumbles and groans when it fires up. That's normal with a furnace older than both of us put together."

"I'll remember." The conversation was ordinary and domestic but even through a gray haze of fatigue, Lori felt a strange sense of connection with this man. He was strong and confident and completely at ease with his surroundings and himself. The way she had always wanted to feel about her life, but never quite managed to accomplish.

Their eyes caught and held for a heartbeat before Matt looked away. "No trouble," he said. He didn't smile, just touched the bill of his cap.

"You'll rest after we leave," Serena ordered. "I've already told Dede to watch out for your little boy at school and to make sure he gets on the right bus back."

"Thank you." What else could she say in the face of such determined friendliness. Besides, she liked this woman. She was accustomed to making quick judgments of people in her work and she trusted her instincts. She liked Serena's son, too, although he was much harder to read, and she didn't trust her intuition where men were concerned as implicitly as she did with women. After all, she'd fallen in love with Kevin Michaelson and that had been the biggest mistake of her life.

"Out, Mom," Matt said, not looking at Lori again.

"Remember, Matt's just a holler away. He's got a place fixed up right next to the workshop. He's there day and night."

"Day and night? I see." Lori almost smiled at the thundercloud frown Matt aimed at the back of his mother's head.

Serena smiled impishly at her scowling son. "Day and night," she murmured. "He doesn't even date."

"That's enough, Mom," Matt said sternly. "My social life is of no concern to Ms. Fenton."

"No, of course not," Serena agreed good-naturedly. "Not the least concern in the world."

BUT AS TIME WENT BY Matt Damschroeder's social life, or lack of one, did concern Lori. She and Danny spent many hours with the Damschroeder family as autumn darkened slowly into the cold and gray of winter. She met the rest of the siblings and extended family and found them all as overpoweringly friendly as Serena. All but Matt, who kept his distance somewhat, but who always, it seemed, had time to spend with her son.

"He's no problem," he'd said when she apologized one day just before Christmas for Danny's always being underfoot at the workshop or in Matt's small cozy apartment in what used to be the milk-processing room of the barn. "Boys his age need a man to talk to once in a while."

"What do you talk about?" she'd asked. She wondered if Matt Damschroeder could know just how much she did worry about appropriate role models for her son.

"Man talk," Matt had said with a smile as he wiped his hands on a cloth. "Just man talk."

"Still, I appreciate the time you spend with him."

"I don't spend time with him because I have to," he said. "I spend time with him because I want to."

The words had come back to Lori again and again over the next few weeks as she lay awake at night and worried what to do to ensure Danny's future when she was in the hospital. Always in the back of her mind was the fear that if something happened to her, Kevin's parents would come and take him to raise and make the same mistakes with Danny that they had with their own son.

She couldn't be as tolerant and far-seeing as Gertrude Bengtson. She couldn't believe good people could raise a bad son. She didn't want Danny to live with Charles and Lydia Michaelson and grow up to be as shallow and selfish and hurtful a man as his father was.

She wanted him to grow up to be—like Matt.

She turned over in bed, looking out the window at the warm yellow rectangle of light shining on the snow that was Matt's living room window. Yes, if anything happened to her so that she could not raise her son, she wanted him to be with a man like Matt, surrounded by a large and loving family cherished, nurtured, protected. Never alone. Never lonely.

But how could she accomplish that? Slowly, slowly over a span of sleepless nights she'd formulated a plan. A plan that would make it almost impossible for Danny's grandparents to take him if she should not survive her surgery. For that reason she was going to do something she would never in a million years believe that she could do. She was not only going to ask Matt Damschroeder to become Danny's legal guardian, temporarily.

She was going to ask him to marry her.

Chapter Two

MATT SAW HER coming across the road from his kitchen window. She always stopped and looked both ways before she crossed. Even after living in the Bengtson house for months and learning that not more than three or four dozen cars passed by her place most days, she still acted as if she expected to be knocked over by a runaway cab or hit by a bus. He supposed it was second nature to someone who'd been born and raised in New York City. He watched her pick her way across the gravel parking lot outside the barn, slippery with half-frozen slush and snow. It had snowed so hard the week before that some schools were still closed and getting around continued to be difficult.

He flipped the switch on the coffeemaker and put a pan of water on the stove to heat. Lori Fenton didn't drink coffee. The doctor had advised her to lay off all caffeine the last time she'd been in for a checkup, or so his mother had told him. But she liked peppermint tea, so he'd brought some tea bags down from the house. Just why, he didn't know. She usually didn't stay more than five minutes when she stopped by the barn, looking for Danny— and he usually didn't encourage her to. He'd sworn off women when his marriage went sour and he sure didn't need this one to complicate his life all over again.

He opened the door before she could knock.

"Oh," she said, looking nervous but determined. "Hi."

"Hi, yourself. I saw you from the kitchen window. C'mon in. It's colder than the devil today."

"It's the wind," she said, unwinding a soft wintery-white scarf from around her head and throat. Her hair was just as soft looking as the scarf, sleek and smooth, brown with the color of chestnuts in its depths. Her eyes were brown, too, with flecks of gold in the center. The same shades of brown and gold that oak leaves turned after the first hard frost.

"Yeah, it's the wind." He'd surprised himself with the poetic turn of his thoughts and he spoke more gruffly than he intended. "Let me take your coat."

She looked at him with a small frown between her brows, as if to judge his mood or his tolerance for female company this early in the day. "The wind blows in New York," she said finally. "But not like this."

"Not much between here and the Mississippi River to stop it."

"I suppose you're right." She held out her coat for him to hang on a hook behind the door. "I mean, the land is mostly flat and open. No wonder it's so windy." She was jabbering, Matt decided. Making nervous small talk. He'd never seen her like this before. She was always so composed, so controlled and sure of herself. He wondered, suddenly, what she wanted of him.

"How about a cup of peppermint tea?" he asked, to give her time to get herself under control.

"Thanks." She looked up at him. "How'd you know that's what I'm drinking these days?"

"Mom told me," he said, smiling to help put her at her ease. She was so skittish that he was beginning to feel decidedly uneasy himself. "Haven't you learned by now there's no such thing as minding your own business around here?" He wasn't wearing shoes and she was, but her head still came to just about level with his chin. He could kiss her on the forehead without bending over—i he'd been inclined to do so, he reminded himself. Not too tall, not too short. She had a nice figure as well, not fat but not as skinny as she'd been when she first moved into the Bengtson place. She had curves now. He'd noticed that for the first time when she and Danny joined the thirty-odd Damschroeders and Hadens, his mother's family, for a party the day after Christmas. Now he noticed every time he saw her. Nice curves in all the right places.

"Privacy is highly overrated, especially when someone cares as much about other people as your mother does."

"I know. She's great. Sugar?" he asked. He motioned her to a seat at the counter that separated his living room from the kitchen.

"Just a little."

She took the teacup from his hand and stared down at it with the frown returning to furrow her forehead. He poured a cup of coffee for himself. She looked up quickly, inhaling deeply. "Ummm, that smells good. This stuff isn't bad, but it's a long way from a good hot cup of coffee," she said wistfully.

"Sorry." He scowled down at the coffee cup he was holding. "I shouldn't be drinking this in front of you."

"Why not? There's nothing wrong with your heart, is there?"

"Not a thing."

The scowl on his face grew even darker. Lori felt a quick stab of apprehension. What was he thinking about that disturbed him so deeply? What had she said to make him look that way? Maybe she was making a terrible mistake coming here, asking him to marry her to give her son a guardian and friend. Her son. Lori unconsciously sat a little straighter on the stool. She'd do anything for her son. Including asking a virtual stranger to marry her.

"Sugar cookie?"

"What? I'm sorry, what did you say?"

"I said would you like a sugar cookie?" The scowl had disappeared from Matt's face. He opened the refrigerator to get milk for his coffee. "They're on the plate beside you," he said. "Help yourself. They're heart shaped. Mom's already baking for Valentine's Day."

"It's coming up soon."

"Two weeks from Monday," he agreed.

The day before her surgery.

She would have to work fast, she thought grimly.

"You know your way around a kitchen," she said because it was too quiet in the small, low-ceilinged room with its light-colored walls and dark, rich wood floors. There was an old-fashioned potbelly stove in one corner and the scent of wood smoke was faint on the air. It was very quiet except for the sound of a radio tuned to an oldies station playing softly somewhere behind her. If Lori didn't know what lay beyond the heavy oak door, she'd never guess she was in a barn.

"I've lived alone for ten years. Ever since I got divorced."

"I see."

"You mean my mother hasn't already informed you about my blighted love life?"

She looked up quickly, her tea bag poised over the cup. He was watching her steadily from beneath those dark, straight brows that drew her gaze so often. He leaned one hip against the counter and waited, it seemed, for her to tell him why she'd come to him in the middle of a weekday morning, alone, while Danny was in school. "No. She only said you were single. She didn't give me any details. I—I did wonder if you'd been married."

"Sixteen months."

"Were there children?"

"No." There was genuine regret in the word. Lori relaxed fractionally and her heart felt a bit lighter. He did love children. She hadn't been deluding herself about that.

"Why didn't your marriage last?" she asked, looking down at her tea bag, not at him. She couldn't believe how hard this was. But she had to do it. She had to know everything there was to know about this man for Danny's sake and her own peace of mind.

"You're getting a tad personal, aren't you?"

"Yes." She looked up, meeting his narrowed gaze without flinching. "But I have a very good reason for asking. Please humor me."

He nodded. "We were . . . geographically incompatible," he said with a smile that was as cold as the north wind blowing around the corner of the barn. "She was from Texas. San Antonio. I met her while I was stationed there in the army. We fell in love and I brought her back here to live. She hated it. She hated the heat and rain and humidity in the summer and the snow and ice in the winter and everything in between. She wanted to go home. At first she wanted me to go along, but I was just as stubborn as she was about staying here. Then later she didn't care. She stuck it out a year and then she pulled up stakes and left."

"I'm sorry."

"Don't be. It was a long time ago. We were both kids. I got over it."

She wasn't so sure that he had.

"What about you?" he asked, pouring himself another cup of coffee.

Lori took a deep breath. She'd known this was coming. "No," she said, lifting her chin. "I've never been married."

"I see." His expression gave little away. He was very good at hiding his feelings when he wanted to. Lori filed that small piece of knowledge away for future reference.

"Does that bother you?" she asked.

"No. Why should it?" He took a swallow of his coffee. "We're not quite as narrow-minded out here as you think, Lori. It's true most people around Willow Creek still get married when they find out they're going to have a baby together. But we've got our share of single mothers, as well, a lot of them just kids not much older than Dede. And no one tars and feathers them or runs them out of town on a rail."

"Sorry," Lori said, breaking her cookie into little pieces. It was lopsided, a reject, a defective heart, just like her own. "I'm a little touchy about it sometimes myself."

"Tell me about Danny's father."

"Now you're getting personal."

He smiled, a real smile this time, she noticed. "You asked first," he reminded her.

"So I did. I met him my senior year in college. I was a business major. He was a music major. He was also everything I was not. Old Long Island family. Handsome, wealthy, not a care in the world. He was also selfish and self-centered and completely unable to make any kind of commitment to me or our child."

"He sounds like a son of a bitch."

Lori's smile was tight. "Exactly. But it was my own fault. I thought he'd grow up once he learned I was pregnant. I was wrong. But that's water under the bridge."

"I hope you took him for everything he's got." Matt was looking out the window, not at her.

"He hasn't got a cent," she said. "The last I heard he was playing bass guitar for a rock band, touring New Zealand. It's his parents who are very well-to-do."

Matt quit looking out the window. One big hand was curled around his coffee mug, one stuck in the front pocket of his jeans. "Why are you telling me this, Lori?" he asked quietly, but his tone of voice let her know he expected the truth, nothing less.

"Because I've come to make you a proposition." Her hands started to shake. She set her teacup down very carefully.

"A proposition?" He sounded wary all of a sudden, like a stag scenting the hunter at the edge of the forest.

"Yes. A business deal, really."

"What is it?"

"I want you to marry me."

Chapter Three

"WHAT?" Matt wasn't sure he'd heard her correctly. "Would you repeat that?" His palms were sweaty. He resisted the urge to put down the coffee mug and rub his hands along his pant legs. His stomach lurched as though someone had just punched him in the gut.

"You're not making this easy, Matt," Lori said, raking her slender fingers through her hair. "I want you to marry me. A business arrangement, that's all," she added hurriedly. She stopped talking abruptly. She folded her hands together in front of her, took a deep breath and started again. "No. Not only a business arrangement. I'm asking you this as a favor. For Danny's sake. And my...my peace of mind."

"Your peace of mind?" He felt like an idiot, repeating every word she said, but she'd thrown him for a loop. He'd expected her to ask him and his family to watch over Danny while she was in the hospital. He'd noticed the way she watched them together when Danny was hanging around the shop. He'd made up his mind to take on the responsibility of temporary guardianship if she asked. But marriage. Marriage had never entered his head.

"Yes. My peace of mind." She lifted her chin. Her color was coming back, a soft, familiar flush to her cheeks. "I'm going to have heart surgery in less than three weeks, in case you've forgotten." He liked her better this way, her usual, no-nonsense, confident self. When she looked and sounded so vulnerable, as she just had, it made him ache to reach out and take her in his arms, take care of her, keep her safe—and that scared the hell out of him.

"Matt?"

"I'm thinking," he said, stalling for time to order his thoughts.

"You don't have any religious objections, do you?"

"Were you planning on a church wedding?"

"No. Of course not."

"People will talk."

"My friends will never need to know, but you may have some explaining to do with your friends and family."

"I'd have to think about it." He ought to turn her down flat and get the hell out of there before he got in over his head. But something, some small traitorous corner of his wary heart, maybe, couldn't let him leave her sitting there high and dry like that. "Why don't you just ask Danny's grandparents to be his guardians while you're in the hospital?"

"No!" She was holding her teacup so tightly between her hands that he thought it would break. She was holding on to her self-control just as tightly. "I don't want them to have Danny. Not even for a little while. They tried to take him from me when he was a baby. They've tried again and again to get me to make them his legal guardians. I don't want them to have him. If something happens to me, I don't want them to raise him to grow up like his father." She was trembling, and he caught a glimpse in the depths of her brown eyes of the very young, helpless and frightened child-woman she must have been when Danny was born. He didn't like what he saw because it made him aware that underneath that Wall Street tough-as-nails facade there was still a little girl who'd grown up too fast, lonely and alone. "Please, Matt. For Danny's sake." She said the words as though they contained the most powerful magic in the world, and he knew for her they did.

"Nothing is going to happen to you, Lori," he said helplessly. He felt her pain all the way through him, try as he might to ignore the ache.

"I can't be sure of that. Maybe I can sweeten the pot. What about money? For your business. Ten thousand dollars? That would help you out, wouldn't it?"

"I don't want your money." He leaned forward, his hand balled into a fist on the countertop.

"You could use it for anything you want." Her desperation was evident in her voice and in her body. "I'll make sure you get it no matter what happens to me—"

"No!" He refused to even consider the possibility that something would go wrong with the surgery. That Lori would die.

"Matt, please. For pity's sake, marry me. Give me some peace. If anything should happen—" She took a deep, shaky breath, reaching out to cover his hand with hers. It was the first time she'd made any move to touch him. He remained very still. Her touch was soft, hesitant, but it affected him like a bolt of electricity racing along his nerve endings. "If I should die I could rest easy knowing Danny was safe and happy and cherished in a family like yours."

"I would watch over him even if we weren't legally married," he said more softly, hoping against hope she would change her mind, give him an out, save him from what he feared would develop into a broken heart of his own. She bowed her head but not before he caught the sheen of unshed tears in her eyes.

"I've told you. His grandparents are wealthy and influential people. You don't have the financial resources to fight them. They'd take him away from you. Just as they've tried to take him away from me. I know they would." She lifted her head, not trying to hide her tears this time.

"Don't cry, Lori." He was lost and he knew it. He reached out and slowly touched the silky fineness of her hair. "Don't cry."

"Please, Matt. Marry me," she whispered once more. "You're the only man in the world I trust enough to give him my son."

THEY WERE MARRIED early on a blustery February morning with only Matt's mother and father as witnesses. Ethan Damschroeder was tall and broad shouldered with thinning, steel gray hair and kind gray eyes, like Matt's. A man of few words. As different from his outgoing and exuberant wife as night is from day. But Lori liked him all the same. He reminded her a lot of his son. He didn't speak often, but when he did he had something worthwhile to say.

It was barely daylight when they arrived at the mayor's office in the brand-new brick municipal building at the edge of town. The wind was so bitingly cold that Lori kept her head down all the way inside the building and didn't notice the florist's box Serena carried until they were inside the mayor's small, crowded office.

She pushed the box into Lori's hands. "Open it, dear."

"Serena, you shouldn't have." She was aware Matt's mother had misgivings about their hurried and unorthodox marriage, but she had kept her opinions to herself and Lori was grateful. She couldn't blame Serena for her concern. Marriages of convenience, business arrangements destined to last no more than a few weeks, were not the kind of matches most mothers wished for their sons.

"Of course I didn't have to. I wanted to. No bride should have to stand up without something to hold in her hands. I never realized until my own marriage why brides carry bouquets. It's so you have something to do with your hands. The florist suggested the colors. It is Valentine's Day, after all. The most romantic day of the year," she added without a trace of irony.

"Serena, calm down. You're chittering like a house sparrow," Ethan said, indulgently patting his wife's hand. "Go on, Lori, open it."

Lori smiled and did as she was bade. Inside the box was a small bouquet, a nosegay, really, of pink and white roses and baby's breath with tiny knots of red ribbon, in honor of the day, scattered here and there among them.

"Oh, Serena. It's beautiful. Thank you very much."

"It matches your dress just fine." Lori was wearing a simple winter white sheath with a gold belt and gold jewelry. The effect was both stylish and classic and she was glad she'd made the effort to look her best, when Matt shrugged out of his heavy coat and she saw he was dressed in a neat dark suit and tie.

He looked very handsome, serious and distinguished as his mother pinned a red rose boutonniere to his jacket lapel. He shook hands with the mayor as she bustled into the room apologizing for being late, and for a moment Lori's breath caught in her throat, as she watched the man who, in a few short minutes, would be her husband. Was she doing the right thing, asking this virtual stranger to marry her? To stand in the place of a parent to her son if the need arose?

Matt turned his head as if sensing her appraisal of him and the sudden confusion that rooted her feet to the floor. He didn't smile but held out his hand. "Come here, Lori. I'd like you to meet Mayor Burgess." She took a step forward and then another. His big hand closed over hers and she felt his strength and his warmth flow through her, banishing the chill from her bones and the worry from her heart.

She had chosen the right man. The best man for her son.

"Congratulations, Lori," the mayor said, studying her with friendly curiosity, as she reached for her reading glasses and the book containing the marriage vows. "Is this a single- or a double-ring ceremony?"

Lori hadn't even considered a ring.

"Just one, Mayor," Matt said, smoothly producing a small blue velvet box from his pocket.

"Matt, you didn't have..."

"I wanted to." He opened the box to hand the mayor a plain gold band. "If you're ready, Mayor, so are we."

The ceremony took only a moment, or so it seemed to Lori. Before she knew it, the mayor had pronounced them husband and wife. "You may kiss the bride," she said, pausing expectantly.

Lori hadn't considered that, either—kissing Matt. Or at least not that she let herself think about. He leaned close, but didn't pull her into his arms. When his lips touched her mouth, she closed her eyes. Matt's head blocked out the light. He was still holding her hand and brought it up between them. She felt the slow steady beat of his heart against her palm. It was very quiet in the small, brightly lighted room. The pressure of the kiss increased. Her lips flowered open beneath his, welcoming him. The tip of his tongue met hers, then withdrew. "Happy Valentine's Day, Mrs. Damschroeder," he said softly and lifted his head.

Lori had nothing to say in return. She stepped backward, away from the beckoning haven of his arms. She liked being kissed by this man. She liked it very much. She liked him very much. Enough to wish for a moment that their marriage was real. But it was only a wish, she told herself sternly, a passing fancy engendered by her vulnerability and her anxiety over an uncertain future. She would have to be very careful to keep her distance and her perspective. Accidentally falling in love with her new husband was something she simply could not allow to happen.

Chapter Four

"GOODBYE, SWEETHEART. Be a good boy and do everything Serena tells you to do."

"I will." Danny clung tearfully to his mother, curling against her in the high hospital bed. Lori held him tight and stroked his blond head. Her eyes were filled with tears, but she refused to let them fall. Matt watched the woman he'd married less than twelve hours earlier struggle with her emotions and was amazed all over again at her courage and strength of will.

"You'll have a good time staying with the Damschroeders," Lori said, her voice husky but under control.

Danny nodded. "Dede's taking me to the high school basketball game tomorrow night. And then the next day, after school, I can come and see you—for a few minutes," he said, sitting up on his knees. "Matt promised." He shot him a gap-toothed grin. Matt smiled back.

Lori had spent a lot of time over the past couple of weeks explaining to her son why she was marrying Matt. In fact, Matt had been there for one of the talks to support them both. Lori had told Danny that she believed marriage should be forever, but now, because she wanted him to be as safe and as happy as he could be while she was in the hospital, she was going to marry Matt, for just a little while. And if anything did happen to her—which it would not!—he could stay with Matt and Serena and Ethan forever.

"I've already okayed your visit with Dr. Scarpelli," Lori said. "Only don't worry if I look a little scary. Like I don't feel very good, you know."

"And have tubes coming out of your arms and lots of beeping machines around you and stuff like Dr. Scarpelli showed us in that other room?"

"Yes," Lori said, smiling. "Exactly like that."

"I won't like it," Danny said fiercely. "But I won't be afraid."

"Good. Now you'd better be going. They said I have to go to sleep very early tonight."

"Earlier than seven-thirty?"

"Earlier than seven-thirty," Lori confirmed.

"Bummer." His mother laughed. Matt smiled, as well, but he was far more worried about Lori than he cared to admit.

"Time to go, Danny," Serena Damschroeder announced, sticking her head in the room. "There's school tomorrow, remember?"

"Okay," Danny said, but he made no move to get down off Lori's bed.

"Go with Serena, honey. Tomorrow this will all be over and next week I'll be back home."

Matt looked at her, wondering if the word "home" had been merely a convention, a figure of speech, or if she might, just possibly, have started thinking of Willow Creek as home. But she had bowed her head to kiss her son and he couldn't see her eyes or her expression. When she looked up again, her face was a pale mask, her eyes carefully concealing bright unshed tears.

"'Bye, sweetie. Be good. I love you."

"I love you, too, Mom. I'll be good. I promise."

Serena held out her arms. "We'll take good care of him, Lori."

"I know you will."

"Are you coming, too, Matt?" Danny asked.

"I thought I'd stay with your mom until she falls asleep."

"Okay," Danny said. "Are you going to be here tomorrow?"

"Yes. I'm staying in Columbus all night so I'll be here first thing tomorrow."

"Good. I'm glad. You can make sure they take care of my mom." He took Serena's outstretched hand and walked out of the room, turning to wave at his mother one more time from the doorway. "Matt will take care of you."

"I know he will, sweetheart."

"Our prayers are with you," Serena said quietly, stepping aside as a nurse entered the room with Lori's sleeping medicine. Serena looked at Lori and then at Matt. "With both of you."

SOMETHING WAS terribly wrong.

Lori had known that from the first moment she awoke from the anesthesia, but there had always been a nurse or a doctor present with a hypodermic and soothing words to lull her back to sleep before she could voice the questions that formed so slowly, so reluctantly in her mind.

"What's wrong?" she managed at last, as she was finally able to force her eyes open to see that Matt was sitting beside her bed. Somehow, even in her pain-filled dreamlike state, she'd known he was always there, close by, waiting for her to come fully awake. He stood up and leaned over her. She was horrified at the sound she made. Her voice was a rusty croak, the words slurred and broken. What had happened to her?

"It's all right, Lori," he said, his tone reassuringly normal. He took her right hand in his and held it tight. "It's all right."

"Please." The effort it took to form the single word was enormous. The muscles on the left side of her face were stiff. Her face tingled as if she had just been to the dentist and the numbness was beginning to wear off. She closed her eyes and almost panicked. The whole left side of her body felt the same way. "What happened?"

"The surgery was a success," another voice said. She turned her head to see her surgeon, Dr. Anthony Scarpelli, standing on the other side of the bed. He was a heavyset man in his early sixties with a big red nose and intense deeply set blue eyes. Lori focused on those eyes and tried to make sense of what he had just said, but the words had already slipped away to the edges of her consciousness, and that frightened her almost as much as not being able to move her arm and leg. "But there was a complication. You had an allergic reaction to the anesthetic—a one in a million occurrence. There was no way we could have predicted or prevented it from happening. Do you understand?"

Lori closed her eyes. This time she had been able to decipher enough words to understand. She nodded, relieved that the simple gesture was not beyond her power. "Yes."

Matt squeezed her hand reassuringly as if he sensed her panic. Dr. Scarpelli kept on talking and Lori struggled to comprehend as much as she could. "As I said, the surgery itself was a success. But afterward, in the recovery room, you suffered a slight stroke."

Lori's eyes flew open. The word echoed over and over inside her aching skull. "No."

"I'm afraid so, my dear. But you will recover completely. You have to believe me when I say that. There is some paralysis on your left side. But it will go away eventually and you'll be good as new."

Lori felt tears form behind her eyelids and she was powerless to stop them. "How long?" she managed to ask, her eyes glued to the doctor's face. She was so achingly tired. It was far too much effort even to think.

"Let's not worry about that just yet."

"How long?" she demanded, forcing back the beckoning darkness.

"Six months. Six months at the very least. But don't worry, my dear. Your husband has already made arrangements to take you home."

"No," Lori said. She looked pale and thin and very, very stubborn sitting in the wheelchair beside the window of her hospital room. "We've been over this again and again. I'm not going home with you."

"Okay," Matt said patiently. "I'll come home with you." He was getting used to arguing with her. In fact, Dr. Scarpelli had encouraged it. Lori was a fighter, he said, and it didn't matter to him if the stimulus to work hard at regaining her health came from within or without. It mattered to Matt, though. He didn't like being the heavy, but he liked seeing Lori sitting in the wheelchair, morose and dejected, even less.

"No!" She swiveled her head in his direction, her brown eyes shooting sparks of gold fire. "I'll hire a nurse." In the three weeks since her surgery, her speech had returned to normal. Only occasionally there remained a slight stutter, a hesitation in her response if she was particularly upset or very tired. Her arm, too, was gaining strength. She could feed herself and brush her hair, hold a pencil and write her name. But the muscles of her left leg had been slow to respond to therapy. She was still confined to a wheelchair most of the time. She hated it. And he knew she hated his seeing her there.

"Yes." He leaned forward, both hands on the padded arms of the chair. "The last thing Danny needs is another stranger in his life. You can move into my place at the barn."

"It's too small." She wouldn't look at him but stared out the window at the gray, rainy day. It was March now. Winter was very reluctantly giving way to spring.

"Okay. I'll move my stuff into your house. We'll set up some sort of intercom system so that you can call me if you need me when I'm working in the barn."

"No, Matt." She rested her head on the palm of her hand. She still tired very quickly. "I don't think it's a good idea for us to be living under the same roof."

"We're married," Matt pointed out. He wasn't sure it was such a good idea, either. The thought of having Lori so close, day and night, was damned appealing—to say the least.

"Don't. Please," she said, looking up at him. Her brown eyes were enormous in her thin face.

Matt felt the muscles in his jaw tighten. She was just about the most stubborn woman he'd ever known. "Okay. We'll compromise. You can move into the big house. Mom's practically insisting on it, anyway."

"I—I...couldn't do that. I don't want to be a burden—" She never finished what she was going to say.

"Hello, Lori." A couple stood in the doorway. The man was average height, slightly overweight. He was wearing a dark suit and trench coat. The woman beside him was a little taller, blond, over sixty, Matt guessed, but very well preserved. She wore a fur coat. A mink. Matt had never seen a mink coat up close, but there was no mistaking the authenticity of this one.

"Lydia. Charles." Lori covered her left hand, the fingers still slightly, involuntarily curved, with her right. "What are you doing here?"

"I had cocktails in the city yesterday with Rachel Finkbeiner's sister. She asked me how you were doing. That she hoped you would recover from the *complications* of the surgery," explained the woman Lori had called Lydia. "She said she hoped you wouldn't be crippled for life. I couldn't imagine what she was talking about, so I called that doctor friend of yours and insisted she tell me exactly what had happened and why we hadn't been notified."

"We've been worried about you," Charles said. "And about our grandson."

"Danny's being well taken care of." Matt had risen when the older couple entered the room. "I'm Matt Damschroeder," he said, holding out his hand.

"Charles Michaelson. This is my wife, Lydia."

"How do you do?" The response was perfunctory. The woman couldn't seem to take her eyes off Lori in her wheelchair.

"Charles and Lydia are Danny's grandparents," Lori said, her back ramrod straight, her voice carefully even. Matt realized how much effort the nonchalant pose was costing her. She was determined not to show weakness in front of Danny's grandparents, but he could see the tension in every line of her body and sense the fear in her heart. He seated himself on the edge of her bed, close but not touching, ready to help if she asked him.

"We've come to take Danny home with us," Lydia said in a tone that revealed she was used to giving orders.

"No." Lori's voice quavered.

"Surely you can see that's what's best for him," Lydia continued, sounding, to Matt's ears, even more agitated than Lori.

"You must come, too, Lori," Charles said.

"Yes," Lydia agreed after a moment's hesitation. "We'll hire whatever help you need, of course. A nurse. A physiotherapist."

"No, thank you," Lori repeated, struggling to stand. "I have a therapist. A good one. I—I d-d-don't want your—"

"Lori." Matt was beside her in the blink of an eye. He put his hand beneath her left elbow, helping her to stand. She flashed him one quick look, a mixture of gratitude and desperation that twisted his heart, then turned to face Danny's grandparents once more. "We're not going back to Long Island with you."

"It's for your own good," Lydia said, her face a mask of good manners and good breeding. Behind the facade Matt wondered exactly what she was thinking.

"No." Lori was trembling harder. She'd just returned from physical therapy and he knew how hard she pushed herself during that hour, how exhausted she must have been. But he also knew somehow that she was trembling more from fear than from fatigue. She was scared, rightly or wrongly, that Danny's grandparents, powerful and influential people she'd called them, were going to take her son away from her. There was no way in hell he intended to let that happen. Matt pulled her close, taking most of her slender weight against him.

"Thanks for the offer, but Danny's staying here with his mother. They're both coming home with me." He hadn't realized until just that moment how very important it was to him to have Lori and her son under his roof.

"Whatever for?"

"I'm glad Lori has made friends here," Charles Michaelson interrupted his wife diplomatically. "But we're the only family Danny has. He belongs with us."

Matt felt a shudder of fear course through Lori's body. He knew how helpless she felt in her present condition. How much she had dreaded exactly what was happening right now.

"You aren't the only family Danny has," Matt told them quietly, forcefully, leaving no room for doubt. "He has me. You see, Danny is my stepson. And Lori is my wife."

Chapter Five

APRIL IN THE COUNTRY could be a very beautiful month, Lori decided, as she watched the dull grays and browns of winter give way to the soft greens and yellows of spring. The weather was as changeable as her moods. From every side she could hear the throaty roar of tractors laboring to pull planters through the rich black fields. And closer above her head in the trees, birds were singing. She looked up at the sky, watching the fleecy, dark-edged clouds for signs of rain before she began walking again. She was turning into a country woman, she thought with amusement. She never watched the clouds in New York, or listened for birdsong or the rush of wind through the trees.

For the past week, when the weather allowed, she'd walked down the lane from the Damschroeder house to meet Danny's school bus and check their mailbox at the end of the lane, going a little farther without stopping to rest each day. It was a symbolic journey, in a way. If she could walk to her own home and back, there was no reason she and Danny couldn't return there to live on their own.

She could not continue to take advantage of the Damschroeders' hospitality. It had been nearly a month since she left the hospital, so unnerved by Danny's grandparents' arrival on the scene that she'd allowed Matt to arrange for her to stay at his parents' house without putting up a fight. And once there she had been so completely surrounded by so much warmth and caring that she'd been unable to break away.

The truth was that when she left the hospital she hadn't been strong enough to manage on her own. But that dark time was past. Every day now she grew stronger and more sure of herself. And soon, very soon, she would be able to leave the down-filled nest the Damschroeders had provided for her and her son. And then, for all their sakes, she must also take the legal steps to free Matt from their marriage of convenience.

Danny's school bus pulled up in front of the barn with a screech of brakes. Danny bounced down the steps and turned to wave goodbye to his friends, waiting for the bus to move on, before he raced across the road to the mail-box.

The big double doors of the barn were open. Matt walked out into the sunlight, wiping his hands on a red shop rag. "What's up, buddy?" he asked, as Danny skidded to a halt in front of the mailbox where a big brown envelope rested in the new grass at the base.

"Do you suppose it's the Space Shuttle model Grandma Lydia promised to send me?" Lori heard him ask as she reached the edge of the roadway and rested a moment with her hand on the trunk of the big oak tree at the edge of the driveway. He picked up the package and gave it a shake, smiling broadly at the satisfying sound it made. "Yep. It's the model. Great!" He spun around. "Mom! Grandma and Grandpa sent me the Space Shuttle, just like they said they would."

"You'll have to send them a thank-you note right away," Lori said, stretching her mouth into a smile.

"I'll call them," Danny announced. "I don't like to write thank-you notes." Lori wisely let the matter rest for the moment. In the two weeks since Charles and Lydia had left Ohio they had spoken frequently on the phone with Danny. Serena had said it was a good thing that her

son and his grandparents were growing closer. Lori tried
to feel the same way, but it was hard to do.

"Matt, will you help me put it together tonight?"

"After you've done your homework."

"Ah, Matt."

"After you've done your homework. C'mon," he said,
motioning toward Lori, still standing beside the oak.
"Let's walk your mom back up to the house. She's looking pretty tired."

"I'm fine," Lori said, defending herself.

"Where's your cane?" Danny asked, bouncing up for
a quick hug before he ricocheted off in another direction,
clutching his precious package in one hand, while his
knapsack swung from its straps in the other.

"I don't need it to walk this far."

"That's not what Dr. Scarpelli says," Matt reminded
her, offering his arm as they turned to follow Danny up
the driveway.

"I should think you'd be glad to see me without that
damned cane," she shot back, letting her nerves get the
better of her. She wasn't used to having her husband this
close, to feeling the rough warmth of his skin beneath her
hand as he tucked her arm in his. "The sooner I'm on my
own and out of your hair, the sooner we can all get our
lives back on track."

"It's only a model airplane, Lori," he said. She could
feel his gray eyes on her and kept her gaze focused on the
ground in front of her feet. She thought she'd hidden her
anxiety over Danny's gift very well. Evidently she was
wrong.

"I can't help thinking it's more than that."

"You're overreacting."

This time Lori did look up, but Matt was watching
Danny as he raced up the driveway ahead of them. "How

do you know that? You've only spent a few hours with Danny's grandparents. I've known them for years."

"And been scared to death of them for years," he answered, coming to a halt when she did.

"You're not the first person to tell me that," she admitted reluctantly. "But it doesn't alter the facts. I was twenty-three years old, unmarried, unemployed and damned near penniless. They tried to take Danny away from me. And his father—their son—never lifted a finger to help me, even though he didn't want to have anything to do with Danny himself. How can you believe that people who raised a son of a bitch like that are fit to raise my son, as well?"

"Good people can have kids that turn out bad. That's a fact of life. Did you ever stop to think about that? Did you ever stop to think that no matter how much you love Danny, how much effort and energy you put into raising him, he just might turn out the same way?"

"No," she said vehemently. "I'd never let that happen to my son."

"I'd bet you a year's pay that Lydia and Charles have said that more than once about Danny's father. Think about it, Lori, before you condemn them out of hand."

"Maybe they are good people who had the misfortune to raise a bad son, but that doesn't make it any easier for me to trust them today than it did in the past." They were almost at the back door. Lori was shaking as much from anger as from fatigue.

"In the past, Lori. Those are the key words here."

"It's not in the past. They were here not three weeks ago, determined to take him back again." She didn't want to talk about it any more. She didn't want to have to listen to any point of view but her own. "How I handle this situation between Danny and his grandparents is none of your business.''

''I see.'' He looked down at her hand, still resting on his forearm. ''You don't want to hear the plain unvarnished truth, even from your husband—is that it?'' Lori had trouble meeting his steady gaze.

She dropped her hand from his arm. ''You're not really my husband, Matt,'' she said softly, amazed at how bereft she felt at the sudden disconnection, and how disturbed she was by the sharp clutch of pain the words sent through her newly reliable heart.

''And you're not the intelligent, caring woman I thought you were,'' he said with what sounded like real regret. Then he turned on his heel and walked away without another word.

''DANNY, how are you coming with those carrots?'' Serena asked Lori's son, as she turned away from the big sink beneath the kitchen window. ''I'll need lots and lots of them for the pot roast I'm planning for supper tonight.''

''I just have two more to scrub,'' the little boy answered proudly, pointing at the big crockery bowl of carrots beside him on the table. ''How about you, Mom? Got the potatoes peeled yet?''

''Almost done.'' Lori put down the half-peeled Idaho she was holding and leaned close. ''Did you ever think the two of us would be helping to cook food for this many people?'' Most of the Damschroeder clan were expected to share the meal, possibly twenty people, in all.

''No,'' Danny giggled. ''It's like cooking for a restaurant. I wish I had one of those big white hats a chef wears.''

''Me too.''

"I've always wanted to own a restaurant," Serena confided, bending down to take two golden brown apple pies from the oven. "This place used to be an inn, you know. A stop on the stagecoach line from Columbus to Cincinnati."

"Matt told me." He'd told her many things about his family as he sat by her bedside hour after hour, those first terrible days after she'd awakened from her drugged sleep. Some of it she remembered. Some she did not. But what she did remember was his voice, low and soothing, always strong, always supportive and always there.

"There are six bedrooms. But of course you know that. Now with only Ethan and I and Dede living at home—"

"And us," Danny piped up.

"And you," Serena corrected herself with a smile. "Most of the time, they're half empty. I'd love to fill them with the antique furniture Ethan's parents left us. It's all still up in the attic. I couldn't let those kids of mine ruin it while they were growing up. If I had my wish I'd bring it down, paint and paper and turn this place into a bed and breakfast."

"Why don't you?" Lori asked, as she dropped the last potato into the pot.

"No time. And no money. Besides, even though we think Willow Creek is one of the prettiest places in the country, there isn't any reason for tourists to come here. It's too far from either Columbus or Cincinnati to attract overnight visitors." She slid the pies onto wire racks on the counter to cool. "But it's a nice dream."

"A very nice dream," Lori agreed. Owning her own business was something she'd never considered. She'd always seen herself at Carter, Finkbeiner and Strauss or a similar firm, working hard, toeing the line, maybe making vice president someday. Someday far in the future. She wondered now, sometimes, if the financial security she'd be buying for herself and Danny would be enough to make up for the loneliness that was surely going to be part of the cost of that success.

Thunder rumbled off in the distance. A spring storm had been threatening since before Danny arrived home from school but now it sounded much nearer.

"I hope Ethan and Matt get that last field planted before the storm hits," Serena said, looking out the window. Matt's brothers were working on fields near their own homes, so Matt had volunteered to help his father finish the planting when he wasn't making work calls of his own.

The big, high-ceilinged kitchen grew darker as the sun disappeared behind the storm clouds. It thundered again. Much nearer than before. "Wow!" Danny exclaimed, his eyes wide with excitement. "That was close."

"Oh, dear," Serena said, still looking out the window. "I left the wash hanging on the line." She was quartering onions to put in the pot roast. "It'll get soaked or blown all over the yard."

"I'll get it," Lori offered, rising from her seat. She rested both hands on the tabletop for a moment to make sure she had her balance and then headed for the back door. Aside from a continuing weakness in her leg and a frustrating tendency to have to search for words when she found herself in a stressful situation, the effects of her stroke had all but disappeared.

"Thanks," Serena said, banishing a wayward strand of curly brown hair off her forehead with a puff of her breath. "I'm already half an hour late getting this roast in the oven."

"No problem," Lori said and smiled. She took one look at her cane and left it sitting by the door.

To tell the truth she was tired of kitchen chores and welcomed the excuse to get outside into the sultry warmth of the late April day. Running an inn might be Serena's dream of a lifetime but it wasn't Lori's. At least not the physical aspects—cooking, cleaning, catering to the whims of your guests. But the financial challenges and opportunities of owning your own business intrigued her more than she cared to admit.

Lightning struck somewhere not too far away with a snap and crackle that made her jump. The thunder that followed was almost instantaneous and a little frightening. Lori couldn't remember being outside in a thunderstorm like this ever before, exposed, unprotected by high walls of stone and steel. She quickened her steps toward the clothesline strung between two metal poles in the backyard.

Beyond the banks of tulips and daffodils that bordered Serena's garden, acres of green winter wheat stretched away toward the river at the bottom of the hill. It seemed as if she could see half the world spread out before her. In the far distance, where the storm clouds hadn't yet dimmed its light, the sun winked off a metal silo. In the other direction Lori could just make out the rain being driven before the wind in silvery sheets that blanketed the countryside in a gray mist.

The rumble of thunder, long and sustained, masked the roar of two big, green tractors as Ethan and Matt hurried to plant the last rows of corn in the field behind the barn. Lori watched them make the final turn and head back. The rows were as straight and precise as though laid down by a giant ruler. She finished taking the sheets and towels down, just as the first big drops of rain began to fall.

Lori noticed the barn doors were closed. Matt and his father would be soaked if they had to get down off the tractors to open them before they could drive the machinery inside. She dropped the last towel in the clothes basket and started across the gravel driveway just as Ethan pulled into the yard. The barn was almost an exact duplicate of the one where Matt lived and worked, except it was even larger. The doors were big and heavy but surprisingly easy to open on their well-oiled track. Lori pushed first one and then the other as far back as they would go.

Ethan drove the big tractor and its attached planter on through to the back. He shut down the noisy, powerful engine and the sudden silence magnified the wind and the beginning tattoo of rain on the metal roof.

"Matt's finishing up the last round," Ethan said, climbing down out of the cab. "Looks like we made it."

"That you did," Lori ageed with a smile. She glanced up at the dark clouds overhead. They looked as if they were being stirred by a giant's spoon. "It's going to rain buckets."

"Yep," Ethan replied. "Buckets. Want to make a run for the house?"

"In a moment. Do you know I'm thirty-two years old and I've never stood outside and watched a thunderstorm in my whole life."

"Is that a fact?" Ethan smiled, a slow, warming smile, very much like his son's. "Well, then maybe you just ought to do that once in a while. I imagine they have thunderstorms even in New York City."

Lori laughed. He was teasing her and she knew it. "Yep," she said, imitating his slow, country drawl. "But somehow, being filtered down through all those towering walls of glass and concrete, they lose something of their fascination."

"You need to see the whole storm spread out over the countryside to appreciate the wonder and power of it all," he agreed. "Mother and I usually watch from the back porch. Join us if you want."

"I'll be along in a moment," Lori said. She was watching the wind drive the new wheat before it like waves on the ocean. "Oh, dear. I left the laundry sitting in the yard."

"I'll pick it up on my way in." She didn't see Ethan smile indulgently and shake his head as he took off for the house at a trot. "We'll make a country woman of you yet," he said, but the rumble of thunder and the approach of Matt's tractor drowned out his words.

The rain was coming down in torrents as Matt drove into the barn. It wasn't until that moment that Lori realized her fascination with the storm had trapped her there alone with him. In a matter of moments the gravel driveway outside the barn had become covered with water. The footing was treacherous. She would have to walk slowly to keep her balance, and by the time she got back to the house she'd be soaking wet. Both Ethan and Serena would know she'd set off in the rain to avoid being alone with their son.

She stayed put, moving a little way into the shadowy interior of the barn to avoid being pelted by raindrops. She owed Matt an apology for her behavior on the walk back from the mailbox the day before. She'd thought a lot about what he'd said to her then. She'd overreacted and she knew it.

And it was time, also, to talk about an annulment of their marriage-in-name-only. Time to sever the ties between them so that Matt, as well as she and Danny, could get on with their lives.

"We did it," Matt called, as he jumped down out of the tractor cab. The sleeves of his shirt were rolled above his elbows. His forearms were strongly muscled, tanned and covered with a light dusting of gold-tipped hair. The dark green brim of his hat kept his face in shadows, but his teeth flashed white in a wide grin. "Everything's in the ground. It can pour all night, for all I care."

"Congratulations." She couldn't help smiling in return. Smiling as well, she realized, because he no longer seemed to be angry at her. "Do you get a trophy or a prize? Is it always such a rush to finish a field of corn?"

"No," he said, suddenly serious. "I haven't thought about farming as winning a race against an opponent with all the rules on their side in a long time. It's just what we Damschroeders do. It's who we are."

"I know."

"Do you?" He was watching her very closely. His gray eyes were as dark and stormy as the rain-filled clouds overhead. He closed the distance between them in three long steps. Lori didn't back away, although he was very close.

"Yes. I've known a great deal of satisfaction in my own work. But the truth is, facts and figures, no matter how large the denomination, are still just letters and numbers on a page. The only deadline I usually have to work against is the closing bell on the stock exchange. I've never had hand-to-hand combat with Mother Nature."

"You've spent all your life working for goals you can't see or touch. Documents that are filed away and forgotten almost before they're signed. Mergers that have no more effect on your life than the change of lettering on the office door," Matt said quietly. "Poor Lori. There's so much more to this world than money and success." He reached out, taking her by the shoulders, and brushed her forehead with his lips in a kiss that was feather light but burned her skin like a brand.

Lightning struck nearby. So close the explosion made her jump. Matt frowned suddenly, fiercely, and pulled her into his arms. Lori sucked in her breath, suddenly dizzy and disoriented. He'd touched her before over the past few weeks, helped her in and out of her wheelchair, supported her when she returned from her therapy sessions exhausted and discouraged. But never like this. Never the way a man touched a woman he desired. A woman he loved. Thunder shook the ground and her knees trembled, as well. Rain beat down, shutting out the world, and her heart beat the same rapid tattoo as the raindrops. "This is incredible," she whispered. "I never..."

"Neither have I," Matt said and lowered his mouth to hers.

Their second kiss was nothing like the first. On their wedding day Matt had been gentle, undemanding. Now his mouth was hungry, insistent, and his arousal excited her. She opened her mouth to the pressure of his lips and his tongue thrust inside. Lori gasped. She hadn't been kissed in years—and never like this. Never as though she were the most desirable woman on earth, as though he couldn't get enough of her. As though he wanted to take her then and there on the damp straw-covered floor of the barn.

"Matt. No," she whispered desperately, when his mouth lifted from hers long enough to allow her to speak. Two minutes earlier she'd been rehearsing the words she would use to tell him it was time to dissolve their marriage of convenience. Now she could think of nothing but his kiss and the pleasure of his arms around her, and she let her thoughts skim past every boundary to fantasize about what it would be like to be his wife in deed, as well as in name. She lifted her hands to his chest to put some small distance between them. "Please stop. This isn't right."

He lifted his hands to frame her face. "It feels very right to me." His eyes were darkly shadowed by his hat. It was almost impossible to read his expression in the twilight gloom of the big barn. He held himself very still. Lori could feel the quick sharp beat of his heart beneath her palm. "I haven't been kissed like that in a long, long time, but it hasn't been so long that I can't tell when a woman wants me as much as I want her."

"It would only complicate matters."

"Why? We're married."

"That's only a technicality."

"We could make it a reality."

Lori didn't know what to make of that statement.

"No," she said sadly, looking around her, admitting for the first time the alienness of her surroundings. They came from different worlds. Even if she could believe he loved her not because he felt responsible for her but because she would make his life complete, she couldn't delude herself into thinking she could build a life in Willow Creek. She didn't belong here any more than his first wife had. "Our marriage is only a business arrangement. We can't make it real."

"I'd be willing to try if you are."

Those were not the words she wanted to hear. "It wouldn't work," she said once more. "I don't belong here." She lifted her eyes to his. "And I want to go home."

"You'll be much closer to Danny's grandparents in Manhattan."

She took a deep breath and nodded. "I know that. I can deal with it."

"I see." He stepped away, denying her the heat and comforting strength of his arms around her. "Has Dr. Scarpelli told you you're well enough to leave here?"

"Not yet. But I'm going to talk to him tomorrow. I can't . . . I can't stay here any longer, Matt," she finished miserably. She had never dreamed it would be this hard to tell him it was time for them to part.

A muscle jumped along the line of his jaw. His face was set and hard. Or perhaps that was only a trick of light and shadow, perhaps he just looked relieved. "Then I won't put any obstacles in your path. As soon as the doctor gives his okay, we'll start the annulment proceedings. Is that what you want?"

She looked down at her hand, at the plain gold band she'd worn since Valentine's Day. If he cared for her enough to want her to stay with him, surely he would say so. She waited. Matt was silent. "It's what I want. As soon as possible."

"Then I'll leave the arrangements up to you," he said. "It's stopped raining. Do you want me to walk you back to the house?"

"I can get there on my own," she said.

"Then I have work to do." He turned and walked into the shadowy interior of the barn. Lori watched him go and felt, oddly, as if her heart were about to break all over again.

Chapter Six

"WHAT DO YOU MEAN, I can't leave Ohio for six more weeks?" Lori clasped her hands together in her lap to keep them from shaking. "Why do I have to stay here that much longer?"

"I can't in good conscience release you before that time," Dr. Scarpelli said quietly, leaning forward over his desk to emphasize his point. "You have been a very sick young woman."

"But, Gertrude. Surely you can transfer me to her care."

"I've already discussed your case with my sister-in-law," he said, still very quietly but with an air of authority that was hard to ignore. "She agrees with me that if you return prematurely to New York and the life-style you led before the surgery, you might do permanent damage to your health."

"What do you mean?" Six weeks. She couldn't stay married to Matt that much longer without running the risk of falling in love with him. Her response to his kiss in the barn the day before had been proof enough to her that she was in danger of doing just that.

"I mean that you may not recover completely from the effects of the stroke."

"Please be more precise." Surely the risks to her physical well-being were not that great? Certainly not as great as the emotional risks to her heart if she stayed.

"By that I mean the hesitation in your speech will not go away. You'll tire easily, find it hard to concentrate under stress. You might never get rid of the cane. Distinct disadvantages in your line of work, Mrs. Damschroeder.''

She sat a little straighter in her chair. He was right, damn it. Her work required that she be razor sharp, ready to act at a moment's notice. Anyone who didn't perform at peak efficiency was passed over, left behind or squeezed out. She'd seen it happen often enough to know that no matter how much Finkbeiner, Carter and Strauss valued her work, they would not wait forever for her to hit her stride again.

"I want to go back to New York," Lori said helplessly.

He rested his elbows on the top of the big desk and steepled his fingers before his lips. "Considering the fact that you know the risks and are intelligent enough to do everything in your power to minimize them, I will reevaluate my decision in three weeks' time. That's the best I can do."

"Then it will have to be good enough. Good afternoon, Dr. Scarpelli." Lori rose from her chair. The doctor stood, as well, moving ahead of her to open the door.

"The time will go quickly, Mrs. Damschroeder. I was raised on a farm in Pennsylvania, so I know there's always something going on. Relax. Enjoy yourself. Heal. And you'll be back in New York before you know it."

"I just hope that's soon enough," Lori said more to herself than to him.

"MATT?"

"Over here," he said, walking out from behind the big John Deere combine he was working on for Art Yoder. "Back from the doctor so soon?" His sister had driven Lori into Columbus for her physio session and her visit to Dr. Scarpelli. She hadn't asked him to accompany her and he hadn't offered to act as chauffeur, as he usually did. In fact, they'd exchanged barely half a dozen words since he'd kissed her in the barn.

"Do you have a moment to talk?" she asked, fixing her gaze on a point somewhere close to his left earlobe.

"Yes." He wiped his hands on the shop rag he'd stuck in the back pocket of his jeans. "How did your session go today?"

"Fine. Almost good as new."

"And your talk with Dr. Scarpelli?"

"Not so good. Even though my health is improving, he doesn't think I should go back to New York for at least another six weeks."

"That isn't what you wanted to hear, is it?"

"No. I—I don't know what to do. I can't impose on your family for that much longer."

"You and Danny are no imposition, believe me. Mom and Dad love having you."

She waited, hoping and dreading that he might have something more personal to add. Matt remained silent. "Thank you for saying so," she said at last, politely, formally. "But nevertheless we'll be moving back into the Bengtson house as soon as possible."

"That's your privilege," he said, equally formal.

"And I'll be making an appointment to see a lawyer about the annulment. The sooner we put this all behind—"

"You might want to hold up on that for a while," Matt interrupted her.

"Why?" Lori's pulse rate speeded up. Was he going to ask her to reconsider her plans, ask her to stay? A montage of nights and days and years stretching ahead into the future with Matt at her side flashed across her mind's eye. The future. Their future together, as a family. It was a lovely thought. What she wanted most—

"Danny's grandparents are coming to visit," Matt said, shattering her unwise fantasy of happily-ever-after as quickly as throwing a rock through a stained-glass window.

"But how do you know they're coming? I haven't heard from them for several weeks."

"Apparently that's why they've decided to make the trip," he said dryly. "They called just after you left this morning. They'll be here sometime tomorrow afternoon."

"So soon."

"Mom's invited them to stay here."

"Oh, dear." Lori felt anxiety pushing against her like a dark wave. "Why did she do that?"

"We've had this conversation before, Lori. They're not bad people," Matt said quietly.

She pushed the dark wave away. She was stronger now. She could handle this. "I know that." She looked up, met his gaze. His eyes were neutral, his expression giving nothing of his thoughts away. "You've made that point more than once." She hesitated a moment, searching for the right words. "And in my heart I know you're right. It's just that I find them intimidating."

"And I find that hard to believe," he said with a smile.

She smiled, too. "I have come a long way in eight years. But where Danny's grandparents are concerned, it seems I have a terrible habit of reverting to a twenty-three-year-old single mother."

"They're older now, too. And probably wiser. Give them a chance."

"I don't have much choice, it seems, thanks to your mother." She smiled to show she wasn't angry with Serena. She wouldn't have expected her to do anything other than offer the hospitality of her home, once Lydia and

Charles had announced their intention of visiting Willow Creek.

"Mom's a great believer in family. And grandchildren. Danny is their only grandchild, isn't he?"

"Yes."

"Children are a powerful magnet."

"Do you want children of your own someday, Matt?" She didn't know why she asked that dangerous and personal question. She just wanted to know.

"Yes," he said, looking down at his hands. "I would. Are there plans for more children in your future?"

"I—I don't know. It's very difficult raising a child alone."

Matt took a step forward. "You're not alone anymore."

"No," she said, looking into his eyes, refusing to read a deeper, more intimate meaning into his words. Their gazes collided and held. "Now I have friends," she said very softly, "people who want what's best for me . . . like your parents."

"I wasn't talking about my parents." His voice was rough and low, sliding across her nerve endings like honey.

"I know," Lori said, her words so soft that she didn't stir the echoes in the big old barn. "I should never have asked the question. It wasn't fair to either of us in the position we're in today."

"We could be more than friends," Matt said, not moving any closer but seeming to block out the sky and the sun until there was nothing else for her to see, nowhere else for her to look but into the depths of his eyes.

"I—I don't know." He bent his head as if to kiss her. Lori tried to still the frenzied beating of her heart, tried equally hard to push away the insistent warnings that kept repeating themselves over and over in her brain. Nothing had changed. They were still from two different worlds and there was no way to merge them into one. She must keep that undeniable reality in mind, even if Matt did not. "It won't work, Matt."

"This works," he said, lowering his mouth to hers, cradling the back of her head in his hand so that she couldn't pull away. "You know there's something between us." It took every ounce of willpower she possessed not to kiss him back. She felt hot tears sting the backs of her eyelids and blinked them away. He lifted his head, stared down at her. "What's wrong?"

"You're confusing caring and responsibility with... something else, Matt," she said. "I don't need your pity." Her voice cracked, and she swallowed hard against the tears that blocked her throat. "I won't let you make that mistake."

"I'm not confusing anything, damn it," he said roughly. "Pity's the last damn thing I'd ever feel for you. I'll prove it."

"No." She put her hand on his chest, holding him away. "I won't let you say something you'll regret. Neither of us can afford to confuse love with gratitude."

"Is that all you feel for me? Gratitude?"

"Yes, Matt. I'm sorry." It was a bald-faced lie but one she felt compelled to tell. Because she did need, and God help her, want, Matthew Damschroeder with all her heart and soul.

"I don't believe you don't want to make this work as much as I do," he said, dropping his hand from the back of her head. Cool air replaced the warmth of his fingers on her skin. She shivered and hoped he didn't notice.

"I never lie," she said, forcing the words past the lump in her throat. She made herself keep looking at him, although the momentary glimpse of despair she imagined she saw in his eyes clawed at her soul. "Never."

Chapter Seven

MAY WAS even more beautiful in the country than April had been. It was a magical time. Plants and flowers seemed to pop up out of the ground, grow and bloom in a matter of hours. Kittens, born in the last cold days of winter, were brought down out of the hayloft by their proud mother and allowed to romp in the sweet green grass. A box full of fluffy yellow chicks arrived by express mail from a hatchery in Arkansas, and Danny was given responsibility for their care and feeding.

Lori had never seen her son quite so taken with anything before. He watched over his little brood of chicks as though he were a mother hen himself. He changed their water, measured out their feed, added vitamin drops to their rations with the meticulous care of a scientist incorporating the final ingredient of his greatest experiment. After school he would shoo them out into the yard, a few at a time, when the dogs and cats were safely shut away, and let them peck at bugs in the grass. He acted as if he'd been born and raised on the farm. He loved every minute of it. And strangest of all was that his most enthusiastic helpers in these endeavors were Charles and Lydia.

Danny's grandparents had been staying with the Damschroeders for almost a week. And all in all, things were going very well. At first Lori had wanted to move back to the Bengtson house immediately, before they arrived, but Serena had insisted she and Danny remain under her roof. It was time, she said, for Lori to stop running away from what couldn't be changed. And Danny, she insisted, deserved to have this time with his grandparents.

"I can't think of anything more terrible than not being allowed to see my grandchildren," Serena said, not for the first time, as she kneaded bread. "It would break my heart not to be part of their lives."

"Matt said that's how you'd feel."

"Matt's a smart boy," his mother said approvingly. "Or should I say, man."

"It's just that Danny's father turned out to be such a wretched human being." Lori laughed a little self-consciously. "At least in my humble opinion. You don't think that was Charles and Lydia's fault?"

Serena brushed aside her objection with a wave of her hand. "That doesn't mean a thing. It takes a whole new set of skills to be a grandparent." She was looking out the kitchen window as she so often did while she worked. "Believe me, I know. I have to stop and switch gears all the time when I'm dealing with the little ones and when I'm dealing with Dede and her brothers and sisters. Besides, you're never too old to learn."

"Is that old saying really true?"

"Yes."

"They tried to take Danny away from me, you know, when he was just born. I've never been so frightened." Serena made a sympathetic clicking sound with her teeth. "When I wouldn't give him up without a fight they offered me money."

"They must have been very frightened, as well."

"How can you say that?"

"You offered Matt money to marry you, I understand." Serena didn't turn away from her chore but her voice held no censure, only understanding.

"Yes. I—I was desperate."

"Exactly. I imagine Charles and Lydia were desperate, too. You can't imagine how responsible you feel for your grandchildren, Lori. You've raised the person that's raising them. Every mistake you made you can see magnified a thousand times in your own children's parenting."

"And everything you've done right, I imagine, too," Lori said softly. Matt had told her that, as well. You couldn't be responsible for everything your children did after they were grown. But you could still *feel* that responsibility. And react accordingly.

"Yes." She could hear the smile in Serena's voice. "Everything you've done right, too. Human beings aren't always at their best when they're thinking with their hearts and not their heads. A lot of the time we do all the wrong things for all the right reasons." She beckoned Lori to the counter. "Look at Lydia. She's taken to gardening like she was born to it." They watched as Danny's grandmother worked among the newly emerged plants in Serena's garden. Charles was nowhere to be seen, and Lori had the sneaking suspicion he was fishing with Ethan in the river at the edge of the woods. "Just imagine. Lydia's never had a garden," Serena had said wonderingly. "I can't imagine living all boxed up in the city that way."

"Charles and Lydia have a lovely home. A condominium on a golf course. The grounds are beautifully landscaped." It was she and Danny who lived all boxed up in a high-rise apartment building.

"It's not the same thing," Serena said, still kneading the bread dough.

"You're right. It's not the same thing at all." The closest she got to a garden in the city were the potted plants at the corner grocery store.

"Why don't you go out and help Lydia with the weeding," Serena suggested, her round, placid face totally devoid of guile.

"I don't know," Lori said reluctantly.

"There'll never be a better time to get to know her. Working in the dirt is a great leveler. Give her a chance. For Danny's sake, if not your own."

"WOULD YOU LIKE some help?" Lori asked, lowering herself carefully to her knees. She still wasn't comfortable enough around Lydia Michaelson to show any sign of weakness. It wouldn't do to lose her balance and topple over into the carrot tops because she was too proud to use her cane in the soft, uneven ground.

"Would you like to help me stake up these tomato plants? Serena says it's going to storm and she doesn't want the wind and rain to break them." Lydia was wearing a baggy white cotton shirt and dark tailored slacks that still managed to look elegant and expensive, even streaked with black topsoil. At one time Lori might have worn a similar outfit herself. Today she had on jeans and a T-shirt with her hair pulled up on top of her head in a loose knot.

"That's a good idea." Lori sat back on her heels and looked up at the hard blue sky. "It is going to storm. I can feel it in the air."

"You can? I've never been weather sensitive, but it's a talent you must pick up fairly quickly, living close to the land this way. Working in the garden, walking in the woods and along the riverbank. Eating Serena's marvelous cooking, sitting in a rocking chair on the porch to watch the sun rise and set. I don't think I've ever enjoyed a vacation more." She pushed a strand of hair off her forehead with the back of her hand, leaving a smudge of black earth behind. "But you didn't come out here to help me stake tomatoes or talk about the weather, did you?"

"No," Lori said, taking a deep breath. "I came to talk to you about Danny."

"He's a wonderful little boy, Lori. Both Charles and I are proud of the way you're raising him." She was looking into Lori's eyes, her hands resting lightly around the roots of a small green tomato plant.

"Thank you." Lori wasn't certain what to say next, but Lydia went right on talking, as though she had thought about what she was going to say for a long time before that afternoon.

"I'm sorry for all the animosity and misunderstanding there's been between us in the past. I wish we could put back the clock and start over. I guess we knew that Kevin was behaving badly but he is our son. We're as much to blame as he is."

"You can't be responsible for the actions of a grown man, Lydia."

"That's what Charles has tried to tell me, but I don't think there's a mother anywhere in the world that can completely divorce herself from her children's actions, even when they're grown. I'm sorry to say that at first I thought that if we had Danny with us, I could make amends for my mistakes with his father. Later—" she looked down at the small plant in front of her; Lori noticed her hands were trembling slightly "—I just wanted some way to keep him close. Please forgive me, Lori. I never knowingly meant to cause you pain."

"There's nothing to forgive," Lori said and meant it. She could dare to look into the future now and forgive and forget the past. "I never looked beyond my own needs, as far as Danny was concerned. I've denied him a chance to learn to know and love the only family he has in the world. I'm as guilty of causing pain as you are."

"I hope someday that we might become friends." Lydia was wearing dark glasses that hid her eyes, but there was a catch in her voice that spoke all too clearly of the depth of her emotion.

"I hope so, too."

Lydia bowed her head over the little tomato plants for a long moment, but when she lifted her eyes her emotions were under control. "How ironic that we should come to this understanding now that you're going to be living six hundred miles away, when all this time we lived so close to each other and almost never got to see Danny at all."

"Danny and I won't be staying in Ohio, Lydia. We'll be returning to New York as soon as Dr. Scarpelli gives his okay." Lori struggled to find the right words. She had no idea it would be so difficult to explain her situation to Lydia. "Matt and I have a marriage in name only. We'll be starting annulment proceedings very soon."

"A marriage of convenience? You married Matt Damschroeder to keep Danny away from us?" Stunned, Lydia stopped with her hands in midair, a tomato stake clutched like a weapon in the left and a ball of white string in the right.

"Yes. I was desperate to secure his future and I knew Matt and the whole wonderful Damschroeder family would be the best thing for Danny, if I didn't pull through. At the time it seemed the only thing to do."

"But, Matt—" Lydia thought better of what she was going to say next. "I'm sorry you felt you had to go to such lengths to keep Danny safe from us."

"So am I," Lori said. "More than you know."

THE STORM Lori had predicted came late that afternoon, far stronger and more menacing than anything this spring. The radio and television both broadcast severe weather warnings, and Ethan and Matthew took up watch on the back porch, searching the sky for funnel clouds. Everyone else remained in the kitchen, ready at a moment's notice to head for the cellar.

Outside, trees twisted in the wind and branches were snapped and hurled across the yard and against the house, as though by an angry demon child in a fit of pique. Charles stood by the open back door and watched the rain come pelting down. Serena went about her work, staying prudently away from the windows. Lydia and Danny were working a jigsaw puzzle at the kitchen table, but Lydia jumped with each and every thunderclap.

"Grandma," Danny laughed. "Don't be such a baby. It's only a storm."

"It's just about the worst storm I've ever been in," Lydia told him. "We don't have storms like this on Long Island. At least not thunderstorms," she corrected herself.

"Maybe there'll be a tornado. I'd like to see one," Danny said, his voice an equal mixture of wishing-for and hoping-against. "I bet it would be just like in *The Wizard of Oz*."

"If that happened, your chicks would probably lose some feathers," Lori warned him.

Danny frowned while he considered this possibility. "It would still be great to see. I could tell the kids at school back in New York. None of them have ever been to the country."

"I think it would be a good idea to head down into the cellar," Ethan said, coming into the kitchen.

"Oh, Ethan." Serena turned pale. "It isn't a tornado, is it? Dede's still at the high school. She was supposed to have a softball game tonight."

"It's not a funnel cloud, Mother," he said. "But it looks like a bad squall line's coming."

"Let's go, everyone," Matt ordered, coming into the kitchen just seconds after his father spoke, but it was already too late. The room turned dark as night as the storm hit with a roar like a freight train. Lori saw the young maple in the side yard bend over almost double. Hailstones rattled against the window and the slate roof. Matt was struggling to shut the back door when a second even more violent gust of wind roared through the yard. With a banshee shriek the roof lifted off the main barn and fell back again with a crash that shook the stone foundation beneath their feet.

Serena gasped and Ethan cursed under his breath. The others remained rooted to their chairs, unnerved by what they'd seen. Before anyone else could move, Matt was out the door. "The electricity's got to be shut off!" he shouted over his shoulder as he ran. "Everyone stay put."

"Oh, dear Lord," Serena moaned, heading for the door.

Ethan held her back. "Don't go out there, Mother. It's not safe."

"But the barn. The hay. What if there's a fire." They'd made the first cutting of the sweet-smelling hay just days before.

"Matt's taking care of that. We'll call the fire department just to be on the safe side."

Serena nodded her agreement. "Yes, we'd better do that just in case. What about the machinery?"

"It's all replaceable. Thank God, no one was hurt."

As quickly as it had come, the squall line moved off to the east, taking the thunder and lightning and stinging hailstones along with it. They all crowded onto the back porch, staring at the ruined barn. The rain continued, heavy and soaking, but Matt didn't return to the house.

"I didn't really mean I wanted to have a tornado come," Danny sniffed, guilt written large on his small, sun-tanned face.

"Of course you didn't, sweetie. It was just a coincidence, that's all. And Ethan said it wasn't a tornado, not really. It wasn't your fault."

"But I did wish it and now the barn's ruined. And where's Matt?"

Lori was asking herself the same question. She thought of all the things she wanted and needed to say to Matt and wondered now if she would ever get the chance. Her arms tightened involuntarily around her son's slender shoulders. She mustn't think like that. "He stayed in the barn to keep out of the rain. Don't worry. He's all right. He knows what he's doing."

"But what if the wind starts up again and the rest of the barn falls on top of him?"

"That won't happen, son," Charles said, patting Danny on top of his head. "Matt's too smart to stay in there if it's dangerous. What do you say—as soon as the rain lets up, we head outside and check on your chicks?"

Danny nodded, looking relieved. "Okay, Grandpa, if you say Matt's okay, I believe you."

"Thank you, Charles," Lori said, grateful that the older man was taking charge of keeping Danny occupied and safely away from the dangerous debris-strewn area around the barn.

"Listen, there's the siren on the fire truck," Serena said. "Thank heaven they're here." She followed her husband into the yard, Lori and the others close on her heels.

The big red fire engine was just turning into the driveway at the foot of the hill. Following it was the sheriff's cruiser and several cars and pickups driven by members

of the volunteer fire department, Lori guessed. Right behind them were Matt's brothers, and off in the distance,
rumbling down the road came the nearest Damschroeder
neighbor, Art Yoder, on the bulldozer he used to dig farm
ponds in the area.

"We radioed the electric company to shut off power till
we get the mess cleaned up," the mayor said, jumping
down out of the cab of the big truck. Lori hardly recognized the small middle-aged woman who had married her
in February wearing a lacy-collared, flowered-print dress,
now wearing the heavy fluorescent yellow turnout coat
and high black boots. But she wasn't at all surprised that
the emblem on Mayor Burgess's helmet proclaimed her
Chief of the Willow Creek Volunteer Fire Department. In
Willow Creek all the residents pulled their weight.

The sound of one more large engine was added to the
already considerable noise in the barnyard, and moments
later Matt drove the big self-propelled combine out of the
ruins of the barn. The cab was partially collapsed and
there appeared to be quite a bit of damage to other parts
of the machine that were too technical for Lori to name,
but it was moving under its own power.

Matt steered it to the side of the yard and jumped down
out of the cab. Lori's knees were suddenly very weak. She
hadn't realized how frightened she'd been for his safety
until just that moment. When she looked up at the barn
roof, the collapsed beams, the scattered and broken slates,
the dangling power lines, her heart jumped into her
throat. What if something had happened to him in there
and she'd never had the chance to say...she loved him?
The realization burst over her with all the fierceness of the
just-past thunderstorm. She loved him. And heaven help
her, there was nothing in the world she could do about it.

"Sorry, Dad," Matt said, coming over to his father who was standing only a few feet away from Lori. "Both the tractors are buried under the roof fall. Most of the rest of the stuff looks okay but it's going to take some heavy equipment to get everything out."

"We'll manage, son," Ethan said, clasping Matt's shoulder. "We've got insurance and we've been through worse than this. I'm just glad to see you out of there, safe and sound. Don't go back inside until the roof's shored up."

"It's not as bad as it looks. We had to get the combine out of the way before they could move anything else. And the main supports look sound enough."

Ethan nodded. "They ought to be. My great-granddad built this barn out of native lumber. Those beams are eighteen inches thick, solid walnut. That barn was built to last a dozen lifetimes."

"It will, Dad, once we get a new roof on it."

"Matt, are you all right?" Serena asked, hurrying across the yard. "I was so worried when you went into the barn. All I could think of was that it would collapse on top of you."

"Not that barn, Mom," Matt said, looking at his father. "It was built to last a dozen lifetimes."

"Well I've aged half that much this afternoon," Serena declared.

"Lori," Matt said, as though seeing her for the first time. "Are you all right?" He moved toward her.

"I'm fine," she said, hiding the true extent of her concern behind a smile. She looked at the damaged barn, the sky, anywhere but at him, afraid that he could read her emotions in her eyes. "What a storm!"

"It was a humdinger," he agreed. "Lori—"

"Yes?" Close by, someone used a CB radio to call for a front-end loader and heavy jacks to shore up the roof beams. Several more pickups, filled with friends and neighbors, drove into the yard.

"I . . . nothing." There were too many people and too much was going on around them. Matt just shook his head.

"Goodness," Serena interrupted, tears of relief and gratitude shining in her eyes. "How will I ever feed all these people with the electricity turned off?"

"You'll manage, Mother," Ethan said, giving her a hug. "Seems like you won't have to do it on your own, either. Look." He lifted his hand in greeting to several members of their church whom Lori had met over the winter. The women were carrying picnic hampers and large containers of ice water and what looked like lemonade.

"Matt. Ethan. We need you over here," Art Yoder called. "Where do you want us to dump all this stuff?"

"Damn, I didn't think of that. Pile it around the side of the barn," Ethan called back. "We'll plan what to do with the mess when it's all cleaned up."

"Make a hell of a bonfire come Halloween," Art hollered, as he climbed back onto the bulldozer. "Hell of a bonfire."

"Don't overdo," Matt told Lori, already moving away. Was that what he'd meant to say to her all along? Or had there been something more? The sudden clarity of her own feelings toward him now colored every word he said. She didn't know if the frown in his gray eyes meant he was worried about her, or that his concern was only habit, an outgrowth of weeks of taking care of her and Danny. Or was his real concern now for the barn and the repairs ahead? *The barn,* she told herself firmly, ignoring the pain the brutally honest assessment caused to her still-healing heart, *only the barn.*

"I'll be careful," Lori promised, barely aware of the words she spoke, struggling to keep her new love hidden away where Matt could never guess it existed. "I won't overdo."

But of course she lied.

Chapter Eight

IT WAS AFTER MIDNIGHT before the last of the Damschroeders' friends and neighbors pulled out of the driveway and the household settled down to sleep. All through the long spring afternoon and evening they'd worked to clear the wreckage of the barn roof, cover and secure the valuable bales of timothy hay in the damaged portion of the loft, free the two big John Deere tractors from the tons of slate and wood under which they'd been buried.

Lori had worked side by side with Lydia and the other women, keeping the workers in cold drinks and hot food. Serena's cooking stove was gas, and someone thought to light the barbecue grill in the backyard. They set up an assembly line of food and drink. And everyone breathed a sigh of relief when power was restored an hour before darkness fell because no one wanted to wash the mountains of dirty plates and silverware by hand when Serena had a perfectly good dishwasher sitting idle.

They were all exhausted by the time they'd called a halt to the cleanup. Everyone else had bathed and gone straight to bed. Everyone but Lori. She'd come back downstairs long after the others were asleep for a last soothing cup of peppermint tea, hoping it would ease the nagging ache in her leg and banish the wearying fatigue from her mind. She was simply too tired to sleep.

The seldom-used front door opened and closed. Lori sat up a little straighter, pulling her light cotton robe more closely about her. She wasn't worried or frightened by the late-night intruder into the sleeping house, although his being there was definitely cause for unease. For some reason or another Matt, too, was awake and must have seen the kitchen light still shining. She turned slightly in her chair, stretching the weary muscles of her face into what she hoped would pass for a smile.

He didn't smile back. "What are you doing awake at this hour?" he asked before she could inquire the same thing of him. His hair was damp, as though he'd just come from the shower, and Lori's fingers itched to touch where it curled slightly just above his collar. His shirt was loosely buttoned, exposing a triangle of bronzed chest covered with a tangle of brown hair. She longed to touch him there with her lips, as well as her hands. He was close enough that she could smell the spicy tang of his aftershave and feel the heat of his skin, warming her like fire through the thin cotton of her nightgown and robe.

"Just having a cup of tea." She indicated the half-empty cup beside her, pleased her voice didn't betray the sensual direction her thoughts had taken. "The water's still hot. Do you want some?"

"No." His tone was husky, rough around the edges, from fatigue or anger, or some other emotion Lori didn't know about. "I saw the light from my kitchen window and wondered who was still up and around."

"Everyone else is sound asleep," Lori admitted.

"Why aren't you sound asleep?" he asked, making no move to join her at the big oak table.

"Too tired, I guess," she made the mistake of saying.

Matt's gray eyes turned as dark as the thunderheads that had stacked up over Willow Creek that afternoon. "I told you not to overtire yourself."

"I didn't," she shot back, but she didn't rise from her seat to confront him, knowing full well her rubbery legs would give her away. "Your mother and father, even

Lydia and Charles, worked much harder than I did today, and they're all very nearly twice my age."

"None of them were at death's door three months ago," he growled, coming closer, towering over her so that Lori had to rise to her feet to keep him from dominating her completely.

"That was three months ago," she countered. "I'm perfectly fine now." But the hand she rested on the table gave the lie to her words. She swayed a little on her feet, hating her healing body for betraying her at such a critical moment.

"The hell you are," he said and pulled her into his arms. "If I let go of you now, you'd crumple in a heap at my feet."

"I would not," she asserted but was horrified to hear her words leave her throat in barely more than a whisper.

The touch of his hard, strong hands on her skin had the same effect as a bolt of lightning. She felt half paralyzed and confused, disoriented, floating free in time and space. If she'd ever thought she could deny what she'd discovered about herself that afternoon, she knew now that it was a hopeless dream. She loved him. Loved him as she'd never loved before, or would ever love again. She couldn't take her eyes from his, but she could read nothing of what he was thinking, of what he felt, in their rain-darkened depths.

He lowered his head to kiss her and Lori felt as if she had been swept up along with Dorothy in the famous tornado that deposited them both somewhere over the rainbow. She curled her hands around his neck, letting her fingers slide through the silky softness of the hair at the nape of his neck, as she'd so often longed to do. She kissed him back, letting her heart rule her head, heedless for one glorious moment of what was right or wrong, what was expedient—what might break her heart.

Matt deepened the kiss, and reluctantly, sadly, Lori came back to earth. "Matt, please don't." She sucked in her breath, hating herself for letting her desire, her need for him, show so clearly.

"Why not?" he asked musingly. "We're married."

"Don't say that again." She stiffened in his arms, determined to be free of his mesmerizing touch. "I should never have let anyone think our marriage was real. It was wrong, but it was just so much easier than trying to explain the truth. I'm sorry. I'm sorry," she repeated, fighting back tears of anguish and longing and fatigue.

"I'm not," he said. He moved his body slightly away from hers, not letting her go, but no longer dominating the small space between them.

"Please don't be kind," Lori said fiercely. "I know how awkward it must be for you. All your friends... Your parents' friends... The women today were asking questions. Friendly questions, but still..." Her voice trailed off. She'd been living in her own little dream world the past few months as she recovered in body and spirit. Her friends and acquaintances were far away—a world away—in New York. She had no one to answer to but herself. She hadn't considered Matt's position carefully enough. How hard it must have been for him to fend off the questions and interested speculation of friends and neighbors. How his convictions, his principles would weigh on him to make this marriage right.

"The hell with the neighbors," Matt said, drawing her close again.

"But your reputation..."

He laughed a little reluctantly, and shook his head. "My reputation? If we're going to turn Victorian all of a sudden, it's your reputation we ought to be concerned with.''

''No one I care about knows we're married. Except Lydia and Charles,'' she added after a moment. ''And I told Lydia the truth this morning. There's no more pressure there.''

''Pressure? What pressure?''

She put her hand on his chest, meeting his stormy gray gaze with steady eyes. ''Our marriage is just pretend, Matt, and it's just between us. Don't let what other people believe make you think you need to make it real,'' she said softly.

''Do you mean to say you'd go to bed with me if we weren't married? But you won't sleep with me because we are?'' There was a hint of amusement in his voice. But his eyes and his expression were as serious as before.

That wasn't the case at all, but if believing that kept him from learning the real truth, she was willing to go along with the deception. ''Yes. I would.''

''Those are your terms?''

''Yes.'' He was silent for a long moment as though waiting for her to say something else. She didn't. There was nothing more to say but I love you. And the words were impossible to speak.

''You're not denying there's something between us?''

''No,'' she said, sadly. ''I can't deny that.''

''Neither can I,'' he said, and if she'd been thinking more clearly she might have heard the sadness in his voice that echoed her own. ''Stop being Lori Fenton, financial wizard, and just be Lori, my wife, and let me love you as you should be loved.''

''But what about tomorrow?'' she asked as his lips came down on hers. He spoke of making love but he did not say he loved her. She ought to have used that critical, heartbreaking omission as a weapon to defend herself from future pain, but it was too late. She could do nothing to save herself.

"Let tomorrow take care of itself."

Could she do as he asked, just this once, not consider the consequences of what she was about to do, let tomorrow take care of itself and enjoy this one precious night with Matt?

"Yes," she said, torn between desire and regret. "Let tomorrow take care of itself."

Without another word Matt scooped her into his arms and carried her into the living room that no one ever used. He placed her on the wide overstuffed sofa and followed her down into its cushioning depths.

"I've always fantasized about making love to a woman on this couch," he said with a chuckle that banished a few more of her doubts and fears. This was Matt, the man who had befriended her son, watched over her with care and tenderness—her husband—her heart whispered to her brain. She had nothing to fear from him, and much to enjoy.

"Just any woman?" she couldn't help asking.

"When I was a teenager it was just about any woman. Lately I've become a lot more selective. Lately it's just been you." He opened her thin robe and undid the dozen tiny buttons down the front of her nightgown with trembling hands. For a moment as the cool night air touched her breasts, Lori's sanity returned.

"I'm not a dream, Matt. I'm Lori. I'm real." She moved restlessly beneath him, but even before she could open her mouth to tell him one more time that this should never be, he lowered his mouth to her breast and Lori, the thinking, logical woman that she thought herself to be, ceased to exist. A new Lori emerged in her place. A woman, eager and desirous. A wanton creature who wanted nothing more than to possess and be possessed by the man beside her.

"I'm not so sure you're not a dream," he murmured against her skin. "And if you are, then I hope to God I never wake up."

"We'll have to wake up," Lori said, wishing for a moment herself that they never would. "We'll have to wake up all too soon."

"Hush, Lori. You talk too much," Matt growled and lifted his mouth from her breast to her lips.

From that moment on she had no breath and no inclination for speech. The only sounds she could form were soft moans of encouragement and satisfaction. The knowledge that Matt's parents and sister, her own son and his grandparents slept just above their heads ceased to matter—nothing mattered except the touch and taste and feel of Matt in her arms.

MATT WATCHED LORI SLEEP. The moon rode low in the sky, dawn already a pale gray curtain in the east. It would never do for his parents to find them wrapped in each other's arms on the living-room couch. It was time for him to leave, let her come to terms with what had happened between them in the night. Although, God knew, he didn't want to go.

He slid off the couch and scooped up his clothes. What they needed was time alone together to talk about themselves, to explore the physical passion they'd discovered last night, to discuss the future, their future, together. The trouble was there was going to be precious little time or privacy for anybody in this house over the next couple of days, and he was too much of a coward to wake her now and ask her if she loved him. Because if she said no, she didn't love him, that she was grateful for his care and kindness but only thought of him as a friend and a lover, that she wanted to go back to New York and the life she'd led before, it would surely break his heart into a million pieces.

And unlike the medical miracle that had mended Lori's broken heart, there was nothing on earth, no doctor, no medicine, no operation, that could ever make his whole again.

Chapter Nine

"LORI!"

"I'm here, Matt," she said, amazed at how steady her voice sounded. She turned away from the cupboard where she was putting away the last of the supper dishes. For almost the first time that day, the kitchen was empty of Damschroeder friends and neighbors. Only Serena was there to act as buffer between her and Matt. She'd been able to avoid him all day with relative ease, as she made her hard choices and her plans to leave Willow Creek, because there had barely been a moment when he was not completely absorbed in overseeing the repairs to the barn roof. It seemed that was no longer the case.

"What's this I hear from Lydia that you and Danny are going back to New York with them tomorrow morning?" Lori's heart sank. She should have known Lydia and Charles would let the information slip. She could hardly blame them. Her actions were as puzzling to them as they would be to everyone else once her plan became public knowledge. "Did you know anything about this, Mom?" he growled, crossing the big room in three quick strides. The old-fashioned wooden screen door slammed shut behind him, punctuating his words with a loud bang.

"Your mother doesn't know anything about it," Lori said. It was true. She hadn't found the courage to say anything to Serena as yet. Telling her and Ethan she was leaving early the next morning would be almost as difficult as telling Matt.

"I know." Serena set the stack of dishes she had just taken from the dishwasher down on the table with a thump. "Lydia told me. She's very upset. She said you didn't explain anything to her or Charles. Only that you must return to New York immediately. I don't understand your hurry. I—I've been looking for an opportunity to talk to you ever since, Lori. Maybe now is as good a time as any?" She glanced uncertainly at her son.

"It is not a good time," he said darkly. "Go on outside, Mom. Please. I want to talk to my wife alone."

"Serena, don't go," Lori begged. It was cowardly and she knew it but she didn't want to be alone with Matt. She could say what had to be said in front of his mother. But she wasn't certain she could bring off her carefully rehearsed little speech if they were alone.

Serena looked from one to the other of them, studying them both. The worried frown Lori realized the older woman had been wearing for most of the afternoon was no longer so pronounced. She gave Lori a slight, apologetic smile. "I think I hear Ethan calling me," she said, making up her mind. "You two settle this between you."

"Why the hell are you sneaking off like this?" Matt demanded almost before his mother had left the room.

"I'm not sneaking off," Lori insisted. "If anyone did anything sneaky it was you. This morning. Leaving before I was even awake." She had felt so lost and unhappy waking to find herself alone that she had known from that very moment that she must leave Willow Creek Farm or be lost forever to her need to be near her husband on whatever terms he wanted her.

"What was I supposed to do with half the town due here in less than an hour—let Danny or my parents find us there together and try to explain to everyone at once?"

"I don't know. No. But you should have said something. Anything."

"Is that why you're leaving? Because I didn't stay? Because I thought we had time to work this out between us?"

"No," she lied. "I'm going back to New York. Back to my career and my life," she said, before the tears that tightened her throat made speech impossible. "Last night—"

"What about last night?" Matt asked, advancing on her, trapping her against the sink.

"Last night should never have happened."

"It's too late for that argument. Last night did happen." He was so close now that she could feel the heat of his body and smell the sawdust that sprinkled his shirt and the golden brown hair on his arms. Lori put her hands on the edge of the sink behind her. Her legs threatened to give way beneath her, not from physical weakness but from the force of her emotions.

"What happened last night doesn't change anything," she said, already drained from the effort to keep her voice even and as normal sounding as possible. She loved this man. Loved him more than life itself, and walking away from him and never looking back was going to be the hardest thing she'd ever done.

"The hell it doesn't." He was looming over her now, and for the first time she saw the formidable Damschroeder temper in full blaze. He framed her face with his hands. His touch was gentle but unyielding, completely at odds with the fury in his gray eyes. "It makes you my wife." Suddenly Lori realized the emotion underlying his harshly spoken words was not fury but fear. Her heart began to pound in her chest. Fear of losing her? She closed her eyes briefly, afraid he could read her emotions as easily as she had just read his.

"I never meant to stay this long. I never meant for us to be married this long. Everything I have, everything I ever wanted is in New York," she whispered, holding herself rigid, lest she give in to the temptation to turn her cheek to his palm and nuzzle like a kitten.

"Are you asking me to leave Willow Creek Farm and come to the city with you?" he asked.

She shook her head. "I know you wouldn't come," she said simply. She wouldn't ask it of him. She loved him too much to try to mold him to a way of life he would hate. "You know yourself too well. You know who you are and where you belong."

He dropped his hands from her face but didn't move away. He was so close that if she took a deep breath her breasts would brush his chest. Lori held herself very still. "Everything I've ever wanted in life is right here." The pain that sliced through Lori's heart was a thousand times sharper than the surgeon's knife. "Everything," he said fiercely, "except you."

"Are you saying you'd leave your home and family, your business, to come to New York with me?"

His gaze was steady, all his heart and soul laid bare for her to see. "With nothing but the clothes on my back, if that's what it takes to convince you I mean what I say."

"What are you saying, Matt?"

"I love you for your courage and determination and the way your eyes light up when you're with Danny and the funny way your nose wrinkles when you laugh. I love you more than I ever thought it was possible to love another human being. I should have come right out and said it weeks ago. I want us to be together. I'll go with you to New York. I'll follow you to the moon, if that's what it takes to prove I love you."

"All the way to the moon." She closed her eyes so that he couldn't see her tears.

"I'm willing to leave the place I love most on earth to be with you and Danny." He gave her a little shake so that she had to open her eyes and look at him. "I love you, damn it. After my divorce I hurt so bad inside I swore I'd never say those words to a woman again. For ten years I've kept that vow. All that time I've been afraid to put my heart and soul on the line. Until today. When Charles told me he was making arrangements for you and Danny to fly back to New York with them, I felt as if my guts had been kicked out. All these months I kept telling myself there was plenty of time to make you love me. That I'd be able to find the right words, the right arguments to get you to stay. Then, all of a sudden, there wasn't any time left. I realized how close I was to losing you forever. I love you, Lori Fenton Damschroeder. Don't break my heart again," he said, pulling her tight against him. "I couldn't stand it. Tell me you love me, too."

"I love you," she said, sliding her arms around his waist, resting her head against the rock hardness of his chest. "I've loved you for weeks and weeks. I just couldn't say so."

"How can anyone so bright and successful be so stupid," he said, giving her a kiss on the nose that took the sting from his words.

"A very confused and uncertain woman," Lori admitted, leaning back in his arms as she touched his lips with the tips of her fingers. "I was just as frightened as you were to risk my heart again. And I meant what I said when I told you we came from different worlds. We do. That hasn't changed." But everything else had. How long ago had she made up her mind that their two worlds could blend, could be made one? "Oh, Matt, what if I don't fit into life at Willow Creek?"

"Fit in at Willow Creek?"

"That's what I said. I'm making you a counter offer."

"Which is?" he asked, his eyes ablaze with love and hope.

"I don't want to go back to New York," she said. "I'll cherish forever the fact that you were willing to leave here for my sake, but the truth is, this is where I want to belong, just as much as you do."

"What about your career?"

"My career." She couldn't conceal the pang of regret that she was afraid he could hear in her voice and read on her face.

"Will you miss the rat race that much?" he asked, stroking her hair.

"I'll miss it," she said, knowing she had to be honest with him. "But not enough to go back."

"I think that within six months you'll be making money hand over fist at something."

"I have to confess I have considered the idea of starting a long-distance financial consultation service," she said, no longer afraid to share her dreams. "I did most of my work on the telephone, anyway. And I have a friend who left Carter, Finkbeiner and Strauss last year. She started her own company. I could give her a call."

"How much do long-distance financial consultants make?" Matt asked with a smile from which all the darkness had fled.

Lori smiled, too. "A lot," she said with satisfaction.

"Great." He bent his head to nuzzle her neck, and Lori's breath caught in her throat. "Because farm mechanics sure don't."

"I'll have to do some traveling," she said, holding him off with a hand against his chest. "It'll take some time to get myself established."

"Mmm." He brushed her lips with his. "We'll work it out. You can do anything you want as long as you promise you'll always come back to me. That you'll bear my children, share my dreams and my sorrows and grow old alongside me."

"Babies? Yes. Oh, yes. As soon as Dr. Scarpelli gives his okay."

"Maybe on our anniversary? Valentine's Day seems a great time to start a baby."

"Yes, it does. It would be perfect." Six months ago she would never have dared to dream of celebrating her anniversary with Matt, never dreamed of being a mother again. She had come to Willow Creek farm reluctantly, in fear of death and the future, intending to stay only as long as necessary. Instead of the temporary marriage of convenience she had planned, she had been granted something much more precious, a family for her and her son, a man she could respect and honor, happiness and love to last a lifetime—all because once upon a time a woman named Lori Fenton had a broken heart.

"What about all the rest?" Matt's lips hovered over hers. His arms held her close, surrounded by his strength, secure in his love.

"We'll have it all," Lori vowed. "Love and laughter. Friends and family. Happiness to last a dozen lifetimes. All of it here, at Willow Creek."

MY COMIC VALENTINE

Muriel Jensen

A Note from Muriel Jensen

Love is in the air. Because publishing demands five months' lead time from completion of a book to its appearance on the shelf, I am surrounded by pumpkins and Indian corn as I write this. But the season doesn't matter.

I believe love is always bright red and heart-shaped within us, though we only honor it specially in the middle of February. I believe when we rid ourselves of fear and suspicion, we're all brimming with love that's eager to spill over, to infect the person next to us, to cause an epidemic.

Every romance reader is a champion of love, and I'd like to invite you to join my army this Valentine's Day. Give smiles, throw hugs, blow kisses, until they're thicker in the air than smog, until the National Weather Service is forced to declare a *love alert!*

Prologue

SHE HAD TO HURRY. In the distance she could see a ribbon of light on the horizon between the blackness of the ocean and the deep blue of the sky. Dawn would soon bathe the sleepy town of Sailor's Beach, and in a matter of minutes, the sprawling home on the high dune where she crouched in hiding would be exposed.

She ducked down behind the classic Jaguar sedan's rear fender, trying to calm herself with the knowledge that her victim had already made this easier for her by having a standard gas-tank cap without a lock. The sound of gasoline drizzling through the syphoning tube from his tank into her gas can calmed her further. It was working. She was going to pull it off—her first caper.

This couldn't really be called a serious caper, she reflected, reevaluating her plan as the tube did its slow work; that implied a theft. In this case—and in those that would follow—her plan was not to steal but to make a point.

Her New Year's resolution had been to take action against men who were getting away with committing the kind of injustices against women that never got to court. The sort of wrong that she'd recently experienced and that had changed her outlook on life, and the course of her future.

Her own shock and pain had made her suddenly more aware of the injustices endured by many of the women in her circle of friends. She knew firsthand of men who were unfaithful to their wives, men who cheated the women they worked with in a dozen insidious ways, tradesmen and professionals who victimized women who sought their services by overcharging or doing shoddy work, and men who got away with countless subtle insults to women's self-esteem day after day. The woods were thick with them, and this wasn't even L.A. or New York. This was rustic Baldwin County on the Oregon coast.

It had taken her a month to research her first case. She'd selected Sean Megrath because of his shameless use of his daily comic strip as a vehicle for illustrating his demeaning, sexist attitude toward women. His widely-syndicated "Brick Banyon, Secret Agent," was essentially the portrayal of a repulsive ongoing battle between the square-jawed, macho all-American hero, Brick, and Goldie Lots, a curvaceous blonde who was mercenary, covetous and self-serving, alternately flirtatious and pouty, continuously in need of rescue, and always, *always* late.

If all went according to plan, Sean Megrath would come sprinting out of his house and into his car at nine-twenty to race the mile to the post office with yet another misogynous installment ready for mass publication.

She had devised the perfect punishment for Megrath. In her research she'd learned that cartoonists were fined hundreds of dollars for strips that arrived late and delayed production. So she'd annoy the hell out of him by syphoning the gas out of his car and making him late for the mail run.

Although the loss of several hundred dollars was hardly "cruel and unusual" punishment for a man of Megrath's wealth, still, he'd hate being outsmarted by a woman—a woman with a sweet, sweet mission of revenge.

The syphoning stopped. She got gingerly to her feet and removed the tubing. From her backpack she took out a note she'd written, tucked it under the windshield wiper, then affixed a foil-wrapped chocolate kiss to it with a piece of tape.

She'd done it! Struggling to contain her euphoria so that she didn't sabotage herself at the last moment, she coiled the tubing and stuffed it into her pack. She carried the gas can into the carport and hid it under a tarp that covered a small boat.

She took one last look around to make certain she'd left no other evidence, then raced down the dune, past the old Victorian house at the bottom and toward her car, which was parked in the shadow of the old cannery.

Once behind the wheel, she relaxed and began to laugh. Slapping a black-gloved hand against the steering wheel, she cried out, "All right, men of Baldwin County, Oregon, it has begun!"

Chapter One

SEAN MEGRATH LOOKED over the panels of his strip with a satisfied grin. Good old Brick. He'd done it again— thwarted the conspiracy to overthrow the democratic Russian administration and reunify the Soviet at all costs, rescued Goldie, who'd been lured to their secret headquarters by promises of receiving Czarina Alexandra's gold-and-diamond bracelet.

"But Brick," Goldie said, wide-eyed, in the third panel. "Don't be angry. I only came to spy for you."

In the last panel, Brick carried the startled-looking blonde off over his shoulder, her pert bottom in its short skirt lavishly illustrated. "That's not what I pay you for, baby," the copy read. He'd captured the arrogance and sexual gleam in Brick's expression. It would require little guesswork on the reader's part to determine just what Goldie's duties were. "Stick to what you know and you won't get into trouble."

Sean signed the strip with his last name in neat block letters. He glanced at the clock as he rolled the sheet and dropped it neatly into the labeled mailing tube. Nine-twenty. Just enough time for a swig of coffee and a doughnut.

Someday he was going to get better organized, he vowed as he stood and pushed the flexible lamp aside. The golden Labrador stretched out under his drawing table lifted his head and regarded Sean with mild interest. Sean reached down to scratch the dog's ears. "We'll walk when I come back, Jiggs."

He went to the bar in his studio that held a coffee-maker and a white bakery bag. While taking a large bite out of a doughnut frosted with colored sprinkles, he poured coffee into a mug with Brick's face on it.

Trademark products had paid for the house, the boat and his costly divorce settlement. Even if he hadn't had a dime, he'd have sold himself into slavery to get Lisa out of his life for good. Of course, if he hadn't had a dime, he'd never have attracted Lisa in the first place.

The alarm on his watch beeped. He took another swallow of coffee and held the doughnut in one hand while he snatched the mailing tube from his table.

Sean pulled keys out of his pocket as he sidestepped through the garage between the boat and the gardening tools leaning up against the wall. Checking the end of the tube to make certain he'd secured the cap, he opened the driver's-side door, tossed the tube in and slid behind the wheel.

He patted the trademark Brick Banyon doll that sat on his dash, and turned the key in the ignition. He was already looking over his shoulder so he could back out without decimating the bare forsythia again when he realized that nothing had happened.

He turned back to the dash, his brow pleated in concern, and tried again. He was rewarded with the same ugly sound—the starter turning the motor with no result.

He patted the leather-upholstered dash as though it were a feminine derriere.

"What is it, sweetheart?" he asked, turning the key a third time. "Are you ill? Hurt? Something upsetting your transm—" He stopped as he noted the needle on the gas gauge indicating Empty.

"Empty?" he said aloud in disbelief. "You should still have about a quarter of a tank." Then he noticed a square of pink paper fluttering under his windshield wiper.

Frowning, he pushed his door open and braced one leg out of the car to retrieve the note.

"What the hell?" A foil-wrapped candy kiss fell out of his hand as he slipped back behind the wheel.

He unfolded the note.

Mr. Megrath,
You are denigrating the image of women in the name of so-called entertainment. Your portrayal of Goldie implies that women are all stupid, selfish, disloyal and untrue—and what's worse, men all across the country who are addicted to your deadly dose of macho bull are buying into it.

Clean up your act, sir—and Goldie's—or you will be hearing from me again. Let your big fine be a reminder of even bigger penalties in store for you in the future if you don't heed my warning.

I am presenting you with this candy kiss. Certainly your attitude will prevent you from receiving *real* ones from any discriminating woman.

Sean stared at the note in disbelief, then cursed loudly. "Men all across the country identify with Brick," he declared, his voice reverberating inside the car, "because *they* know women are selfish, disloyal and untrue. I never said they were *stupid*. There's nothing stupid about selfishness."

He took a moment to accept that he'd just been threatened, and had his gas tank syphoned by some hard-talking babe.

Anger flared in him. She'd wanted him to be late with his strip and have to pay the fine. Well, she wasn't going to succeed. This *babe* apparently didn't know she was dealing with the star of Northwestern's track team. He glanced at his watch as he snatched up his strip and got out of the car. Nine twenty-five. He could still make it.

CLUTCHING HER SCREAMING three-year-old to her left hip, Abby Stafford groped in the purse dangling from her right shoulder for her keys.

"No! No!" Molly screamed, pushing against her and kicking. Her plump cheeks, already flushed with fever, were turning purple with rage.

"I'm sorry I mentioned the doctor!" Judy Grover, who'd come to sit with Abby's grandmother, shouted over the screams. "I thought she knew that was where she was going!"

Abby, finally finding her keys, fumbled for the right one. "I never tell her because I always get this reaction."

Judy helped her pull the car door open, apologizing again.

Abby glanced toward the railed porch and saw her grandmother waving in the open doorway.

"Judy, run back to Gran," she said urgently. "I'll be fine."

Judy looked over her shoulder, saw the old woman begin to totter onto the porch and groaned. "God!" she shouted at Abby as she ran toward the house. "How *do* you cope?"

If I stopped to think about it, Abby told herself, *I'd lose my sanity.*

Molly was now leaning backward out of Abby's arms and in real danger of landing both of them under the car rather than in it.

Abby mustered all her strength to pull her back up, only to have Molly stretch out both arms and grasp the roof and the side of the car, still screaming at full volume. "No! No! No!"

Abby sent up a silent prayer. "Lord, please. If you care for me at all, *do something.*"

Chapter Two

SEAN HAD SPRINTED AS FAR as the bottom of the dune when he realized that his stardom in the 800 meter had been fifteen sedentary, vice-laden years ago. He hadn't eaten doughnuts then, or had a fondness for Sam Adams beer.

Screaming coming from the front of his neighbor's house slowed his pace. An open car door and the potential it offered brought him to a stop.

The woman he occasionally saw over his back fence was struggling with the child over whom Jiggs always made a complete fool of himself. Though a fence separated them, Jiggs would lie on his back as close to the fence as he could wriggle so that the little girl could reach through and scratch his stomach—proof that even the most aloof male could fall victim to the wiles of a woman.

"Hello," he said.

The woman didn't hear him. The child bucked, knocking her off-balance. He stepped sideways just in time to catch her as she reeled backward with her screeching burden.

There was instant, heavy silence. Sean righted the woman and found himself the object of the scrutiny of two pairs of brown eyes precisely the same espresso color.

The child's index finger jabbed out to point at him. "Man!" she cried with recognition.

No. Abby closed her eyes. It was *him*. Sean Megrath. Her neighbor. The man she'd lusted after with vivid, uncharacteristic, unwidow-like fantasies. The man for whom she put on lipstick when she put garbage out the back or called Molly in from the yard, on the off chance he might be watching from his kitchen window or working on his car.

Once, she'd waved at him from across the street when she'd seen him downtown, but so far they'd never spoken. She had hoped that would happen one sunny morning when she was dressed to open her shop or go to church. Not when she was without makeup, her hair stuffed into a beret and her child behaving like someone possessed—right out of *The Exorcist.*

He was sexy and dangerously good-looking—the kind of man mothers warned their daughters against. She knew that in all probability nothing could ever develop between them. That didn't stop her from dreaming and hoping.

"Good morning," he said. "Can I help?"

Abby tried to pull herself together, but she simply couldn't stop staring at her neighbor. He was tall—tall enough that the slightest inclination of her forehead would have placed it against his formidable shoulder. His hair was dark brown—not a particularly remarkable shade, but thick and shiny. She imagined it would be springy, wiry to the touch.

His eyes were dark blue, and his gaze direct—not assessing or calculating like the first glance of so many men.

"Oh, no," she said, embarrassed that she'd been staring at him. "Thank you, though." She put a hand to her daughter's cheek. "Molly has a fever and we're on our way to the—" She stopped herself just in time and spelled, "*D-O-C-T-O-R.*"

Molly was still looking at him—or rather, at the half-eaten doughnut in his hand. He hated to admit it, but he had a particular weakness for females at this stage: innocent, unspoiled, all wide eyes and pink cheeks.

"Ah..." he said, smiling again. Abby felt her knees go weak. "Maybe we could help each other here. If I can get Molly into the car, would you consider taking me along? I'm on my way to the post office, right across from the clinic." He held up the tube. "I waited until the last minute and then my car...wouldn't start. I have to get this off express mail by nine-thirty. I'll be fined if it doesn't make it." He looked at his watch as he spoke, and found to his dismay that it was now nine thirty-one.

"Oh, sh—" he exclaimed, biting back the curse just in time.

She said quickly, briskly, "Don't worry about the time." She handed him Molly, then placed a protective hand on the top of his head as she pushed him down into the passenger seat. "When you get to the post office, ask for Sylvie. She prepares the pouch. The deadline is posted as nine-thirty, but the driver often doesn't pick up until nine forty-five. I know because I sell a lot of things mail-order and the occasional customer is in a hurry." She closed his door and ran around the hood to the driver's side. How she had dreamed of this!

As Abby started the car and pulled away from the curb, Molly's chin began to quiver dangerously. Sean quickly handed her what remained of his doughnut. She grabbed it with immediate interest, turned it over in both hands, and took a bite. Colored sprinkles flew everywhere. She chewed and gazed up at him as he belatedly yanked out the seat belt and fastened it around both of them.

"Good?" he asked. She was a beautiful child.

She pointed to a sprinkle caught on the chest of his black leather jacket. "Yel-low," she said clearly.

He pointed to another perched on his arm, preferring not to watch the road and their alarmingly swift progress down it.

"Red!" she exclaimed.

"Close," he corrected. "It's pink."

She looked at it and looked at him. "Red," she insisted.

He nodded, letting her have her way. That was what life always came down to, anyway, if a man spent time with a woman. Lisa had always insisted on it, and made his life miserable when he held out against her.

She pointed to his eyes. "Blue!" He caught her tiny finger just in time to avoid a jab to his cornea.

He pointed at hers, gently poking the plump cheek just below it. "Brown," he said.

She giggled with delight. "Brown," she agreed.

Then she wriggled around under the confining seat belt, stood on his thigh and rested her face on his shoulder.

Abby glanced away from the road apologetically as she turned onto the main street of Sailor's Beach. "I'm sorry. I hope escaping the fine is worth getting a dose of flu germs. She isn't usually that . . . cuddly with strangers."

"We're not exactly strangers," he said, securing his wraparound grip on Molly. "She and my dog are good friends. I've seen her out there when I've been working on my car."

I know. She comes in babbling about the 'man' and the 'doggie.'" *And I've seen you. How can you be even more handsome close up? Because you're holding my daughter, and she and I both miss her father so much?*

She screeched to a stop, almost passing the clinic in her sudden confusion, and proceeded to parallel park with a precision that surprised him after the erratic drive to town.

Then she unbuckled his seat belt and tried to take the child from him. He felt little razorlike fingernails dig into the shoulder of his jacket as Molly spoke a firm "No!" into his ear.

"Molly," Abby said reasonably, "Mr. Megrath has to go to the post office and we have to go see . . . the toys in the clinic."

"No! Man. Molly."

"Maybe it'll be easier out of the car," Sean suggested, opening his door. Holding the child to him, he climbed out onto the sidewalk. Abby came around and reached in for his mailing tube.

"All right, now, Molly," she said gently as she pried a little hand open. "You have to let go."

Molly clutched him with her other hand. "Mine!"

"No, he's not ours," she said, prying the second hand off. Then she realized what she'd said. "I mean...yours," she amended quickly, guiltily. He was looking at her with those direct blue eyes.

Molly was leaning out of her arms, her tiny hands reaching toward Sean as she screamed, "Man! Molly's!"

For an instant, Sean couldn't move. It occurred to him that precious seconds ticked away and he still held the tube. But he'd never had this experience before—a child screaming for him, pleading for him with outstretched arms.

He told himself reasonably that Molly was just a baby—and a feverish, cranky one at that. She didn't know what she was doing. She didn't know *him*. This wasn't genuine feeling; it was the result of a half a doughnut and a pair of arms she'd seemed to enjoy having wrapped around her. He'd never seen a man at Abby's house. The child was probably hungry for a father figure.

Abby saw the distress in his eyes at Molly's reaction and tried to reassure him. What must he think of them? Molly sobbing for him, and she staring at him like some love-starved single mother.

"It's all right," she said, forcing herself to get a grip on herself and Molly. "She'll be fine once I get her inside."

She cradled Molly in her arms and was backing toward the clinic door. "Thanks for the help. Don't forget to ask for Sylvie. Bye." And she disappeared inside, somehow juggling child, purse, and the heavy glass door.

He stood where he was for another moment, trying to assimilate all that had happened to him in the last fifteen minutes. He'd had his gas syphoned, his character criticized, a threat leveled against him. Then he'd finally met his very attractive neighbor and gotten a look from her that would have melted a more susceptible man, and had been romanced by her three-year-old daughter.

God, he thought, finally turning in the direction of the post office. Even Brick Banyon would have been hard-pressed to keep his cool in such a scenario.

Chapter Three

ABBY ROCKED MOLLY, who continued to scream after having been examined and given a shot.

"She'll live." Dr. Baines, a thin, bespectacled man in a light blue lab coat studied her over the rims of his glasses as he wrote a prescription. "But I'm getting a little concerned about you. You look awful. You know, the world wouldn't come to an end if you called your brother and admitted you need help with Eloise. He'd come through for you."

Mercifully, Molly was beginning to tire and her screams to diminish. Abby smiled at the doctor as she retied the hood of her coat.

"Of course he would. But he's always on the road, and Janice has her hands full with her new restaurant. They'd have to put Gran in a care facility and I just can't do that yet. She's always been such an important part of our lives."

"You don't consider that *you* have your hands full?"

"Sure. But I work out of my home. It's more conveninent for me to care for an older person than it would be for most people." Molly securely bundled, Abby smiled at the man who'd been *her* pediatrician. "End of lecture?"

He shook his head at her and handed her the prescription. "I guess so, since you aren't even listening. Just remember that if you wear yourself out, there won't be anyone to care for either Molly or Eloise."

"I know. I take care of myself. I just didn't have time for makeup this morning, so I look a little rough. Thanks for fitting us in."

"Anytime."

Abby crossed the hall to the pharmacy attached to the clinic, and had the prescription filled.

Molly was now fast asleep and a dead weight in her arms. As she turned to leave, she came face-to-face with Sean Megrath. He held a bouquet of flowers in one hand and a teddy bear in the other.

She stared at him with astonishment. She'd been fairly sure after their brief encounter earlier that she'd never see him again except from across their backyards.

"How is she?" he asked.

"Ah...fine. Well, that is, she will be. It's just the flu."

Sean studied her. She'd taken off the beret and thick dark hair fringed her forehead and fell to her shoulders. The ends curved inward, against her face, creating a silky inviting cavern toward the back of her neck. He experienced a flash of sensation as he imagined exploring that path with his lips.

He'd been celibate too long, he decided, if the mere sight of a woman's neck excited him.

"I thought you might need a cup of coffee," he said, transferring the bear to the other arm so that he could open the door.

She stepped outside. Although her heart raced at the invitation, she assumed an air of outward calm. "Thank you, but I have a gift shop in my home and I have to open in about fifteen minutes. Can I give you a lift home?"

"Is that what Sweet Violets is?" he asked. "I've noticed your sign. I wondered if you had a nursery. Here, let me carry Molly and you take these."

He scooped the child away from her in one arm as she relieved him of the flowers and the bear.

Her eyes widened. "Are these for us?"

Molly settled against his shoulder without waking. "A thank-you," he said, following as she led the way to the car. "For saving me from the fine. You were right. The driver was due at any moment and Sylvie got me taken care of in time."

"I hope nothing serious is wrong with your car."

"Someone syphoned my gas."

She gave him a sympathetic look as she unlocked the car. "Kids, I suppose."

"No, I don't think so. Whoever did it left a very acerbic note." He related loosely the note's contents.

After placing the bear in the infant seat in the back and the flowers beside it, she straightened to frown at him. "You mean someone—some woman—did it deliberately as a protest against your strip?"

He nodded, loving the way she touched the top of his head again as he ducked into the passenger seat with the still-sleeping Molly. "That's what she said."

Abby closed his door, then came around to slide in behind the wheel, her expression puzzled. "I know everyone in this town. I can't imagine who would have done that."

"She thinks I'm sexist and irresponsible."

Abby turned to him with a teasing smile as she started the station wagon. "I think Brick Banyon is, but that could just be a ploy you use to sell newspapers, gain notoriety and achieve success. It doesn't mean *you* are."

He sensed diplomatically-couched disapproval.

"You read my strip?"

She pulled away from the curb and drove through town toward the beach.

With a candid glance, she admitted, "I started when you moved here and the *Sentinel* did a story on you. Usually I don't even have time to read the front page, but someone in the shop pointed it out to me and since you live just beyond my back fence I thought it was only neighborly to know something about your work."

"And you don't disapprove?"

"Of course not. I imagine even the comics page falls under the right to free speech."

"You don't agree with the sentiments expressed in the note?"

She shrugged as she stopped at a light. Her profile, he noted, was in perfect silhouette.

"Depends on your point of view, I guess. Women who've had bad experiences with men are probably primed to criticize any word or action that suggests we aren't man's equal. Then there are those of us who've had wonderful men in our lives and will never feel threatened by anything."

She glanced at him as the light turned green and she pulled away. "Does that make any sense?"

He'd never known a woman this rational. Having had his theory on the sexes challenged, he struck back, but gently.

"I haven't noticed a man in your life," he said.

"No, there's just Molly and my dear-but-drifty grandmother." She hesitated a moment before she added, "My husband died two years ago on a fishing boat that went down in bad weather."

He'd suspected something like that. Somehow she didn't seem like a divorcée.

"I'm sorry." Unconsciously, he stroked Molly's back.

"Thank you. But I was deliriously happy for almost five years," she said philosophically. "I can make it last a lifetime. What about you? The behavior of Goldie in your strip suggests that a woman has 'done you wrong.'" Her voice softened to add emphasis to the old phrase that meant heartbreak.

He nodded as Molly clutched his thumb in her sleep. He closed his hand around her little one, almost covering her arm to her elbow.

"My mother was first," he said in a tone intended to suggest it didn't matter. "She left my father with a failing dairy farm and me. I was eight. Then there was my wife. She took off with an apprentice who'd been working with me for a year. They took a new strip I'd been developing."

Abby heard in his voice that it *did* matter. She sent him a sympathetic glance. "I'm sorry. Were you able to get the strip back?"

He shook his head. "I'd been at the point of deciding it was flawed, anyway. I just let it go. And I was frankly relieved to be rid of Lisa. I was taken in by beauty and sophistication at a time when I was just starting to make it big and I was vulnerable to adulation. I quickly learned that she was just after money and the good life. When even that got boring, she opted for adventure." He sighed and added ruefully, "That's not something I usually admit on fifteen minutes' acquaintance."

"Why not?" she asked. "It doesn't sound like any part of it was your fault."

Sean felt a stab of very old pain—pain he'd thought he'd dealt with and dismissed long ago.

"It's hard to tell someone," he said quietly, "that your mother thought so little of you, she walked away. Or to admit that with that experience behind you, you grew up and chose to love a woman just like her."

Abby pulled into his driveway and let the engine idle. "All you're admitting is that your mother made a selfish choice that had nothing to do with your value as an individual, and that you later had a very predictable reaction to that. You missed her and wanted her back and unconsciously found a woman like her to accomplish that. I suppose a psychologist would have a term for it."

He shook his head grimly. "I made a stupid mistake."

She shrugged. "You're human. It's allowed. Just don't make it a second time."

"That's a decision I've already reached." Sean got out of the car, propped Molly upright and readjusted her seat belt. Then he smiled at Abby across the seat. "Thanks for the chauffeur service." He wanted to add something else—something that would leave possibilities open—but he couldn't think of anything and knew that would be foolish, anyway. Neither of them was what the other wanted or needed.

"Bye," he said, then straightened and closed the door. He waved and she tapped the horn as she headed down the dune.

THERE'D BEEN NO SIGN of Abby or Molly since Abby had dropped him off six hours before. Sean stood at the window that looked out on the Stafford backyard and nursed a cup of coffee. Jiggs, who had followed him into the kitchen, probably anticipating that the white bag on the bar contained a second sprinkled doughnut, had given up and now rested his head on Sean's foot.

Molly was probably confined to bed, and Abby's shop was open. Of course, neither of them would be wandering into the backyard. He didn't understand why he was disappointed, but he was.

He was serious about his stand on women. He didn't trust them. Abby was pretty and sweet—but they all seemed that way at first. A man didn't discover the truth until he was already trapped.

All he wanted from a woman was witty, intelligent companionship and good sex.

He wondered what Abby wanted from a man. He knew her heart was committed to the husband she'd lost, but every woman had needs that couldn't be filled by a ghost—however much his memory was beloved.

"So what do you think, Jiggs?" Sean asked, wiggling the foot under which the dog lay. "Should I do the gentlemanly thing and continue to wonder, or should I be the real me and scope it out?"

Jiggs rolled off Sean's foot and snuffled. Sean took the dog's response as a go-ahead.

ABBY STOOD ON A ROUGH board bench, tying heart-shaped lace-covered sachets to a red ribbon strung across the mirror atop the mantel in the library that served as her shop. Half an hour before closing, the shop was empty, but the tearoom in the conservatory through the French doors still buzzed with the conversation of shopkeepers on a break, women loaded down with packages, men talking business.

Judy, dressed in a ruffly white apron and cap, circulated among them with a silver coffeepot.

Abby was pleased Judy had volunteered to stay this morning and help in the tearoom. Most days, Abby could handle both shop and tearoom herself simply by keeping the doors open and running back and forth; she was glad she hadn't had to do that today.

She felt glum and headachy, attributing her mood to a rapidly approaching Valentine's Day and its romantic theme. Hearts and cupids were everywhere, and couples were beginning to look at each other with a special gleam in their eyes.

Abby doubted she would ever adjust to her solitude. She loved Molly, and she would die for her in a moment, and she would keep her grandmother at home for as long as it was possible, but she would always long for the soul mate Craig had been. She needed a man in her life. She need to be touched, to be held, to talk for long hours in the darkness, to walk hand in hand, to be caressed with tenderness and made love to with passion. She needed to be married to the right man.

One of the sachet hearts now dangled lopsidedly in the wrong direction. She took it down and retied it.

She couldn't imagine why these thoughts were troubling her so much now. After the first year without Craig, she'd accepted the emptiness in her life and had functioned fairly well. But lately she had experienced a powerful longing for love and companionship. And right now, with her shop filled with lace and dried roses, potpourri hearts and a new line of silky underthings, she felt terribly, terribly alone.

SEAN WALKED THROUGH the French doors and hesitated there. He felt as though he had entered a bygone era. The shop was filled with pastel colors, the fragrances of herbs and flowers, and a warm glow of candlelight that brightened the overcast afternoon.

The sight of Abby standing against a mirror made him catch his breath. A good six inches of lacy white slip were revealed over her high-buttoned shoes as she stood on tiptoe on a flimsy narrow bench. One foot kicked out and up slightly, revealing a little of the shadow inside the slip.

For the second time that day, Sean found himself having to control his sexual response to Abby.

As the doors clicked closed behind him, Abby turned with a smile for what she probably assumed was a customer—and caught her hair in a bunch of thistle protruding from a tall vase on the mantel.

The smile changed to a gasp of distress, then a scream as she tottered dangerously on the bench.

Sean was across the room in a flash, reaching up to enclose her. It was an accident, he told himself, that one hand cupped her bottom and the index finger of the other hooked a small, round breast as he steadied her. He felt the shock of her softness to his very core.

For Abby, who hadn't been touched intimately in two years, the experience was both heavenly and disturbing. Heavenly because his hands were strong and competent and, despite where they'd been placed, somehow respectful. And disturbing, because she experienced a wildly delicious rush.

"Steady?" he asked.

"Yes," she breathed. "But my hair's caught in . . ."

"I know. Don't move."

With swift, athletic grace he was beside her on her narrow perch, caught her arms and wrapped them around his waist.

"Hold on to me," he said, "while I get you free."

Free. Free would be good, she thought. *And the confinement I feel has nothing to do with my hair and the thistle.* It had everything to do with the waist around which her arms were wrapped.

It occurred to her that it was strange to feel ensnared when *she* was the one holding *him*—and rediscovering long-forgotten sensations.

For a moment the sense of security was even more overpowering than her stirring sexual awareness. It had been so long since she'd had a shoulder to lean on, and she was particularly susceptible to it today—headachy and anxious and just a little unsure of her ability to cope.

It couldn't hurt, she thought, to indulge herself for a few seconds.

Sean's usually deft fingers were surprisingly clumsy. It should be a simple task to untangle several strands of hair from the thistle, but so far, Abby's hair remained caught.

Or it could be that he wasn't concentrating. The moment he'd placed her arms around him for the sake of her safety, he realized he'd placed himself in grave danger.

He felt every soft, round inch of her against him. Her cheek against his collarbone was tantalizing, her breasts fitted into the hollow of his ribs caused a shiver, and the inclination of her lower body against that part of him straining for control was creating a memory that would keep him awake tonight, he was certain.

Then, just when he'd freed the last strand, he felt her small hands open against his back and a ragged sigh expand her chest as she leaned her weight into him.

It was a gesture of acceptance, of trust. He couldn't remember ever having been granted either by a woman. He even entertained the flattering notion that she was inviting response.

Knowing instinctively that even if he was right about that, the invitation extended only so far, he repressed the thought—for now—and wrapped both arms around her.

Abby felt his embrace close around her like the haven she'd been seeking for the past year. She absorbed the sweetness of it, wondering if this could really be happening to her, and after a total of only about twenty minutes in his company.

The possibility was more than her already woozy head could deal with. It began to spin.

Sean heard her gasp and pulled her away from him to look into her eyes. Had he misread her, after all?

He knew immediately that that wasn't the problem here. The brown eyes looking up at him were unfocused and suddenly she was very pale. She brought a hand from around him to put it to her head.

"What is it?" he asked urgently.

"I don't... I feel..."

He leapt off the bench, arms extended, just in time to catch her as she crumpled.

Chapter Four

DECIDING IT WOULD NOT be good form to carry the owner's inert body into the tearoom, Sean headed in the other direction in search of help.

In a comfortable living room free of the Victorian fussiness he'd seen in the other rooms, Sean encountered a thin old woman seated in an upholstered chair and wrapped in a blanket. She was watching a soap opera, and looked up in concern as he walked in carrying Abby.

Then her frown turned to a smile. "David!" she exclaimed in pleased surprise. "You're home. How nice. What's happened? Has Abigail fallen off the swing again? I swear, we're going to have to confine that child to her room for her own protection."

Sean carried Abby to a sofa across the room, wondering who the hell David was. He remembered Abby had said something that morning about having a dear but "drifty" grandmother. She had turned back to the television. He seemed to be on his own, here.

Propping a small decorative pillow under Abby's head, he hurried into the next room, which mercifully was a kitchen. Water. A wet cloth on the forehead. That always worked on television. He opened drawers until he found linens and soaked what looked like a dish towel under the cold tap, then returned to Abby with it.

He placed it on her forehead and sat beside her on the edge of the sofa. She groaned softly but didn't open her eyes. He began to feel panicky. Could this be something serious? He knew so little about her.

He felt mild relief when he noted that her bosom in its formfitting lacy white blouse was moving gently up and down. She was breathing.

He reached up to unbutton the top few buttons of the high neckline. That was something else they always did on television. Curiously, his fingers, which had been clumsy untangling her hair, moved competently now.

He turned the towel over and she stirred again.

"Abby!" he said, leaning over her. "Abby, can you hear me?"

Her eyelashes fluttered.

"Abby!" he said more loudly, putting a hand to her cheek and tapping lightly. "Wake up, Abby!"

"Man!"

Molly, apparently just up from a nap, shuffled sleepily into the room and started to clamber onto his knees. She was dressed in a faded pink sweat suit with the Little Mermaid on her chest and the teddy bear he'd bought that morning clutched in the crook of her arm. She was clearly delighted to see him.

Then Molly noticed her mother and leaned out of his grasp, apparently trusting him not to let her fall. She slapped Abby soundly on the arm. "Mommy! Up!"

"Molly, no." Sean drew her little hand back as she poised to strike again. Then, miraculously, Abby came to.

It took her a moment to focus on him and her daughter. "Hi," she said weakly. "What...? Oh, no." She put a hand over her eyes and groaned again.

Sean caught her hand and squeezed it lightly.

"Are you all right? How do you feel?"

"Embarrassed," she admitted. "I've been a little dizzy this afternoon. I probably should never have gotten up on the bench, but Valentine's Day is coming and I have to..."

Abby hesitated as she used Sean's grip on her hand to pull herself to a sitting position, then clutched at his arm as the room began to spin.

Molly nudged her face between her mother's head and Sean's shoulder. "Mommy. Milk and cookie," she reminded.

Abby stroked her daughter's pudgy pink cheek. "You look a lot better than you did this morning, pumpkin." Suddenly she tensed and asked in alarm, "Where's Gran?"

Sean pointed to the armchair. "Right there, deeply engrossed in some soap. She thought you'd fallen off the swing again."

Abby smiled indulgently. "That's where she lives now," she said. "In my childhood."

"She called me Dave."

"That's my brother. I was always trying to keep up with him, and he was always carrying me back, wounded."

Molly shook Abby's shoulder impatiently. "Mommy! Milk!"

"Right." Abby pushed gently on Sean. "Come on. I'll get her a snack and get you a cup of coffee and one of my famous white-chocolate brownies."

He resisted. "Why don't you let me get the snack?"

"No, I'm fine. I just didn't have time for breakfast this morning, then I was worried about getting the shop open and decorated and forgot to have lunch." She smiled winningly at him. "If you'll let me up, I'll eat something."

He studied her for a moment, reluctant to break the intimacy of their position. But Molly was getting restless, and he was getting too involved. It would be dangerous to let either situation go unchecked.

He tried to put Molly down on her feet but she clung to him with a firm "No."

"Her father was very single-minded." Abby explained to him with a grin.

Sean stood, slipping Molly to his hip where she seemed happy to settle. He offered Abby a hand up and stayed close behind her as he followed her into the kitchen.

He was relieved to see that, though still pale, at least she seemed steady. She pointed him to the breakfast nook in the corner. In a moment she produced a cup with a lid and a straw and a small plate holding three frosted animal crackers.

Molly immediately clambered off his lap to get to her snack, dumping the bear on its head in the corner of the booth.

As Abby came back to the table with two mugs of coffee, Molly made an indistinguishable exclamation and stood up on the seat, pointing back toward the living room.

"Okay," Abby said, lifting her out of the booth, then passing her the cup and plate. "But, please, be careful. Try not to spill."

"What does she want?" Sean asked as Abby went back to a commercial pie case in a corner of the kitchen.

She indicated the noise coming from the television. "Cartoons," she replied with a smile, pulling a plate out of the case. "A mother's salvation. Cream or sugar?"

"No, thanks."

Molly came running, pointing urgently past Sean, demanding, "Bear!"

That he understood. He reached for the teddy bear still in yoga position and passed it over.

"Thank—you," Molly said, snatching it from him and running back to her cartoons.

Abby placed a glass plate in front of him. In the center of it, on a red heart-shaped doily, was a heart-shaped piece of thick white cake. On top were nuts and chunks of white chocolate.

"This looks like there should be a law against it," he said, poising his fork over it.

She smiled across the table at him as she pulled her half sandwich toward her. "I'm glad there isn't. I get four dollars and fifty cents apiece for those. What do you think?"

He took a bite. Ordinarily, his morning doughnut was as close as he got to sweets. He usually found decadent desserts nauseatingly rich. But this had a different quality—the tang of sour cream or cream cheese under the sweetness.

"Exceptional," he declared. "What do you call it?"

"Heart's Delight," she replied. Her voice came out in a breathy whisper.

She didn't know why it happened. One moment they were talking companionably, and the next, something in his gaze coiled around her and made her feel as though she'd been drawn right inside him.

She felt his energy, his intelligence, his humor, and the dangerous force of his sensuality. She remembered vividly everything she'd experienced with her arms wrapped around him.

And she felt something else—warmth, comfort, protection; all the things women felt in the presence of the right man. She wondered if he had any idea he exuded those qualities.

She made herself pull back. She took a bite of her sandwich, then took his coffee cup to the counter to refill it. The physical act of walking away from him, if only for a few seconds, helped release her from his spell.

She brought the cup back and gave him a very casual smile. She knew she was falling in love, but it was important to her that he knew she wasn't the kind of woman on whom a man could use magic. She needed the real thing. She'd had it once, and she'd have it again—or she'd have nothing.

Sean read her eyes. A cartoonist made people laugh by poking fun at their common vulnerabilities. That sounded simple, but to spot humankind's fallibilities, one had to study people closely. He was constantly observing, analyzing, concluding.

He saw her loneliness, and realized that she saw him as the man who could give her back what she'd once had.

It wasn't arrogance on his part, it was understanding. He felt precisely the same way. Sort of. He was certain they had much to offer each other—on a casual and temporary basis. The trick would be to make her see it that way.

He could tell she was a woman who'd always been handled carefully. He had to do this slowly, or risk failure. And he didn't deal well with failure.

Having finished the sweet, he asked amiably, "You're sure you're going to be all right? I hate to leave you if you're still feeling faint."

Abby sensed a slight shift in his approach. She didn't know what it meant. It was as though he'd deliberately banked the interest she'd seen in his eyes. Of course, hadn't she just done the same thing?

Interesting. Apparently they were evenly matched.

"I'll be fine," she assured him easily, standing as he did. "Judy, my friend who mans the tearoom for me, will be closing up in a minute and staying for dinner. Here, I'll let you out the back door and all you have to do is cross our yards."

She opened the lace-curtained back door. He hesitated on the threshold, knowing he had to leave her with something to keep her as sleepless that night as he would be.

He caught her chin in his hand, turning her face up to his, letting her think his interest was simply diagnostic. Then he kissed her gently but lengthily, in complete control, tracing the line of her bottom lip with the tip of his tongue.

He smiled down into her eyes and said softly, "Shout across the yards if you need anything," and took off at a sprint.

You're cool, Megrath, he congratulated himself as he ate up the distance between the two houses. She'd been startled when he left her, off-balance, even in a dither. That was good. Now she'd lie awake tonight, wanting more.

Yes. It was no longer popular for a man to want control of a relationship, but he'd made that kind of man the hero in his strip, and he intended to conduct his own relationships in just the same way.

It was all about taking charge and holding on to it. Simple. Elemental. Expedient. And he had the knack.

He opened his back door, heading for a well-deserved beer, and promptly fell over Jiggs who was sprawled out on the kitchen floor.

Chapter Five

SHE HADN'T EXPECTED to work in daylight, but this was simply too good an opportunity to pass up. And so far, she'd seen no evidence that Megrath was taking her seriously. She intended to take further action, but she hadn't expected the opportunity to fall into her lap.

She looked around the campus, now quiet with afternoon classes in session, and saw no one in sight. She reached into the half-open window of the Jaguar, opened the door and let herself into the leather-upholstered interior.

What could she do, she wondered, to tweak his sexist nose? Then it came to her.

It took less than a minute. She wrote a quick note, attached a candy kiss, then slipped out of the car and walked away, chuckling to herself. That had been too easy.

AS THE COMMUNITY college's campanile rang out three o'clock, Dan Fogel, head of the art department, called for order among the students clustered around Sean as he signed autographs, answered questions, and avoided the seductive glances of a little brunette in fatigues.

"I appreciate your enthusiasm, people," Fogel said, extracting Sean from their midst, "but we've already kept him an hour overtime. Thank you for sharing with us, Mr. Megrath."

The students applauded warmly, and the little brunette was hauled away by a tall, thin boy in glasses. Then a young man with a military haircut stepped out of the stream of departing students to shake his hand.

"Thanks," he said. "And if the broad who syphoned your gas gives you any more trouble, let me know. I'll get my criminal-justice buddies on it. She had no call to do that to you."

"I appreciate it, Bender. And if you get that idea for a strip together and want some feedback, come and see me."

The boy beamed. "Thanks, Mr. Megrath."

When the last student had left, Fogel helped Sean pack up the sample strip he'd brought. "I'm sorry that had to come up," he said, obviously embarrassed. "But you know how young people are. No one's feelings are sacred, even a guest in the classroom."

Sean snapped the tab on his portfolio. "Don't be concerned. I called the police to report the theft, and showed them the note, hoping it would help them determine who wrote it. That makes it all a matter of public record."

Fogel walked him to the door. "I think the *Sentinel* making it a front-page story was a bit much, but I suppose that's the price of fame."

Sean laughed and offered his hand. "It's the price of challenging a current standard of behavior. Women take themselves very seriously today. Men are expected to revere that."

Fogel shook his hand. "I salute your courage. Can I invite you back again?"

"Anytime."

"Good luck with Brick," he called as Sean started down the hall. "And watch your back with the ladies."

Sean stopped just outside Shelton Hall to put his collar up and stuff his free hand in his pocket. It had rained all morning, but now the clouds just hung menacingly close to the treetops on the knoll on which the college stood.

The sky was already darkening and fog wound its way through the campus, seeming to string the evergreens and the buildings together. Student traffic appeared to be thin at that hour, and the quiet landscape took on an eerie quality.

Sean laughed at the thought, wondering if he should give up the strip and start writing mysteries. "It was a dark and stormy afternoon...."

He was putting his portfolio in his car when he noticed that his Brick doll was standing on its head in the litter bag that hung from his radio dial.

He began to smile at the sight, until it occurred to him that it couldn't have happened accidentally. Someone had put it there. Then he saw the candy kiss atop the folded pink note on his dash and realized who was responsible.

"You little..." He snatched the candy and the note and read the neatly block-printed message.

Have seen no improvement in your strip. Presuming you work ahead, I'm giving you one more week to prove yourself responsible. I'm watching you!

Sean slammed the car door closed, muttering profanities under his breath. Now she was guilty of breaking and entering. He looked down at the window he'd left half open and amended that thought. She hadn't broken in, but she had entered.

Glancing around for signs of the perpetrator, he looked up at the Gothic library that stood on the topmost point of the knoll. A slate walk lined with trees sloped down toward a parking lot just off the street. Running down it was a figure in a black hooded cape.

The full-length cape floating out as the figure ran suited the moment and the setting so perfectly, he almost couldn't believe his eyes. He watched, both angry and fascinated, and tensed for battle.

The light, graceful step of the running figure indicated a woman. He began to run toward her as he drew the obvious conclusion: She was a woman who saw herself as some kind of vengeful force; the woman who had syphoned his gas tank and forced him to explain to a classroom filled with young people why she had bested him; the woman who had dumped his Brick doll on its head.

He was waiting at the bottom of the slope as she ran the last few yards, carefully watching her feet. Her face was obscured by the hood.

She noticed him at the last moment, and, unable to stop, ran into his arms with a shriek.

He stared into the shocked brown eyes further shadowed by the hood, then reached a hand in between her hair and the black silk lining and swept the hood back to make sure.

"Sean!" Abby gasped. Free of the hood, her face was ruddy with the cold, her eyes startled. "What are you doing here?" Then a possibile reason for his unexpected presence seemed to occur to her and she grabbed his arm. "Did something happen? Is Molly...?"

"No. No, nothing's wrong," he said quickly, anxious to reassure her, but completely unable to escape the conviction that had made him intercept her. "At least, nothing's wrong at home. What are *you* doing here?"

She blinked, apparently surprised by the question. "I teach a class here."

He looked skeptical. "In what?"

"Fashion history," she replied, her lips pursing in annoyance at his authoritative tone. "One to three every Wednesday."

He absorbed that information without reaction. "Does that have something to do with the getup?"

She drew a slow, careful breath. Her eyes looked ready to ignite and what was probably a formidable temper was held in check by yet another breath. Excitement stirred inside him, apart from the anger.

"I have an extensive collection of vintage clothing," she answered, her voice deadly but calm. "I wear a different piece to every class so my students can see and handle the real thing. The temperature today seemed to call for this cape. It's nineteenth-century. Velvet and silk. Anything else you'd like to know?"

"Where were you going in such a hurry?" he demanded.

"Home!" she snapped at him, her control decimated.

"You aren't by any chance escaping the scene of the crime?"

"What 'crime'?"

"Someone let herself into my car."

That did it. In one hand she held a folder stuffed with papers. She placed the other squarely in the middle of his chest and tried to push him aside. He moved simply so she wouldn't break her wrist, but caught her arm before she could get past him.

"Answer me, please," he said.

She yanked her arm free and gave him a look that would have braided steel. "I did *not* break into your car!" she shouted, finally losing all control. "And I resent the suggestion that I would do such a thing! I just this moment came out of class. You can check with the drama teacher, if you like. She came to talk to me about costuming for a period play.''

His anger began to deflate. What he knew of her made his suspicions seem absurd. But she *was* here and she had been running away.

''Then, why were you running?''

''Because I'm cold!'' she shouted. ''This cape is romantic, but not very warm. In the spirit of interrogation, what are *you* doing here?''

''I was asked to speak to the drawing class,'' he replied.

''Then why are you behaving like a cretin?''

For a moment, he didn't know what to tell her. He was wrong, of course. He didn't know how to explain his behavior except that at the moment, and in his state of frustrated anger, she had seemed a likely suspect.

Unwilling to admit he'd been a jerk, he tried the trick Brick always used. He grasped the loose knot of hair at the back of her head and pulled it back. For reasons he didn't understand, because generally he appreciated amenable women, he wanted to taste her temper. He thought it might be because he felt he deserved her fury, but he had no need for a reason when he closed his mouth over hers. He held her firmly in place, lured her into capitulating for one exciting moment, then she shoved away and glared up at him while her papers spilled over the grass.

''Listen to me,'' she ordered quietly, the promise of a threat in her tone. ''I have never understood women who suffer abuse—physical *or* verbal—one moment, then fall into the man's arms the next. I know Brick Banyon doesn't have a grasp on that, but if you're going to live out my back door, *you* had better understand it. Not that I ever want to see you again. If you come anywhere near—"

"I thought you were the woman who left me the note," he interrupted, suspecting that her threat could go on for some time.

She stopped. He thought all might be lost when her anger appeared to grow. Fortunately, curiosity diluted it.

"What on earth for?"

He explained what he'd thought when he'd seen her running down the walk in her cape. "At first I didn't know it was you, then when I did, it seemed as though it might fit. You had proximity, ample opportunity—"

"Oh, right. That was the night Molly got the flu. I entertained myself by syphoning your gas between pacing the floor with a screaming child, changing her bedding, and trying to catch an hour's sleep that night myself." With a glance of disgust, she leaned down to collect her papers.

He got down to help. "I'm sorry," he admitted sincerely, "I knew I was wrong almost immediately, but you're so pretty when you're angry, I kept it up."

She straightened, stuffing a disordered pile of damp papers into her grass-stained folder. That confession did not seem to have earned him any points.

"Play games with somebody else, Sean."

He straightened the pages he'd collected against a raised knee. "Come on," he chided with a grin. "I'm a cartoonist. I have a playful approach to almost everything." He handed her the sheets, retaining his hold on them when she tried to snatch them away. He looked into her eyes. "I imagine you don't get much chance to play at all."

He saw her eyes soften, her mouth turn down. He was right, and it must affect her even more than he'd realized. He felt a desperate need to change that.

This was not the man who'd eaten Heart's Delight in her kitchen the week before, Abby thought. This man thought her capable of theft—even if it was just a tank of gasoline—and he found it amusing to taunt her because he thought she looked pretty in a temper! She felt angry, confused, off-balance. How could she have been so wrong about a man? The second question was, did she need this aggravation in her life?

"By way of apology," he said, "let me take you home with me for a cup of coffee."

She was still annoyed enough to be ungracious. "I have an elegant tearoom and the ability to make every sophisticated coffee drink known to man. Why would I want to go home with you for a cup of coffee?"

He reached out to pull her hood up and settle it lightly on her hair. He tucked a loose strand in with gentle fingertips.

"Because it would give you a different perspective," he said. "I have a panoramic view of the ocean, and my dune blocks your view." He'd saved this for the last, and he played it out with what he considered laudable nonchalance. "And because I have a box of old things I inherited from my aunt and I haven't known what to do with them. Maybe you'll have an idea."

Her interest was piqued. "What kinds of old things?"

He shrugged. "Clothes. Trinkets."

She eyed him suspiciously. "Why didn't you mention this the other day?"

"I didn't know you collected clothes the other day."

She sighed. Perhaps she could make allowances for his boorish behavior. Perhaps if someone had syphoned her gas tank and written her a scathing note that had ended up on the front page of the *Sentinel,* she'd be suspicious and rude, too.

And his touch did things to her. She'd had good instincts about that when she'd fallen in love with Craig. Could she be that wrong this time? She had at least a fifty-fifty chance.

"Come on," he coaxed, putting an arm around her shoulders and leading her toward her car. "Meet me at my place. I'll show you the stuff my aunt left, and we'll make a deal over a cup of coffee."

She smiled faintly, deciding that even odds were probably better than those life offered in most things. "All right."

"Good." He waited until she'd unlocked her door, held it open for her, then locked it. "Drive carefully," he cautioned and pushed the door closed.

As she drove away, he felt the barest twinge of guilt at not mentioning that the deal he had in mind had nothing to do with his aunt's things.

Chapter Six

SEAN'S STUDIO HAD A magnificent view. Sky met ocean, making it seem as though infinity lay just beyond the window.

"Looks like the edge of doom, doesn't it?" Sean asked, putting a steaming mug of coffee on the drawing table beside her. "Sometimes I miss New York. It's always lit up like a Christmas tree, even in the middle of the night."

"You probably never see the sun rise in New York," she observed, turning away from the window to pick up her cup. "We have magnificent ones. Just the other morning it looked like the day was being pushed up right out of the ocean."

Abby sipped at her coffee and discovered it had been laced. "Mmm," she said. "Brandy."

"Since I kept you out in the cold," he explained, taking her arm and leading her toward the living room, "I felt the responsibility to warm you up again."

"Well, who's this?" Abby dropped to her knees to pat the large yellow dog under the coffee table.

"That's Jiggs," Sean replied. "He approves all my work."

Sean gestured toward the sofa and Abby sat on the middle cushion.

The large living room was dark blue and beige with touches of red. Oak woodwork, undraped windows that looked out on the ocean, and simple, rustic furnishings gave the decor the look of Colonial America combined with contemporary comfort.

He put on the soft light of a table lamp shaped like a coach lantern. "Make yourself comfortable," he said. "I'll get the box."

He disappeared into the corridor leading to the bedrooms, and was back in a moment.

She moved her cup aside to make room for the deep, wide box he placed on the coffee table. He leaned over to part the white tissue. Her attention was immediately captured by a small beaded bag in a bright, berry shade.

Exclaiming over it, Abby reached in to pick it up and admire its perfect condition, then opened it to find a worn but sound lining fitted with a silver comb and a flowered compact.

"Do you mind if I open it?"

"Of course not." He smiled, all annoyance gone. She looked charmingly avaricious. It was an aspect of her he was pleased to discover—like the earlier glimpse of her temper. He didn't want her to be as perfect as she seemed, or she wouldn't consider the deal he was about to offer.

She opened the compact. A trickle of loose powder escaped as a long-closed clasp resisted, then jerked open. It surprised him to catch a still-fragrant scent.

Abby held up the compact to look into the spotted mirror. "Was your aunt a blonde?"

He leaned over to look with her. "How did you know?"

"The shade of the powder." She closed the compact reverently and replaced it with care, then fastened the bag, tracing its pattern of beads with the tip of her finger.

"Wouldn't you love to see the dress this went with?" she said.

"It's at the bottom, I think."

"It is?" She began digging in earnest, turning up several pairs of gloves, a marabou stole, a smaller box of Art

Nouveau jewelry, and a painted fan before finally coming to the wasp-waisted gown that was a slightly paler color than the bag but decorated with the same color, size and shape of beads.

He watched as she stood to shake it out and instinctively held it against her.

The beaded bodice and top of the skirt caught the lamplight, and for a moment Sean could see Abby in the dress, being twirled on some Victorian dance floor by a handsome man in formal dress.

He was surprised to feel a sharp stab of jealousy for a man who existed purely in his own imagination.

He had lured her with the box, but he suddenly resented how completely its contents had captured her attention. He'd brought her here for a purpose and it was time he got to it.

But before he could speak, he noticed her looking around for a mirror.

"There's one in my bedroom," he suggested innocently.

He hadn't fooled her. She grinned knowingly and crossed to the entertainment center with its long glass doors. "I'll make do with this, thank you."

"You are *so* lucky to have this," she said, holding out the side of the skirt and doing a turn.

He leaned an elbow on the back of the sofa, his expression bland. "Yes, I know. I thought I'd wear it to the chamber-of-commerce awards banquet in March."

She came back to him, laughing. "I meant that this is exciting, to have a dress and bag in your possession that certainly belonged to a lady of grace and style. She may even have made it herself. There's no label inside, and it was quite common in those days for women to make their own gowns and a purse to match. The purses came in a sort of kit with the frame and a pattern.''

She folded it carefully back into the box. "I have acid-free tissue paper. I'll bring you some. This should be wrapped in it so that one day *your* grandchildren can see that everything wonderful doesn't come with batteries.''

"I was thinking of giving you the dress," he said.

She stopped in the process of folding the paper over, her lips parted, her eyes saucer-size. "What?" she breathed.

He had her. He proceeded carefully. "Would you like to have it?"

She hesitated a moment. "No," she finally replied, then hastily amended, "I mean, yes, of course. Who wouldn't? But it's yours. I mean, it should stay in your family."

He shrugged. "I'm it. My father's gone, no siblings. Lisa and I fortunately had no children." He looked into her eyes as he said the words and saw her answering empathy. He felt his own aloneness, coupled with a sharp awareness of need—a need for Abby.

Abby was breathless. There was something happening here that she didn't understand.

"Why would you want to give it to me?" she asked.

He held her gaze. He wouldn't lie, but he had to do this carefully.

"Because you love old things. Because you would appreciate it and care for it. Because," he said with complete truth, "I care for you."

His eyes were steady, gentle, honest. Her heart began to thrum, her pulse grew erratic. Did he really feel it, too? Could she have been right? Had she found the right man a second time in just a matter of hours?

"You do?" Abby whispered.

Sean took her hands, still poised over the box, and turned her to face him. They were trembling. He vacillated for just an instant, then looked into her velvet-brown eyes and decided he had to have her—whatever it took.

"I do," he told her, placing both her hands in one of his and covering them with the other. "I'm sorry about this afternoon. You can understand how my attitude toward women got a little skewed."

She was willing, eager to be generous. "Yes, but you have to look around you and realize that all women don't run when things are difficult. Most of us have amazing staying power."

He leaned sideways against the back of the sofa, pulling her with him so that his arms enfolded her. She looked wary but interested.

"Is that a promise?" he asked, shaping her cheek in one hand and tracing her cheekbone with his thumb. She was so soft. Softer than any woman he'd ever touched.

"I can't speak for other women," she said. He could feel the warmth in her eyes.

"I want you to speak for you," he said. Deep down, his mind retained a firm hold on the purpose of this encounter, but the parts of it that involved sensation—the parts that fantasized—were running wild. His hands were steady, but everything inside him was trembling. He could see Abby in his bed.

Abby's thoughts were spinning out of control, but she had more than herself to think about. She fought to keep a hold on common sense.

"It would take a very special man . . ."

"Holding you," he heard himself say, "makes me feel very special." He didn't know where that had come from. It was true, but he hadn't planned to say it, and he'd thought this over very carefully. It was time to get to the point.

"Abby," he said. He heard the urgency in his own voice. "Let me tell you what I have in mind."

Abby heard the first warning bell. What he had in mind? As though this wasn't spontaneous? As though it had been somehow calculated?

That couldn't be what he meant, she told herself. He was nervous. She was nervous. Discovering love could be scary stuff—particularly for a man who'd known so little of it from the women in his life. She leaned her head back against his arm and asked trustingly, "What do you have in mind?"

"A sort of...partnership." He had no idea why that had been so difficult to get out. The last word stuck and had to be willed into sound.

Her pulse accelerated. She snuggled closer. "Partnership?"

"You and me."

She was beginning to hear music. She linked her fingers in the hand he had over her shoulder. "Together," she said.

There was an instant's hesitation, then he said, "Right," and she heard the second warning bell. The tone would have been much more appropriate for "Wrong!"

She didn't move, afraid to shatter the moment, should the joy and excitement she felt be proved a mistake. "Together," she repeated, encouraging him to go on.

He was experiencing the same sensation he'd known on the bench when he'd held her against him. It was suddenly desperately important that he not fail in this.

"My experience has proved," he said, thinking that he sounded like a scientific paper, but unable to stop now that he'd started, "that it's foolish to risk your heart in a relationship." That made perfect sense to him, but it suddenly seemed imperative that he justify the statement.

"Two very different people promising to spend a lifetime together when each will see and feel things in a completely different way from the other is demanding the impossible."

Full alert! Disappointment ran over Abby like an ice shower, but she didn't move. She sensed she should conserve energy for what was to come. She waited.

"You were fortunate enough to have had a good marriage," he went on, taking her silence for encouragement. "But now you're alone and I..." *I'm lonely.* Why was that so hard to admit? He chose what he considered the more honest explanation. "I need a woman. You."

She could no longer remain still. If she did, she would give him a one-two punch to the solar plexus. She stood and went to the window. In that short amount of time, darkness had fallen. She smiled grimly to herself. How appropriate.

He was behind her immediately, his hands on her shoulders, his lips close to her ear.

"I know it sounds...calculating...out of context, but when you think about it, it's very practical. I'm in a position to..." Another phrase he had to force out. He did it, irritated with himself—and with something else he couldn't quite pinpoint. "To help you financially," he said firmly. "And you're in a position to...please me."

He closed his eyes, thinking he'd made himself sound like some Eastern potentate.

She remained silent, staring out the window. *You've blown it, Megrath,* he told himself. *She's going to turn around in a minute, slap your face, and storm out of the house and you'll never see her again except when she empties her garbage.*

Abby felt the firmness of his hands on her shoulders as he pulled her back against him and kissed her temple.

"Do you understand?" he whispered.

She did. He was the sad victim of a dearth of love and repeated betrayal, and she was going to save him from himself. She just hoped she had the guts.

She turned, smiling as warmly as she could manage when she felt like ice clear through. She looped her arms around his neck and pulled him down for a quick kiss.

"Of course I understand," she said amiably. "You want to pay me for sex."

Chapter Seven

THE WORDS reverberating around him in that sweet tone sounded obscene.

"Well, I wouldn't put it that way, precisely," he said with a frown.

"Well, there's no point in mincing words, Sean," she replied, taking his hand and leading him back to the sofa. She urged him to sit, then took her place right beside him, her knees wedged against the side of his thigh. She looped her arms around his neck and laughed softly, happily. "We're both adults. You don't have to decorate it with lace for me. I understand completely."

She put her head on his shoulder and heaved a heartfelt sigh. "In fact, I've been waiting for some time for a man in a tux and a top hat to come along and simplify my life."

Simplify? he wondered. Suddenly things seemed inexplicably complicated.

Abby raised her head to fold her hands on his shoulder and smile into his wary eyes. Somewhere under the anger and the need for retribution, she was almost enjoying herself.

She kissed the tense line of his jaw and smiled. "I just didn't expect him to be a cartoon."

"Cartoon*ist*," he corrected. "Brick Banyon is the cartoon, I'm the cartoonist."

"Of course." She couldn't help the dry sound of the words. His frown deepened and he studied her closely, looking, she suspected, for a sign of condescension in her eyes.

She maintained an innocent stare and asked with anticipation, "What do you intend to pay me?"

He expelled a gasp of exasperation or surprise—she wasn't sure which. "Well...you can be sure I'll...I'll be generous."

"Of course." She nodded agreeably. "That's not the kind of thing you can decide without knowing how I'll...you know...how well I perform."

"Abby..." He groaned out the word.

"It's all right," she reassured him with a quick hug. "Let The Buyer Beware. I understand. I'm a businesswoman, remember? I won't put good money down for any product that hasn't proven itself."

Sean was beginning to feel as though he were drowning in a manure pile that had the properties of quicksand. He hadn't expected her to react this way. He had hoped for agreement and cooperation, certainly, but he hadn't expected such zealous exploration of the basic elements of the deal.

He stood and pulled her to her feet.

"Why don't we go into the details another time," he said, feeling as though he were choking.

She looked upset. "But don't you want to...?" Her index finger pointed in the direction of the bedrooms.

"Abby!" He caught her shoulders, frustrated and irritated. She looked up at him with big, wounded eyes and he resisted the impulse to shake her. Caressing her upper arms instead, he said more quietly. "No. Right now I want you to take the dress and the bag home, and...and I'll pick you up tomorrow night. We'll take a walk or go to a movie, then we'll come back here for dinner. Then we'll see...how you feel."

Tomorrow. That would be good. Maybe they'd both be back to normal tomorrow.

Something passed over her eyes, something that cast a shadow over their brightness. He tried to analyze it, but it was gone in an instant.

"You're sure you want me to have the dress?" she asked.

"Absolutely." He tried to put the dress and bag back into the box. Apparently unhappy with the way he was doing it, she pushed him aside and folded the dress with loving care, tucking the bag between its folds.

If her plan didn't work, she thought, he wasn't getting the dress back. He wouldn't deserve to have it.

He helped her into her cape and carried the box for her to the door.

She turned to take it, smiling into his eyes with all the affection that had been growing inside her before he'd bruised it so badly.

She saw his eyes react to hers. She wondered if he even realized he liked her better this way. Maybe there was hope for him. Time would tell.

"Thank you for the dress," she said softly.

"You're welcome." His lips came within an inch of hers, his eyes roving her face, feature by feature. "You're not angry?"

"Of course not." She put a hand to his cheek and stood on tiptoe to plant a gentle, lingering kiss on his lips. He let her retain control of it, seeming to drink it in as some kind of reassurance.

When she drew away, he smiled, looking relaxed and confident again.

"And you know what?" she asked softly, tauntingly.

He fell like a ripe fruit. "What?" he asked with anticipation.

"The dress is so beautiful," she said with a flirtatious shrug of her shoulder, "that I won't even charge you for the first time. See you tomorrow night."

He was leaning against the molding, a hand over his eyes, when she turned to wink at him.

THEY WALKED OUT OF THE movie theater hand in hand. It was after ten o'clock and Sailor's Beach was quiet, except for the hum of neon signs and the drumming of rain on the cars parked along the main street.

"I'm sorry the rain prevented us from taking a walk," Abby said as they stopped under the marquee to watch it pour, "but I thought the movie was wonderful!"

The film had been a contemporary piece about a high-powered businesswoman who'd left her career in Los Angeles to marry a doctor from a small town in the midwest.

Sean gave her an indulgent smile as he helped her pull up her hood. "It was all right if you believe in fairy tales. Stay here. I'll get the car."

She caught his arm. "It's just at the end of the block," she protested, tugging him out from under the theater marquee and into the rain. "I'll come with you. And, yes, I *do* like fairy tales. Doesn't everyone?"

He pulled her close, trying to shield her from the downpour. "I guess they're okay for children."

She grinned up at him. "You might say that about comics, but they have a message for everyone."

He gave her shoulder a scolding pinch. "The movie was completely unrealistic."

"Because they fell in love?"

"Because she gave up what she wanted for him. That just doesn't happen."

"Love can make anything happen," she insisted as they ran to the corner. "It can make real life out of fairy tales and dreams come true."

They stopped at the corner, waiting for the light to change, the rain hissing around them like a living thing. "For the average person, a dream come true is nothing more than comfort, contentment, and compatibility with a mate. It isn't love. Love doesn't exist."

"It does," she said firmly. "I've known it."

"Abby..." he began with good-humored impatience. Then the light changed to Walk and they ran across the street, the argument suspended.

Sean pulled her close again. "Let's go home," he cajoled, "have brandy by the fire, and plan what to do with the rest of the evening."

All right, she thought. *I gave you your chance.*

They hurried to the Jaguar parked near the mailbox and the newspaper dispenser. The headline caught Abby's eyes and she bought a paper while Sean unlocked the door.

"'She Strikes Again,'" Abby read, pointing out the bold headline to Sean as he helped her into the car.

He groaned. "Don't tell me the press found out she'd gotten into my car."

Abby waited until Sean slipped in behind the wheel, then read the news story aloud.

"The angry woman to whom local celebrity Sean Megrath fell victim late last week has struck again. This time her target was Robert Folk, a young Coast Guard engineer assigned to the cutter *Laurel*. His new Camaro, scheduled to be shipped to northern California where Folk has been transferred, had disappeared. Folk reports that he left it parked on the dock where Gerald Bishop, a friend of Folk's promised to pick it up and drive it to Seattle for transport.

"Bishop, unable to locate the car, arranged a ship-to-shore call to Folk, who assured him he had left it in the parking lot. Bishop reported the car missing.

"Folk reports having received a padded envelope that contained a note explaining that his car had been 'reassigned.' He refused to share the details of the note, but says that it did include a chocolate kiss—the same signature attached to Sean Megrath's note.

"This mysterious woman—this 'Sweet Avenger'—seems to be embarking on a serious crusade."

The article went on but Abby stopped, turning to Sean with a disbelieving smile.

"Wow! She has such courage. They're calling her the Sweet Avenger."

With a frown, he took the paper from her and tossed it into the back seat.

He put an arm around her and pushing her hood back, caught a strand of her hair between his fingers. "I thought you were willing to believe that Brick didn't necessarily reflect the real me."

She gently traced the line of his jaw with her fingertip. "But you proved me wrong on that, didn't you?" Her tone made it sound like anything but an indictment. He heard it anyway.

He caught her chin between his thumb and forefinger and looked into her eyes. "Are you sure you want to come home with me?"

You can do this, Abby told herself firmly. *Don't be concerned about his feelings.*

Actually, most of her reluctance to follow through with her plan came from her own feelings. She had them—and they were all for this gorgeous, sometimes-sweet, some-times-funny, always-exasperating man. She should be able to indulge them, explore them, give them free rein. Instead, he was forcing her to squelch them and pretend to fall in with what he had "in mind."

She wrapped her arms around his neck in that way she had that always narrowed his focus and swamped his senses so that his vision, his nostrils, his...space were filled with her. She took his bottom lip between her teeth and tugged. His backbone turned to pudding.

"Oh, yes," she said in a seductive whisper. She added something else that didn't quite register because she was now almost in his lap.

She kissed him like he'd never been kissed before. He felt her lips, her tongue, her teeth. They were ruthlessly passionate, disarmingly gentle, surprisingly creative, and he felt as though she could draw out of him every thought, sensation and dream he'd ever known.

She was pulling his sweater up, and he felt her finger-tips against the cotton of his T-shirt, when the significance of the words she'd spoken a moment ago suddenly registered.

He caught her wrist and pushed her down beside him.

"What," he asked stiffly, "did you say?"

She frowned, perplexed. "When?"

"When I asked you if you were sure you wanted to do this."

She thought back. Then she gave him that innocent look he was growing to distrust more and more.

"I said yes," she replied. "What...?"

"After that," he barked.

"I said that you had promised you'd be generous."

He was the picture of affronted dignity. "So our conversation went, 'You're sure you want to do this?'" Sean put a hand to his chest to indicate that he had spoken the words.

She nodded.

"And the reply—" he pointed to her "—was, 'Oh, yes. You promised you'd be generous.' Is that about right?"

She nodded, that innocent look still in place. "I believe that's verbatim, but I don't unders—"

He started the car, screeched out of the parking spot and raced out of town toward the beach.

"Will you please tell me what the problem is?" she asked quietly. "If you're upset because I'm doing it for the money, that doesn't make sense. It was your idea to begin with."

"This could have been handled," he said angrily, "with a lot more finesse."

"How," she asked, "do you finesse an offer of money for my..."

"Don't say it!" he ordered, casting her a dark glance as he screeched to a halt in front of her house.

Before she knew what had happened, they were standing on her front porch.

"Where's your key?" he asked.

"I didn't bring one. Judy's with Gr—"

"Then knock."

She didn't have to. The door swung open, and a smiling Judy greeted them, a very wide-awake Molly on her hip. Judy sobered instantly at the expressions on their faces.

"Man!" Molly said gleefully, reaching both arms out to him.

For a moment Abby thought he wouldn't respond. Then, without a loosening of his taut, angry features, he reached out to engulf one little hand in his and say with surprising gentleness, "Hi, button."

Then he turned to Abby with a look she read clearly: disappointment. And he stalked away.

Judy pulled her inside as Abby took Molly from her and held her closely.

"I take it things didn't go well," Judy said with concern.

Abby sniffed as her eyes brimmed. "Actually," she said grimly, "they went precisely according to plan."

She just hadn't suspected there'd be so little satisfaction in success.

Chapter Eight

"SHE WAS DOING IT for the money!" Sean shouted aloud to no one in particular. He lay on his back in the dark on the sofa where Abby's scent still lingered. Jiggs had forced his way between Sean's body and the sofa back. At Sean's outburst, he looked up.

"I know I offered her money," Sean went on. "And I fully intended to give it to her, not because I wanted to *pay* her, but because I thought she'd want something back and I really don't have anything else to give her. God."

He dropped his forearm over his eyes and tried to blot out the sight of her, face-to-face with him, looking at him as though she desired nothing in this world more than she desired him. And all the time it had been because she wanted the money.

Reason reminded him for the tenth time since he'd left her on her porch, *But you* offered *her money.*

He thought about that for a moment, then reason took the notion a step farther: *You admitted that you don't have love to give her. What in the hell made you think she has love to give you? She lost the man she loved. You're just what she's settling for. Good sex and a wallet. Almost the same things you want. So, why the indignation?*

He had no idea. He used to see the world so clearly, but everything seemed to be shifting on him lately.

He could remember her kissing him, her fingertips on his T-shirt just above his belt buckle, and felt a shudder run through him.

All Sean knew for certain was that he had to have her in his arms and—this was hard to accept—even if it meant taking back the proposition. He'd figure her out or die trying.

In his mind he began to draw tombstones.

ABBY FITTED THE BOUQUET of silk violets into the round starched doily and pulled the stiff lace up to the base of the flowers to create a nosegay. She tied narrow silk ribbon under the doily, leaving the ends long and knotting them an inch from the bottom. The effect was romantic—a gift from long ago.

Abby sat in the living room, violets, lace and ribbons strewn about her on the sofa and the coffee table. Molly played with her collection of toys and kitchen containers at her feet, and her grandmother sat across from her in the recliner, watching a 1930s musical on television.

I'm perfectly happy with this, Abby told herself. *This is my family. I love them more than my life. I don't need a man to make me feel like a woman. I don't need...*

She sighed as she stuffed violets into another doily. *Maybe I don't need it, but I certainly did like it.* When Sean wasn't being a jerk, he made her feel the way Craig had made her feel—special, cherished, desirable. She would miss that.

That's what you get for overplaying your hand, she told herself. *You should have told him in the beginning where to go instead of having the arrogance to try to play the heroine—determined to save him from himself. Particularly since you did that to save him* for *yourself.*

Live and learn, she thought philosophically, attaching ribbon to the nosegay.

The ring of the doorbell had her scooping things off her lap and dropping them beside her on the sofa. Molly beat her to the front door.

She pulled it open to find herself face-to-petal with a dozen roses. They were interspersed with fern and baby's breath to make up a fat bouquet. It was Molly who noticed the bearer.

She wrapped her arms around a jeans-clad thigh and exclaimed delightedly, "Man!"

Abby took the flowers, unmasking Sean in a leather jacket over a black turtleneck. She noticed that his dark clothing emphasized the blue of his eyes.

She was thrilled to see him, particularly with what appeared to be a peace offering. Anxious to consider that his presence meant she'd been right to take on his sexist attitude in the first place, she found herself willing to take up the challenge again.

She sniffed the roses.

He leaned down to lift Molly onto his hip. "Hi," he said. "Can we forget everything I've said so far, and let me tell you what I really meant when I...?" He groped for the right phrase, then finally finished the sentence with a desperate gesture of his free hand.

"When you offered me money," she said plainly.

He sighed. "Yes," he replied. "I did that because relationships that work require give and take and since I don't have love to give, I've found that many women are often just as happy with..." He watched her darkening expression, stopped, and quickly took another tack. "But now that we've established you're not in that category, we can renegotiate."

This didn't sound hopeful, Abby thought. That is, he was still unwilling to give the only thing she wanted, but he was apologizing for his crass proposition. She was grasping at straws, she knew, but something told her that turning him around was going to be a bloody, uphill struggle and she was going to have to take her small victories where she found them.

"All right," she said. "Would you like to use my breakfast nook as a conference table?"

He shook his head. "I think we need neutral ground. I'll make reservations for tomorrow night at the Sailor's Beach Inn. Can you get someone to watch Molly and your grandmother?"

"I think so."

"Good. I'll pick you up at seven."

"Good."

He was angry, Abby realized, despite the fact that he'd come to apologize. She imagined it wasn't easy for a man like him to admit to a woman that he was wrong, but she suspected it was more than that. It was almost as though he was even more angry with himself. She couldn't decide if that was good or bad where *she* was concerned.

He set Molly down on her slippered feet. She took his hand and tried to drag him into the house.

He stood firm. "No, Molly. I have to go home."

"In!" she insisted, pointing to the warm, lamplit living room beyond the open door.

Eloise leaned sideways in her chair to wave at him. "Come in, David," she called. "You're late for dinner."

Sean waved back, then grinned at Abby. "Nobody around here seems to understand who I really am," he said.

She pulled a recalcitrant Molly away from him and picked her up, letting her hold the flowers. "I think you're the one who doesn't understand who you really are."

He wasn't sure what she meant, but he was reluctant to ask. He had difficulty escaping their discussions unscathed. And he'd just gotten her to agree to see him tomorrow. He wanted nothing to interfere with that.

He reached out to pinch Molly's chin. "Bye, button," he said.

"Kiss!" she ordered, and leaned out of Abby's arms toward him, her little Cupid's-bow mouth puckered. He leaned down and received a noisy kiss on his cheek. Then he returned it.

She smelled of baby powder and cocoa and her mother's spicy rose fragrance.

"Seven," he reminded Abby.

"Seven," she repeated, her voice thin, her control wavering dangerously under her smiling facade. "Thank you for the flowers."

He disappeared into the night while Molly called more bye-byes. He didn't know himself at all, she thought. He didn't know how good he'd be as a husband and father—and he didn't know how good they'd be for him. It would be such a loss if she couldn't make him see that.

THE INN WAS DOWNTOWN. Some turn-of-the-century entrepreneur had added turrets to every corner of a very functional, square, three-story building that had once housed a glove factory, and turned it into a comfortable hotel and restaurant.

The lobby continued the medieval theme with a great stone fireplace, colorful heraldic banners, and several thronelike chairs set around the room.

Abby dropped the hood of her cape as they walked across the lobby toward the restaurant. "This place always makes me feel as though I'm Princess Aleta waiting for Prince Valiant to come home from his adventures."

Sean took the cape from her. "Now there's a work to respect. Harold Foster was one of the best artists ever to create a strip."

The maître d' greeted them with a formal flourish, then apologized that their table wasn't ready.

"Everyone is dawdling over dinner tonight." He winked and leaned a gray head conspiratorially toward them. "Two days until Valentine's Day and love is in the air. May I take the lady's coat and page you in the lounge?"

They found a semicircular booth in a quiet corner near the stone fireplace. A waiter dressed like a medieval page took Sean's order of a bottle of champagne.

"Champagne?" Abby questioned. "Are you celebrating?"

He reached an arm along the back of the booth and touched her hair. "You're sparkling," he said quietly. "I thought champagne seemed appropriate."

Abby had taken special pains with her appearance tonight. She'd worn her hair loose, and her simple black dress fit like a glove. But she knew it was more than that. What she felt for Sean made her features glow.

She drew a breath, determined to set an easy pace for this evening.

"Any news on your gasoline thief?" she asked. "Even KATU in Portland had something on her on last night's news."

"No kidding. No, I've been bound to the drawing table for the past few days. What did they say?"

"Seems the Coast Guardsman's car was found in Seattle. Apparently someone had put it on a car carrier that had been parked in front of Beach Motors after having delivered several new cars. The driver stayed the night here at the inn, then hopped into his truck the next morning without noticing the strange car under the four he still had to deliver to Seattle. They didn't discover the car until he off-loaded at the Seattle dealership."

He shook his head. "Maybe you could get word to her that I've had a change of heart before she hits me again."

Abby looked into his watchful expression. "What makes you think I'd know who she is?"

"It's someone in Sailor's Beach. I doubt that she'd come from down the coast to do her work in the middle of the night. I got home from Portland with a quarter of a tank that night. At nine-twenty the next morning it was empty. I doubt she'd have done it after sunrise. I am a little remote up there, but I'm always up early. I have a feeling she knew that."

She met his direct gaze. "And you're suggesting that I'm close enough to watch your comings and goings."

"You also mentioned having seen the sunrise that morning."

"When?"

"When I brought you home to see the contents of Aunt Adelle's box. I complained about the view looking like the edge of doom, and you mentioned the beautiful sunrise just the other morning. The morning my tank was syphoned."

She closed her eyes, trying to summon patience. "I did not steal your gas."

He nodded amiably. "I know. But you know everyone in town. I'll bet you know her, you just don't know she's who she is."

She frowned, working that out. "How do you know it wasn't me?"

"Because," he said, turning to face her. His fingertips reached under her hair to caress her shoulder. "I've seen you in operation. You're not so directly vengeful. You're much more subtle."

Despite her effort to stop it, color filled her cheeks. He'd figured out her plan.

He grinned and added, "No less effective a strategy, mind you, but not so hands-on."

She made herself meet his gaze. "I wasn't sure you understood."

"I didn't," he admitted. "Not right away. I'm much more used to manipulating than being manipulated. It took me until yesterday to figure out that your cheerful acceptance of my terms wasn't that at all."

"Sean," she said gravely, turning toward him, "I was just beginning to really...like you, and you offered me *money!*" She lowered her voice at the last, looking around to make certain they hadn't been overheard.

He leaned his elbow on the table and put a hand over his eyes. "I know. I'm sorry. But my past experience has been that it worked. And like I explained last night, I have no love to give you. I was sure you'd want something back." He lowered his hand and sighed. "If I tell you I'm sorry all to hell, can we start again from the moment I had you interested in being with me?"

The waiter brought their champagne, popped the cork, poured, placed the bottle back in its ice bucket and disappeared again.

You mean from the moment I first saw you with the realtor, she thought, *looking over the property.* When she spoke aloud, she tried to be less direct, though the subject made it difficult.

"You still want to make love to me?"

He didn't hesitate a second, even leaned a little closer. "Yes."

"Have you considered why?" she asked. "I mean, if I don't want money, what could I be after?"

He understood the point she was trying to make. He had to make it clear there was no hope in that direction.

"The obvious," he replied, unembarrassed. "Good lovemaking. The pleasure and the closeness nothing else can give you. Have you had that since your husband?"

She didn't resent his asking. She knew he was trying to make his point, just as she was.

"No," she replied candidly. "I haven't wanted it with anyone else."

He looked her in the eye. "You want it with me. I see it in your face when you look at me." He let her absorb that for a moment, then added mercilessly, "It can't be for love, Abby. We've spent a total of about five hours together."

She wouldn't deny what she felt. But this would be so much simpler if he understood what *he* felt. "You're telling me it's just my libido that needs you?"

He thought a moment. "Yes. I guess that says it."

She shook her head at him with tolerant indulgence. "And on the basis of that you want me to tell the Sweet Avenger that you've reformed? She might drop an anvil on you next time."

With a roll of his eyes, he clicked the rim of his glass against hers. "To man and woman," he said.

Abby drank to that—one of life's loveliest equations.

"It's just a matter of practicality," Sean said, placing his glass on the table, his long fingers turning it absently. "Man and woman were made to mate. It's in the grand design. Why complicate what exists perfectly at its most simple? It's pleasure. Why do we have to justify a sexual relationship by attaching marriage to it?"

They ate as the argument continued. Abby watched him, a smart man in his prime, and thought it sad that the ability to give love was really all he lacked. She'd be foolish to try to change him and she'd only get hurt again. Yet

her heart told her he was worth the risk. And this was the
season of hearts, wasn't it?

"So." He poured more champagne into her glass, then
topped off his own. He combed a hand through the side
of her hair. "Are you hungry?" he asked.

The last thing on Abby's mind at the moment was food.
She shook her head. "No."

"Then, why don't we cancel our dinner reservation?
We'll dance, then take a room. Decide for yourself which
one of us is right."

Her pulse was pounding and her mouth was dry. She'd
arranged for Judy to stay the night on just such a contin-
gency.

She reached for her champagne, her smile bright, but
her heart uncertain. "You're on," she said.

Chapter Nine

THE MUSIC WAS MOODY and slow. Abby was locked against Sean, her body to his. The heat of his hand splayed over her lower back was turning her spine to liquid. Her breasts were pressed to him, just beneath the jut of his ribs, their tips sensitized, so that every movement of him against her was sweet torture.

Her legs moved languidly with his, his knee making a continuous stroke against the inside of her thigh.

Then the piece was over and they stood together on the dark dance floor, unwilling—or unable—to move. She felt a part of him, as though she wanted everything he wanted.

Why couldn't they simply make love together and fill the void of loneliness that haunted them both? What point was there in cluttering their relationship with the emotion and promises that so often tore people apart?

The band struck up "My Funny Valentine"—a romantic, bluesy arrangement of it—and she remembered why. Because she knew the demands of a relationship built to last could contribute as much to those involved as it would cost. Because she knew love could be wonderful. Because under the strong attraction she felt for Sean, under the desire, was love. No matter what they did or didn't do, she was motivated by love; and nothing could change that.

They began to dance again, though the sudden crowding on the floor made it impossible to do more than sway in place.

Sean was sure that one more moment of this would render him unconscious. When Abby wrapped her arms around his neck and leaned her forehead against his shoulder he felt the world around him begin to dissolve.

It worried him more than a little as he strained to draw a steady breath, blinked to clear his eyes. He was a man who could give himself fearlessly to passion, but he could never remember losing himself to it. Some part of him was always aware, always completely in control of his mind and his body.

But he was rapidly losing that awareness now.

Then Abby raised her head to look into his eyes, hers focused on him with an intensity of need and wanting that pushed him to the brink of insanity.

Up on the small stage, the saxophone fairly wept its notes.

"Will you come with me?" Sean whispered.

He felt her sigh against his cheek. "Yes," she said.

Sean retrieved her cape, went to the desk clerk, and had a key in a matter of moments.

In the elevator they stood arm in arm, staring into each other's eyes for the brief ride to the second floor. Sean unlocked the door and let Abby pass before him into the cool, dark room.

He flipped on a light, then closed and locked the door. Abby stood waiting for him at the foot of a bed curtained in medieval heraldic red and gold.

Neither paid attention to the pseudo Middle Ages decor. They came together, arms straining, lips meeting, bodies fitting perfectly against each other.

Abby felt Sean's hands all over her. With tender urgency they traced her spine and slid over her hip, hesitating there to press her even closer.

She felt his arousal and moved ever so slightly in welcome.

He groaned, and while she continued to hold him, he yanked off his jacket and tossed it aside. He found the zipper of her dress and pulled it down.

She stepped back long enough to let the garment fall to her feet, then reached for him again.

He parted the heavy curtains surrounding the bed, then braced a knee on the mattress and, holding her to him, guided them down to the blankets.

"Abby," he whispered desperately. He felt filled with need, filled with emotion, filled with a kind of anxious urgency he'd never experienced before. He said her name again, but had no coherent thought to follow it. He simply felt as though he needed her complete attention.

Abby clutched at reason, feeling it drift farther and farther away as his hands moved on her, slipping down the thin straps of her ivory silk teddy. His lips on the swell of her breast almost vanquished her. But not quite.

Sean looked up from a fascinated perusal of the beaded tip of her breast—and encountered her dark velvet gaze. She appeared heartbroken. A solitary tear spilled over and trickled down into her hair spread out on the covers.

Passion, desire, the edgy excitement—all came to a sudden halt.

Bracing himself up on an elbow, he frowned down at her, more startled than angry.

"What is it?" he demanded.

"Oh, God." Abby sat up, wiping the tear away, straightening the silk straps. She was embarrassed and angry with herself for having taken such a foolish chance, and for subjecting Sean to what must seem like some coy thoughtless tease.

Now she had to explain it. She wrapped her arms around herself, suddenly feeling very cold.

"I'm sorry," she whispered, forcing herself into control, making herself look at him. "I can't do this."

The longing and frustration were as clear in her eyes as they were within him. So what was this about?

He reached behind her to yank at the blankets. He wrapped them around her shoulders and held them together in front of her. "Are you afraid?" he asked gently.

She looked at him with genuine puzzlement. "Of what?"

Okay, that wasn't it. He felt relieved—and further confused.

"Are you thinking about your husband?"

She shook her head, her eyes apologetic. "I'm thinking about you."

He couldn't help an ironic lift of his eyebrow. "By drawing away from me?"

Her hands inside the blanket tightened on the edges of it as she huddled a little farther into them. She stuck one hand out to wipe away another tear.

"You don't want it this way," she said, her voice tight and strained. "And it wouldn't be fair of me to go through with it, pretending otherwise."

He tried to make sense of that and couldn't. "What way, Abby?" he asked. "What are you pretending?"

She sighed and sat up, squaring her shoulders under the protective blanket.

"I'm pretending that I'm doing this for all the reasons *you* believe a man and woman should make love. Because nature ordained it, because attaching commitment to it only harms it, because . . ."

"Okay, okay." He stopped her with a fingertip to her lips. "I understand what you're pretending. What I want to know is—what are you *feeling?*"

She shook her head apologetically. "Love, Sean. I'm feeling love."

He felt the words like a tangible blow that made his gut ache. "Abby..."

"I know, I know," she said with wry fatalism. "That's why I had to stop you. I'm sorry about the price of the room. The owner and I have worked together on vintage fashion shows, so I know her fairly well. Maybe I can work out a trade and pay her off in desserts for the restaurant."

Sean lay on his back beside her, staring at the shadowy underside of the canopy. An incredible truth was crowding in on him—something that had been trying to make itself known for a week or more. He'd been turning away from it, sure he was the victim of his own sentimentality over a sweet and drifty little old lady who called him David and a love-crazed little girl who knew him only as "Man," but who seemed wild about him all the same.

But it was more than that. It was a chord this woman had touched. It made him feel things he'd once thought impossible. It had made him fall in love. But, could he ever make her believe *that* after all his pompous oratory—particularly at this moment?

"You know what I'm feeling?" he asked, reaching a hand up to rub her blanketed back.

She uttered a grim little laugh without turning to look at him. "Frustration?" she guessed.

"Besides that."

She turned, bringing the covers with her. Her eyes were wary, but with a spark of interest deep down. "What?" she asked.

He gently caught her cheek and pulled her down to him. "Love, Abby," he said. "Love for you."

Cradled in his arm, she frowned up at him. "Don't tease me, Sean."

"I'm not," he assured her. "I think I've felt it since the day you took me to the post office, since the first time I held Molly and your grandmother mistook me for your brother. You have to forgive me for not recognizing it. I haven't had a lot of it."

She was scanning his eyes, trying desperately to read them, needing to see to the heart of him before this went one step farther.

He guessed what was on her mind.

"It's very new to me, and I'm not even sure I can do what it requires of a man. So, for now, all I can do is tell you truthfully that I love you. The future isn't anything I can promise."

Abby felt joy flare inside her and all cause for concern slip away. He was capable of the promise—he just didn't know he was. Just as he hadn't known he loved her. He would come through. He might put her through a nervous collapse before he did, but he'd come through. It was all she needed.

"Then . . ." she said softly. "Where were we?"

He had no trouble remembering that he'd been divesting her of the teddy. He inched it down her legs and off, uncovering an expanse of skin as silky and as ivory as the garment.

He knelt over her, mesmerized.

She caught the tail of his tie and used it to pull him down to her. As he braced himself over her, staring with awe into her totally loving, trusting eyes, she untied the expensive silk and tossed it aside. Then she unbuttoned his shirt, tugged it out of his pants, and waited patiently while he rose to his knees and pulled it off. A round-necked T-shirt followed.

Boldly, she undid his belt and slid his zipper down.

Sean felt himself swamped by a myriad of new sensations. Or maybe they were all the old familiar sensations, heightened and magnified because this was Abby he was about to make love with—the woman who looked like a figure out of Romantic history, and who had love for him in her eyes.

His desire was at once hotter and gentler, his passion deeper yet sensitizing him to every nuance of her touch. The desperate greed of a body soon to be satisfied was tempered by a need just as desperate to give her every pleasure he knew.

His slacks and shorts tossed over the side, he lifted her to the center of the bed, untangled the blankets, and pulled them up to cover both of them.

Abby wriggled against him, eager to feel his warmth against her. She shuddered with pleasure as his hands swept up and down her, first in long smooth strokes that lit a fiery path from her toes to her chin, then tracing circles on her that mimicked her spinning senses. It occurred to her in one last moment of rationality that *this* was lovemaking, love literally *being made*—being created out of feelings and trust and the knowledge that it would remain intact the next day.

With a groaning little sigh, Abby surrendered completely, rubbing her knee up Sean's thigh.

He captured it and pulled her leg over him, reaching inside her. She caught her breath, as a dark whirl of delicious tension started to build. For an interminable moment she lay poised on the brink of the long-forgotten pleasure.

Then Sean was over her and inside her. Waves of sensation rolled over and over her and she surrendered herself willingly to it.

Sean felt it coming. As Abby trembled in his arms, his own release lay teasingly beyond him, building even as it remained elusively out of reach.

He was intensely aware of everything that touched his sensitized body—the blankets against his back, the warm sheet against his legs, the pillows under his forearms. And Abby. Her flesh was now feverishly hot against his, every curve smoothed against his weight, her hair like warm silk over his arm, and every little shudder of her body rippled along him like white water.

And suddenly he saw clearly the difference between making love and being in love. For as long as he could remember he'd participated in the ritual of sex in an interested but removed fashion; he'd felt pleasure slam against him, pin him for a moment or two with its power, then leave him feeling less than satisfied.

But what he felt at this moment was greater than anything in his sexual experience. And when release came, it did so with the same force, but then went on and on and on. And when it was over, he was more than satisfied: He knew he was in love.

"Oh, Sean," she whispered against his throat.

"Yeah, I know." He kissed the top of her head as he settled her on his shoulder and tucked the blankets around her. "That was so perfect it was almost scary."

"Love flavors everything."

"Is that a delicately stated 'I told you so?'"

She yawned. "Absolutely." She hooked an arm around his neck and snuggled closer. "I can't believe I have the whole night free. I won't have to get up for glasses of water, or to see why Gran is wandering around, or because I suddenly got a brainstorm about something I should do in the shop. A whole night free!"

Sean laughed softly and stroked her hair. "Not precisely free. I intend to have you up a few times, but you can rest for now."

"I warn you. I'm a bear when I first wake up."

"But I've just learned a few things about you. I can change you from a grizzly to a teddy bear with just the right touch—right here."

He stroked a hand teasingly over her hip and she moaned softly against him, her need to sleep dissolving.

"But you wouldn't take advantage of that, would you?"

"Most certainly."

Chapter Ten

SEAN WOKE UP aware that Abby was no longer beside him. And, worse, he felt as though he might die if he didn't get her back immediately.

He sat up in the middle of the bed, rubbing a hand over his rough chin and experiencing the vaguely hung-over feeling of the morning after a night of repeated lovemaking.

He groaned as he remembered telling her he loved her. Not that it wasn't true, but he didn't like this new feeling of vulnerability. Because he'd never been loved by a woman, he'd learned to never need one. But now he did. And he didn't like awakening and feeling incomplete because she wasn't there.

Where was she, anyway? Was she just in the shower, or had she decided it had all been a mistake and gone home on her own? When he listened for the sound of water running, he heard the rustle of clothing from beyond the draperies surrounding the bed.

A sense of relief washed over him, and he reached for his pants that had fallen between the bed and the drapes and lay back to slip them on.

"Hi!" a cheerful voice said. "I didn't know you were awake. After last night, you should sleep until April."

He felt a little less vulnerable with his trousers on and swept the curtains back, prepared to explain his emotional position once again. Instead, he simply stared.

Abby was wearing a wedding gown. *No. She couldn't be!*

He blinked. Yes. She *was* wearing a wedding gown, all bows and lace and flowery doodads, and a veil that hung to the floor and stretched out several feet behind her.

Once he'd established that fact, he forgot to consider the incongruity of the situation, and knew only the sudden fear that clutched at all his vital organs.

She turned away from the mirror, a glowing smile on her face. The veil twisted with her to enfold her in a graceful curve of lace and gauzy fabric. Her softness threatened to swamp him, but his anger quickly assumed control.

"No!" he said, springing to his feet, tossing the draperies aside so violently that they bunched up on the bed. "Oh, no. Don't even think about it! It's not going to happen. I told you last night that I wasn't promising anything beyond..."

Sean's glower blackened Abby's sunny mood. Rooted to the spot, she began reasonably, "Sean, I—"

"Last night was just an object lesson, wasn't it?" He advanced on her. "Teach him that he can only love you on your terms!"

Then she understood. He'd misinterpreted the wedding dress. The idea was so absurd that for a moment, she couldn't quite absorb it. She tried reason again.

"You think that this...?"

"I don't think—I know," he said, now towering over her. "I know how women work, how you get what you want by giving over. I just forgot."

Abby heard the words in disbelief, the beautiful night they'd shared disintegrating in her mind.

"Giving over," she echoed, hurt and anger brewing in the pit of her stomach. "You consider what I did with you last night as 'giving over'?" Then she doubled her fist and hit him as hard as she could in the upper arm. "You idiot!

And what in the hell was it I was supposed to want so badly that I slept with you for it?''

He folded his arms, wincing a little as he brought up the left one.

''A husband,'' he said stiffly.

She shook her head pityingly. ''And I suppose this dress is what brought you to that conclusion.''

Two things occurred to him simultaneously—that she was magnificent in a rage, and that her question was probably loaded. He didn't care. She'd had no right to manipulate him like that.

''Yes.''

''Jerk,'' she muttered under her breath, whipping the veil off and gathering up yards and yards of fabric and dropping it on the bed. Only then did he notice that the back of the dress wasn't fastened. There was a good foot and a half of tiny lace buttons she apparently hadn't been able to reach.

She pulled her way angrily but carefully out of the snug sleeves, wriggled the waist down to her knees, then stepped out of the dress.

She grabbed it up and held it under his nose so quickly he didn't have time to indulge the moment's distraction she presented in the ivory teddy.

''Look at it!'' she commanded.

When he frowned in confusion, trying to push it away, she shoved it back at him. ''Look—at—it!''

He obliged, afraid her rising voice would awaken everyone else on the floor.

''All right,'' he said. ''I'm looking. For what?''

She rolled her eyes. ''God. And to think men from coast to coast revere you and Brick as role models. I fear for the species. You don't notice that the color has yellowed, that the silk is shattered, that the lace has a few holes in it?''

When he still didn't get it, she explained sharply, "It's old, Megrath. It's a vintage piece. If you'll recall, I mentioned last night that the woman who owns this hotel with her husband has worked with me on several vintage fashion shows because she has some old things of her grandmother's.''

The dread inside him suddenly had a new face—his own stupidity.

"I awoke feeling wonderful," she said, "and called room service, thinking you might enjoy breakfast in bed before we left." She indicated the tray of food that had long since grown cold. "When the owner saw that I was awake, she sent the dress up with room service. She had promised to lend it to me for my class.''

He stared at her in stupefaction, unwilling to believe he'd misunderstood so completely.

"If you find that hard to believe," she said, tossing the dress on the bed and yanking her own dress on over her head, "you might consider that I had no wedding dress when we came into this room last night, so if you mistook it for a contemporary one that I would have bought in the flush of matrimonial fervor after having made love to you . . .'' She paused in her proposal to stop before him and deliver the rest of it right into his face. "I'd have to have bought it during the night, which I couldn't have done because we both know I was otherwise occupied much of the time. Or I could have bought it after you fell asleep. What time was that? About four in the morning?" She glanced at her watch. "But that would be presuming you know a bridal shop anywhere in the continental United States that would be open for business before dawn!'' The last was spoken at full volume.

He winced. "I get the point. Look, I—"

"No, you don't," she interrupted, shaking one shoe at him as she slipped into the other. "You don't begin to get the point. You don't seem to understand that Brick isn't real. A whole country of men may laugh and applaud his behavior because commitment and responsibility do get nerve-racking and tiresome, but they don't confuse his 'life' with their real lives like you do. You and Brick aren't trailblazing the future, Megrath. You're dinosaurs. You're extinct!"

"Abby..."

She was folding the dress into its box but turned to glare at him over her shoulder and interrupt.

"Most of today's men are smart and caring, and willing to give to a relationship every bit as much as they get. But there are still some like you, who use love to get sex—the old stereotypical holdover from the Stone Age."

She turned back to fold the veil into the box. He watched her in silence, completely at a loss to explain himself or to begin to know how to apologize.

She shrugged into her cape, shouldered her purse, and picked up the box. She confronted him for the last time in the middle of the room.

"I hope the Sweet Avenger gets every damn one of you. Goodbye."

He didn't try to get the door for her. She was moving under a head of steam he didn't dare intercept.

"SO THAT'S PRETTY MUCH what happened." Sean was sprawled out on the sofa, with Jiggs wedged in his customary spot between him and the sofa back. "And you know what the worst part is?"

Jiggs, his head on the waistband of Sean's sweat bottoms, seemed to be waiting for the answer.

"Everything she said was right. I fell in love with her and got scared to death, so I gave her all these precautions about needing time and space. Then when I saw her in the wedding dress— For an instant I knew that was precisely what I wanted. But I also knew it had the potential for hurting me again in all the same old ways.

"What I discounted was that this time I'm in love with Abby Stafford, so the potential doesn't exist. She loves me back. You know what, Jiggs? If I could have her back, I'd marry her this minute, on the spot." Sean sighed heavily. Jigg's head rose and fell with his master's diaphragm. Sean ruffled his ears. "But that chance is pretty slim. I think it's just you and me, pal."

"ABBY, THAT DRESS IS dynamite," Judy said, turning the gift shop sign from Closed to Open while Abby unlocked the register and slipped in the cash drawer.

Abby fluffed the off-the-shoulder sleeves of the berry-colored dress that had been Sean's Great-Aunt Adelle's. Though it fit her beautifully, it almost hurt to wear it, considering what had happened that morning several days ago. But, as she'd told herself when he'd given her the dress, she wasn't giving it back even though they had decided to go their separate ways. He didn't deserve to own anything so wonderful and so definitive of the romance he simply didn't understand.

So she wore it today, Valentine's Day, as a slap in the face to his ignorance. *She* knew what love was all about, and even if she might never again find the right man with whom to share it, she would hold it in her heart anyway.

Abby dabbed at her eyes with a tissue as she went to straighten a table of lace-edged linens.

"And the color," Judy said, coming to put a commiserating arm around her shoulders, "matches your nose."

Abby sniffed and sighed and balled the tissue into her palm.

"He'll come around." Judy gave her an encouraging squeeze.

Abby squared her shoulders and lifted her chin. "He'd better not if he wants to continue breathing."

"Give him a break. You said he's had trouble with women all his life."

"Now I see why," Abby retorted mercilessly. "He's completely incapable of giving."

"We're all basically selfish. We have to be taught to give. Usually by our mothers. You said his left."

Abby frowned at her friend. "Judy, if you're going to take his side, you can just go home."

Just as Abby spoke the last word, a crowd of six or seven midmorning coffee-breakers burst into the tearoom, their breath puffing ahead of them, hats and scarves coming off as they took the large table in the corner. Two of the women shouted their orders to those left behind as they wandered into the gift shop, rubbing their hands together.

Abby grinned wryly at Judy. "But not until we close."

And that was the last time they had an opportunity to speak to each other. Abby sold everything in the shop shaped like a heart—from lace potpourris to chocolate. Her table filled with nosegays of violets was bare by lunchtime and after that there was a run on anything with roses, lace, ruffles or angels.

Taking advantage of the heavy shopping traffic, Abby had positioned her grandmother in a rocker near the cash register, from which she handed out business cards to everyone who made a purchase or simply wandered through.

Molly, dressed in a frilly white dress, carried a basket with cookie samples. The vast amount of attention, hugs, pats on the head and extravagant compliments she received kept her interested in her task.

Business slowed down mildly in the middle of the afternoon, then burgeoned again later when last-minute shoppers stopped by before heading home from work.

Abby was engrossed in wrapping a two-foot-high cupid she'd never expected to sell but ordered for visual interest, when Judy emerged from the tearoom. "How long shall we stay open? It's twenty minutes after closing already."

"As long as there are customers, if you can stay. Do you have a date tonight?"

"Not until eight."

"Great. Things should slow down in another few minutes."

Judy hurried back to the still-half-filled tearoom, and Abby handed the cupid to her customer, hoping his wife would be pleased with it. Then she noticed Sean.

He stood in the doorway, wearing a tux and a top hat and a lethal smile. He stepped aside to let the man with the cupid through, tipped his hat at a pair of women who followed, staring after him, then closed the door.

He stepped toward the counter, flourishing a cane.

He made a gorgeous figure, she noted, her heart thudding out of control. Reason shouted over and over in her mind. *This doesn't mean anything. Don't be swayed. He's tricky.*

He stopped on the customer side of the counter, tipping the cane over his shoulder. His eyes were filled with mischief and, she noted with another thud of her heart, love.

"Hello, David," Gran said, rocking and smiling.

He turned to tip his hat at her. "Hi, Gran. You look beautiful today."

The old woman beamed. Sean turned to Abby.

"I once heard you say," he said, making no effort to speak quietly, "that you were waiting for a man to appear in a tux and a top hat to save you from your daily drudgery."

He looked around the beautiful, cheerful shop, where four or five undecided customers still lingered, then turned back to her with a smile. "But this is such a wonderful atmosphere, I can't imagine you'd want to leave it."

Everyone had turned to look.

Abby glanced their way, then turned a warning look on Sean and replied quietly, threateningly: "I meant from the drudgery of worrying and making big decisions alone. I didn't mean I wanted to leave my shop and tearoom."

He swept off his hat and placed it on the counter, his eyes dark and focused intently on hers. "That's what I thought. So, here I am, ready to serve."

She raised an eyebrow. "In what capacity?"

"Why, as husband, of course. To help you worry and make big decisions. To spoil Gran and love Molly and make you the happiest woman alive."

No one even pretended to shop. They had gathered a little closer, and the doors to the tearoom had opened and half a dozen people, Judy included, gawked from there.

Molly, who'd gone in for a glass of milk, spotted Sean and came running toward him.

"Man!" she called excitedly as he lifted her into his arms.

"Not man," he said. "Daddy. Can you say Daddy?"

Abby swatted his arm. "Don't tell her that."

Molly turned on her mother with an indignant frown and swatted her arm. Then she turned to Sean and said loudly and clearly, "Dad-dy."

"Very good," he told her.

"Sean," Abby said, doing her best to put the interested onlookers out of her mind, "you will not bully me into this."

"Of course not. I've come to charm you into it."

"I won't listen," she insisted stubbornly.

He inclined his head apologetically. "I'm afraid you'll have to." He held up his free hand from which dangled the second bracelet of a pair of handcuffs, the first of which was clasped around his wrist. He hooked the other around a side spindle of Gran's rocking chair and snapped it locked.

"Sean!" Abby exclaimed.

"All you have to do is accept my proposal," he said implacably.

"I accepted your proposition once," she whispered harshly, "and look what happened!"

He leaned toward her as far as he could with one arm attached to her grandmother's chair and the other supporting her daughter.

"But this is a *proposal*," he enunciated carefully. "As in, 'Will you marry me?'"

"You're not doing this because you want to make a commitment," she challenged. "You're doing it because you've been thwarted."

"I'm doing it because I've fallen in love," he corrected quietly, gravely. "I'm doing it because I lay awake last night, feeling sorry for myself, hating myself for being stupid about the other morning, sure you'd never want to hear from me again, much less see me."

He sighed. Molly, seeming to sense he needed comfort, leaned her head against his shoulder. He kissed the top of her head.

"Then I remembered," he went on, "that you're a woman who knows all there is to know about love. You know that it isn't always soft and round and edged with lace. Sometimes its hard and rough and peeling, but it's still there."

He sighed, as though going on was difficult. "That was the kind of love I had. When you expected love from me..." He hesitated. A collective breath was held. "I told you I couldn't do it, because I truly thought I couldn't. Then I got to know you and...we had the other night...."

Sean and Abby stared at each other, his eyes desperate for understanding, hers reflecting his pain and her own.

"Now, what's inside me is very different," he said. "It's softer and stronger and... It's the damnedest thing—it's growing. Abby, please..."

She flew into his arms, sobbing, and crushing her daughter between them. Her grandmother tried to give them a business card.

One of the customers—her eyes brimming as she watched the interested audience cheer and gather around Abby and Sean—thought that this wasn't quite the way she'd intended to straighten him out, but it had worked. In this morning's strip, Brick had told Goldy that he loved her.

So Sweet Avenger—case number one—was closed. She dropped a bill on the counter to cover the price of her purchase and walked out the door as everyone else continued, unknowingly, to applaud her first success.

She walked away, the sound reverberating pleasantly in her ears. It was a good start. A *very* good start.